VALOR

CASEY L. BOND

VALOR

Dragon. Warrior. Woman.

ISBN: 9798793226691 (paperback)
ISBN: 978-1-0880-1451-6 (hardcover)

Book Cover designed by AC Graphics
Edited by The Girl with the Red Pen
Character Art Illustration by @ArtbySteffani

THE GODS

NAMINA – GODDESS OF ALL CREATURES

Oro – God of the Cursed Dead
Rata – Goddess of Fire & Light
Urit – God of Storms & Lightning
Ventus – God of Wind & Air
Yenza – God of Earth & Stone
Zairitus – God of Great Waters

CHARACTER NAME PRONUNCIATION GUIDE

Asra – Az-ruh
Cassius – Cass-yus
Estin – Es-tin
Favian – Fay-vee-uhn
Gaila – Gay-luh
Grady – Gray-dee
Indri – In-dree
Kaan – Kahn
Kirsi – Kur-see
Satira – Sat-ee-ru
Strieg – St-reeg
Thanias – Than-eye-us
Vayl – Vay-uhl
Zaire – Zay-r

CHAPTER 1

Mother once told me that if I'd been born a boy, she would have named me Valor.

We were taking turns scrubbing clothes on the washboard when she said it out of the blue as if she spoke of nothing more than the warm air and billowy white clouds lazily drifting overhead.

We didn't have but a pinch of soap shavings with which to wash. No bubbles clustered on the surface and the water didn't cloud at all, despite our efforts that bright spring afternoon. But Mother always did the best she could with what little we had. She was always content.

She smiled wistfully, as if she admired the name. But I couldn't smile with her. In my heart, I worried she didn't love me as much as she would have if I had been born a boy, like Zaire.

Boys were coveted. They were the wish placed upon every swollen belly.

Girls were disappointments.

Mouths to feed. Too weak to help with the demands that life in the countryside required. The heavy hardship of her dowry was an apparition, haunting her family from the moment of her birth to betrothal, because even paltry sums were too much to afford.

That was why many a baby girl appeared on the steps of the gods' temples, abandoned. Mother had not cast me away, though. She did love me. She told me every night when she tucked me into bed. If she had asked what I felt about being a girl, I might have told her I was happy, the life she provided was a good one, and that I hoped she loved me *as much* as she loved my brother.

Most of that was true. But I would never admit that in the shadowed corners of my heart, I hoped she loved me more.

That day, I asked Mother what valor meant and for a moment, she stopped working my dress over the ridges. Her eyes searched the pale blue sky as if a perfect description was written in the blue sky in ink made from clouds. "It means to be fearless and brave. Always."

She went back to scrubbing, already seemingly lost in thought, but I had to know. "Do you regret that I was born a girl? Do you wish I was Valor?"

"Vayl," she said, locking eyes with me as her fingers tightened on the pale blue fabric. "Valor lies within you, even if I did not name you for it. There is nothing about you that I would ever change. You are exactly who you were born to be, and I am proud of all you will one day do and the woman you will become."

I had no idea what she meant, or how she could even imagine what I might be capable of in the future, so I didn't ask any other questions. I only knew that women weren't destined for greatness, only for perpetuating male lineages.

I helped her scrub and hang the wash until our basket emptied and my fingers shriveled. Until the laundry line was full of pale articles that snapped in the wind like flags being waved in surrender.

CHAPTER 2

I threw the threadbare blanket off my clammy skin and scrambled out of bed before rushing across the floor, dizzy and disoriented. My heart pounded in my chest. My lungs were full of smoke. Coughing and gasping and nearly ripping down the curtain that separated my half of the room from my brother's, I fled the house. Heat pressed against my back as I shoved the door open, hinges squealing. The frail wooden door frame vibrated like a bell after it slammed against the house.

Father didn't notice. His rattling snore never broke its predictable rhythm.

With trembling hands, I patted my gown over my thighs, stomach, arms, lips... I touched my hair. Nothing was burning. Nothing had been singed, though my shift was soaked through with sweat at the small of my back. I plucked it off my skin.

The material wasn't dry and flame-eaten. It was only a dream. *Only a dream.*

The night wind licked cool tendrils across my body as if Ventus, god of the wind and air, wished to further reassure me. But all Ventus's cool touch ever did was remind me that he had not claimed me. And as I wasn't his, he didn't care if I broke apart each night, only to piece myself back together each morning.

I blew out a shuddering breath and raked my hair away from my face, holding it there until my arms weakened.

"Do you still taste the smoke when you dream of her?" a voice sadly asked from the darkness. Zaire slouched atop a fence post in the yard, looking like the weight of the world lay on his shoulders.

My brother was the only one who remembered that night as I did. The only one who understood the terror. He was also the only man who treated me as an equal. In Zaire's presence, I could speak freely, as I had when I was alone with Mother.

"When did you get home?"

My brother shrugged. "I haven't been here long."

I looked to the house. Perched in one of the sills was a stubby, almost burnt-out candle. The flame flickered weakly. I lit one for him every night despite my fear of fire – whispering a nightly prayer to his god, Zairitus, to keep him safe, and hoping that mine delivered my words to him.

It was the only beacon I could offer. Zaire knew the empire better than most. He knew the paths that led home. But somehow, the lit candle made me feel like if he ever lost his way in the darkness, he would find the light and it would guide him back to us. "Why didn't you come in?"

"You were sleeping. I didn't want to wake you," he let the simple lie roll off his tongue. The truth was more complicated. Zaire didn't come in because he didn't want to wake Father and bear his scorn. As courageous as my brother was, when it came to dealing with our father, he was a coward.

We sized one another up the way siblings did when there was much to say, but no point in saying it. When there had been too much time and distance and pain between them for far too long. When words were more likely to be used as weapons than a soothing balm. When the only thing left between them was the bond of loyalty that siblings uniquely shared, forged in the innocence of childhood before maturity hacked away at their limited perspectives to reveal the cruel world they would face as adults.

Venomous words perched on my tongue. I wouldn't tell Father he'd come home this time. Knowing Zaire had come so close but chose to keep his distance would hurt him. He would never admit it aloud, but the pain was evident in the crevices marring his brow. And whenever Zaire's name was mentioned, in the depths of his eyes, regret often swam.

The two hadn't spoken since Zaire left home to join the Imperial Army, an act Father had expressly forbidden. Zaire defied him and set off to carve his own future anyway, with neither Father's permission nor his blessing.

"I can feel you shaking from here," my brother said, a sad smile tugging at his lips.

I held a hand out in front of me and watched it tremble.

"I still dream about it, too," Zaire admitted. He jumped down from the post and crossed the space between us. Something was tucked tightly beneath one of his arms. He awkwardly pulled me in for a one-armed hug, and as I felt my heart soften, I let him. "How is he?" he asked of Father.

"Not well."

He laid his chin on the top of my head. "I'm sorry you bear this burden alone."

Father was not a burden. He was alive, and that was enough.

Zaire released me and stepped away. He did not climb onto the post again, but leaned his back against it as he scrubbed a hand down his face. He was exhausted and in need of rest, but I knew he would not come inside to lie in his bed.

I'd seen him a handful of times since he left, and only when I slept lightly enough so his footsteps outside woke me up. Most of the time I slept soundly, and he came and went without saying a word. The only reason I knew he'd been home was by the pile of tokens he left for me to find the next day.

Once, he left a hand-scrawled note on parchment that smelled like the sea. He'd stuffed it into a corked bottle. It took me hours to coax the paper out of it. When I told Zaire later how long it had taken me to remove, he laughed, surprised I hadn't just smashed the bottle to retrieve it. But I didn't want to break the elegant glass. It was long and slender, and curved unlike any bottle I'd seen.

And it was from him. I missed him.

It still sat upon my crooked dresser.

Sometimes he would leave bundles of spices and coin to help us buy what the garden would not produce. There was the occasional spool of thread and needles I needed. I always lost those. Or a strand of vibrant red ribbon, a match to one I left behind long ago. I think he remembered that day every time he saw one, and wanted me to know he hadn't forgotten either.

Sometimes he would leave a bottle of corn liquor, nasty smelling stuff, but it helped Father sleep when the pain made him miserable.

A few times he left bouquets of lavender he collected when crossing the miles of purple fields. If a mere handful smelled that good, I was certain even the gods took their time drifting above or strolling the lavender fields to enjoy their heady fragrance.

"I should go," he rasped, staring at the boulder looming large even in the darkness. He looked at his feet. "Vayl, it'll be a long time before I can come back again. A very long time."

I swallowed thickly, hugging myself, already feeling the loss of him though he stood before me. "Why?"

"My duties carry me elsewhere for now. For the foreseeable future."

He never divulged what his orders were or where he was being sent, but he'd never warned me like this before. I wondered if duty was truly taking him away, or if he was finally choosing to let us go and start a life of his own. As it was, he'd barely held on after leaving, the thread tethering him to us slowly unraveling with each passing day. I could almost see it – taut and weak between him and this life.

He gestured to the hills behind our farm and smiled wistfully. His eyes crinkled at the sides mischievously. "Hey, you know the boulders we used to jump across as kids?"

"Yes." I nodded, trying to smile. He always did this. Tried to make me smile when I felt like the skies were falling.

"Mother hated us jumping across their tops." Whenever he mentioned her, he knew I would listen. He'd used the tactic against me often enough that I should have developed a defense, but I couldn't and he knew it. He waited until my eyes lifted to his. "If you see or hear anything strange – anything at all that seems *off* – I need you to run and hide there."

My lips parted. "I can't leave Father." He stayed quiet because he knew I was right. I stepped closer to my brother. "What's happening, Zaire?"

He looked off into the darkness as if he could see through the foothills all the way to those boulders. "I'm probably just worrying for nothing. It's just that when I'm gone, I won't be able to check on you." He forced a smile. "It would give me peace of mind if you promised, though. You always keep your word. People who might bother a young woman wouldn't bother an old man, so you needn't worry about Father. You have to honor your own safety, Vayl."

The way he spoke reminded me of a looming storm rolling over the sky, ready to drench us all, wind howling, tearing limbs and leaves sideways with its angry gusts. I swallowed thickly around the knot forming in my throat. "Then I promise. But promise *me* you'll be careful."

"Always," he replied with a tired smile.

Zaire was not one to worry without cause, so the fact that something had spooked him this badly set me on edge. I had already lost my mother, and my father was dying. I didn't want to lose my brother, too. Not to war... and not to worse.

He finally brought out what he'd kept tucked beneath his arm. Even in the moonlight, the folds of red were vibrant.

"What is this?" I asked as he held it out to me. My lips parted. It was a generous measure of silk. Smooth, cool, red silk. Silk so fine, there was only one place in the empire it could be found. "This came from the Imperial City," I breathed.

"You've outgrown hair ribbons." He stuffed his hands in his pockets. "I wanted you to have something special for once. Something that's just yours and that you don't have to share. I wanted to make this gift count."

My heart cracked at his repeated warning. It felt like goodbye;

like a loss so great I wasn't sure how to envision, let alone cope with. I hugged the fabric to my chest. As angry as he made me, I would welcome that anger to keep him close. "It's beautiful."

He nodded at the vibrant red ream. "Make yourself a dress. Take care of Father. And don't worry over me, I'll be fine. I love you, Vayl," he told me boldly. "I'm proud of you. I hope that you'll be proud of me someday."

A knot formed in my throat and blocked the words pouring from my heart. I was already proud of him. As a brother. As a man. As a soldier.

He glanced at the house. Zaire wanted me to be proud of him, yes, but he also coveted our father's love. Hastily, he hugged me once more before striding away, blending into the night like a wraith.

Not only had I failed to tell him I was proud of him, I didn't even tell him I loved him. I refused to acknowledge this as goodbye – even if he meant it to be.

Sometimes I wondered if Mother's spirit pushed Zaire toward us when he drifted too far away. Just as I wondered if she sent the nightmarish memory of that night so we wouldn't forget how she fought for us and take each other for granted now that she wasn't there to save us again, even from ourselves.

I refused to let her memory fade. Every day, I tried to recall something she said, some small moment that passed between us when she lived. I could never forget how she died, but it was the small moments that could be buried by the hourglass's sand.

Like the joy that shone in her eyes at the simplest things. She would grin if she found a blooming daisy and loved listening to the trills of songbirds. She always wore a smile – small and content, or radiant and beaming. I didn't know how much it had comforted me until she and her smile were gone.

From afar, women envied and men admired her long black, silken hair, her perfect rosebud lips. She was a faithful wife and a gentle mother, offering only kind corrections, though Zaire and I did many things that should have provoked her anger.

When Father returned from war injured, she didn't complain about taking on his chores along with her own. She was just happy he had survived and came home to us. When pain overwhelmed him and made it impossible for him to raise from the bed or walk across the room, she assured him that in time, he would heal.

She believed even when he doubted. She was strong when he was weak.

She once told me that it was the duty of a woman to be a pillar, to hold up the roof when storms raged against it. I wasn't impressed by her analogy. I thought pillars were functional but purposeless until the night the beams that held our roof up began to snap and the true pillar of our family fell to the flames.

Seven years ago, Mother walked to a nearby village to help an old friend harvest the first of summer's crops. Our garden hadn't flourished as quickly as we'd hoped, despite the long hours she spent toiling in it, dragging buckets of water from the stream to keep the soil around the shoots moist. Time had gnarled her friend's hands so badly she had trouble gripping anything, so Mother helped her plant and tend her crops when she could spare the time. Now, she would see that they were plucked, prepared, and put away for winter.

She fixed our supper early in the morning and before she left, told us to expect her home just before dark. I missed her, even though I knew she wasn't far. Father and Zaire argued all afternoon but after dark, when she was supposed to come home, I was finally free from the beastly tension they both fed. After Father shouted for Zaire to leave his sight, my brother stomped into our bedroom, his eyes red from crying. Not that he let Father see. Later, Zaire had fallen asleep on his cot, curled into a ball.

The only noise came from crickets singing outside and the squeaks from my cot when I shifted my weight as I tried to find a comfortable spot. In truth, I didn't want to go to sleep. Darkness deepened outside my window, but I wanted to hear when Mother came back home. I was lying on my bed wondering when she would open the door or if she might stay with her friend – it was scary to walk alone in the darkness – when I smelled smoke.

It billowed into mine and Zaire's room, and on the heels of the acrid, suffocating plumes, nipped the flames.

I screamed to wake my brother. He startled. Fire let itself into our room and climbed the walls before either of us could get to our feet. Fear sparked in his eyes like a blade striking flint. We made quick plans to run outside and draw water to douse what we could, but flames were everywhere. As we tried to run through the door, my nightgown caught. I rolled around on the ground to put it out.

Zaire panicked when he saw the blisters on my skin and ran back inside where the flames weren't as thick, but the fire was spreading in his direction. I yelled for him to come to me, but he refused. I begged him, but he would not budge. He only shook his head rapidly and made himself smaller.

Smoke thickened, filling the space so that only a sliver of clear air remained along the ground. I cowered on the floor, crying; partially from the pain of being burnt, and also because I didn't know what to do or how to get out. I knew Zaire and I were going to die.

Flames rippled over the walls and furniture, arching over the ceiling, and soon the whole of it was engulfed. I screamed for Father again and again, knowing he likely wouldn't be able to get to us and if he managed it, that he wouldn't be strong enough to get us out.

The dark smoke grew even denser. I couldn't see further than my arm could stretch, and my eyes watered from the intense heat. My throat dried so that all I could do was cough.

Deeper into the house, Father coughed, too.

He was still alive...

He wouldn't be able to stand up on his own.

If we didn't help him, he would burn to death.

But we were helpless against the inferno charring our home, scorching our lungs.

I lay on my belly on the dirt floor and slid beneath my bed where a wisp of clean air remained.

Just then, a great crash sounded as Mother burst through the door. Smoke rushed toward her, eager to escape, obscuring her from sight. I don't remember a single time when she raised her voice until that night when she called out for us. She pushed through the flames and rippling heat for her children.

Fate pressed her hidden courage forward like the insides of grapes bursting from their skins. She was determined despite her fear, relentless despite the danger.

Before our world burnt away, I had considered her weak. She'd always been so mild-mannered, subservient to our father's wishes and will. But that night she proved her strength, and my ignorance, by dragging us out of our engulfed home, one by one.

I was ten and Zaire was only eleven. His voice had not yet deepened, and he had barely begun to grow to the height he'd finally settled at. She found him first, crouched in the corner of the room, his body folded as small as he could manage. Most of the time, Zaire was a bold, arrogant boy, fearless to the point of recklessness.

Relief and desperation washed over his sooty, sweat-slickened face as he reached out for Mother, only to pull his hands back into his body as the heat pressed down upon him like the heavy earth upon a newly filled grave. The fire raced across and up the walls on either side of where he'd sought refuge, melting the thick curtains Mother had scrimped and saved for months to buy.

Mother scooped him up as if he was a small child and not nearly as tall as she, tucked his face into her neck, and hurried outside.

She returned a moment later and found me lying beneath my cot as the fire spread across it over my head. It had only been a moment since she'd left with Zaire and in that scant time, the inferno built into a great beast, roaring and consuming. Never satiated.

I could still taste the smoke, and not only when I dreamed or thought of that night. It never truly went away. The smell had tattooed itself forever on my tongue.

Mother waved me out from beneath the cot and when I didn't move quick enough, she caught my wrist and dragged me. Then she lifted me up and tucked my face into her neck as she'd done with Zaire and quickly brought me outside to sit with my brother in the cool mud. She started back toward the house but stopped short. The main beam holding up our roof snapped. It would buckle, as would the smaller pillars. Their splintering and ensuing crashes still echoed in my ears at night when I dreamed of her.

The feeling of panic came with those nightmares, knowing that Father was still inside.

As the smoke plumed so thick that even though we were a safe distance from the blaze, it choked us, and despite the danger that awaited with the knowledge that our roof would soon fall, Mother rushed back inside for her husband. She was a slight woman, and she'd always seemed so delicate. But she lifted him easily that day. Hooking his arm over her shoulders, she pushed forward, walking him through the flames until he was out of the fire's greedy clutches.

She walked him from our home with her teeth gritted together, just as the entire structure collapsed. She wore fire-eaten silk, what was left melted to her skin. Her scream still sent shivers up my spine when I remembered that night.

The sound was full of agony, desperate and final. But there was relief in her tone as well.

She dropped Father on the muddy soil beside us before she swayed sideways, her knees buckling. She rolled to her back, wheezing and gasping. Her mouth opened and closed like a fish on land, desperate for water. Smoke oozed from between her cracked, charred lips.

I still remembered the smell of her burnt hair and skin, and how her beauty melted away. I remembered how my knees smarted as I crawled over the dirt to her and how I vowed to crawl a thousand miles if the gods would spare her life.

But the gods, not even Yenza who had claimed her, was willing to bargain with me. Their silence roared in my ears as I tried to comfort her, terrified to touch her for fear that I would cause her more pain, and afraid not to for the same reason.

She lay dying, yet I didn't take her hand or comb my fingers through what was left of her hair, threads of it leaking smoke. I did not kiss her shiny, blistered lips or the small patches of skin that weren't charred on her cheeks or forehead.

Instead, I told her I loved her. I told her a dozen times, two dozen, three... I couldn't tell her enough because I knew I would never be able to tell her again. She had to know it. She had to know I was there and she wasn't alone.

She was afraid. I could see it in the tension that filled her as she fought to stay alive and with us. She strained to breathe, struggled and gulped and coughed and gasped. And then suddenly, the fight left her. Her arms went limp and her breaths shallowed, then slowed. She knew she was dying. I saw the realization in her eyes and knew she had accepted her fate. She understood my words and felt my presence. Her eyes were aware, though her lashes had burnt away.

In my heart, I begged her not to leave us, but dared not speak those selfish words. She deserved as peaceful a death as she'd made our lives. She didn't need to worry for us anymore. She'd saved us and now we would live, knowing she'd given everything so we could see another day.

She died as I told her I loved her, hovering so close I heard her last breath escape her in the form of a hushed groan.

When her heart went still, mine shattered.

Zaire quietly cried nearby, his tears leaving clean paths on his sooty cheeks. He'd scooted closer, but not close enough that she would've seen him. He didn't tell her he loved her, but Mother knew the sound of her children's cries. She knew his sorrow and heard his despair. She felt the weight and depth of his love.

Father never chastised me for speaking, for shouting, or sobbing. For hours, he sat alone in the mud staring at the house.

Eventually, the rest of the roof gave way and collapsed with a harsh roar. The sound was final.

If my heart didn't already lay in pieces, it would have crumbled in that moment.

Numb, I sat by Mother and watched the fire whittle what charred wood remained into skeletal, brittle spindles, still coughing from the smoke that had tried to suffocate us all.

CHAPTER 3

T***wo weeks after Zaire's last visit...***

As I worked in the garden, pulling the relentless weeds that daily attempted to rise and suffocate our autumn vegetables, still too far slight to eat, my eyes caught on the fence post Zaire had last perched upon. I worried for him. The life of a soldier was nomadic. He went where he was commanded and did what he was told, when he was told to do it. Sometimes months would pass without a sign he'd visited.

It had only been a couple of weeks, I told myself. And he said it would be a very long time before he could return. If he ever did...

I blew out a breath, feeling ridiculous for worrying.

Zaire was fine. Probably making his way back through Kaan toward the Imperial City. I pictured him bent over picking lavender, stuffing the purple into his pockets and enduring the teasing of his friends over it. Or maybe the smell was so heavenly, they didn't laugh at all and instead took some sprigs for themselves.

Father's rattling cough snapped me from my thoughts. I pinched a stubborn weed, pricking my thumb on one of its hidden thorns, muttering a curse beneath my breath when blood pooled and mixed with the dirt on my hands.

"Vayl!" Father called for me, his cough severing my name.

His rusted voice carried as far as the garden, but not far beyond it, so I stayed close most days until necessity mandated I leave him for a short time.

I dusted my dirty hands on my apron and rose from where I knelt, then walked through the stretching shadow cast when the beams of golden light broke over the great boulder that had come so close to smashing us all.

Between the fire and the boulder, I couldn't help but wonder what we'd done to anger the gods of fire and earth, and why the three of us were spared when Mother wasn't. If there was a good and innocent one among us, it was her.

Maybe their punishment for us was leaving us here to toil in a life without her.

Father's cough turned violent. He called for me again, impatient.

I wasn't allowed to shout back that I was coming, though in my mind, I barked an irritated reply. He never gave me time to reach him before calling out again, and again...

As much as the garden reminded me of Mother, the boulder was a marker that belonged to Father alone. He had lamented that rock for years. It hung precariously on the cliff above the house when we came to this place, but our desperation for shelter outweighed the risk of that great rock crushing us as we slept. Though he'd told us it might more times than I could count.

The rock had likely clung to that cliff for longer than any of us had been alive. There was no reason to think it would fall in our lifetimes, but fall it did, just as he'd predicted.

Perhaps Yenza, god of earth and stone, heard him speak about it so many times he grew annoyed and flicked the stone toward us just to shut Father up.

When the boulder finally broke away, Father felt the earth tremble from inside the home. He heard thunderous booms as it hit the earth, tumbling toward the valley. He told us that he'd clutched the arms of his chair and braced for death.

Zaire and I were outside. I was collecting eggs, getting ready to spread a too-thin layer of feed for the hens, while Zaire teased the goat, running about his pen to taunt the grumpy old thing.

It sounded like the sky rent in two when the boulder finally separated from the cliff. Zaire's eyes grew wide. He leaped the fence and raced toward me. "Run!" he shouted, clasping my hand. I made the mistake of looking over my shoulder to spot the danger he'd already seen.

Panic made my heart race faster than my feet. We sprinted toward the east river as fast as our legs would work as the boulder crashed southward. I clung to his hand, straining to keep up with his longer strides.

When we were safe, we turned and watched it tumble toward the house, eyes wide, hearts in our throats. Had Father been right? Would it smash the house and him in it?

I could only cover my mouth and hope that Yenza would stop the great rock. Perhaps he heard my shouting, because it stopped rolling and settled just shy of our home.

All was quiet for a long moment, Zaire and I staring at the settled stone as if it might begin rolling again, until Father shouted our names to make sure we hadn't been crushed in the yard.

"Vayl!" I hurried toward the house.

My basket was nearly empty. In its bottom were a few bitter but edible leaves, some worm-eaten spinach, and a scrawny beet. There was still time for things to grow before the cold came. If Father hadn't needed to eat something to keep up what little strength he had, I wouldn't have dragged anything out of the soil. I'd chewed on some grass to keep the hunger pangs at bay, knowing he needed the sustenance more than I did.

The spring and summer harvests were meager and though we reduced the amount we ate to tuck more away, what we'd managed to store wouldn't sustain both of us through the winter. The stores may not even feed one.

We still had chickens and one tough old goat to keep us from starving this year. What we would do next year if our fortune didn't change, I wasn't sure.

I stomped the dirt off my boots outside the front door so he'd know I was near and stop shouting for me. The hinges shrieked when I opened the rickety wooden door.

Inside our modest, darkened home, Father reclined in a chair whose back was obviously broken. One day while glancing out the window, he spotted it outside our closest neighbor's dwelling and asked Zaire to drag it to ours. It leaned to the right, constantly threatening to empty him onto the dirt floor.

Behind him, tattered blankets covered the two windows. At first glance, one might think their bottoms were lined in lace, but only because mice had chewed through the fabric here and there. The only light they allowed in was from a tiny seam where some of the stitches had begun to separate. They were nothing like the delicate, sheer curtains Mother had loved. Those freely allowed Rata's light to shine in and brighten the home.

Father said the light hurt his head. It was truer that reminders of Mother hurt his heart.

I folded my hands in front of me. He did not invite me to speak, so I kept quiet and waited.

In Kaan, it was a husband's duty to rule over his household and teach his son to do the same. It was a wife's honor to submit to his judgment and teach her daughter to keep her thoughts to herself, to only speak when granted permission and only convey the minimal necessary. Women were to work and be seen, not heard. They were to obey, to relent. Never were they to rule; they were to be ruled.

Zaire may have treated me as his equal, but Father didn't approve of it. Zaire was careful in his presence to spare both of us punishment.

Father believed in the rules established by the gods, and he once told me that the gods thought women were fools who were unable to think without committing some horrible act of sedition against them. I wondered if they repressed us, not for our own good, but for theirs. It was blasphemy to even think such a thing, but I wondered if the gods feared the minds and strength of women most of all.

From his breast pocket, Father pulled out and pressed a threadbare handkerchief to his mouth. It came away speckled with blood. He took a generous drink from a half-empty bottle of corn liquor and hissed after it went down. He was no drunkard, but only partook when the pain needed to be drowned. It must be unbearable today. Would it worsen?

I had traded a chicken for that bottle. I couldn't afford to trade another, or else...

"The healer came today," he said. "Death's rattle is in my lungs. Oro draws near."

My ribs tightened uncomfortably. The god of the cursed dead was coming to claim him, and not for the reason most would assume. Oro claimed few, but my father was among their number.

At last winter's harsh end, after many freezing nights, Father fell ill. Spring came and summer went, but neither the seasons nor time eased his cough or the weakness that had eaten its way into his strength like worms wriggling into an apple's core. The healer had warned me many times over the past few months when he'd come to look him over that his time on earth was drawing to an end.

I would have known it even if the healer hadn't told me.

He'd thinned so much that his collar and breast bones protruded. His cheeks were sunken. His skin was sallow and dark circles lay heavily under his eyes. Only wisps of graying hair remained. The rest had fallen out, whether from the sickness or starvation.

"I must see that you're taken care of." He toyed with the handkerchief. "I know you won't understand, but I need you to know that I've given much thought to your future, Vayl. I want you to live a life where your time isn't spent fighting for every kernel." He choked on the last word, but composed himself again, and then, "You are of age to marry."

My back stiffened. I swallowed thickly. My lashes fluttered as if his words were a gnat they could bat away.

He noticed and his lips pursed, sour. "I've been corresponding with the matchmaker of Starcrest."

Since when? How had he done so without me knowing? Unless the healer had been carrying the letters back and forth for him.

"The opportunity she offers is hard for people like us to imagine. You should be grateful," he added. "When I am gone, you will have no one to care for you. You should not squander the chance given you."

My brows furrowed and I bristled. I didn't need to be cared for! I was a woman. I'd cared for this house and the land it sat upon for as many years as I'd cared for *him*. Besides, Zaire could claim custody of me as my eldest brother. I may be of age to marry, but that didn't mean I must.

As if intuiting my thoughts, he added, "The healer said that the Emperor has ordered the army to the wall. There have been changes of late. Zaire may not return before winter. He may not return at all."

Was that why my brother was so troubled? He hadn't mentioned the wall when he was here last.

I couldn't imagine what sort of changes would make the Emperor draw his army to the wall. It had held strong since the elven wars had ended.

The wall dividing the empire of Kaan from the kingdom of Thanias, land of the elves, was as wide as ten men standing side by side with their arms outstretched. It was tall as the great mountain pines that clung to the mountains, the wind pushing their branches northward. Beyond its width and height, it was suffused by a layer of magic with which our emperor had procured and protected us for many years.

Father shifted to sit up straighter, wheezing until his breathing cleared again. Then he continued, "Zaire is a young man. A soldier, beholden to the Emperor, who will one day be husband to a wife. Placing you in his care, even for a short time, would place a hardship upon his budding life. I won't write to him on your behalf when the gods have offered another path for you to take." His eyes finally rose to mine. His mind was made up. He wouldn't let me speak or try to sway his opinion.

Anger tore through me.

He noticed, his eyes hardening.

Our conversations largely consisted of my thoughts and retorts raging over my features while he said what he pleased.

He lifted a parchment, its red wax seal teetering on the edge of the paper. "The Emperor wishes to take a new concubine. He'll take more than one if the women are worthy. If you are passed over, the matchmaker will see that you are wed quickly." He punctuated the sentence with a harsh cough. "But if he accepts you, your life would be one of leisure and riches untold."

My gritted teeth could not contain my fury. I spoke, his will be damned. "I would rather die than become one of them. I don't want *that* kind of life."

"Refuse, daughter, and you might get what you prefer. The Emperor is not one to be trifled with. His brother, the Lion of Kaan, expects to see you next week at the matchmaker's house when he passes through. The matchmaker will spend time grooming you in the days between now and then." He laid his head against the broken chair back and closed his eyes, the matter finished in his mind. "You leave at dawn so she can get you ready to meet him."

My mouth gaped. *Tomorrow?* "What will you do if I'm not here? You can't even stand without help." I threw a hand toward the door. "You cannot walk outside to draw water, or carry it, or cook, or wash or mend your clothing!"

"You forget yourself!" he snapped angrily, coughs wracking his frail form. He held out a rolled piece of parchment. "*I* am the head of this household. You will do as *I* say. You *will* leave at dawn and you *will* give this to her."

He'd signed me over to the mystery woman like one might sell property or livestock. I vibrated with anger as I snatched it from his hand.

"Mother would never approve of this and you know it," I seethed.

I turned my back on him and left the room to gather my thoughts before packing my things.

~

RATA SANK in a brilliant swath of gold. Zaire once told me that if you watched closely enough, you could catch the last ray of Raya's fiery light, a flash so bright it was nearly invisible, and so fast, one almost always missed it. Careful not to blink, I stared at the hill as Rata passed behind it. But the last ray eluded me as it always had, and the shadows descended as they always did.

The trees are almost bare, I noted as I angrily wrapped a blanket around my shoulders and paced back and forth along the path my frustration and feet had, over the years, worn down to the dirt.

I was angry. Livid, actually. The Emperor had an entire palace brimming with concubines. How could he possibly need more?

I *couldn't* leave.

If I went tomorrow, who would care for Father? Who would bury him when the stubborn fool died because he couldn't take care of himself?

How would Zaire ever know what happened to me? I could try to send word through the matchmaker, but missives to soldiers often went undelivered.

I could refuse to go...

Father was certainly in no condition to make me. I could see that he was cared for until he took his last breath, and then I could bury him in secret and pretend that he still lived. We had no friends and our nearest neighbors were too concerned with their own survival to have compassion for anyone else. No one had checked on us in years. They wouldn't begin now.

The matchmaker couldn't drag me away. She didn't yet have the letter Father penned that signed me over into her care. It still lay on my bed. I could bury it with him or toss it into Rata's flames. I knew more than most how adept they were at devouring.

"Vayl!" Father called out. My worried feet stopped. His voice sounded strange. Thin and desperate.

A dull thud, followed by a loud crash came next.

I hurried back into the house. The top hinge broke off when I wrenched the door open.

Father had fallen out of his chair into the floor, knocking over the table that sat next to him. The bottle of corn liquor rolled over the dirt floor, spilling and sloshing its contents. I kicked it out of the way and scooted the table over to reach him.

He clutched his chest, gasping. "Can't breathe."

Suddenly, neither could I. "Let's get you back up into the chair."

"No," he protested, feebly batting at my hands. "Don't move me."

His back hurt, I knew, but he needed to sit up to catch his breath. He couldn't lay flat. The healer said it would smother him. I hooked my forearms under his armpits and tried to lift him, but he cried out.

"Stop!"

I laid him back down and crouched beside him, wincing with him as his face contorted in pain. I felt so helpless. Useless. "Father, what do I do? Should I run and get the healer? What can I do?"

He shook his head, his breathing heavy and thick. "You do nothing, Vayl. You let me die."

Needles pricked at the back of my throat. My nose stung as I fought away tears. "No. Father... no."

"I'm sorry," he wheezed. In the next second, what little strength he had bled from his muscles and he slumped slowly to the floor, his eyes turning to glass.

I SPENT hours that night digging a hole deep enough to cradle him. One snick of the shovel at a time, one sliver of thick soil tossed to the side, followed by another. I buried him next to Yenza's boulder. Despite Oro's chill, so deep I could see my breath, the ground remained unfrozen.

~

I SLEPT through the dawn and when I woke, my first instinct wasn't to go to the matchmaker, as Father had insisted. The letter he'd given me to provide her lay discarded on the floor beside me when I woke. I was muddy, covered in sweat, and completely numb.

If I chose to go at all, she'd have a few less days to prepare me for the Emperor's brother.

I didn't leave the house until Rata hovered directly over my head. The goat tried to ram me when I brought hay out to him, so I left it scattered on the ground and scrambled back out of his pen, vowing to eat him first when the winter hunger was too strong to ignore.

Checking under each of the six hens we had left, I came away with only two eggs. Some were too scrawny now to bear them. Scattering a handful of feed on the ground, they rushed down to peck as much of it as they could before it was all gone, clucking desperately as they darted from kernel to kernel.

My eyes and throat stung. This... this was what Father said he didn't want for me. To fight over each morsel as I slowly starved.

The muscles in my arms and back were sore from digging. Every small, inconsequential movement hurt. With the livestock cared for, I decided to care for myself. The pangs in my stomach could no longer be sated with blades of grass. I plucked what I wanted from the garden and ate until the cramping in my stomach faded. Deep down, I knew I wouldn't be able to stay here, yet I couldn't bring myself to venture far from the boulder, as if it was an anchor and I a ship that would drift away without its steady strength.

It was strange. I loved my father, even though he was difficult to love sometimes. I respected him because that was what my mother would have wanted. But now that he was gone and I could consider what I might want for my life for even a minute, I had no idea what *I* wanted... And what did my wants matter in the grand scheme of things?

I hadn't wanted my brother to leave or my parents to die, yet now they both lay in the ground and Zaire was gone. I was alone.

No, I didn't know what I wanted, but fiercely knew what I *didn't* want.

The last thing I wanted was to become something the Emperor would use and discard as he pleased. I decided to persuade the matchmaker to find a husband for me instead. Marrying someone I didn't know seemed nominally better than being a concubine, even nestled in riches among the many he kept.

I sat beside the boulder as Rata, god of fire and light, was caught by the great darkness and wrenched from the sky, never catching sight of the last ray Zaire talked about. Maybe the last ray didn't exist and it was foolish hope that kept me looking, longing to see something bright in a dreary world.

I should have known it was childish to look for such things.

The sands in the hourglass that once felt so sluggish rushed through to the bottom in an instant, and soon cool, gray shadow flooded the valley and washed over me. I went inside the house and tore the blanket from my bed, wrapping it around my shoulders to stave off the chill. I didn't want to stay inside alone, so I would sleep beside the boulder. Beside him.

Then my eye caught on Father's chair and the inferno inside me raged. I dropped the blanket and left it laying in the floor.

I stomped toward the chair and took hold of the unreliable, miserable, horrid, broken thing and dragged it to the door. I had to lay it on its side to get it through the frame. Sweating and angry, I tugged and pulled until it was far from the house, far from the fences and pens in the middle of a muddy field.

My father deserved better than this, even though he never believed it. When Mother promised to scrimp enough to get him something sturdier, he forbade it. When Zaire told him he could use cut wood to at least brace the damn thing, he refused his help.

Even as inch by inch, year by year after she was gone, it sank like a ship slowly taking on water, and he – the sailor – too full of despair to bother using the bucket sitting in front of him to bail it out.

I hated the smell of smoke as much as I hated the sound of flames and the too-dry heat that fire poured over my skin, but I returned to the house and took up the tongs, plucking a coal from our fireplace. Carrying it back out to the field, I placed it on the fabric of that damned chair and watched it char and burn and catch.

Then I went back for my blanket and stood far away where the heat and fire couldn't touch me, watching it burn. Fire did what fire does. It consumed. Destroyed. Laid waste.

When only tendrils of smoke remained and the bulky piece was reduced to ash, I noticed movement in the murky twilight. Something caught my eye. From the hills, someone emerged. I squinted to see who it was, a shiver running up my spine.

Zaire's warning to run and hide among the boulders resurfaced.

"Vayl!" a voice cried.

I knew that voice in my soul.

I ran, my arms pumping and heart thundering, past the smoke that curled toward my brother. "Zaire?" He was limping. As I got nearer, I could see he was covered in blood. "My gods, what happened to you?" I put his arm over my shoulder and became his crutch. I didn't tell him about Father or explain the fire as I walked him around it.

"They'll find me. You can't stay here." A sheen of sweat, soot, and smeared blood covered his ashen face. "You have to run. But first, I need your help," he wheezed, clutching his side. We passed the pens and garden, the boulder and the place where I'd laid our father to rest.

"I'll help you. Let's just get you inside first, hmm?" I tried to calm him.

"You have to help me!" he repeated frantically, pain lancing his voice.

"I'm here, and I'll help you, I swear. Were you at the wall?"

Just a few more strides to the house. He shook his head. "Not the wall. I was assigned to the palace dungeons, but..."

My ankle turned in a sunken spot and I stumbled, almost missing a step. After the elven wars, the Emperor ordered his armies to collect the elves and all those who remained behind in Kaan who had been bestowed with gifts from the gods, prisoner. He kept them beneath the fine palace he and his concubines resided in, high in the snow-capped mountains perched above the Imperial City where an escape would mean a frigid, slow death to any who attempted it.

He cried out, hissing with each step. "I heard something I wasn't supposed to hear, and then I was caught spying. I was a fool to think Favian wasn't watching! He has eyes everywhere." He let out an agonizing groan.

Spying? What had he done? What did he learn? "What –"

"Stop," he panted, bracing a hand on the door frame after I wrenched the door that was barely hanging on back so we could fit through it. "Stop."

He tried to catch his breath, swaying forward. I pressed a hand against his chest so he didn't topple forward. His head lolled. "You've lost too much blood. You need to lie down, but not here. You have to keep moving. We're almost there."

There was no way I could carry Zaire. He was much larger than Father. Taller. Broader. Heavier. If he didn't help me, I'd have to lay him on the floor.

He leaned harder against me, but pushed closer to his bed where he gingerly sat on its edge and doubled over, clutching his side. I wasn't sure how he was able to sit in the shape he was in, or how he hadn't collapsed yet.

"I can't lay flat. I can't," he breathed, hissing and writhing. "Where is Father?" he asked, looking out the doorway of our room, suddenly noticing his absence.

I thanked the gods he couldn't see the empty spot where his chair used to sit. Instead of answering, I announced, "I'll get some cold water and cloths. I need to see your wounds."

Dipping water from the bucket that sat just outside the house, I brought it into the room we used to share, tearing the curtain back to allow more room. I pulled one of his shirts from the dresser and wet one, then brought it to his shoulder where a sliver of flesh gaped. The wound was mostly healed. It was his side that was bleeding afresh. "Let me see your side."

Zaire shook his head. "Don't touch it," he begged. He rocked shallowly, clutching the wound. "Father!" he cried out, craning his head toward the doorway where our father should be sitting, eyes as tight as his abdomen as he curled in on himself. "I almost had it."

"Had what?" I asked, trying to keep him talking, if for no other reason than to distract him from Father's absence. I ran out of the room and took up the bottle of corn liquor, then grabbed the back of an old, wooden chair and dragged it across the packed dirt floor, leaving fresh tracks.

"An elven elixir that would heal him. I was going to buy it off one of the..." He coughed. "I know who wounded him," he gritted when I sat beside him, pouring the alcohol onto the clean shirt and dabbing it onto the cut on his shoulder that sliced all the way across his chest. I needed to cut his filthy shirt away to see what his side looked like. That was what he kept protecting; that was where the worst wound lay.

His eyes were bloodshot and glassy. I put the back of my hand to his head and realized he was burning up with fever. No wonder he was saying such outlandish things. He was obviously hallucinating.

His pitch rose. "I almost had it!"

"If such a thing were real, I would give anything if I could give it to you now," I told him, heart battering my chest.

He brought his fist to his mouth. "Father!" he cried. "I'm sorry. I regretted the angry words I spoke to you the moment they left my mouth and have regretted them every moment since. I didn't enlist to *spite* you. I enlisted to *avenge* you."

His words and energy spent, Zaire slumped forward and almost fell. His head landed against my stomach.

"I need you to lie down, Zaire."

He nodded weakly, then let me ease him onto the cot. When he didn't cry out or protest when I laid him back, icy fear flooded my veins. I ran to find a sharp knife and began the work of gently, but quickly, cutting his shirt away, trying to speak to him so he wouldn't pass out.

"What happened to Father, Zaire?"

I knew Father had taken a sword to the back during the elven wars, a blow so close to his spine that if he had so much as breathed, it might have slid sideways and severed it.

A pool of Zaire's blood was forming under his cot, drop by drop. His face was as pale as the sheets he lay upon. Dry lips peeled apart, his skin was pale as snow. His fingers found my wrist and tightened around it. "An elf didn't injure him. Lord Favian thrust his sword into our father's back," he whispered, blinking lazily and relaxing his grip, his consciousness buoyed.

My ribs tightened in surprise. "Lord Favian? The Emperor's brother; the Lion of Kaan? Why would he do that? Stay with me, Zaire," I said sharply, turning his head toward me and smacking his cheeks a little to rouse him.

"Because Father questioned the orders he gave."

As I peeled the shirt away from the wound he'd been clutching, my stomach turned at the sight. A sword had bitten far into his side.

"How do you know it was Lord Favian?" I asked calmly. He groaned and his eyelids closed. I smacked his cheek again. "Stay with me, Zaire. Stay awake. How do you know it was Lord Favian?"

"Father told me," he slurred. "When I told him I wanted to enlist, he told me what happened and forbade it. He didn't want me anywhere near the Lion. I went anyway. I went to kill Favian, but all this time Father thought I'd betrayed him... or maybe he knew and didn't think I could do it. I don't know what's true anymore. I think I'm dying, Vayl."

"No, you're not. You are *not* going to die on me. Do you hear?"

"Father?" he rasped.

I dabbed alcohol beneath Zaire's nose like I'd seen the healer do when Father had a spell. It seemed to rouse him a little. Zaire had managed to stanch the bleeding enough to allow him to travel home, but the edges of the wound were angry and red streaks radiated from it, a sure sign of infection. "How did you walk so far like this?" I breathed.

"Didn't," he slurred. "Stole the Emperor's horse."

The Emperor's horse. By all the gods' gifts.

He licked his peeling lips. "I need your help."

"Of course," I vowed, trying not to cry. Trying to calm him down. His eyes were feverish and frantic.

His pupils flared and retracted again. "You must go to Starcrest, to the matchmaker. She's a trusted friend. Tell her... tell her that you have a message for the Dragon."

I nodded, trying to calm him down, pressing the alcohol-soaked shirt to his side. "I can do that."

He weakly clasped my hand with his. "Promise. This is important."

"I promise."

He withdrew a sharp, clear glacieris stone from his pocket.

"Zaire," I breathed as my heart stuttered. Where had he gotten such a stone? Glacieris was rare. It was so coveted that certainly no one of Zaire's station could afford it. Had he stolen it from the Emperor as well?

"I must write it on your skin," he said.

I swallowed thickly, then offered him my arm. He shook his head. "Your back. No one will look there. Show *no one* but the Dragon. Not even the matchmaker. Tell her to send for him. Don't ride the horse into Starcrest. The Emperor's men will know him. The horse is a rare breed."

"By the time I get to Starcrest, my sweat will have removed your message."

He weakly shook his head. "The mark of glacieris cannot be removed so easily. The Dragon will help."

I lifted my gown at the back and sat on the edge of the bed so he could reach my skin. He carefully wrote a few words with the frigid stone. Suddenly, the glacieris stone hit the ground, tumbled, and settled between my feet.

"Zaire?" I whispered. I twisted and held his face in my hands. My fingers gripped his head. "Look at me. *Look* at me, brother."

Zaire blinked slowly. His dry lips parted. "Take the dagger from my boot. Show it to the Dragon and he will know." He batted my hands away. "Take it."

I loosened his left boot. There was nothing inside. But in the right was a sleek, silver dagger engraved with an intricate, fire-breathing dragon. My heart faltered.

Before he drew his last breath, my brother cried out. Tears streamed from his fear-soaked eyes into his hair. He held my hand like he did when we were children and I was afraid of the monsters I was convinced lurked in the darkness of my imagination. Thumbs hooked, hands wrapped around each other.

"I need you to go, Vayl," he told me. "To Starcrest. To the matchmaker. Give no one your name."

I managed to speak around the knot lodged in my throat. "I won't. I promise."

His words were melting together. Tears glistened in his eyes, gathering in their corners. "I'm sorry I left you in the fire."

I shook my head, my tears matching my brother's. "You didn't leave me."

A slow blink. "I ran. I was afraid."

"We were young," I told him, my voice shattering. "You can't blame yourself for any of it."

"I'm not young anymore, but I'm leaving you again." His eyes slowly drifted closed.

I sniffled, unable to hold back my tears but unwilling to release his hand. "I don't want you to leave me," I told him, still that selfish, weak girl I was when it was Mother I sat beside.

"Go," was the last word he slurred before death claimed him, too.

I didn't wait to see whether Oro would collect him, or if I felt the presence of my father, given his first soul to reap.

CHAPTER 4

I stumbled outside, barely able to see through my tears. No matter how many times I swiped them, more were there to take their place.

I didn't want to leave. Everything in me screamed to stay, but whatever message this was... it couldn't wait. I could feel it in the intensity of his words. I felt it in my heart.

Zaire wasn't hallucinating. He was lucid, even as his spirit drifted away.

Just as Zaire had said, there was a stark white stallion tied to a tree on the hill where the trees began their ascent. It took a moment for the horse to warm to me, but soon, my hand glided down his neck and he leaned into my touch. He bent to help me climb on and I guided him through the darkness, but we didn't head straight to Starcrest. First, I stopped at the healer's home and woke him.

The healer's hair was a curled mop of gray locks, wild from sleep, beneath his pale cap. His wife's brown and silver was also mussed. She was shorter than him by more than a head and clutched her chest at the sight of me as she stood behind him in their doorway. Her eyes drifted beyond me to the stark white stallion. The Emperor's horse.

Women weren't supposed to ride horses. And they certainly weren't supposed to knock on doors after dark.

Placing his spectacles on the bridge of his pointed nose, he squinted. "Vayl? Has your father passed away?"

"Yes, sir," I replied steadily despite the sorrow thrumming through my body, making my hands tremble. "I buried him last night."

"Then why –?"

"I'm here because my brother came home this evening with a mortal wound and has died as well," my voice cracked. "Someone must bury him, but unfortunately I must leave. The matchmaker is expecting me. It's a matter of urgency, or I wouldn't have bothered you."

I could have informed him that the Lion wished to meet with me. That would've struck fear in his heart. But too much fear would freeze it and he wouldn't help me at all.

His lips parted. "Vayl, if Zaire deserted his position in the Emperor's army, I'm afraid I cannot get involved."

"I can pay you handsomely," I told him, holding my chin up higher. I didn't want him to see how desperate I was... or maybe I did. I didn't know how to handle this.

He sighed. "It isn't about the payment."

"Isn't it?" I asked, holding the glacieris stone out for him to see.

He choked. "Where did you get this?"

His wife's eyes locked on the stone as if it was the only thing on this earth that meant a thing.

"If you give me your word you will personally see that my brother is laid to rest beneath the boulder beside our father, I will give you this piece of glacieris. This stone is worth more than the time and effort for which I'm asking. It's worth more than you'll make in your lifetime in this poor province, and no one needs to know who buried them if you dig the grave tonight." Tears swelled. I wasn't too proud to beg if it came down to it.

He swallowed, eyeballing the stone before gingerly taking the crystal from my palm. "I can go first thing in the morning."

"You must go now," I corrected.

"Vayl, I haven't a horse to pull my wagon and I cannot walk. My foot is still healing from where I broke it. I can borrow one at first light, but if I wake someone at this hour, it will draw attention."

"My brother did not desert his post," I asserted.

"What is the Emperor's opinion?" he challenged, crossing his arms.

It would mean slower travel, but... "I have a horse, but you won't want to keep him around when you've finished. I borrowed him from someone who will want him back. He knows the way home."

He sighed and his gray, worried eyes slid to mine. "Do I want to ask from whom you've borrowed the horse?" He peeked over my shoulder at the radiant, obviously well-bred stallion, tied to the lowest branch of a scraggly pine.

"No, sir."

He heaved a heavy breath. "I see."

He was going to deny me. I caught the sorrowful look he flashed his greedy wife. His fear was the only thing I had left to play on.

"Please, sir? I buried my father last night and had to leave my brother behind, though it pained me greatly. I'm not strong enough to dig another grave. Not physically, and not –" The words caught in my throat. "Please help me. I would do it if I could; however, Father made arrangements for me with the matchmaker this morning. Lord Favian wants to see me, to determine if I might be His Majesty's next concubine."

His lips parted and his eyes grew fractionally larger. "If the Lion of Kaan expects you, you must not tarry. We don't want him coming to look for you here."

Often called the Lion of Kaan, Lord Favian was the Emperor's brother. He was also the man my brother left home to hunt down. The man who thrust his sword into my father's back many years ago, and the same who cleaved my brother's side for eavesdropping. With one sword, Lord Favian had taken them both away from me.

The healer's eyes softened. "I'll see that he's buried. Where did you lay your father to rest?"

"Near the boulder. You'll see the fresh mound of dirt," I whispered, turning to leave. "You may also take the goat and chickens, but could I ask you to secure the house? I may return one day..."

"Of course," he agreed. He patted his chest once. "May the gods keep you, Vayl."

"The gods don't hear my prayers, healer. Maybe they'll listen to yours."

THE CITY of Starcrest was formed like its namesake with five sharp points jutting from its core. I arrived at one tip as Rata once again dawned behind a thick blanket of gray clouds, carrying a sack containing a few articles of clothing and some vegetables that would keep for a day or so – in case some calamity found me along the way. I almost wish it had. But I arrived in Starcrest unscathed, the hem of my dress soaked and muddy, looking as awful and exhausted as I felt.

In the heart of the town, larger buildings loomed and the rich dwelled in fine homes surrounded by stone walls and windows with clear panes that didn't warp or bend reflections. I'd never coveted pure glass, and if it was possible, I wished for it even less now. Distorted glass would conceal my flushed face, sweat-soaked, tangled hair, and the heartrending sorrow etched across my features. Despair hung in the dark circles beneath my eyes, in the slumped hunch of my shoulders, and rested in the down-turned corners of my lips.

Rumors hinted that the matchmaker had her finger on the pulse of this place and far beyond. Perhaps they were right. Even Father knew where and how to reach her. I assumed her home would be located in the finest part of the city, but found no sign proclaiming her profession outside any home or building.

Despite the number of people hurrying by, I might as well have been alone on the street's side. Men rushed in opposing directions, crossing roads traversed by great, lumbering carriages, and ducked into shops, eager to conduct business. Some carried crates up wide stone steps where colorfully painted doors opened for them, but then nudged them shut too quickly for me to peer inside.

Curiously, I noticed no women were walking about, though they could be seen through the clear glass window panes, dressed in frilly gowns and with perfectly arranged hair. Nothing like my mud-stained rags and unruly tangles. They wore pleasant expressions and held their backs so straight, I wondered if they were in more pain than I was.

The scent of fresh horse dung wafted from the streets, but a kaleidoscope of pleasant smells swirled from the buildings all around me. Recently baked breads and sweets, and freshly butchered meat mingled with heady cigar smoke. Outside the local tailor's shop hung a sign fashioned out of wood to look like a spool of golden thread. A girl sat in the shop's window, painstakingly sewing an incredibly intricate, pink-petalled tree onto red silk.

I recognized the cherry tree at once, the harbinger of Spring and new growth. Those trees were my favorite. In Spring, winds frolicked through the countryside like children, tumbling and carefree, plucking those pale pink blossoms from the trees where they would swirl through the air and dance along the ground, piling around fence posts and at the bases of walls. I used to wonder how such beauty could exist alongside such plainness, but our region was full of the flowering trees.

For a few weeks each year, they doused the tangy farmland with their light fragrance and littered soft petals all over the thatched roofs of our small village like colorful confetti thrown in celebration.

For a season, the winds painted over us with strokes from nature's delicate palette. As Spring faded to Summer and those buds died, bright, new leaves claimed dominion. Once the blossoms were overcome and everything returned to its normal dingy state, I missed them and wished for time to hurry so we could enjoy them again.

The girl sewing in the window smiled when she caught me watching and held up her work for me to see. A tall man in the back of the room noticed me, then her. His gruff voice made her flinch as he reminded her to focus on her threadwork. I left so she wouldn't get into more trouble, and wondered – if her thread could weave the words Zaire had painted on my skin, what would his message say?

Some of Starcrest's buildings were taller than four of my homes stacked on top of each other. In the distance, some loomed even larger, but I wasn't there to sightsee. With rising anxiety, I realized I was hopelessly lost. Not only could I not find the matchmaker, I had gotten turned around and wasn't sure which of the star's points I'd already visited and which I still needed to search.

A boy my age approached with his hands in his pockets and a contented look on his face. He looked nice enough. I met his eye and he stopped. A kind, playful grin revealed a broken front tooth. "You look utterly lost," he remarked.

I remained quiet. It was a statement, not a question or an invitation to converse. I wasn't sure how the citizens of Starcrest treated women who spoke out of turn. Father said the Emperor allowed horrible punishments for those who didn't follow the rules.

Sensing my discomfort, the boy entreated, "Excuse my manners, miss. Please do speak."

"Thank you. Where can I find the matchmaker?"

He smiled. "That's easy enough. She lives this way. Come on, I'll show you."

When he waved for me to follow him, I had no choice. My hands tightened on my bag as he started down a narrow alleyway cut between buildings and I halted, my feet rooted in the dirt. Zaire had cautioned me that alleys bred trouble. There were too many shadows even in daylight, he'd often warned.

The memory of him bleeding and broken just last night rose,

as if to remind me that he wasn't there to ask for help anymore. I was the one he was depending on to deliver this urgent message. I would not let him down.

I was suddenly glad to have his dagger tucked into the side of my boot. It was a piece of him, not to mention protection from those who might hurt me.

Noticing my stance, the boy paused. "It's a shortcut," he assured me, his brows lifting as he nodded pleasantly.

What choice did I have but to trust this stranger? I hurried to catch up and keep up with his longer strides. I noticed the sour smell of the dirt underfoot as I stepped from Rata's light into heavy shade. We were halfway through the narrow pass when abruptly, the boy turned and grabbed my bag, ripping it from my hands and pushing me down in the scuffle. He upended it and shook my things out onto the street before rummaging through it all, patting the bag to make sure he hadn't missed something sewn into the scratchy sack. A runty beet rolled out and came to rest against my boot. "Nothing," he gritted. "*Nothing* worth taking."

I thought of drawing the dagger but was afraid the boy would wrest it away and take it from me to sell, and maybe even stab me for good measure before leaving me in the alley to die.

As the boy angrily stalked away, I stood and dusted myself off. I never should have trusted his smile. I should have noticed the gleam of hunger in his eyes and trusted *it*. Hunger never lied. It hollowed cheeks and stretched skin too tightly over bone. Hunger boasted its power. I knew what it felt like to be starved and desperate, but I'd never steal from someone with the same features. At least, I didn't think I could. Maybe if the pangs were intense enough, I *would*.

It was easier to say what you would or wouldn't do when you weren't in the situation you were considering. Until something happened to you, you just didn't know how you'd truly react. Before the fire, I would've said that Zaire and I easily could have escaped on our own. How proud and terribly wrong I would have been.

Gathering my clothes, the few spindly carrots, and the beet at my boot, I stuffed them back into my bag and left the alley and shadows behind. Merging back into the crowd was easy. Finding the matchmaker proved much harder. I walked every street in every direction, peeking in windows and peering down more alleyways, until the shadows shrank with Rata directly overhead. Despite the cloud cover, a sheen of sweat coated every inch of my skin. I was sure I'd passed every shop at least three times and never had I seen a single dwelling or structure that looked like it would house the matchmaker.

My throat was dry and I had no water.

Worse than that, my heart hurt and I had no remedy.

I stopped and leaned a shoulder against a stone wall near the entrance of a broad marketplace, each stall covered with bright fabric that formed a beautiful patchwork quilt. I was tired of walking in circles, desperate to find this woman and deliver the message so important to Zaire, and then what – I wasn't sure. All I knew was that I couldn't go on like this, with the acrid tang of smoke tattooed on my tongue and hands that hadn't stop trembling since Zaire took his last breath.

My chest felt like it might cave in. When I was on the verge of tears once more, I noticed a man in tattered robes who sat at the entrance of the colorful market holding a worn, wooden bowl out for people to take pity on him. When someone gave him a coin, he slid it into his pocket, emptying the bowl again.

He did this several times.

I smiled to myself, hoping his pockets were full. I hoped he'd sewn extra ones into the garment to keep what he'd been given hidden and safe. That he'd never met a boy who would tear that coat from him and shake his coins into the dirt at his feet before taking them away from him.

The man's hair was gunmetal gray and his dark skin was deeply wrinkled, but his most striking feature was the pale gray film clouding his eyes. Even blind, his head swiveled to the sound of feet approaching and walking past. He sensed and saw with his ears.

Another man dropped a coin into his bowl. It disappeared, safely tucked into his jacket pocket with the last, a small clink the only noise emerging from the exchange.

I wondered if *he* would offer help since he, too, sought help from others. Pushing off the wall, I walked over to him and stopped beside him. He stared at me for a long moment, unseeing. I crouched in front of him so he didn't have to crane his head.

"Excuse me, sir. I've been walking all morning in search of the matchmaker's home."

The man's head tilted at the sound of my voice. "A young woman, looking for the matchmaker..." He stretched his bowl out in my direction.

"I have no coin or valuables."

He retracted his bowl. "A strong spirit is more valuable than gold." I wasn't sure what he meant. "May I ask you a question?"

"You may."

He grinned. "Why do you seek directions from a blind man?"

I looked around at those who passed by without even noticing us. "Because I doubt the men buzzing around here with their vision intact know it better than your feet."

"Too true," he heartily agreed. "The matchmaker owns the deep teal home due east from here." He pointed in the direction. "The house and fence are trimmed in paint with real gold flake in it – a gift from the Emperor himself. She found the Emperor's last three concubines, you know. She's become quite famous for having the favor, and the ear, of our ruler."

"Thank you," I told him gratefully, pushing up to stand.

"She seeks yet another young woman to send to the palace. Is that the life for which you hope?" he asked shrewdly as I turned to walk away. "To be drowned in silk and belong to the most powerful man in the Empire?"

"I belong only to myself," I answered, straightening my spine.

He smiled and slowly nodded, as if he could see that I meant it. That if I could, I would weave those words into a shield so strong, not even the gods might pierce it.

"Never forget that truth. This world was built to silence you. Don't let it claim your voice."

I swallowed thickly. "Perhaps someone should tear such a world down and build a new one."

He chuckled and sat his bowl down, staring at the muted, gray sky with unseeing eyes. "Perhaps that someone is you," he mused.

I wondered if he saw any light at all, or only felt the change in temperature from the orb that rose with daylight and fell with dusk. I envisioned a mountain of pink petals gathered around him like the dried leaves were. "I'm sorry I can't give you something in return for the directions."

"But you did," he insisted. "You gave me something that filled more than this bowl could ever hold." He grinned widely. "You gave me hope."

With a sad smile, I left him on the street with his broad smile, coin-laden jacket, and occasionally empty bowl.

Father had believed that only the weak and ignorant dared to hope, claiming that hoping for something you didn't have was a fruitless waste of time. Yet, I did exactly that time and time again. I was always disappointed when it proved its fickle nature and my father right. Every time I let myself grasp it, hope was jerked from my hands and emptied onto the ground, scattered like the boy had littered my clothes and food. As if to show me that what I possessed was worthless and hope, pointless.

The blind man didn't give me hope, but he did show me kindness. And that alone eased the ache in my chest ever so slightly.

Mother once told me that even the people we passed on the road were meant to be in our lives, if only for that brief moment. The blind man and I were meant to meet today. Perhaps it was a blessing to us both that he couldn't see me. I certainly wouldn't inspire hope then. I was as starved and desperate as everyone else.

I *knew* Father was dead.

I knew Zaire was dead.

I knew Mother was dead.

My mind remembered. My heart felt their absence. But the earth still spun as if nothing had happened. That was the thing that made breathing and walking and... *living*... so hard.

I took a deep breath, feeling my lip quiver as tears pricked at my eyes. I had a never-ending supply of spilling sadness, it seemed. And just when something took my mind off all that had happened, something else would remind me how deep and fresh the wounds truly were. It was such a cruel cycle for the living.

Yet the dead had their own.

The gods who claimed Mother and Zaire would collect their souls and usher them into the Solace, a place of beauty and rest where they would spend time garnering wisdom and guidance based upon their experiences. Eventually, they would be trusted to watch over their heirs from beyond, guiding when necessary, providing gentle nudges in the form of gut feelings.

Mother belonged to Yenza, god of the very soil in which my family lay. I imagined her walking with Yenza in a beautiful field of wildflowers where the petals grazed their palms with a whisper-soft touch. She used to pluck bouquets for the god of earth and soil, winking at me and telling me that wild and untamed things that grew from the earth were Yenza's favorite. She would leave them at the edge of her garden at night, and they would be gone when we walked outside the next morning.

There was no lovely offering for the god of the cursed dead, save the surrendering of one's spirit in eternal servitude. Oro chose few, but those he claimed were destined to be the ushers of cursed souls.

I wondered when Oro had come to him. Whether it was on the field of battle during the fierce Elven wars, where the spirits of the fallen were collected and Oro walked the blood-soaked soil to take those who belonged to him, or while Favian tore his sword from his flesh, coming so close to severing his life that Oro must have stood beside Father – deciding whether to spare him.

Did he feel the rumored chill of Oro's presence when the god appeared?

Father would have no rest. He would not see the Solace. Those whom Oro claimed would become ushers, collectors of cursed souls. Father would see them to Oro's fields and plant them there until their very essence shriveled. A shudder passed through me at the thought, but I remembered all Father did for the gods that governed the living. Mother and I waded into the creek one summer afternoon and I told her I knew that Father belonged to Oro. She told me I was right, but she told me to watch him more closely. So, I did.

As he had nothing to give his god until he passed from this life into the next, Father quietly honored all the rest when he was able.

When we had a milk goat, he would ask Zaire to set a bowl of warm milk in front of the animal pens outside for Namina, god of all creatures. When lightning flickered and bolted from the sky, he threw salt into the yard to honor Urit.

Once a year, in the Spring before the rains came, he asked Zaire to paint the windowsills with water from the stream so that Zairitus, the god of great waters, after whom my brother was named, would protect our farm from his floods, but deliver enough rain to nourish our crops and help them grow. When Zaire left, the task was left to me. I wondered if Father thought my handling of the ritual would somehow dilute it since I wasn't Zairitus's chosen and I was only a girl.

My brother was disappointed when Zairitus claimed him. He'd always been fascinated by Trayton, the great dragon warrior of the night. *Each pale white flicker of light in the sky is a scale on his back*, Zaire told me more times than I could count when we were little and still lifted our eyes at night. Trayton shielded us as he fought the darkness to free his love, Rata.

I wasn't sure why Zaire was unimpressed with Zairitus. He controlled the fathomless, raging seas and vast, churning lakes, and was the god of simple, quiet ponds and powerful, rushing rivers. Of life-giving streams and calm, trickling brooks. My brother loved water, but never appreciated how the god's favor allowed him to swim like a fish and hold his breath beneath the water far longer than anyone claimed by another god. To him,

Zairitus had only claimed him because of his name, because of vanity, not because he was extraordinary. And Zaire had always longed to be remarkable.

If a flood had washed over our family and overtaken our home, even as a boy, Zaire could and would have saved us all.

I could do nothing when the fire came. The favor of my god came too late, and it wasn't powerful enough to make a difference in the outcome that night.

The matchmaker's house was east, straight down the road, like the blind man said. It was just as opulent as he'd described, with freshly painted teal walls and windows trimmed in gold like the Emperor's finely tailored clothes. From between the balusters of the tall, golden fence surrounding the home, I spotted lush, verdant grass that hadn't turned brown and brittle despite the cool air.

My modest home was made of dried mud bricks we didn't form with pieces of straw we didn't cut holding them together. My family had squatted in the house no one else wanted until we made it our own, waiting each day to see if anyone would come to lay claim to it in the name of the dead man we'd taken it from and leave us without the pathetically thatched, rotting roof over our heads. Father couldn't climb to fix it and Zaire had tried many times over the years, but the roof leaked all the same. Certain things, once ruined, were unfixable, no matter how much effort you put in.

I lifted the gate's latch and let myself into the yard. Despite the neat walkway paved with flat, gray stones that sparkled in defiance of the dull sky, each of my steps felt heavier than the last, like I was slogging through the thick, suctioning mud that came with the early deluge of spring rains and daily threatened to swallow the only boots I owned.

Twin ponds lay on either side of the walkway with matching fountains, providing a home for several fat bellied koi, their orange, black, and white backs sleek beneath the water's surface. The remnants of flowering bushes and manicured trees had been delicately arranged with painstaking effort. An animal shrieked, startling me. My heart hammering, I stopped to watch as a beautiful peacock strutted toward me over the grass, strolling as if he were king of this place and his only duty was to display his splendid, colorful tail to me, his sole subject. He fanned his feathers and they shivered in delight.

A door slid open.

"I assume you're Vayl," an older woman barked from the doorway. "It's a good thing you're as beautiful as I was told, or I would send you back home. My time is worth more than everything you're gawking at, girl. And you are very, *very* late."

Blinking at her sharp tone, I realized I'd forgotten that Father had sent me there. In my sorrow-fueled haste to leave, I'd forgotten his letter and imagined it lying on the floor, trampled by the healer as he moved Zaire from the bed to his grave.

The matchmaker wore her dark hair in a tight bun that made her features appear even more severe. Her silken robes were vibrant red, trimmed in gold. She pursed her painted lips, displeased. They were thin, set into a face she'd painted to look as pale as plaster, with the exception of demure rosy cheeks and twin kohl streaks rimming her eyes. I wondered how Zaire came to know and trust such a woman.

How could she be so bitter amongst this much beauty and bounty? The beggar who helped me here had little to nothing but the coin he could garner from a kind hand, yet he'd smiled like he was the richest man alive. This woman frowned like she was the most miserable, even though she had more riches than anyone I knew.

I, on the other hand, felt like a reed near the edge of a pond, bent and ready to break.

The matchmaker's lip curled as she took in the state of my hair, mud-stained clothes, and the rumpled feed sack I clenched in my arms. When I paused at the bottom of her steps, she huffed, "Come inside to bathe. The layer of grime on your skin is at least a meter thick."

I ignored the jab, welcoming the anger she provoked – at least it was something different from the sadness – and took the three raised steps to stand beside her on the marble landing of her pristine home. I had no intention of staying longer than it took to deliver my brother's message. I would go home, I decided. I didn't want to become a concubine and certainly didn't want to become the wife of anyone someone so sour might find me.

"I need your help," I told her, keeping my voice low.

"I know that," she clipped, rolling her eyes.

"You don't understand, I –"

"I understand perfectly well, girl," she snipped, turning her back.

I waited until she realized I wasn't following and retraced her hurried steps. "Having second thoughts?"

I was sick of her condescension. "I have a message for the Dragon."

Her sharp eyes cut to mine. "Inside. Now." She opened the front door to reveal a beautiful foyer with a floor of inlaid wood. The instant the door snapped shut behind us, she quietly demanded, "What do you know of the Dragon?"

"I have a message for him, and I know you can reach him."

She crossed her arms and regarded me carefully. "What is your message?"

I raised my chin. "Perhaps you didn't hear me. The message is for the *Dragon*. Not for you."

Her eyes narrowed. "Very well. Remove your filthy boots and put the bag with them. I'll burn it all."

"But this is all I have!" I argued, clutching my things to my chest. "You aren't burning any of it."

"That is all you *had*," she corrected, then pinched the bridge of her nose. "I'll send for the Dragon, but you must still meet the Lion. He chooses his brother's concubines, and he's expecting you. Tomorrow."

My stomach dropped. "Tomorrow?"

"You are late, and I received word today that now he plans to arrive early, which leaves us *very* little time to prepare you for his visit." Though she was clearly upset, I didn't take the opportunity to explain the reason for my tardiness. I didn't want her anger, but I sure as hell didn't want her pity, either. "He likes to try upsetting me and catching me off guard. As if I would allow him to fluster me," the matchmaker added under her breath.

"I don't want to see him. I don't want to be considered," I told her.

She laughed. "Don't you understand, Vayl? What *you* want no longer matters. The Lion is coming, and he expects to see the girl I described. If said girl isn't here, he will find her."

I swallowed thickly.

"Does Lord Favian know who I am or of my family?" I asked carefully. It wasn't like he could hurt them again, but he could use this meeting as a reason to cut me down like he had my father and brother.

"I gave him a false name."

"Why?" I asked.

"Because *I* know who you are, and I care about your loved ones. Is the message you carry from Zaire?" she guessed.

I nodded, my chest suddenly feeling heavy with the knowledge that she cared. "I need to know the story you wove for him about me," I told her as I unlaced my boots, bending over to hide my tears as best I could. They splashed onto the floor, but she didn't notice. Or if she did, she graciously kept quiet. In case she threw my boots away like she'd threatened, I slid Zaire's blade from my boot and tucked it up my sleeve.

Her voice softened when she saw the tears I couldn't stop. "I know how this works, Vayl, and I will tell you. But first, I think you should bathe and take a moment to relax. Catch your breath, dear."

CHAPTER 5

Still in the foyer, she clapped her hands and six... make that seven... girls appeared, stepping out from behind columns on which vases were perched, slipping from curtains and out from behind doors, where they had blended into walls. I hadn't seen them there at all, which unsettled me because I should have noticed at least one of them.

The matchmaker seemed pleased by my startled expression. "My attendants are talented at blending with their surroundings."

The girls hurried out of the main room at one command: "Prepare a fire beneath the tub." The matchmaker looked me over. "It'll take steaming hot water to melt some of this off you."

I gritted my teeth.

She locked eyes with me. "I was *far* dirtier when I arrived at *my* matchmaker's house. I don't say it to offend you. I am only here to help."

Her shoulders straightened and her chin rose as she tucked her past away where it belonged. I wondered if she regretted the vulnerable moment she'd shared with me. Had it been genuinely offered, or strategically given to earn my trust? If Zaire had *fully* trusted her, he would have told me to deliver the message to her to pass on to the Dragon. But since he didn't...

Curious, I asked, "How did you come to take her job?"

A fierce glint entered her eyes. "I kept my mouth shut and my ears open, and when the opportunity came, I seized it first."

She led me to a room where split wood was being tossed onto a bed of flaring coals in a pit that lay beneath an enormous golden tub, its gilded feet fashioned to look like claws. The matchmaker's attendants silently carried buckets of water to fill the tub.

I stared at the catching flames, hating them and the smell of the smoke they bore. "The fire heats the water quickly," the matchmaker shared, "but the flames can't spread because the stones underneath contain it."

She must have seen the question and accusation in my eyes. "Zaire told me what happened to your mother."

He trusted her that much?

One girl tended the charred pieces of fragrant wood, crouching beside them as they thinned, became brittle, and burnt away, completely turned to ash by the hot coals beneath them. "Is that a special kind of wood to burn so quickly?" I asked the girl.

Startled, the attendant glanced at the matchmaker, who dismissed the girl with a sharp nod. The girl quickly left the room and my question unanswered.

I turned my attention back to the golden tub, mesmerized by the fragrant steam rising from the surface. "We don't intend to boil you," the matchmaker teased. Only one attendant remained in the room, holding a golden pitcher. "Douse it and leave us," she ordered the girl, who poured water over the coals, making them hiss. Steam billowed as the girl departed.

The matchmaker turned her attention to me. "Do you need help bathing?"

"I can manage," I answered tightly.

She gestured to a sparkling counter that gleamed with an array of bathing implements. "There are scrub brushes of every kind. Use them all. I don't want to see any dirt on your body the next time I see you. There are soaps and salves. Use those, too.

Scrub and comb your hair until it's clean and untangled," she instructed.

I almost groaned, knowing there was no way she'd think my definition of clean was good enough to match her obviously high standards. The only thing that kept me on my feet was the promise the hot water whispered in the steam wafting into the air. I felt the unmistakable need to feel something other than pain. I cleared my throat. "What am I to wear?"

"Dress in the robe hanging over the screen for now. I'll bring you something fresh soon enough."

I nodded once, glancing toward the folded screen in the corner. I'd never seen such an opulent room divider; a far cry from the tattered sheet I'd used back home to provide privacy. Carefully stitched red and teal dragons slid over its shimmering yellow panels. Lotus flowers blossomed and pink petaled branches slithered in from the corners.

The robe laying over the top of the screen's edge was fuchsia silk, trimmed in gold like the matchmaker's robes. My thoughts returned to the girl I'd seen carefully stitching the cherry blossoms in the shop window and I couldn't help but wonder whose fingers had worked the garment.

It was reminiscent of the ream of fabric Zaire had pressed into my hands before he left that night. My chest ached at the thought of leaving it behind. I vowed to retrieve it as soon as I could. I'd hidden it away under the mattress of my cot. The healer agreed to secure the house after burying Zaire.

As long as no one tossed the place or moved in, I could go back for it. I had to. I'd regretted leaving it, but now was glad I hadn't carried it to Starcrest with me. If I had, the boy in the alley would have stolen it and it would be lost forever.

The matchmaker walked purposefully toward the door. "Work quickly while the water is hot. In the meantime, I'll see that something is prepared for you to eat."

My eyes snapped to her, belying the hunger that warred beneath my anxiety. I was starving.

She lingered annoyingly. "Do you need anything else?"

I fought the urge to scream at her to leave me be, but wondered if she saw it in my eyes because hers narrowed. Sliding a narrow-paneled door from the wall, she stepped through before sliding it shut silently behind her. I slipped Zaire's dagger from my sleeve and carefully laid it on the golden counter.

Tired to the bone, I stripped off my dress, underthings, and stockings and stepped into the hot water. Zaire said his message would not leave my skin so easily, but I hesitated, wondering if I should scrub what I could while standing and hope the match-maker accepted the attempt.

Unfortunately, the tub's bottom was slick. The sole of my right foot slid to the side, then when I tried to catch myself with the left one, it scooted to the other side and a second later, I was lying in the water on my back. The indecision of *to bathe or not to bathe* was stripped from me as I wiped water from my eyes and face. I hoped Zaire was right and that my sweat and this warm water couldn't wash away his message. He'd never lied to me before; I was just afraid I'd made a blunder in carrying out his final request. I lost my footing in the creek once and fell into a deeper puddle. He laughed and teased me about it for days. He would tease me now for being so paranoid. It was glacieris, for the gods' sake.

Fully submerged, I allowed the water to melt and coax the dirt and sweat from my hair. Tears were already falling when I finally lifted my face above the water. I let them fall and the sorrow flowed as I sat in the water, feeling a rush of too many emotions to possibly describe.

Some of the tears were for Mother, some for Father, some for Zaire.

I wondered if Zairitus felt the tears cried on my brother's behalf. Could he feel how much I'd loved him? How much I missed him?

I cleaned myself as well as I could, using the brushes and soaps before me. Gently scented soaps lay on a small table beside the tub. Two bars were gritty; they raked roughly, removing enough layers of dirt that my skin glowed red. The third bar was smooth; it left my abraded skin feeling soft. I used a pale cream on my head that smelled of jasmine and worked the knots from my hair, combing it with my fingers until it was smooth enough to use a comb.

I brushed my cuticles until only the slightest stain lay in the corners, then scoured my feet until no stains remained on my heels. When the water was tepid and murky and the grime settled at the bottom, I stood and wrapped myself in the plush towel she'd left.

A myriad of jars lay on the counter where I'd left Zaire's blade. Investigating each salve was easy, but I didn't know which one to use or for what purpose each was intended. Some were greasy, others were thick and creamy, while still others were all the consistencies in between. One jade colored jar's creamy blend smelled of flowers. A ruby one containing thick, pink sugary grit smelled of cherries. A sapphire jar held an oil with a pungent scent so strong, it stung my nose. I couldn't quite place it, but knew I'd smelled it before. I certainly didn't want to wear it on my skin.

I exchanged my towel for the silk robe and sat on a stool, waiting for the matchmaker to return and idly wondering if I'd cleaned myself well enough for her exacting standards.

Just then, the matchmaker slid the door open, carrying a simple gown folded over her arm. I heaved a sigh of relief and sat up straighter. The dress looked comfortable, unlike the complicated, stiff frocks she and her attendants wore. She looked from me to the jars, then sniffed the air. "Which one did you use?"

"None. I don't know what they are." *And I don't trust what I don't know.* That was true, not only of her creams and salves, but of her. As much faith as Zaire put in this woman, I couldn't bring myself to just yet.

She smiled, but I couldn't tell if she thought me wise or simple. She patted the garment she carried. "This dress may be a bit loose, but it's the best we have to offer at present. My seamstress is already altering a few items for you, including the gown you'll wear to meet the Lion tomorrow."

"When can I see the Dragon?"

She blew out a long breath and pursed her lips. "My message should have reached him by now. I would guess he'll come before dawn, but there's no way to tell exactly when he will arrive."

I wondered which one of her invisible attendants had sought him out while I bathed.

Fighting the chill on my skin, my teeth chattered. I lifted my eyes to hers. "I need your help."

"So you've said," she quipped.

"I need the Lion to take me to the Emperor. I need him to choose me."

She paused and for a moment, she looked past my pain and the freshly scrubbed skin, as if she could envision making me into a woman an emperor wouldn't be able to resist.

"Your father said you would likely resist becoming a concubine."

True, I had no intention of becoming the Emperor's plaything. But I had every intention of killing Lord Favian and the Emperor himself, if need be.

She pressed a hand to her chest and inhaled sharply, as if reading my traitorous thoughts. When I took a step toward her, she held out a hand to stop me. Her eyes shone with fear and something else. Hope? No... hunger. Her chest heaved.

"I'll leave you to dress. Come to the courtyard. Dinner is ready. Your lessons begin the moment you step out of this door, Vayl."

She was going to help me.

Sliding the thin door closed with a whisper, she left me alone.

Tugging on my chemise and tying the corset as tightly as I could on my own, my fingers worked quickly over the buttons of my new dress, stumbling over one of them in my impatience. I tucked the short dagger into the space between my breasts and hoped I didn't bend over too far and accidentally stab myself. The scent of cooked meat and vegetables met me in the hall, causing my mouth to water. I hurried from the room, chasing the scent of food and the spices that adorned it. Turmeric, cumin... cinnamon?

The matchmaker primly sat at a small table in an intimate

courtyard surrounded by a thick curtain of sweet-smelling vines with bell-shaped, white blooms that provided cover from the rest of the yard. Dragonflies buzzed in the air, ducking and darting this way and that. In the last rays of sunlight that spread over her yard, they almost seemed to glow.

"Sit," she ordered, gesturing to the chair I was already walking toward.

I pulled it out and sank gratefully against its curved back.

"Sit up straight. Concubines do not slouch."

I straightened my spine.

"We can speak freely here," the matchmaker advised.

I noticed the girls she employed and wondered how anything could truly be kept secret with so many hovering, ready to jump at her every command.

"You need to learn to harden your expression. I know what you're planning. To gain true, private access to either of them, you need them to believe you *want* to be there. You must *become* a true concubine. The Emperor and Lion must believe it, as must the other women he keeps. Especially his two favored. The twins are very protective..."

Twins?

One of the matchmaker's attendants rolled a cart toward us. She sat a plate of steaming food in front of the matchmaker and poured glasses of water and wine for her. She took her time serving me next.

I felt taut, like a drawn bow string ready to be released. My trembling fingers twitched to reach out and grab something off the table. Everything in me roared to devour every morsel left on the plate, but I waited until the matchmaker unfolded her napkin and daintily laid it in her lap, rearranged her golden cutlery – just so, and calmly took a sip of water.

"Now, your turn."

This was a lesson. In humility. In self-restraint. A lesson I considered purposely failing just to fill the uncomfortable, desperate void gnawing in my stomach. But I remembered the blind man and his ebullient hope and thought if he could see something beautiful amid all that was tarnished and broken in this world, I could certainly summon enough restraint to refrain from eating like a starved dog.

I slowly unfolded my cloth napkin and lay it on my lap, pretending I'd done it a thousand times before, righted a crooked fork among the line of golden cutlery, and took a dainty sip from my water glass.

"When the Emperor is near, your head stays down until and unless he tells you to raise it. Your mouth stays closed unless he tells you to speak. Whatever he utters is the law that governs you at any given time. You do not have the option to refuse him – in anything," she warned. "If I send you, he will – in time – make you his ally. If you go through with your plan, you'll become his greatest enemy."

We stared at one another over the table, through the tension, distrust, and steam curling between us. She swilled the wine in her glass.

"What plan?" I asked.

She rolled her eyes. "When you stepped onto my porch, rage and resolve were painted over every inch of your face. Thank goodness you will learn to school your features before the Lion notices. Your plans for *him* are clear enough. What you haven't settled on is whether you should kill the Emperor as well."

"Why help me, then? It's murder. Treason." It was insanity.

She shrugged. "Some destinies cannot be stopped, and some futures are worth risking everything for." She sawed her meat into tiny pieces, delicately chewing each bite and sipping her wine. "You must know that the chances of you succeeding are slim."

I knew that. I just didn't care. "Then I'll die knowing I tried my best, and that will be enough."

She pointed her fork at my plate. "Eat. Stop worrying about being proper right now and fill yourself. I wager it's been a long time since you've had a nutritious meal."

"I've never eaten like this," I admitted before taking a large bite of steaming broccoli. For the next half hour, I didn't worry about propriety or anything but filling my stomach with meat and vegetables and a sweet, red-orange sauce that was indescribably delicious. I drank glasses of cherry wine and accepted a second plate of food, nearly finishing it, too. I ate so much I nearly made myself sick, but it was worth it.

I finally felt full, and that sensation chased the despair and fear and anger away that had dogged my steps for many years. For a moment, I feared my drowsiness was the result of the matchmaker drugging me, but soon realized it was my full stomach that made me want to curl into a ball and sleep like a bear cub beside her mother.

Noticing my drooping eyelids, the matchmaker announced that a room had been made ready for me and led me back inside.

"Is it true that the Emperor has moved part of our army to the wall?" I asked, keeping my voice low. Starcrest was near enough to the wall that if the rumor was true, she would know.

"He has," she confirmed. "The sheer number of soldiers makes it seem as though he's sent the entire army, not just part."

"Do you know why?"

"The elves have been testing the strength of the wall," she revealed.

"Testing its strength? Or testing it for weaknesses?"

She glanced back at me for a moment. "The magic has held, so their intentions do not matter. Don't worry, Vayl. You are safe here."

Did she mean I was safe here at her home, or here in Starcrest? Or did she mean all of Kaan was safe?

She should tell the Emperor not to worry. He obviously had reason for concern if he'd sent the full force of the empire to the wall.

Many years ago, Zaire and I found an old game board tucked into a cupboard in our house, left behind and forgotten by the family who'd built and owned it before we claimed it. Together, we determined rules to a game that only he and I knew and played. In the Game of Scales, as we'd dubbed it, one could move their pieces across the green and blue diamond patterns one at a time, overtaking the other's game pieces by skipping over them going forward or backward.

My favorite strategy was to push all my men toward the greatest threat, while Zaire scattered his across the board to protect as much of his half of the territory as possible. If I took one of his lands, he still had the others. If he overtook mine, my kingdom fell into his hands.

He once told me that I positioned my armies to form a wall. One only needed to find or make a fissure and the wall could be breached. Once it was, I'd already lost.

I sometimes altered my battle plan depending on his moves, but Zaire was steady and consistently won our fabled skirmishes, while I was stubborn and foolhardy, convinced my bullheaded initiative would stop him. If life imitated the Game of Scales, the Emperor was making a mistake in sending all his men to one location, or even lining the true wall with men ready to fight.

The matchmaker stopped near a door and slid it back into its pocket in the wall. "Vayl," she began carefully, "why didn't Zaire deliver the message himself?"

My hands began to tremble and a knot the size of a fist choked me. I pressed my eyes closed.

"You're not ready to talk about it."

I might never be.

"I'm not ready for the Lion," I rasped, "but I need him to want me."

She smiled sadly, lifting a piece of my damp hair. "Oh, darling. I have no doubt that he will." She let out a heavy sigh and her shoulders fell, suddenly weary. "I'm sorry," she said, letting her hand linger. She knew what I could not admit. She knew Zaire was gone, and she was sorry. She had known him and cared for him.

It struck me how little I knew of my brother's life beyond his brief visits home. The thought made me even sadder. I had asked, but he never gave clear answers. He kept his life tucked away from me, but not from others. The matchmaker had been a part of it, however small.

"Both of us need rest. Tomorrow morning, we will wake early so there's time to prepare for Lord Favian's arrival."

I stepped into the room and slid the door closed behind me, then listened as the matchmaker's steps faded back down the hall. The room was immaculate and brightly decorated, like everything else she owned. The walls were canary yellow, the silk screens fuchsia, covered with more golden dragons, their wings outstretched. Bold paintings of peacocks adorned the walls and the bed covers were silk, the color of plums.

For a long while, I sat on the edge of the bed and worried about tomorrow, so distraught about the past few days I couldn't stop shaking. I wondered if the trembling would ever go away. Like how the taste of smoke still lingered on my tongue, a constant and ever-present reminder that Mother was gone, perhaps the trembling would stay so I wouldn't forget Father and Zaire.

Finally, I tucked Zaire's blade beneath the bed where the silken bed skirt covered it and laid down, trying to calm my thoughts and still my hands. As my body sank into the plush mattress, I marveled at how soft and full the blanket down was and wondered if Zaire had ever slept in something so fine while he was away from home. Eventually, I drifted to sleep on a pillow that cradled my neck, the silk of my fine dress soft against my skin.

CHAPTER 6

The matchmaker woke me while Rata was still drowned in darkness and the dragon god Trayton still fought for her – for us – and shoved me toward another steaming tub of water.

The dragon god was present, though the Dragon I needed to speak to had not shown up for his message yet.

"I sense your question and all I can say is that he has not yet come or sent word."

I nodded.

"Lord Favian slept at an inn not far from here last night."

"How do you know?"

She smirked in response, keeping her secret source close to her chest.

I tried to wake and absorb the information as she instructed me on the purpose of each salve and cream and lotion and told me to use them this time – but advised never to use any at the palace that I didn't bring with me and lock or hide away.

"Concubines have been poisoned through their skin before," she admitted. I blinked at the admission.

The matchmaker prattled. It was clever, she said, to use a poison that must be absorbed over time. The girl would fall ill, eventually becoming weaker and sicker, until she died. It would look like a natural death to those who did not know to look for the telltale signs: discolored nail beds, hardened soft parts, no odor of death, and a lack of decay in general.

"The last girl I sent was poisoned. She was found in a dress she'd put on four days prior, but was preserved so well, she looked to be alive. They called for three physicians to confirm she was, indeed, dead," the matchmaker explained. "Hundreds of flies lay dead around her body. They'd been poisoned, too, through the toxin still present on her skin."

"No one suspected that she'd been murdered at that point?"

She shrugged. "I'm sure some did, but no one wanted to upset the Emperor. There are whispers that she was last seen with the twins I mentioned. The Emperor favors them over all the rest. He whispers his secrets to them both, and they do not like to feel threatened. The girl I sent was beautiful, like you. I believe they were jealous of her. She took his attention from them and they put a stop to it."

And put a stop to her heart...

I quickly bathed again before the matchmaker returned bearing a golden gown in her arms. She hung it on the folding screen where I could better see the garment. It reminded me of the gates surrounding the matchmaker's opulent grounds, painted with real gold flake, if the blind man was correct.

The brilliant hue matched the gaudy rings adorning the matchmaker's every finger and the settings that hugged the colorful, precious stones studding the lobes of her ears.

She waved me over, pressing a more rigid corset into my hands. "We won't lace it tightly, except at the top. You certainly don't need to look skinnier, but this will plump your breasts," she explained as she worked the laces.

I studied the gown hanging beside me, wondering if it would fit or billow as the plain dress had on me yesterday. I might as well have worn a shapeless sack. I was far too thin.

"It will fit," she promised, pulling it down from the dressing screen and holding it up over my head so I could dive inside. "My seamstress darted it in a few places and sewed hidden strings in so we can cinch it to make it smaller if needed."

I noticed the matchmaker fidgeted when her hands weren't busy. She bit the corner of her lip. Her eyes occasionally darted to the door. Her nervousness spread to me, making the tightness I felt in the bones of my ribs contract even further until they felt like they might splinter.

Tugging the gown down and into place, she tucked the layers that had been mussed and fastened the back. She glanced toward the window from which gentle morning light poured. Rata's fire was weakest right after she was set free. It took all day for her to regain the strength she'd lost and would lose again in this perpetual push and pull of day versus night.

"I will comb and pin your hair back. There is no time to let it dry in Rata's light."

I sat on a stool and allowed her to comb my tangles out, hissing when she tore strands from my scalp. "The story I fed Lord Favian is that a fever took your mother years ago, and that age and illness claimed your father. I told him you have no siblings or extended family to take you in, and that is why you came to me for help. I told him that I sent word to him the moment I saw you, knowing the Emperor's tastes."

I tucked my shaking hands beneath my arms, hugging myself in an effort to calm my nerves. She noticed, and her eyes looked worried. "I have something that should ease it."

I nodded, unable to speak.

Seated before a golden mirror, I watched her work my hair into twists and pin them together in intricate coils, her hands deft and sure.

Her dark brown eyes met mine in the glass. "Favian knows all of the concubines. I'm not sure how well..." she trailed off. "He also knows what his brother prefers."

I swallowed the bile that inched up the back of my throat. "What does he like?" I asked, afraid she might answer and afraid she wouldn't.

"The Emperor is attracted to submissive women, but that's

not what Favian hopes to find for him. He is looking for a woman who can survive the others. He didn't say it outright, but I believe he suspects one of the concubines is responsible for killing the newest ones sent to the palace."

My head ticked back in surprise. "Newest *ones*? You only mentioned the last girl you sent."

"There have been at least a dozen," she admitted, her hands stilling on one strand of hair. "What you are about to do is not without risk."

"But with that risk comes the only reward I covet," I rasped, fiercely determined. It was all I had now, the seething hatred I felt for the man who took my loved ones away.

Her eyes met my reflection's. "You must make Favian believe that you are such a woman, but you also must be careful not to provoke his anger. You'll be teetering on a precipice. One wrong step, Vayl..." she warned.

"I know."

She finally finished coiling and pinning. Satisfied with my hair, she added a few decorative pins, each with a golden peacock festooned at its end. She painted my lips and smoothed powder over the skin of my face and neck. She swiped shimmer over my eyelids and spritzed me with a heady perfume.

"Why is he called the Lion?"

"*Some* would say that Favian bears the title because he ferociously leads Kaan's armies and is second in line to the throne, as Emperor Cassius has no heirs."

"You said *some* would say that. What is your opinion?" I asked shrewdly.

Her brows rose as she tucked two golden slippers onto my feet. "I would say it's because he devours anyone who stands in his way." She held her hands out for me to take, then pulled me to my feet. "Lord Favian believes his time is more valuable than gold, and he isn't one to waste it. He will abruptly leave if he thinks for one second that you can't survive the other women. Do not be a lamb in the presence of the Lion," she advised. "He can smell fear, they say." With that warning ringing in my ears, she called for an attendant to bring a special concoction of tea. "It will calm your hands and ease your heart."

"There is nothing in this world that could possibly do the latter," I told her honestly.

She inclined her head. "Even so."

The girl soon returned with a steaming cup of tea. In the amber water swam a few herbs I could name and some I didn't recognize. I smelled chamomile and lavender. Rosemary. But something bitter lurked behind the sweet notes.

I sipped it anyway, knowing she wouldn't poison me before I met the Lion. Even the matchmaker feared him. By the time I finished sipping, the tremors had mostly quieted. I was about to ask what was in the mix when an attendant knocked lightly on the door. "Madame, Lord Favian has arrived. He just entered the gate. His men wait beyond it on horseback."

"He's early, and he didn't stable his horses," she whispered to me. "That means he will not tarry long. Make an impression and make it quickly."

I stood and followed her as she rushed to meet him, her silk skirts billowing behind her.

My pulse pounded in my ears. Fury, not blood, rushed through my veins.

Time slowed as we approached the door.

"Look at him like that and he'll kill us both," she snapped into my ear, smiling as he crossed the yard. I smiled, too, hiding away what lay in my heart. I smiled at the thought of seeing him take his last breath...

She slid the door open.

He climbed the few steps.

"Lord Favian," she welcomed warmly, confidently holding her shoulder blades back.

He greeted her with a single nod. "Heart Reader."

My breath hitched. *The matchmaker was gifted? No wonder she's so intuitive...*

Favian wasn't young. Faint lines cut into the pale skin around his eyes and lips. A few creased his forehead. He was taller than me, as most were, but where I was thin and starved, he was husky, muscular, and stout beneath the honey-brown leather armor he wore. His leathers had been crafted beneath a skilled hand that had painstakingly etched a lion onto his breast plate. The beast stood proudly, his mouth parted to reveal sharp teeth.

The armor was well used. Like a good book, the leather hide was worn soft at its edges. Friction had faded the thick panels under his arms. It had been sliced and gouged, but here he stood. He'd won or escaped his battles thus far.

Favian smelled faintly of mint soap and his fair hair, still damp from his bath, was tied at the nape of his neck. Strands alternated in shades of honeysuckle, pale and darker yellow. Like his brother's were rumored to be, his features were handsome enough. A square jaw, sharp brows.

His eyes caught mine. And held. They were a deep, unsettling blue with no striations radiating in them at all. Their solid color reminded me of the nights where Trayton's great back did not shimmer. They were cold and calculating, the eyes of a man with raw, indisputable power.

I expected him to trace my form and take in the gown and peacock hair pins the matchmaker had selected, or perhaps take note of the shape and red hue of my lips.

If he noticed any of it, he didn't give it away. A strange stand-off silently unfolded between us. Who would be the first to blink? To look away?

He tilted his head, intensely staring, curious. In his eyes was both threat and dare, and I willingly danced with them both. "Heart Reader, you have done well."

The matchmaker pressed a hand to her chest and bowed at her waist. "Thank you, my lord."

"What is her name?" Favian asked the matchmaker, as if I didn't have the wits to answer his question myself. He moved closer.

One step.

Two.

"Her name is Valor, Lord Favian," she answered. The hair on

the back of my neck rose at the mention of the name my mother had chosen to name me if I had been born a boy. The matchmaker was gifted. Though human, some amount of elvish blood coursed through her veins and granted her some power, however weak or strong.

Heart Readers could intuit a person's intentions, but as far as I knew, they could not read their minds or memories. How did she know my mother's intended name for me?

I finally looked away, my eyes catching on the woman in question as the matchmaker moved closer to him. Her eyes flashed a warning. *Careful, girl...* I could almost hear her say. Did she know the meaning of the false name she'd given me? Didn't she know predators did not bow to their prey?

I heeded her warning, softening my lips and blinking as if I'd forgotten myself in his presence, bolstering the masculine pride that practically rippled from him like cologne.

I needed him to choose me. And that need was so overwhelming, it nearly made my knees weak.

Choose me, I silently told him, *and I will deliver a cut for every day my father spent in pain, for how he wasted away, for how he lived in fear and hid it so we didn't bear it with him, for every mile my brother traversed trying to reach home as he was dying.*

The way Favian carried himself sparked a rush of hatred so forceful, I worried he might see it burning in my eyes, a remnant of the fire that took what the Lion standing before me hadn't. Then, the untouchable Favian finally let his eyes drift over me.

He thought the world was his to do with as he pleased and that he had any say in my destiny. I almost laughed.

My future, my destiny, was worth going to war with the Emperor over simply because it was mine and would *never* be his.

His eyes met mine again, victory lighting them. He thought he'd conquered me, or wanted to still. "There are certain matters I must see to before I can return for her," he finally said, his voice clipped and sure.

"You won't dispatch a carriage for her? Like the others?"

A smile played at the corner of his lips. "My men and I will personally deliver her to the Emperor, to ensure her protection, of course." My skin crawled. "I'll be back to collect her within a fortnight. She'll need a riding dress."

If Favian is going to see me to the palace, there might be opportunity for me to end him somewhere along the way... I'll kill him, then run.

It would depend on how many of his soldiers traveled with us and what opportunities revealed themselves.

She bowed to him. "I'll see to it, my lord."

The matchmaker beamed a smile as he reached into his satchel and pulled out a large bag of coin, placing it into her outstretched, greedy hands. She rattled the bag. The clinking coins were so loud they drowned out the sound of the small rolled parchment hitting the floor, and she swept her gown's train across the floor, concealing the silent, hidden girl whose toes reached out and tucked it away. The attendant closed her eyes and shrank into the wall once more, giving no indication she had stolen from the Emperor's brother. Her dress perfectly matched the rich, purple curtains framing the small window beside her.

I wasn't sure if the girl had stolen the paper for the matchmaker or me, but already I itched to read what was printed on that small scroll.

"I'll come for you soon, Valor," he promised me, a darkness slithering through his gaze.

The matchmaker thanked Lord Favian profusely and followed him to the door. He had already forgotten her and quickly strode across her yard, spitting into the grass before opening the golden gate and leaving it wide open behind him.

After dispatching an attendant to close the gate, she tossed the bag to the girl who was brave enough to steal from the Lion. The little thief didn't take the opportunity to mention what happened, instead catching the coin bag and walking away with it, disappearing into a room farther down the hall. The small scroll still lay beneath the curtain she had been hidden behind.

"I have a riding dress that can be altered to fit you. I'll bring it to your room along with several others you'll need. There is much to do and no time to waste."

The matchmaker's attendants fell into step behind her, leaving me near the door. I bent to collect the scroll, then followed, stepping into my room and easing the door closed as they rifled for the dress. The scroll was sealed with wax bearing the Emperor's crest.

I wanted so badly to crack the seal, but just then I heard footsteps in the hall. I hid the scroll beneath my pillow and turned to face the matchmaker, who pushed into the room holding a gown that was yards too long.

Another of her attendants carried in a wooden crate. "Put the dress on, then stand atop this so we can place the pins," the matchmaker ordered.

I took the dress from her hands and walked behind the dressing screen. I took a moment to breathe before exchanging the golden gown for the one I would wear to the palace.

The next hour was a blur of hurried, but careful adjustments. The girls lamented how much fabric would be lost when all was done, as I was quite shorter than they'd expected. They discussed what alterations would flatter my form and hide the sharp jut of my hip bones, whether it was possible to fatten me up in such a short time, how my hair should be arranged on the day I was to leave, and what hues most flattered my complexion.

When the decisions were settled upon and all the gowns and dresses pinned, I slipped behind the screen and changed into a plain, moss-green dress that flared from my hips to where it kissed the ground. I itched to hide Zaire's blade back in my corset, worried something would happen and I would accidentally leave it behind.

I listened as the matchmaker instructed one of the youngest girls on how to sew the alterations. She dismissed the few that lingered, ready to help, from the room. I stepped out as they followed the tiny seamstress away.

The matchmaker turned to me. "Well done, Vayl."

"Why didn't you tell me you were a Heart Reader?"

She quirked a brow. "That isn't something I announce upon first meeting someone. Do you have any idea how dangerous it is to have a gift? Especially one the Emperor and his brother make a sport of exploiting?"

"I thought the gifted were all prisoners of war."

Her lips pinched. "I am not in the dungeons beneath the palace, but do not think for one second I am not caged, Vayl."

The gifted were the products of unions between humans and elves. Such relationships hadn't existed since before the war, but gifts were inherited, passed down through bloodlines. Her ears were as round as mine. No one could tell she was part elf. So, how did the Emperor know? Had she tried to garner his favor by telling him and instead found herself caught up in a game she couldn't possibly win? No, that couldn't be it. She would have read his heart and seen his intent to use her gift against her.

Could she be manipulating *him* instead?

A woman with her means and wit could easily arrange to disappear and resettle in some remote place among the far-flung reaches of the empire. She might even be welcomed in Thanias, kingdom of the elves. Then again, maybe her human-like features would cast her as a pariah in that fabled kingdom.

"I need to go to the market for some provisions you'll need to carry with you."

"Should I go as well?" I asked.

She shook her head. "I'd rather you stay here. The Lion has eyes on my home."

I startled. "Do you mean he'll watch until I leave?"

She nodded. "He's always watching."

I met her eyes. "May I go outside? I'd like to see the gardens. I've only seen them from the windows and the barest glimpse from the courtyard."

Her eyes narrowed, assessing my motives. "Of course you can.

I would just warn you not to run. Lord Favian would be alerted at once."

Tipping my chin, I replied, "I have no plans to run. I told you. I *want* him to take me there."

She watched me for a long moment. Satisfied with what she saw, she gave a firm nod. "I'm sure you're hungry. I'll ask for a small meal to be prepared for you now, and a larger one for us to enjoy tonight."

She'd sensed my aching stomach; an intuition borne of someone who was all too familiar with the feeling, though years ago it must have been for her. "Thank you," I told her. "I truly mean it."

"And I'll have some tea ground for you to take on your journey."

I nodded in thanks, unable to speak, needles pricking at my throat again. Even now, my hands remained mostly still from the concoction she'd brewed for me earlier. When I held them in front of me, I couldn't discern the vibration I still felt humming through them, and that was all that mattered – appearances. The truth could always be denied without visible or tangible proof.

The matchmaker made her way to the front door, delivering final instructions to the girls waiting in the hall. I tiptoed to my room and slipped the scroll into my sleeve and Zaire's knife into my corset, then let myself out the back and into the garden where roses climbed to form an arbor over my head.

It was like stepping into another world, one untouched by the Emperor. There was a golden table with matching chairs nestled beneath it, trails of colorful rocks twisting into swirling patterns underfoot, more fountains, and fat bellied koi skimming along each pond. This garden was where the beautiful peacocks truly roamed. I counted six before another cried out from the iron aviary where they made their homes. The structure was taller than the house, with a tangle of gilded perches inside.

There was such beauty here. Plants with leaves as broad as an elephant's ear, spindly grasses with lion's tail tufts sprouting from their middles, sweet-smelling lavender, and heady jasmine.

It wasn't orderly like the front yard. There was a glorious chaos to the place, as if the matchmaker built it little by little and lacked the planning that would have made it appear more cohesive. But it was the disorder that made me want to sit and rest and maybe lose myself for a little while. Perfection was boring. Flaws were the ink with which great stories were penned.

One of the attendants, bearing a sweet demeanor and a heart-shaped face to match, brought me a basket of small rolls with sweet butter to slather onto them, and a tall carafe of water. I ate the rolls, pinching tiny pieces for the pea chicks who dared come close enough, only to scurry away to keep up with their pea fowl mothers as the majestic creatures strolled along the curling pathways.

When no bread remained to share, I stood and dusted myself off, then walked to the aviary and sat with my back to its pretty bars. The taller plants that surrounded it would provide the cover I needed. When I was fairly certain none of the matchmaker's attendants was lurking, I removed the scroll and broke the seal with my thumb.

After I read the words, my hands began to tremble again.

CHAPTER 7

I watched the pea chicks in the yard for a long while, contemplating the heavy rose blossoms that swayed in the breeze, their stems arcing beneath their weight, and considered the message on the scroll until my thoughts strayed once more to the Lion. How would I manage to kill such a formidable soldier? Before he enlisted, Zaire taught me how to shoot his bow, throw a knife, and hold a sword, but my skills hadn't been tested. I'd never seen battle or defended my life against one who would claim it in one swift slice.

It had to be something done in a way the Lion wouldn't expect....

The instant the matchmaker arrived back home, a flurry of chattering and movement erupted inside the house. I stood up and tucked the scroll into my corset, in front of the blade, flattening the paper I desperately wanted to burn despite my fear of fire.

I numbly walked across the yard and considered whether to ask the matchmaker for more tea now. My hands...

The moment I took hold of the door's handle, a loud explosion rocked the earth. I stumbled sideways, falling into a thorny rose bush. I couldn't hear my own hissing from the small pricks of pain shooting in my palms and leg where I tried and failed to catch myself. My ears rang, tinny and loud.

The matchmaker's house seemed to sway. I stood and backed away from the structure, stumbling into the grass just before an unseen force hit me in the chest and knocked me off my feet. The back of my head smacked part of the rocky walkway.

The blast knocked the breath out of me and I gasped, trying to draw in air. For a moment, I worried Zaire's blade had been run into me, but there was no blood or wound that I could see. The matchmaker's house wasn't moving anymore. The terrible sound was gone. The peacocks cried out, feathers rattling in warning. The majestic creatures rushed to the aviary and hid inside its strong bars, seeking solace.

Suddenly, the matchmaker was in front of me. "Vayl!" she shouted, her voice muffled as if she was underwater. She took hold of my upper arms and gave me a shake. "Are you injured?" she enunciated.

I shook my head slowly, trying to gain my bearings. "I'm fine. What was *that*?"

"The elves tried to breach the wall."

Before I could ask how she knew that, another boom knocked us both over into a row of lavender plants. The moment we tried to stand, another burst of power swayed us. The onslaught was intense and aggressive, so we stayed on the ground to see if it would pass.

The matchmaker's usual confidence was gone, replaced by fear as she clutched her chest. "They aren't stopping this time. They usually stop."

A loud crack resonated from the matchmaker's lovely house. Her attendants spilled onto the lawn around us, shielding their heads. A crevice opened near the foundation and spread upward, inching toward the roof with each surge of energy. We could only watch numbly as her home crumbled.

The sight tore at the fresh wound that lay across my heart. Fire wasn't the only thing that could destroy a home. She said that as a gifted, she was caged, but the detail and work that went into this home and lawn indicated she loved it anyway.

The home was just a structure, one of thousands within the village of Starcrest, but what it provided for her and her attendants was invaluable. Meaningful. Vital.

The matchmaker blankly watched, bracing her body for impact after shuddering impact. Just then, something in the roof of her home popped. Window panes exploded, salting the lawn.

And as unexpectedly as it had come, the attack stopped.

Heart in my throat, I waited to be sure it was truly over. The matchmaker took a few staggering steps toward her home, shrewdly surveying the damage. Her attendants flocked around her like goslings would their mother.

"Matchmaker!" a male voice called out from within the house. A young man appeared in the doorway and the matchmaker rushed to him, throwing her arms around his neck.

"Are you okay?" he asked, glancing around at the attendants. His eyes caught on me and he tilted his head. He was a head taller than I was. His curly auburn hair was tied back at his nape, and on his cheeks were more freckles than there were roses in the matchmaker's garden. He slowly released her, turning his attention to the structure of the house when she asked him to make sure it was safe.

He examined the crack, then walked inside and checked the ceiling for her. We waited nervously outside. "It seems fine enough," he called out.

"Are you sure, Asra?" she asked, wary.

Asra...

"You tell me," he challenged with a smile. I saw the moment her eyes softened. She read his heart and was instantly put at ease. His gait was easy when he walked to her.

Tension seeped from the matchmaker's shoulder and she cupped her elbow.

"Are you hurt?" the stranger assessed.

"I fell, but I'm fine. It's just sore," she told him. She looked to her gaggle of girls and told them that if Asra said the house was safe, it was. "Please see to the mess and then get back to work. We've no time to waste."

"What sort of work do you have for them?" he asked. His eyes found me again, curious.

The matchmaker waved me inside where I followed the two into the sitting room. Asra moved gracefully. He wore no shirt beneath his dark green tunic, the sleeves rolled to his elbows. A few burgundy curls escaped his leather and bounced near his jaw. He tucked them behind his ear.

"This young lady is the Emperor's newest concubine," she said proudly, glancing over her shoulder at me with a secret, knowing look. "Favian confirmed her today."

Asra's cheeks flushed as they stopped, turning to face me. He bent at his waist. "I offer you my congratulations."

"And," the matchmaker lilted, "she carries the message for your brother."

Asra's brows shot up. "*You* called for him?" he asked me incredulously.

"Where is he?" I asked.

He puffed his chest a little. "He sent me to collect the message."

If anger were heat, it would have rippled from my skin, distorting the air all around me. "No."

His chest deflated and he ticked his head back. "No?"

"No," I hissed. "I gave my word. I won't give the message to anyone but the Dragon."

"I'm his brother," he argued, his easy smile returning.

"Firstly, I don't know you or if you're lying. Secondly, I wouldn't care if you were the Emperor himself. I gave my word and I intend to keep it."

His lips gaped in surprise. The matchmaker smirked at the flustered young man. He gestured to me. "Can't you vouch for me?"

"She cannot," I told him. "I don't know her well enough to trust her, either."

The Heart Reader shrugged at her visitor. "She gave her word."

Asra let out a playful growl. "He's not going to like this. He's tracking the Lion."

"Is he?" I asked.

Asra folded his arms over his chest. "Indeed."

"Or is the Lion tracking him?"

"Pardon me?" the boy asked, his brows slanting. His eyes tracked my hand as it dipped between my breasts to retrieve the scroll Lord Favian had dropped and the attendant had artfully swiped. He unfolded and smoothed the paper, his eyes tearing over the words before flashing to mine, green, with the barest hints of blue streaked with gold. Asra's pupils reminded me of geodes. "Where did you get this?"

I shrugged. "The Lion should be more careful with his missives."

He glanced at the matchmaker, whose mouth gaped.

Asra waved the scroll. "I'll be back with him as soon as I can."

"Tell him to hurry. The Lion is returning for her within the fortnight. I need every second to prepare her for what she's walking into," the matchmaker warned.

Asra took her proffered hand and brought it to his lips, placing a chaste kiss on the back, then turned to me and waited to see if I would accept his hand and kiss as well. When he felt the trembling, his eyes slid to mine. His soft lips brushed my skin before he brought my hand down, squeezing it reassuringly before letting it go. He looked back toward the house.

"He'll be here before dawn," Asra promised.

"That's what I told her last night," the matchmaker quipped.

"I'll see to it," he vowed, rushing from the room.

Though I listened intently, he did not run outside. *Where did he go?*

The matchmaker turned to me. "What was on that scroll?"

"A list of locations where *dragons* have been sighted."

"There are many dragons, but only one who leads them. Lord

Favian hunts them all, but covets the kill of the strongest, of course."

"Who are they?"

She smiled tightly. "Those who would dare stand against the Emperor. I won't discourage you if you figure out how to do what you're planning... but I would warn you of its consequences. As his concubine, you will become Emperor Cassius's ally, but you won't have his trust. Trust must be earned over time. His favored concubines have been loyal to him for years. They've killed for him. Patience is the sharpest weapon you can wield. If you're going to do this, you can't just go in wildly swinging the dagger you've tucked between your breasts. You'll have to bide your time. Earn his favor. Make him drop his guard. Allow Favian to drop his guard... You'll need to wait for a moment alone with Favian when he's unarmed and no one else is around to see you approach him, and then slip away before anyone sees what you've done. And that, my dear, is a nearly impossible feat."

My eyes slid to the Heart Reader's. "Zaire was a dragon. Wasn't he?"

"Yes and no. I'll let Asra and his brother explain when they return," she told me. "I need to help the girls, but I won't be far if you need me. I can feel the ache in your heart, Vayl. It's overwhelming to me, so I can't imagine what it feels like to you. It takes great strength to continue on after all you love is gone, but it takes courage to do what you did today."

Tears pricked at my eyes.

"You faced him," she said. "You made a fool out of him. He just doesn't know it yet. Oh, but imagine the moment when the Lion realizes you are no lamb..."

She turned and left me in the sitting room where I sat among the beauty of her gilded furnishings. The memories – the pain – flowed over me in crushing waves. It never ebbed too far away.

I walked outside to better breathe, hoping that this time, the world wouldn't tilt.

~

DUSK FELL and the smell of freshly cooked food wafted into the yard, finally drawing me inside. My eyes were swollen, but the tears had finally stopped. The house was immaculate once again. The tile floors shone like glass. I paused just inside the door, my feet leaving prints. I looked for a rug to wipe my bare feet upon.

"It's okay," one of the attendants nearby quietly told me. It was the little thief. "I'll wash them away."

"What you did was incredibly brave."

"It ended well," she said breezily, shrugging a narrow shoulder. She pointed down the hall. "She's waiting for you. She told me to come and get you. I was on my way, but saw you stand and walk this way."

I started down the hall in search of food, completely exhausted even though I hadn't done much today. The tiredness I felt was deep, like it had burrowed into mind and bone alike. Like it might never leave.

"It will always hurt, but it won't always hurt so much," the girl quietly said behind me.

I looked at her over my shoulder and saw in her eyes that she knew pain, too. "Thank you."

She gently inclined her head.

Following my nose, I had no trouble finding the kitchen. The matchmaker was already there. We ate at a small table that had been pushed into a corner. With no gold flake or gilt, it was the most modest piece of furniture I'd seen in the house. I felt more comfortable in the moments we sat at it than I had since stepping foot across the matchmaker's threshold. Finally, something I wouldn't muddy or mar.

The wood table was worn, and my fingers traced the scars on its top as we quietly ate a meal of venison, creamy potatoes, hunks of soft cheese, and an array of fruits I'd never seen and couldn't name.

The matchmaker didn't press me on manners. She seemed tired, too. Between bites I sipped the special tea she'd had made for me and waited for the tremors to stop. How long would I need to drink it? How many times a day? I had to make them stop for good somehow. Someone – Lord Favian or the Emperor or one of his favored concubines – would notice if I went to the palace trembling like a terrified puppy just separated from its mother.

If Lord Favian thought something was wrong with me physically, I'd never see the palace. He'd likely leave me someplace between Starcrest and the frigid peaks we would have to cross.

"I'm sorry your home was damaged," I told her after taking another warm sip of calming tea, watching her over the rim of my cup.

She brushed a strand of hair out of her eyes. Her usually tight bun lay loose atop her head. Her carefully painted makeup had mostly worn away. "We were fortunate. Some houses fell today."

"If you don't want to groom me for this, I understand. If I fail, or even if I succeed, you could be targeted."

"I know," she admitted softly, straightening the silverware she hadn't even used. "But I am ready. Let them come."

A young attendant brought out a tray with a delicate assortment of plates, each holding something sweet. A slice of cake, a sliver of pie, a square of bread with cinnamon and sugar dusting the top in a crunchy coat. I had just finished my meal but couldn't tear my eyes from the tray. Everything was so beautiful.

The matchmaker claimed she was ready, but her actions would also put these girls in danger. She knew that and was prepared to risk their lives, too. But were they aware of the threat?

"You need to eat as much as you can, and often. You're far too thin, but besides that, you must get stronger before you leave here."

The girl slid the tray between us and the matchmaker and I shared the desserts at my insistence, though she only took a couple of bites to appease me before putting her fork down.

After supper, I went to my room and lay on the bed, my stomach full and heart torn. The Dragon would come before dawn, according to Asra, but trying to stay awake was futile. I soon lost the battle and drifted off to sleep.

CHAPTER 8

I'm standing outside my house beside the boulder where Father now rests, my scratchy blanket wrapped snugly around my shoulders. In the distance, from the hills, there is movement.

"Vayl!" Zaire shouts. He limps as fast as he can toward me, but I am already running to meet him. To help him. The blanket drifts to the ground, forgotten.

I almost reach him.

The sound of horses galloping and their ragged, strained breaths come from every direction. Soldiers surround us. One swings down from the saddle. Lord Favian.

I look at my brother. "I'm sorry, Vayl," he says forlornly.

I scream as they cut him down and continue screaming until they wrench me away and sever my throat, leaving me to choke as I die, staring at Trayton in the sky. He still fights, but not for me.

Someone was speaking, but I couldn't make out their words.

"She's caught in a nightmare. Wake her gently..."

"Vayl," the matchmaker urged. "You're only dreaming. You're safe."

My heart thundered. My eyes flew open and I sat up, scooting to the head of the bed before tossing the covers off and leaping to my feet. Lightning flashed beneath my skin; I could not bear the sensation.

"Vayl," she tried to calm me, standing with her hands out as if I were a dangerous, cornered animal. As if I was a threat.

My chest heaved. Sweat cooled on my skin and a shiver slid up my spine. Soaked hair clung to my face and neck. My knees shook and my eyes burned. I was so tired of crying, but too weak to stop the sting of more tears.

So tired of my hands, which still shook uncontrollably. Then the trembling spread – through my stomach to my knees, and upward to my shoulders and lips.

Candles burned throughout the room in holders on tables and in the hands of the matchmaker's worried attendants. Asra was here. And behind him... someone else lurked in the shadows. I couldn't see his face.

"Give her some space," the stranger ordered. His voice was smooth and rich and deep. The attendants bled from the room, taking their candles with them. The room dimmed, for which I was glad.

Asra lingered, his gaze tracking my every step as I paced, desperate to rid myself of this crackling energy, emotion, and... fear.

The stranger looked at him, then jerked his chin to the door. Asra slowly stepped from the room.

I had a feeling he wouldn't go far.

Only the matchmaker and the Dragon remained.

"I need some tea," I told her, my teeth chattering over the words.

She nodded. "Of course." With hurried steps, the matchmaker left the room.

"Thank you," I whispered. I felt like I might be sick and wasn't sure I could stomach the tea, but she needed a task and I needed... something. I just didn't know what.

Actually, I *did* know. I needed my brother, my father, and my mother back. I needed this crushing, heavy weight to be removed from my chest. To breathe. To keep my head above the water that kept rising, relentlessly consuming without ceasing.

The Dragon quietly stepped to the door and slid it shut. He came closer, but was careful to keep his distance, giving me the space he'd told the others to provide. My frenetic pacing began to calm.

There was only one candle left burning. I would have pinched the wick and put it out if he weren't there. Instead, I used its light to see him better. The tiny flame cast a warm glow over his skin. Like Asra, he was tall and well-built, as any dragon should be. I could see his handsome face and the sculpted physique that lay beneath the simple white shirt he wore. His powerful legs filled black trousers. His clothes were plain and unassuming, but he wasn't.

He and Asra shared the same pointed chin and freckles, but where Asra's curly, burgundy hair was cropped at his broad shoulders, the Dragon wore his dark hair short. Where Asra's eyes were more green than blue, with hints of gold, the Dragon's were green with bursts of gray. The color of an angry sky just before a storm, I noticed as he stepped closer into the twitching firelight.

Where Asra's demeanor was affable and easy, the Dragon's was commanding and confident. More than the darkness, his presence filled the room.

"How do you know of me?" he asked. "I've never met you."

For a moment, I couldn't think because he was in front of me. I hadn't even realized I'd stopped crying and pacing the floor.

"You remember everyone you've ever met?" I rasped, rubbing the chill bumps on my arms. I looked away.

"I wouldn't have forgotten you," he softly answered.

My heart faltered.

"You have a message for me?" he asked.

"I promised my brother I would deliver it to you," I told him, the memory surfacing. The feel of the cold glacieris stone on my back as Zaire hurried to scrawl something on my skin, even as his strength waned. Whatever he wrote was important and secret enough that he only trusted me and the Dragon with it. Maybe it was something only the Dragon would be able to read and decipher.

"Who is your brother?"

A new tear fell, following the same dried path as the thousands before it. "Zaire Halifex."

The Dragon went completely rigid. For a long, horrible moment, I could tell he felt a glimmer of what I did, and for the first time since Zaire died, I didn't feel completely alone. The matchmaker and those in her employ had gone beyond what was expected. They'd been kind and compassionate. But the Dragon had loved my brother. He grieved for him.

His pained stare comforted me. "Is he dead?" he asked, his voice shredding.

More unchecked tears ran down my face. I pressed my eyes closed and pushed the bitter truth off my tongue. "Yes."

"Vayl?" he tested. My name was a whisper. A prayer on his lips. A cruelty.

I nodded, watching as he scrubbed his hand over his lips, then tugged at his hair. He strode toward the door. I lunged forward, reaching toward him, ready to tell him not to leave. I still needed to give him Zaire's message. But the Dragon didn't slide the door open. He let out a terrible, guttural roar. I stopped short, watching as he drove his fist into the canary yellow wall again and again. The paneling splintered before he painted it with blood from his torn knuckles.

Asra burst into the room with wide eyes, searching between the Dragon, the wall, and me. "Stop it!" he shouted at the Dragon, pushing him away from the wall before he could strike it again. "Stop."

My feet carried me toward him without even realizing it. His outburst, his anger, was as deep as mine. Would he appreciate the rage we shared? I wasn't so sure. Before I knew I'd moved again, the backs of my thighs bumped against the bed's fine mattress. When the wooden frame thumped against the wall, the men remembered I was there.

The Dragon hastily wiped his tears away and took a deep

breath, striding purposefully toward me. When I stepped sideways, he stopped. "I would never hurt you."

I cleared my throat and nodded to the wall that now bore a hole the size of his fist. He blinked as if waking. In the doorway, the matchmaker clutched her chest.

"I'll see that it's fixed right away. I'm sorry," the Dragon promised her. He flexed his injured hand, the knuckles raw. He turned his attention back to me. "I'm sorry. I didn't mean to scare you."

The little thief with strawberry blonde hair squeezed into the room holding a cup of tea and a clean, white towel. She laid the towel on the table beside me, a distance from the fire, then placed the cup in my hand and exited again.

I sipped the steaming tea, impatient for it to provide its calming assurance. The Dragon noticed the amber liquid ripple inside the delicate china. He rubbed his forehead with his injured hand. If the cuts bothered him, he didn't let on.

"I'm sorry," he rasped again.

"You didn't cause the tremors. They started after Zaire died. The tea helps ease them," I told him, sipping again.

The matchmaker heaved a sigh. "Now that things are settled, we'll leave you be."

The Dragon thanked her before quietly asking Asra to wait for him outside again. His brother slid the door closed. He and I stared at the door's panels for a long moment in silence. Finally, he spoke.

"Asra and I owe our lives to Zaire."

I sat the empty tea cup down on the table beside the fire, my eyes catching on the flames that crackled in the hearth, startled that I hadn't even thought of the danger it posed. I was almost always aware of my proximity to it, but the Dragon had distracted me with his rage and pain. Withdrawing my hands, I hugged my middle. My bones still vibrated uncomfortably.

"What happened to him?" he managed.

I looked to the ceiling and collected my thoughts. I didn't

want to relive his last moments, but if he and Zaire were as close as he claimed, he deserved to know.

"I buried our father beside a great boulder that had broken off from a nearby mountain and tumbled toward our house, stopping just short of it."

"I know the rock," he quietly acknowledged. "I visited your home with him on a few occasions."

My throat became painfully tight. "I knew Father was dying, but I expected it, so in a way, it was easier to handle. But I didn't expect Zaire to limp from the tree line, covered in blood the very next evening."

The Dragon did not breathe.

"I took him inside and tried to help, but the wound was infected and he'd lost too much blood. He... before he..." I took a deep breath before continuing. "He left a message for you."

The Dragon's chest finally began to rise and fall. "What is it?"

"He used glacieris to write it, but I don't know what he wrote. I can't see it." The thought occurred that maybe Zaire only wanted me to deliver it, not to know what it said. "He told me no one would find it, or look for it, where he wrote it."

The Dragon's head tilted. "Where is it written?"

"On the skin of my back."

"I need to see it," he rasped. "Do you want the matchmaker to be in here with us? I don't want to ruin –"

I cut him off. "My reputation doesn't matter. I won't be matched. I've been claimed by the Emperor."

I've seen fire and flame catch and roar and spread, though never in someone's eyes. But that was exactly what I saw in the Dragon's. A savage, intense burn; a flame for once I didn't fear at all.

Was he Rata's, too, despite his title?

I lowered my eyes and picked at my nails, or tried to. The tea hadn't helped as much as it did the last time I drank it. Maybe I needed another cup. "Lord Favian is returning to take me to the palace within the fortnight."

"Zaire would kill him."

Zaire would have tried. "Lord Favian is to blame for Zaire's death," I told him.

His steely eyes glinted, and I thought he might pound the wall again. Fury rippled through his body, his corded muscles flexing beneath his clothes as if he would stalk out and hunt the one who took away his friend, his brother.

"I plan to kill Lord Favian, and I'm willing to die if it means that he dies with me," I told the Dragon. *And if I can't manage it, maybe the dragon will avenge Zaire for both of us...*

"How?" His tone wasn't placating; he truly wanted to know.

"I'm not sure what chance fortune will provide, but when it does, I will take it."

He nodded thoughtfully.

The dressing robe, red and stitched with dragons and pink petals, still lay over the screen. I told him to wait, stepped behind it, and removed my dress, pulling it over my head to reveal my brother's message. I eased Zaire's blade from my corset and placed it on the narrow window sill in the corner, then tried to loosen the corset's knotted strings. They held firm and would not relent, no matter which way I twisted to tug at them.

I needed help.

I took the robe and held it to my front to cover myself from breast to ankle.

"My brother trusted you, so I'll trust you," I told him, my throat aching.

With a softly murmured *Thank you,* his shadow moved from behind the screen as he shifted his weight. His eyes caught on me the moment I moved out from behind the screen.

"The corset strings are knotted. I can't loosen them."

His dark lashes fluttered.

My heart flitted in response. I swallowed thickly.

Would he see my mother's features, or only the product of time and circumstance? I was nothing more than skin stretched over bone. Sorrow stretched over rage. Lord Favian knew me as Valor. My mother should have considered naming me Wrath instead.

The Dragon's deft fingers found each knot and worked it loose, then tugged at the strings, tearing them from the eyelets until the torturous corset eased its grip. He peeled it from my body like rind from the flesh of an orange. "I won't tell anyone of this," he said, his voice low.

"I told you my reputation doesn't matter now."

His warm breath stirred my wild hair. "It matters to me."

I turned my head to meet his eye and the flutter in my heart moved to my stomach. The strings were finally undone. "Turn around," I told him, my mouth dry.

He pivoted so I could remove the corset and pull my chemise down to my hips, draping the silken robe across my chest and holding the chemise so it didn't fall to my feet. "Okay."

The fabric of his clothes rustled when he moved. His warm fingers tugged the chemise down a little further, raking the soft fabric over skin even Rata's light had not tanned. Men could remove their shirts when they were hot, but women were never allowed to bare their backs.

He read the words my brother had scrawled in his last moments. Breathed them in as if he were taking in the air from that horrible, tragic moment.

Then his fingers drifted over my skin, eliciting a shower of goosebumps. "It's gone," he choked a second before falling to his knees behind me. His touch had erased the last thing Zaire had written and while I knew my brother not only expected, but wanted them gone, I couldn't help but feel their loss.

I turned to find that he'd buried his head in his hands and was rocking back and forth. I discreetly pulled my chemise back up and slid my arms through the robe, tying it sloppily at my waist before kneeling.

Waiting.

Wondering.

He was obviously distraught, in so much pain it gagged him. I put my hand on his shoulder and he lifted his head, then hugged me to his enormous body, rocking us both back and forth, the floor boards flexing beneath his weight. "He found her," he breathed into my hair. "Thank you, Vayl. Thank you for bringing this message to me after all you've been through."

I squeezed him a fraction tighter and his hands and arms responded in kind. One of his hands moved to cradle the back of my head and held it to his shoulder. It was the way Mother held us as she carried us from our house that night.

But he didn't smell like smoke and sorrow, regret and pain. He smelled like the earth just before a thunderstorm. Fresh and vibrant and alive, buzzing with anticipation for the rain and giddy for the bolts charging the air.

Eventually, his breathing calmed and he slowly slid his hand off my head. I raised it to see his face, my heart still thumping wildly. No one had ever hugged me like that; like I was the only thing keeping them on the ground when they might otherwise float dangerously adrift.

"I'll never be able to repay you for this."

"I never asked you to," I quietly replied.

I didn't want anything from him. The only thing I wanted was to kill the men who took everything from me.

"Zaire gave me something, but I think it might belong to you." I stood and stepped behind the screen again, removing the corset but pulling the dress back on. The dragon blade waited where I'd left it. I brought it to him.

He was quiet for a moment, then pulled a matching dagger from his boot. "All of the dragons have one. They were forged together from the same silver, in the same coals, by the same elvish hands." He handed it back to me. "He earned it. You should keep it."

I tilted the knife back and forth, mesmerized by the candlelight that shone over the engraving. "Elvish?"

Sitting back on his haunches, he pointed to the top curve of his ear. I laid Zaire's knife down and reached out. A thick scar met my fingertip before I even knew I'd touched him. He swallowed thickly.

"This is what Favian did to every elf captured after the wars, at his brother's order."

My heart thundered, incited to rage once more. I ran my thumbs over his scars. "Why?"

His brows slanted. "To shame us. Elves are very proud of the points of their ears. Each is a little different than everyone else's. They're also the only thing that outwardly sets us apart from human. He did much worse to the gifted. He considered them abominations. The torment he inflicted upon them..." With great effort, he tried to blink away the memories. I had tried to do the same more times than I could possibly recall.

Between us, a strange bond began to form. Like the knives forged from the same metal in the same coals, by the same capable hands, his and my destiny tangled. But now that I'd delivered Zaire's message, our paths would diverge again. Our destinies would unweave.

Suddenly, my mind filled with questions. What had Zaire done for him? Why did he give him the knife and now entrust me with it? He knew my name. What else had Zaire told him about me?

More than anything, I wanted to know what my brother had died for. I needed to hear it, to know, to feel like it was somehow worth it even though I couldn't fathom how.

I pulled my trembling hands away and tucked them into my lap. His eyes tracked the movement.

"The shaking will stop. Eventually."

"I haven't the luxury of time and healing," I scoffed. "I must make it stop before Favian comes back for me." I needed him to want me enough to take me to the palace and declare me his brother's property. That was the only way I could get close enough to slaughter them. "It makes me look weak."

Because I *was* weak. And I hated it.

"You're not weak, Vayl."

My muscles stiffened. "You don't know me."

"Zaire spoke of you so often, it feels like I do."

I snorted. "He never mentioned you to me. To me, you're a stranger. I don't even know your name."

He didn't give it to me. Instead, he tilted his head appraisingly. "Do you know why the Elven wars stopped?" he asked, watching me closely.

I knew the reason the Emperor would provide, but I was fairly certain the elves had their own perspective. I was curious to know what it was. He leaned closer, sharing the secret and baring his truth, his soul.

"Cassius insists that the might of Kaan's armies drove us out of the empire, but you know the powers we possess. You know it's a lie."

I waited, watching his body for any hint he was lying. The Dragon never flinched.

"The wars ended when a particularly mighty elf switched sides and sealed out the entire army of the Kingdom of Thanias with her magic. When she erected the barrier, those on the other side of it were stuck here in Kaan."

How could one elf be stronger than the sum of them? "Who is she?"

"Her name is Kirsi, and not only is she mine and Asra's sister, she is our future queen." He noticed my widening eyes and explained, "Think of our people – our kingdom – like a hive of bees. We all work for her. Contribute to her vision. Together, we are strong, but not strong enough to destroy her magic."

My mind whirled with what I'd just learned, but it still didn't make sense. Why had she forsaken her own people? Her duty to them? "Why is she helping Cassius?"

He grimaced. "Because she loves him." He was quiet for a moment. "The note on your back revealed that Zaire found our sister. With that knowledge, I will find a way to set her free. It's been my every breath's purpose since she pushed our armies out."

My stomach sank. If this elven princess loved Cassius, she would never take down her wall. When you loved someone, you protected them at all costs. "Why do you insist on freeing someone who prefers her cage?"

I remembered how the peacocks fled to their aviary during the attack, even when they could have taken flight and escaped the danger. Their home was familiar. They felt safe there.

I thought of how the matchmaker said she was caged, but the care she took with it anyway.

"Because she's our sister." He pressed his eyes closed. "Kirsi was young and impressionable when our mother insisted upon dragging us all to Kaan. Kirsi had ceased the assault upon your empire and hoped to finally make peace with Cassius, because the elves had failed to do so when his father ruled. Cassius allowed a small entourage to enter Kaan with us. Our armies were already positioned and ready at the border, poised to attack if anything went awry. And it did, but not in the way we expected. Cassius was charismatic. He wooed Kirsi and convinced her that our mother would never let them be together."

Ah, so she found a way by constructing a wall and pushing those who might oppose their relationship outside it.

"We escaped the dungeons, and Favian, a few years ago with your brother's help. He was our guard, but he wasn't like the others they'd posted outside the cells. He was kind. He snuck food to us because we were so starved, we couldn't lift a ladle to our lips. He told us stories, of you sometimes, to keep us sane. Eventually, he saw an opportunity and dropped a special tool into the cell. We couldn't pick the locks, but we could remove the bolt that allowed the hinges to swing. The moment we were free, though, Cassius began moving Kirsi from place to place to evade us."

I gasped. "Zaire told me he heard something he wasn't supposed to hear and was caught spying. That's how he found her."

The Dragon settled onto his backside, bending a leg and propping his forearm on his knee. "If she stays put long enough, you just might meet her. You'll recognize her right away if you look closely. She, Asra, and I don't share every trait, but we do carry our mother's smile."

CHAPTER 9

The Dragon explained that his sister, Kirsi, was housed in the palace with the concubines, which happened to be the most remote and well-guarded structure in the entire empire. Not only were soldiers positioned within and all around it, if the matchmaker was to be believed, the concubines themselves were not to be trifled with.

Before he died, Zaire told me he was caught spying. Had he actually tried to set her free? Had the other concubines caught him snooping around, looking for Thanias's queen?

"If Favian doesn't know that Zaire died and thinks he'll inform you of the location, Cassius might move her – just in case. But then again...maybe not," I mused, tasting the strategy as I talked it out. It was like the Game of Scales. With this knowledge, the balance was being tipped in the elves' direction. "Cassius expects a war at the border, but why? Kirsi's magic has proven impenetrable over the years." I looked to him to confirm, but he shook his head.

"My sister's strength wanes."

"Why?"

He shook his head. "I don't want to speculate. Every possibility infuriates me."

My eyes flicked to the wall scarred by his fist.

"Our mother is waiting for it to weaken enough so she can break through Kirsi's magic. When it fails, the wall will be obliterated and there will be no way for anyone to stop the elven army from charging into Kaan."

My head ticked back in surprise. "Your mother still lives? Isn't *she* your queen? Why is she weaker than your sister?"

"Every thousand years a queen is born, endowed with enough magic to carry forward to the next thousand. Kirsi is that queen. That's why it was so important for our mother to take Kirsi with her on the peace mission. Kirsi had to approve of the plans because she was next in line and far more powerful."

The thousandth queen, infused with so much power, was weakening. Was she ill? Injured, perhaps?

"If we can just reach Kirsi, free her, and take her back to Thanias, war will wait, at least for now," the Dragon posed. "But if something happens to her, my mother – our people – will show no mercy. When the strength of the wall fails, nothing will resist her. The elves will sweep over these lands and claim the Empire of Kaan for Thanias in penance for Cassius's role in all of this."

I suddenly knew why Trayton, the mighty dragon god with his infinite lit scales, fought the darkness for Rata. He fought to free his lover, but he could do that from anywhere. He positioned himself across the sky to protect *us*.

I met his eyes. "Let me help from within the palace."

"What about Favian?"

"I can learn to be patient. I cannot survive a war."

He shook his head. "It's far too dangerous."

"Is it any more a danger to my people than your mother and her armies will be if I don't?" He was quiet. "You can't stop me, now that I know," I insisted stubbornly.

His brows drew in. I'd seen him grieve and punch a hole into a sturdy wall, so I wasn't sure whether this calm was the harbinger of another storm or if he was only thinking. He could accept my help or not, but if I could free this girl, I would. And if she didn't want to be freed, I'd have to lie to her. I would beg, cheat, borrow or steal to get her out of there and avoid the tide of elven soldiers that would stain our soil red.

The Dragon claimed his sister loved Cassius. Many years had passed since the wars ended; perhaps it wasn't her power that was eroding, but her love and loyalty instead. Perhaps, she was considering dropping the magic that protected Kaan. Maybe she didn't want to protect Cassius anymore.

"Estin," he said out of the blue.

Confused, I raised my eyes to his. "Estin?"

He cleared his throat. "My name is Estin, though I'd appreciate it if you'd refer to me as Dragon when we're not alone."

I nodded. That wouldn't be hard. I wouldn't be alone with him again, so Dragon it would be. I tucked his name into a small place in my heart and locked it away.

"Asra and Zaire were also close," he began. "I understand if you don't want to be here when I speak to him."

"I do," I assured him. Picking at my nails, I frowned. "It probably doesn't make sense, but it helps knowing that someone else loved him."

He wet his bottom lip. "It makes perfect sense. You feel less alone." With a nod, he called for his brother.

Estin kept his posture poised and straight as he told him, but when Asra's eyes welled with tears, Estin's spine finally bent and he placed an arm around Asra's shoulder, fighting to stay strong for him.

"I knew you looked familiar," Asra finally said, looking at me sadly. He crossed the room and hugged me so tightly, my feet left the ground. "You're so... short," he laughed. "And tiny. Zaire said you were a runt."

My mouth popped open, offended. "I am *not* a runt."

He quirked a brow, wiping the moisture from beneath his eyes and trying to smile.

"Not everyone can be as tall as oaks," I teased him. "Besides, you're not as tall as Estin." His eyes glistened with unshed tears, but he clung to me with a watery smile, almost as if he had forgotten he was holding me or didn't want to let go; I wasn't sure which one. "You can put me down now, Asra."

"Of course." Asra lowered me to the ground, sobering again. "Sorry."

"No apology is necessary."

He shook his head. "No, I am sincerely sorry. Not for hugging you, but..." He paused before continuing. I understood the fast turn of emotions. "I'm sorry you were alone when he died."

"I didn't have time to bury him," I told them, remembering. "He wanted me to leave so badly. He was... panicked. I gave the healer the glacieris and asked him to lay Zaire to rest that night beside Father. The healer wanted to wait to bury him the next morning, but I gave him the Emperor's horse that Zaire had stolen and told him to do it under cover of darkness."

Both men went still, then their shoulders began to shake, wide smiles splitting their faces. "Are you saying Zaire stole the white, pure-bred stallion?"

I nodded. "He did."

"He's an elvish horse. He once belonged to my sister, but she gifted him to the Emperor soon after shutting Thanias's armies out of Kaan," Estin explained. "You managed to set him free."

I'd seen Asra's playful grin, but not Estin's. They were eerily alike. I imagined what it might look like if their mother stood between them, beaming her smile along with her sons'. Estin quickly tucked his smile away, but amusement still lit his sharp, handsome features. Amusement, and maybe hope.

I wanted to tell him it was only a horse. That having hope was foolish, like Father had often warned. But a greater need arose in my heart that defeated the urge to break his hopeful expression into a thousand useless pieces, and I didn't want to erase that smile now that it graced his face.

The brothers soon turned their attention to Zaire's message. Estin didn't tell him the method my brother had used to deliver the princess's location, though Asra studiously ignored the robe I wore instead of the dress in which he'd last seen me garbed. They discussed my stubbornness and the unique opportunity I had in being sent to the palace where their sister might still be hidden.

Estin glanced at me, a question stretching between us. He wouldn't tell Asra my true intentions unless he had my blessing.

I took up Zaire's blade and placed it on the table beside the cup and fire. Then I told him I wanted Favian dead and planned to ask my father to take his soul to the cursed fields of Oro, where he would slowly fade. His memories. His sanity. Until nothing remained and he became one of the shadows that clawed to welcome others into the realm.

Asra sat on the edge of my bed and propped his elbows on his knees, the floor suddenly something he seemed intent on studying. "Zaire wouldn't want you to risk such an endeavor," he softly told me. "Lord Favian has spilled more blood than I'd like to imagine. He's skilled in the art of warfare."

"Well, Zaire's not here."

He looked to Estin for help, but his brother remained quiet.

I straightened my spine. "I'm not asking for your permission. This is *my* life, and I will do with it as I please. There is no hope for me to ever be matched, so I'll have no husband to obey... and I refuse to be used by Cassius without knowing that in the end, his wretched brother will die by my hand. Perhaps he will, too," I added. My heart's rhythm suddenly felt wobbly. I pushed a hand against the bottom of my rib cage as my stance wavered.

Asra jumped up, his hand steadying my arm on one side, but Estin was already there with one hand on the small of my back, the other extended to catch me if I fell.

I pushed them away. "I'm fine." Though sweat pebbled on my brow and upper lip, I felt cold.

"You're not," Asra gently argued. "I know, because none of us are."

Estin remained close. "Let us help you. Let us teach you how to kill a man. While we wait for the Lion's return, the matchmaker will teach you the graces a concubine should possess, while we teach you to be a warrior."

"Can such a thing be taught in less than two weeks?"

"What other choice is there?" Asra replied. His brows raised questioningly, seeming to ask, *Are you up to the task? Are you in?*

"We'll have to talk to the matchmaker first," I conceded. "She knows what I intend to do."

Estin glanced toward the door. "Asra –"

His brother went to retrieve the woman who somehow managed to stand in the center of us all as we orbited around her. Then we hatched a plan to divide my time between lessons in the arts of etiquette and murder.

CHAPTER 10

The following morning, I learned that beyond the brief familial history, the matchmaker had established certain expectations with Lord Favian. He knew I was from the countryside, a farm girl. He knew I was simple and unrefined. That would work to our advantage. She would teach me only the basics of what was expected of a concubine when Cassius was not present in the palace, and what would be expected of me when he was. Most of the time, I would not have his attention; I would merely be one girl in a sea of dozens. But as his newest concubine, he would likely quickly make it a priority for us to get to know one another.

The thought turned my stomach.

When he wasn't around, I would have to survive among the women he had chosen before me – especially the notoriously vicious favored twins.

Until Favian came, I would spend my time with Estin, Asra, and a few other dragons who were skilled in specific areas that might prove helpful to me. We couldn't, however, work at the matchmaker's house, or in Starcrest. Too many prying eyes.

I shouldn't have been surprised to learn there were tunnels

hewn beneath the city, or that the matchmaker had arranged to have one carved beneath her home to intersect with the subterranean labyrinth. Dragons took advantage of the darkness, Asra explained.

The tunnels are what allowed him to appear from inside and disappear into the matchmaker's house again the day of the elves' attack.

He wanted to light a torch to help me see as we traversed the darkened corridor, but the thought of flame in such an enclosed space made me panic. "Don't worry. We don't need it. My eyesight is keen in the dark," Asra said. "I was only thinking of you, but if you trust me to guide you through, you can just take my hand and we'll be out in no time. Estin will be waiting on the other side."

There was debris within the labyrinth, but Asra promised to let me know when and where to avoid it. We stood at the entrance and peered inside, cool air licking our skin. The few feet I could see revealed rock walls that had been steadily chipped away. Some edges were sharp. In places, Asra warned, the ceiling had been braced with wood to prevent its collapse.

His hand swallowed my shaking one. "Ready?" he asked, giving it a comforting squeeze.

Asra ducked as he entered the narrow corridor. He teased that it would be a long walk – for me. I swatted his back. I wasn't *that* short.

The matchmaker shoved a brimming full basket into my hand. Whatever she and her girls had prepared smelled heavenly. I was sorely tempted to peek beneath the cloth but refrained.

"We can feed her!" he laughed, shaking his head as he tugged me into the darkness.

"Not as well as we can!" the matchmaker called out after us.

At night, there was darkness, but there was often the light of the moon or Trayton's great, silvery scales that flickered scant illumination just bright enough to outline one's surroundings. Even when the clouds obscured them, it wasn't absolute blackness. The tunnel was a different story. After bumping along the sharp edges of the tunnel and cutting my forearms and elbows, knees and hips, I tugged on Asra's hand to slow him.

"Do you need me to carry you?" he teased.

"Could you?" I asked pleasantly.

"No."

I groaned and let him tug me along. Eventually the tunnel emptied, spitting us out between sharp boulders that could have been the stony teeth of a great monster. In a glorious display, Rata painted the earth a vibrant orange gold. It washed over my skin comfortingly as my eyes adjusted, watering against its brilliance.

Estin emerged from behind one of the boulders. The Dragon – not Estin. I had to remember not to use his true name. I almost wished he hadn't given it to me at all.

His dark hair was damp and divided in thick rows, like he'd just raked his fingers through it. I suddenly realized the candlelight in my room hadn't done him justice. He was handsome. His brother was, too. Perhaps all the elves were.

And his eyes... I was right about the gray and green. Each shade battled for dominance, though they were perfectly and evenly matched. They slid over me, assessing. I was certain they found me lacking. Even now, he was probably wondering why, beyond his loyalty to my brother, he'd offered to help me.

Desperate people did desperate things, I reminded myself. He needed to remove his sister from Cassius's influence, one way or another, and I might be able to help him achieve that goal.

The vulnerable, hurt man I saw last night was gone, replaced by the confident man who stood before me now. In the newness of day, his brokenness had been fortified and determination shone from his demeanor. He was quiet again, which unnerved me more than it should. Was this the Dragon who would punch a hole through a perfectly docile wall, or the Dragon who would rock and cry and mourn my brother almost as fervently as he might his own?

"You're bleeding," he said, taking hold of my arm and rotating it to better see my elbow where blood had seeped through the pale fabric of my sleeve.

"I couldn't see in the tunnels," I admitted.

"Why didn't you bring a torch?" he asked Asra sharply.

Asra's eyes flicked to me.

"I can't stomach the fire." I looked at the fields beyond the large boulders and gingerly pulled my arm away. "I'm fine. It's just a scrape."

As his hand drifted back to his side, I noticed that his knuckles had already scabbed over. A long moment of awkward silence stretched uncomfortably, and then I raised the basket.

"The matchmaker sent food."

Asra snatched the handle from my hand and jogged a few steps away with it, peeling away the cloth and stuffing a pastry into his mouth, groaning. "Strawberry," he managed around his mouthful.

Asra provided levity, while the Dragon's grave demeanor was almost stifling, as if he was a force of nature and all the world waited to see what he might command.

Asra held one up for me. "Want a bite?"

"I would never wrest your strawberry pastry from you. I'll find one you haven't half-eaten in one bite, thank you very much," I teased.

He gave me a haughty, playful look and handed the basket back to me. "And how long does it take for someone so tiny to eat a strawberry pastry? Three days? Four?"

In response, I ate one in three bites just to shut him up, then licked the crumbs from my lips and thumb. Estin watched with the slightest smile playing at the corner of his lips.

Asra choked a laugh. "That just happened."

"I may not be a giant, Asra, but until recently, I knew constant hunger. The matchmaker has fed me more since I met her than I've probably eaten all year." A slight exaggeration. I'd only been teasing him, but he didn't laugh. I noticed the ghost of a smile the Dragon had allowed through was gone. I cleared my throat, plucking an apple pastry from the basket. "Where are we going?"

Asra deferred to his brother, but when the Dragon didn't speak, he informed me, "To a secluded spot."

To be honest, I wasn't sure if Estin had changed his mind about helping me. Not a sliver of him seemed welcoming. If today was awful, I wouldn't bother returning tomorrow, I decided. I wouldn't waste time they could better spend tormenting Favian and moving their friends out of his reach now that we knew he had information about their whereabouts.

Without another word, the brothers started walking down a well-worn path through the hillside. Clutching the basket handle to busy my quivering hands, I kept pace with them and remained quiet.

Fields of harvested grain crunched beneath our feet as we marched across their shorn amber stalks. Not far off, within an island of trees, three horses waited. We rode them through the sea of stretching fields to the edge of the vast, blue ocean where two tents had been pitched on the sand to provide cover from Rata's bright rays and protect against the cool winds that constantly dragged off the water.

In the morning light, the sea glittered. Dazzled. My breath left me in whispers as I took in my first sight of the undulating waters. I barely remembered Asra taking the reins of the horse I'd ridden, helping me down from the saddle with another joke about my height, and my boots sinking into the malleable, forgiving sand.

I wasn't sure how long I stood there watching the merger of sea and sky. It could have been one minute or several. I was lost in the very sight of it, only regaining my senses when a shadow fell over me and I looked up into the craggy face of a stranger, a behemoth of a man. His head was bare, like his barrel-broad chest. The knife sheathed on his belt was as long as his arm, the tip grazing his knee.

The stranger held up a length of rope with several dead fish dangling from it. Their pungent smell hit my nose the instant before he focused on something over my shoulder. I turned to find

Estin there. "We'll feast tonight!" the giant proudly announced, holding up his catch.

"Well done." Estin nodded at me. "Grady, I'd like you to meet Vayl."

The giant man clamped his free hand over his heart. "I'm sorry for your loss. Zaire told us a lot about you."

I tried to smile. "Thank you."

Grady inclined his head, then told Estin, "I'll come 'round once I'm finished with these." With that, he took off with the fish toward a fire built further down the shore.

"You're going to learn how to incapacitate Grady. If you can shut down someone his size, you can handle anyone smaller."

My lips parted in surprise. I looked at the man blazing a path through the sand, still looming large despite the distance he'd put between us. "There's no way!" I scoffed.

Estin raised his chin. "There is. I'll teach you."

I watched Grady. "Is he an elf, too?"

Estin shook his head. "No, but he's gifted."

I cocked my head to the side, suddenly curious. "What is his gift? What's your power, and Asra's?"

"We aren't allowed to speak it, lest the gods take the gifts away. But we can confirm your suspicions *if* you were to guess." Estin's eyes sparkled in challenge. "Let me know when you figure them out."

Glancing up, I noticed Asra watching us from the double horse troughs. He'd already fed the horses hay, and now he hurried into the thin pines with a bucket.

"There's a stream nearby," Estin explained. Asra returned moments later, his bucket heavy. When he'd watered the horses, he jogged back to us. "You must tell me what's motivating you this morning. I'll certainly try to replicate the condition," Estin told Asra, who shot him a fierce look. "I'm just saying that was the fastest you've ever cared for them, brother," Estin remarked. "Could it be that a certain female is here to help Vayl?"

"Nah, I just don't want to miss it when Vayl bests the Dragon himself," he explained, an easy smile on his face.

As Asra tucked burgundy curls behind his ears, I imagined them pointed, a pang of sorrow tunneling into my chest at the thought of the pain he'd endured. My dress rapped in the wind as a gust rushed over us.

Asra shook his head. "She needs something else to wear. She can't train in that."

"See if Indri has something that might work," Estin told him. "I know you're already trying to find an excuse to talk to her."

He saluted his brother. "And this will be the perfect one, thank you." Asra waved for me to follow him and we walked up the shore to one of the white tents. "Indri?" he called out.

A girl with rich dark skin and a curious smile stepped outside, drying her hands on a towel. Her hair was carefully braided, threaded with rows of pale shells like vertebrae in a spine. They clinked together when they struck one another. She was taller than me, but not quite as tall as Asra.

Asra asked how she was doing and made small talk for a moment. He flirted, and Indri flirted back. His eyes fell on her chest, but he didn't let them linger there. Just a glance, but she noticed and allowed her gaze to brush over him, too, soft as drifting fingertips.

She wore a flowy white shirt that was cut low and bared her taut stomach, along with trousers that hugged her hips. His eyes flitted to the curve of them, too, before drifting back up. I'd never worn anything but dresses. Father never would have allowed it.

"Indri – Vayl, Vayl – Indri," he deftly introduced. "Do you have pants and a shirt or tunic she can wear?"

Indri smiled. "I have some things that will work." She waved for me to follow her. "Come inside."

Her tent smelled rich and sweet. On a wide piece of bark, incense burned. She'd laid a carpet on the sand beneath her bedroll. It still bore the curl from having been rolled. "I've just begun to unpack," she explained. "Not that I have much. You can only take with you what you can carry."

She rifled through a generous satchel and pulled out a pair of trousers. "You're thinner than I am, but I think we can make these work. And... she glanced at me and plunged her hand back into the bag. "There's this." She pulled out a small, fitted vest the color of the deep blue of the ocean that roiled past the sand breaks. "You can have it if you want. It doesn't fit me, and it makes my breasts look like squashed potatoes; flat in the middle and billowing at the seams."

I laughed. When she tossed the vest to me, I caught it.

She clapped, then stood. "Okay, I'll leave you to change clothes."

"Won't my corset show from under the vest?" I asked.

"Lose it," she answered. "The chemise, too. You won't need them, and you'll thank me later when you're soaked in sweat." She tilted her head, looking me over. "You good?"

I gave her a nod and she ducked outside to flirt with Asra some more.

I tugged my dress off, and luckily, I was able to unknot the tied strings of my corset myself this time. I lay it and the chemise on the corner of the rug, then stepped into the unfamiliar trousers, drawing them up my legs. They were loose on my hips and a little too long, but after rolling up the pant legs, they were passable.

My hands still shook, but I found that if I kept busy, the trembling didn't become so distracting that it was the only thing I could think about. When Asra had removed the cloth from the basket, I'd noticed small sachets tucked down between the delicious cakes. The matchmaker had sent tea.

The vest fit snugly. My upper chest and arms were bare, as were a few inches of stomach and back as well, but Indri looked the same, so no one would think I looked out of place if I dressed like her. I was about to fold my dress when whispers came from outside.

"How is she – really?" Indri asked.

"She's been through a lot in a short time," Asra answered, keeping his voice low.

"What weapon does she favor?"

"I need your help with that, among other things..." I heard the shifting of his feet on the sand. "I think she needs a woman to talk to about what to expect when Cassius comes to her."

Humiliation washed over me. I knew *some* things. I wasn't completely ignorant or innocent.

"Fourteen days isn't nearly enough time to prepare her for what she's about to face." I could hear the hope in Indri's voice drain away, like a wave that rushed the shore only to be dragged back into the depths.

"Two weeks is all we have," Asra answered.

It was less than two weeks, actually. Favian said within the fortnight, and the matchmaker said he was notorious for arriving early.

Shaking my dress until the fabric snapped quieted their conversation. I lifted the tent flap and joined them outside. Asra smiled as if he hadn't just been whispering about me. "You look like one of us, now. You look like a dragon."

I glanced down at my borrowed clothes. I didn't *feel* like a dragon. I felt small and weak. Like a little girl trying on her mother's dress. But that would end today. Right now, I was a shapeless piece of silver. The next few days and weeks would have to be enough to form and fashion me into a sharpened sword. And when Favian came for me, I would be ready.

Just outside the flap of Indri's tent was a chest I hadn't noticed before. She threw open the lid to reveal a trove of weapons neatly tucked inside. Throwing knives were fitted into the blue velvet lining while a bristling array of weapons consumed the rest of the space: daggers, short swords, long swords, sai sabers, maces, a crossbow, and the smallest recurve bow I'd ever seen.

She saw me admiring it and grinned. "That's my favorite. It was made to fit me, and since we're close to the same size, you'll have no trouble drawing back her string."

Indri handed the bow to me and I ran a finger over the sleek wood. "I used to shoot with Zaire."

Indri's eyes lit. "Good. That bow? She's unassuming and diminutive, quiet and accurate. And when angered, she's deadly."

Catching movement in my periphery, I glanced up to see Estin hefting the weight of a large dummy as he strode toward us. Indri held her hand out for the bow; I offered it and she returned it to her trunk, then tossed a string of leather toward me.

"Tie your hair back – like mine."

As I did as she instructed, Indri waved for Asra to follow her. They jogged across the sand toward the trees, searching for one with a straight enough trunk to tie the dummy. This proved to be more difficult than you'd think. Most of the palms curved this way or that, or playfully swooped to the sand and jutted up toward the sky.

Estin was lost in thought as he approached. He barely glanced at me when he asked where I wanted him to place the practice dummy.

I shrugged. "Indri and Asra are choosing a tree." I pointed him in their direction, but his head didn't swivel to follow their progress. It snapped toward the sound of my voice and his eyes climbed over my skin and Indri's borrowed clothes like ivy crawling slowly up a wall.

I was suddenly hyper-aware of my body. My bones jutted too sharply, the result of too many starved months. Compared to Indri's beautiful flesh, my skin was far too pale. After I met the blind man, I was glad he couldn't see me because he said I'd given him hope. That hope would have dried up like a riverbed in summer if he knew what I looked like. Now, I wished Estin couldn't see me either.

Asra had beamed when I emerged from Indri's tent and cooed that I looked like a dragon.

I didn't. *Yet.*

But I vowed to get stronger and earn the title. And fast.

This was the first morning I hadn't cried, which was probably a result of the dragons welcoming me into their fold...for a time, at least. I wouldn't waste the opportunity or the fact that for now, I had a new purpose.

Not only an end goal, I was fitted into a life my brother led in secret and learning things about him I never imagined. Being here was a gift.

When Asra shouted for Estin, he carried the straw-stuffed dummy to Indri, who pointed him to the tree she'd chosen. He and Asra used frayed scraps of rope to secure the dummy's stuffed form to the trunk, then he left us without a word.

"Go," Indri ordered Asra.

Asra's mouth popped open. "But I'm here to help!"

"We don't need you," she informed him haughtily. "We need girl time."

"Girl time," he scoffed, scuffing his boot on the sand. "Fine, then. I can take a hint. I know when my presence isn't wanted." He turned to leave, looking like a scolded pup.

"Asra?" Indri called. He stopped to look back at her once more. "I'm glad you know when your presence isn't *wanted*, but I wonder if you know when it's *needed*..." She quirked a suggestive brow.

His cheeks turned pink and I wished for Rata to cast the same hue upon the sea one evening while I was here to see it. It would be a glorious color over Zairitus's watery facets.

Indri gave a throaty chuckle as he left us, his head held high and a new spring in his step.

"You and Asra?" I asked.

She shrugged a shoulder, watching him as he walked down the beach to Grady. "We've been dancing around it for months, but the past few weeks, something has shifted between us. I don't know if it's because things feel direr now or what. Our kind have always been hunted, and being a dragon means there's always a target on our backs. I entered the dragons knowing the risks and have lived with the constant threat. But now Cassius is nervous, the elven army once again pounds at the wall, and you're about to get very close to our future queen. Teetering on the cusp of change always makes me just as excited as I am nervous. So, yeah. Me and Asra." She turned away, perhaps regretful of speaking so openly. "Help me carry the weapons trunk."

~

Indri didn't bother with the bow, crossbow, or any of the long-bladed swords, knowing I needed to learn to use something small and easy to conceal. I would have to keep it hidden from the guards, the other concubines – especially the twins – Lord Favian, and the Emperor himself.

When I imagined killing Favian, I used Zaire's dragon blade.

I told Indri as much and she grinned, in love with the idea.

Using one meant that I had to be fast and cunning. If he saw it coming, he could easily overpower me and turn the blade on me instead.

"Tell me," she led, "was Favian attracted to you?"

"I'm not sure."

She bit the inside of her cheek. "Because if you think he might be, or if you can convince him to be, it might be easier to get him alone. No one is immune to seduction; there simply has to be attraction and opportunity. It's a few days' journey to reach the palace on horseback when the weather is good. And this time of year, it may not be."

The thought of seducing Favian turned my stomach, but she was right. If I wanted to kill Favian and live to take my next breath, I had to get him alone. I could kill him and run if I found a way to get him away from his soldiers on the way to the palace. Once we reached the palace, I wasn't sure there would be another chance for us to see each other.

Using blunt wooden daggers, Indri taught me how to stand and guard my core, how to execute various strikes, and showed me ways to defend myself against another blade. On the straw-stuffed dummy, she taught me where to plant the blade to inflict the most damage. Stuffing escaped from the wounds we practiced delivering.

It wasn't an exhaustive course. It was as fast and desperate as this entire hastily constructed plan. Rata beat down on our faces and shoulders as Zairitus's sea spray and Ventus's wind slid over our sweat-soaked skin and clothes.

My muscles burned, but for the first time in a very long time, I felt good. I felt alive.

Useful.

Like I'd found my purpose and was running toward it as fast as my feet could carry me.

I also felt guilty for feeling the tiniest flicker of happiness.

CHAPTER 11

Giant Grady, true to his word, came to us at midday after he'd finished preparing and cooking all the fish. Though he arrived with food, that wasn't why he was there. The Dragon asked him to help teach me how to defend myself. Oddly enough, Estin was nowhere to be found.

Asra joined us, following the delicious aroma. Grady told us to eat and fill our bellies, promising to take over in attempting to teach me the unteachable.

Indri blessed the food, muttering an elvish saying. I felt the air charge with her magic, and after we'd eaten, I felt different. The soreness working its way into my muscles was gone. The fatigue that had become a constant friend was replaced by renewed energy.

"What did you do to my food?" I asked incredulously.

She flicked a glance to Asra, who gave a subtle shrug.

I tilted my head. "Is that your gift? To make the food taste better? Or make it fill us faster?"

"Not exactly," she hedged. Apparently, I'd come close enough. Asra gave her a nod and she explained, "I made it more nourishing so you can grow stronger, faster. It's only a small enhancement. I wish I could do more."

"It's incredible!" I laughed, rolling my shoulders and finding no stress in the muscles there.

Grady stood and stretched his arms over his head. "It's time," he directed at me.

I couldn't stop the nervous laughter that bubbled out. "I honestly don't think I'll ever be able to best someone your size."

"You'd be wrong," he said in a friendly, gentle tone. "It's important that you learn this above all things, Vayl. At some point in your life, likely sooner than you'd like, you'll have to defend yourself, and you'll have to do it well and against someone whose hands are stained by the blood of his enemies."

I would never resign myself to the life of a concubine, and it seemed Grady knew that. Asra and Indri, too. I took a deep breath and stood, walking to him. "Please don't kill me."

Grady's booming laugh drowned out the sound of the sea for a moment, then we walked further down the beach to a spot with deeper, soft sand.

He turned to face me. "When you defend yourself, Vayl, remember that nothing is off limits. Fight hard and fight dirty." With that, he lunged at me.

Without thinking, I ran. "What are you *doing*?" I shrieked.

"Pretending I'm going to throttle you!" he bellowed.

Grady was faster than he looked, not to mention a brilliant pretender. His enormous feet pounded the sand so hard I felt it reverberate in the soles of my feet. He caught up to me quickly and pushed me from behind. I pitched forward, catching myself on my hands and knees. I spat, trying to get the grit out of my mouth. He was already walking away when I stood and dusted myself off. "What was *that*?"

"That was you dying. Figuratively, of course," he chuckled.

He thought he was funny.

He faced me and waved for me to come toward him. I thought he was going to tell me what I did wrong and what to do right next time, but Grady was no teacher. He was a clever fox. The moment I got near enough, he rushed me.

I cursed and tried to run again, this time altering my direction to make it harder for him. It didn't work. One shove and I was splayed out on my stomach on the sand. This time, there wasn't a *little* grit in my teeth. I'd taken an entire mouth full of sand. I took time to spit out what I could.

Asra, his eyes lit with unshed laughter, brought me a cup of fresh water. "Here. But don't tell my brother I showed you any sort of kindness."

"Why?" I asked, taking a drink and swishing the water around to catch what sand was left.

"He wouldn't like it. He'd say it would stunt your growth, but something clearly got to you before I did. You haven't grown since you were five." I'd just taken a drink, so I spat it at him. He leaped backward with wild eyes. "I helped you, and *this* is how I'm repaid?" Indri was doubled over laughing. "It's your fault!" Asra announced, turning his ire to her. "You gave her new clothes and showed her how to use blades and now she's ready to pick a fight."

"No, she ain't," Grady teased. "She's scared."

"Of course I'm afraid – of *you*," I joked to the giant. "I'm not afraid of Asra in the least."

Asra's mouth gaped. He clutched his chest in mock offense.

Grady tapped his temple. "Quit worrying about the difference in our size and start thinking of how to plant me on my arse. I got one, same as everyone else. Zaire was taller than you, but not exceptionally so. He was bigger, sure, but he was nowhere near as broad as any of us. Even so, he didn't just fight as well as we do, he fought better. He started out like you, angrily chewing grains of bread, followed by grains of sand. But he used his unique attributes to his benefit. When you figure out how to use yours, you'll truly follow in his footsteps."

I expected them to taunt me and try to make me mad, not encourage me by saying I could do the same things Zaire could and earn their respect as he had.

"Fight. Dirty," Grady advised again, emphasizing each word. "No rules apply when your life is at stake."

This time, when Grady came at me, I didn't turn my back and run. I waited until he thought he had me, then ducked out of his arms and caught his ankle. He went down on one knee, but caught himself, rising with a half-proud, half-aggravated look in his eyes.

I'd used the same move on Zaire when he and I fought years ago.

"There you go!" he chirped sharply.

He rose and we circled one another warily, but he caught my wrist before I had a chance to lunge away. I was too focused on his barrel chest, watching for when his muscles would bunch as he came for me. It was what he'd done every time.

"What you *don't* expect can get you killed," he chided. "Now, how are you going to get out of this predicament?"

I tugged and pulled, hissing when the bones of my wrist threatened to separate. Then, when he tried to adjust his grip because his meaty hand was sweaty, I twisted, hard. It didn't break his grip entirely, but it allowed me enough movement to slide behind him. He pivoted, trying to get me back in front of him. I couldn't let that happen.

I jumped on his back, trying to hook my ankles around his waist, but couldn't get them around his wide body. Then, the world tipped and I landed on my back...*hard*...with Grady on top of me. The impact knocked the breath from my lungs and I struggled and gasped as he scrambled off.

"Vayl? Oh, no. I'm so sorry. I lost my balance."

Suddenly, Asra was there, lifting my head off the sand. Indri told me to calm down, that air would come soon enough. Sand flew as Estin slid to a stop in front of me.

"We've got her," Asra told him.

"I told you to train her, not kill her," the Dragon snarled.

Grady wrung his hands and apologized profusely. "I am so sorry, Vayl. He's right. I could have hurt you."

The air slowly came as Indri said it would. "I'm fine," I told them. Asra leapt up and wrapped an arm around my waist, trying to lift me to my feet, but I pushed him away. "I don't need your help. I'm not glass."

The Dragon looked like he could use a wall to pound. I dusted myself off, then walked to Grady, who was still apologizing. I waved for him to bend down and wrapped my arms around his neck, hugging him.

"I'm fine."

He raised back to his full height. "I didn't mean to."

"I know, but I'm glad you did. Now, I need you to teach me how to defend myself if something like that happens again."

He shook his head, flicking his eyes over my shoulder. I knew what they would find. The hulking, moody dragon lurking. He was probably shaking his head, daring Grady to continue. But the Dragon could go back to wherever he'd been this morning and mind his own affairs. I needed Grady's help.

Estin moved to stand at my side. "Perhaps that's enough for today," he proposed.

"I don't have many days, so I will respectfully disagree," I argued.

"You could get hurt."

"And if I don't learn, I'll be killed," I volleyed.

Estin fumed and raked a hand through his hair.

My attention was suddenly diverted by his appearance. "What are you wearing?" I looked him over, studying his armor. It stretched from mid-neck all the way down to his wrists and ankles and was constructed of small pieces of metal with a faint teal sheen to it, fastened together at the joints. It looked impenetrable and gave the illusion that he truly was part dragon... "Is it elvish made?"

He nodded. "You'll take Indri's with you to the palace. Another suit is being forged for her."

I shook my head. "I can't do that. Where could I possibly hide it? It would be visible beneath any of the dresses the matchmaker is having altered for me. They're... rather revealing." Describing them as *revealing* was generous. They were beautiful, yes. But they weren't made with comfort in mind. They were made for the

Emperor to enjoy and would conceal very little. "Besides, if it was discovered..."

"Asra is building a false bottom in the trunk the matchmaker will send ahead of your arrival at the palace," he told me. "He'll seal it with magic so that only you can open the panel. We'll put your armor inside and you can store small weapons within the compartment as well."

It sounded like the perfect place to hide Zaire's blade, which was something else I'd been worried about. I looked at Asra. He hadn't mentioned his endeavor to me, but I wasn't surprised. They'd obviously discussed it ahead of time.

"That's very clever," I complimented.

Asra nodded to Estin. "His idea."

The Dragon didn't take time to soak in the compliment. He looked at Grady, Indri, and his brother. "Feel like taking a run?"

Indri groaned. "Now?"

"Now," he confirmed.

I gestured to his armor. "Are you able to run in that?"

He answered with a grin. "What good is armor if you can't move in it?"

All the metal armor I'd seen was clunky and awkward. Leather armor, like the Lion wore, allowed for movement, but it was thick and I'd imagine incredibly heavy. It had to be, to stop or slow a blade. But comfort was second to functionality.

"Where are we running, Grady? It's your turn to pick," Asra told him, waiting.

Grady smiled. "The peak. We jog together to the base, then break apart so Vayl doesn't get lost before the ascent."

In the distance loomed the top of a tall mountain. It wasn't dusted in snow, being this far south, but it was formidable, even from this far away. Grady waved for us to go ahead, and as we jogged down the shore before cutting into the woods, he fell into step behind us, motivating us with shouts of encouragement. Those faded to chastisement when we hit the mountain's base. "It's a race to the top! Move your slow, sorry arses!" he boomed.

Grady stayed close, likely afraid I'd lose my way, as if there was any other way to go but up. He clapped his hands and roared that if the Emperor's soldiers were giving chase, we'd already be dead. He didn't aim the comment at the dragons. It was aimed at me. I wasn't fast enough.

A flash of Asra's burgundy hair to my right fueled my steps, even as the trees thickened and the briars tore at the trousers Indri loaned me. I pretended Asra was Zaire and we were racing, which was the fuel I needed to push harder, the muscles in my legs burning as I pumped my arms. I hated losing to my brother in anything.

The higher we climbed, the more difficult it became to maintain that initial burst of speed. My legs tired, but I continued to push into the thinning air with straining lungs. Asra was gone, likely far ahead of me now. The others had probably passed me by.

Grady's motivating shouts faded away.

I ground to a stop, needing to catch my breath for a moment. Panting, I braced my hands on my knees, ignoring how they shook, though the tremors in my palms had finally gone quiet. I wiped my face, even as sweat trickled down my neck, chest, and back.

I stood and pushed on, higher. Higher.

There was never a question of who would arrive last, but I made it to the top, meeting Grady's astonished face.

"You did it!"

"You seem surprised," I panted.

"I am. No other human dragon has pushed to the peak on their first try," he answered.

"Not.... even.... Zaire?" I panted.

"Definitely not!" he whooped, clapping my shoulder.

I promptly collapsed and laid there for a moment, staring at the sky. Asra and Indri hovered above me. "I think you broke her, Grady," Indri teased.

I laughed and hugged my ribs, still trying to calm my breathing. "I know your gift, Grady," I teased.

He smirked. "Oh yeah?"

"Torture," I told him. The dragons chortled. "Am I close?"

Grady smiled. "Not close at all, though I thoroughly enjoy it."

Eventually, when my lungs stopped panicking, Grady offered me a hand and helped me up. "You're missing the best part about running to the peak."

"What's that?"

He gestured to an opening in the trees. From the top of the mountain, you could see dozens more jutting into the distance as far as the eye could see. At home, the trees were almost bare, but here, they blazed with color in riotous shades of yellow, bronze, and red. It made the mountains appear to be on fire.

"Autumn robs us of too many daylight hours," the Dragon noted from behind us. I turned to find him looking out over the mountains before his green-gray eyes met mine.

I lingered, trying to commit the sight to memory. Over his shoulder, Grady, Indri, and Asra trailed away, beginning their trek back down the mountain.

"We need to get you back to the matchmaker. She's expecting you for dinner."

"Where she'll provide a rousing lesson on place settings, I'm sure," I joked. "How many forks must one have for each meal? Seven? Ten?"

He fought a grin. "I didn't say it would be fun."

"Thank you for today. For everything, Estin. You didn't have to volunteer yourself and your friends to help me." I looked out at the beautiful mountains with a heart that was a little less empty than it was that morning.

"It isn't entirely altruistic," he argued. "I'm hoping you can help us as well."

"I will, even if you didn't have time to go to these lengths."

His eyes flicked to mine, that smile still restrained on his lips. "So you threatened." He waved for me to walk with him, remaining quiet – pensive – as we balanced our steps on fallen, moss-covered logs, taking advantage of the narrow trails cut by the hooves of deer whose coats were darkening with the season.

Leaves crunched beneath our feet; the rustling became a song, harmonizing with that of the wind and sea. I heard the ocean's distinct voice at the top of the peak as a churning, infinite roar straight from the throat of the god of waters, for whom my brother had been named. For a moment, I imagined him at home in the dark depths. Then I imagined him cheering my efforts, encouraging every creature alive in his great watery body to writhe for me.

I walked to the shoreline and watched the tide ebb and flow, marveling at the tremendous, terrible power. One droplet of water was harmless, but when too many to number combined, they were an unstoppable force.

Mighty Zairitus, steady my hands and mind. Make me as powerful as the waves. Help me crush my enemy, the Lion. Where there once was Ventus's air, let him breathe in my wrath and drown in me, knowing that I am his judgment. And when I free the elvish queen, make my feet as quick as the currents tearing from your heart. And if, in the end I live, let me do so having earned the friendship of people such as these. Let me live freely and with the hope of being content one day.

Asra and Indri had waded into the water. Grady hovered on the shore just beyond the reach of their splashes, bellowing for them to cut it out.

He was such a gentle giant. I wasn't sure if he didn't like water or if the cool temperature bothered him.

I ducked into Indri's tent to undress and quickly slid my chemise back on, added the corset and loosely knotted the ends, then tugged my dress over my head. It was such a cumbersome thing. Now that I'd worn pants, I was ruined. Pants were so much more comfortable, not to mention practical.

I walked to the shore. "Is there time for me to wash these?" I called out, holding up the folded stack of borrowed clothes, which were wet with sweat.

"I'll wash them when I wash mine and hang them all to dry," Indri offered, squealing when Asra lunged for her and dragged her beneath the surface. His head popped back up, but hers didn't. He laughed, but as the seconds ticked away, he moved this way and that, dragging his arms through the water and shouting her name, suddenly afraid for her.

She surfaced behind him, then swept his legs out from under him.

He popped up with a menacing grin and dove after her. Indri shrieked excitedly. Grady was now in to his knees and taking tentative steps forward, shivering despite Rata's warmth. He looked at Estin. "Want me to see her back?"

"I'll take her," the Dragon informed him.

I shook my head stubbornly. "I can make it back on my own."

"Even with a torch, it's easy to get turned around if you don't know the way. Other tunnels converge with the one we take... and I know how you feel about fire."

I hated relying on them too heavily. They were busy enough without wasting time escorting me back and forth, but what choice did I have? "Okay, then."

Asra shouted a goodbye to me and Indri waved just before a wave broke over her head. Grady waded in to mid-thigh and threw a hand up in farewell, but doggedly watched the sea.

Thus decided, Estin and I took two horses and rode them to the same island of trees and tied them there. The rest of the journey would be made on foot. Estin was quiet across the plains, his eyes darting toward every sound. The instant before we stepped between the large boulders that guarded the entrance and entered the dark corridor, he paused to let my eyes adjust as much as they could.

"None of us mind," he rasped.

"Mind what?"

"Seeing you to and from the matchmaker's. It's the least we can do."

I looked down. "Estin, I may not be able to free her."

"It has nothing to do with Kirsi. You carried Zaire's message to us. You left him when everything in you must have screamed not to. If you never lay eyes on our sister, it's still enough. I meant it when I said I could never repay you."

"And I meant it when I said you don't have to."

He brushed away a hair that had escaped my braid and tucked it behind my ear. A fluttering sensation swept through my stomach, like the dragonflies that graced the matchmaker's gardens were flying in circles within me.

Without another word, he turned and began walking through the darkness. For miles we walked the jagged corridors in silence until eventually, he abruptly stopped and I smashed into him so hard, my nose stung. Tears pricked at my eyes as I began to laugh, covering my nose and checking to see if it would bleed.

"I'm so sorry," Estin said from where he stood in front of me, closer than I expected. "There was a rock in the pathway that I didn't want you to trip over, so I stopped to move it."

"Thank you."

He blew out a frustrated breath. "I wish you could see."

"I can't see, but I can feel," I told him. "The first time through the tunnel, Asra held onto my hand and if he needed to slow down or we were going to turn, he squeezed mine a little."

His clothing rustled as he shifted his weight. "Here."

I felt in his direction, but instead of his hand, found scales beneath my fingers. I brushed my fingertips over a few of the scales, soft and smooth and cool to the touch. His hand softly covered mine.

"Are you hurt?" His lips, his voice, were at my ear now, his warm breath fanning it. It migrated toward my lips and I was suddenly very aware of how close he was, as well as the fact that his heightened elvish senses allowed him to see me even though I couldn't see him.

"I'm fine," I rasped.

"You sure?" He nudged my chin, then let his thumb ghost down the column of my throat, stopping at the hollow at the base.

My mouth was dry, my skin hot. I nodded. "I'm sure."

His hand gently clasped mine and he turned and began walking.

I drifted behind him like a kite soaring along in a gentle wind. It took a moment for my mind's fog to clear. While we walked together through the darkness, I recalled the feel of his armor and the warmth beneath it, the barely there skimming of his thumb. The skipping beat of my heart.

Estin was quiet until we reached the matchmaker's cellar. And I was glad because I didn't know what to say or make of the moment we'd shared.

One of the oldest of the attendants, a girl with tawny hair and a curvy frame, was waiting when we emerged in the damp, dark room, holding a candle holder, the taper's flame casting warm light over the room. "Dragon," she greeted with a courteous bow. "The matchmaker would like to invite you to dine with her and Vayl this evening."

He still held tightly to my hand, as if he'd forgotten he was holding it. I pulled away and he apologized. "I'm afraid I can't this evening or tomorrow, but would be happy to stay later in the week if she'll have me."

"She will be delighted," the girl assured him, clapping her hands together. "She extends her invitation to Asra and any other dragons, too, of course."

"Of course. Thank you," he said politely. I noticed tension turn his shoulders to stone as he turned to me. "One of us will meet you in the morning, though I'd like to get an earlier start. We can walk through the dark before dawn."

The attendant held out a basket for him to take and he peeked inside. "What's this?"

"Eggs, cheese, bread, and wine for your dragons to enjoy."

His brows rose. "Thank your mistress for me."

The attendant bobbed a curtsy. "I certainly will." Her eyes caught on the scales hugging his powerful body.

He cleared his throat. "Get some rest," he said pointedly, nudging my shoulder with his before ducking into the darkness again.

The attendant waited until he'd disappeared before adding, "Your bath water is already hot, Vayl."

"Of course it is," I muttered. It wasn't that I was ungrateful. I knew I needed to bathe before my second set of lessons could begin. I was sweaty, sandy, and grimy – just as the matchmaker had so eloquently labeled me the day I arrived. But I was also starving and would love to eat before sinking into the warmth – if only to spend more time in the deliciously hot water. My muscles weren't as sore as they should have been, thanks to Indri's magic, but held on to a whisper of an ache that came from a hard day's work.

The girl closed the wooden door over the tunnel's entrance to seal it, then barricaded it with a piece of wood.

Upstairs, I scrubbed myself clean until a layer of sand settled at the bottom of the tub when I'd finished. I smiled at the grains, remembering the day as I dried my hair with a thin cloth, then tugged on a loose, blue dress and followed the scent of delicious food downstairs.

We were dining inside tonight, in a dining room that was small and intimate. Though I was sure it was lovely before they'd decorated it, the matchmaker and her attendants had outdone themselves tonight. There were potted plants tucked in the corners, their blooms perfuming the air in delicate notes. The table was covered by a golden cloth that stretched across its top and dramatically plunged to the floor in a gilded waterfall.

There were five stemmed glasses at each place setting, all filled with wine – white, blush, a burgundy richer than Asra's unruly tresses, one of the deepest plum, and one as dark as night itself. The empty plates were brushed gold. There were five golden forks in a range of sizes, four knives, and three spoons. The matchmaker watched as I approached the table.

"Head down. Look at your feet, but keep your posture straight and your shoulders back. You want to look regal, but you will bow to the Emperor until he invites you to sit. You never sit until he allows it. That's very important."

I nodded, holding my shoulders back and my head pressed down.

"Fold your hands in front of you."

I did so and noticed that the trembling which I had forgotten while working today had returned.

The matchmaker smoothed her severe bun and called for an attendant to brew some tea for me. "Did you drink some today?" she asked.

I shook my head.

"You may sit," she instructed. "But wait until someone arrives to pull your chair out, then gracefully sit as they push the seat in for you." One of her attendants played the role and I sat before her. "Head down until he asks for you to look at him."

"How do you know he will?"

"Because if he invited you to dinner, he'll want to look at more than the crown of your head. And he'll want conversation. That is when you should make him feel important. All men crave validation and praise. They love to feel wanted and, beyond that, to feel needed. Desired." She paused. "You may raise your head, Valor," she allowed, using the name that was mine, even though it wasn't.

The thought of having to make Cassius feel that I cherished and honored him, let alone desired him, turned my stomach.

"School your features," she snapped.

I thought of clear blue skies filled with lazily drifting clouds. Of how I would feel when I shoved my blade into Favian's heart. A soothing calmness washed over me.

"Good," she said, releasing the table and smoothing the golden fabric.

The matchmaker proceeded to explain what each knife, fork, and spoon was to be used for, then she quizzed me. I quickly learned most of them, much to her relief, and managed to keep my expressions reined.

Together, we swilled, smelled, and sipped each goblet of wine. "Some poisons are odorless," she warned. "Do not leave your drink unattended, and never sip at all unless someone else drinks from the same bottle first."

I raised my eyes to hers. "I don't think it's wise for me to drink wine at all. It dulls the mind, and in a place such as the palace, there could be deadly consequences for a moment of letting my guard down. It's not worth it."

She looked pleased. "I was going to tell you that next, though you'll have no choice if the Emperor toasts or is toasted."

Our food was brought out on lush trays, each plate covered with a golden dome to seal in the steam and heat. The matchmaker showed me how to daintily saw meat into tiny, chewable bites, then how to eat delicately and slowly.

"What did you learn today?" she asked conversationally.

"How to defend myself against a man three times my size, how to push forward without giving up, how the sand feels between my toes, how the ocean looks with Rata reflecting on every facet, and how the mountain ranges look from one of the peaks. Oh, and that pants are far more comfortable and convenient than dresses."

The matchmaker's wine glass hovered halfway between the table and her lips – lips that slowly stretched into a smile. "You didn't need the tea?"

"I was too busy to dwell in my thoughts."

"And now?" she asked, her eyes cautious and curious.

I hated to admit it. Hated to let her down. Hated letting her know that I hadn't made as much progress as I'd liked. "Now they're trembling again."

She sat her glass down and used her knuckles to sharply rap on the table. "Tomorrow is another day," she said confidently. "Tomorrow, the shaking will stop."

I wondered how many tomorrows would pass and how many times she would hope for the same before her wishes actually came true.

Just then, Ventus sent a robust wind careening outside. It howled and rattled the windows. Climbing roses raked at the few glass panes that were still intact and clawed at the wood boards covering the panels that hadn't fared so well during the elves' latest attack on the wall.

The bath had relaxed me, but a full stomach made it difficult to concentrate on my lessons. My eyelids felt heavy.

"We need you to try on a few of the dresses we're altering. Would you rather do it in the morning?"

I nodded sleepily. "I would...though the Dragon or Asra will arrive a little earlier tomorrow to continue my lessons."

"I'll see that you're up in time to slip these on for Sylvie," the matchmaker conceded. "She's the one who will alter your wardrobe. Some of the gowns' fabric is very delicate, so she needs to be sure of her stitches and seams." Bestowing a firm nod, she said, "Get some rest, Vayl."

CHAPTER 12

Thirteen days.

Less than thirteen days until Favian returned for me.

I didn't remember what I dreamed about, but the next morning my skin was covered with a sheen of sweat so cold, I shivered all over.

One of the attendants – Sylvie, the seamstress – came to wake me, but found me pacing the floor when she arrived. "Are you alright?" she asked, her eyes flicking to the door.

"Yes, just nervous," I told her with a smile I hoped would put her at ease.

Thankfully, she didn't run and tell the matchmaker I was losing my mind before leading me down the hall to try on the dresses. After stepping into the room, a gaggle of girls slowly filled the space, followed by the matchmaker. While they chatted about what tasks they had to do today to help prepare me, the matchmaker fretted about the possibility that Favian might arrive early and unannounced, and that I'd be off with the dragons when he came.

The tiny seamstress Sylvie placed several pins between her lips and worked quickly to tuck and secure the dress so that every inch of it fit me perfectly. I watched her in the mirrors positioned all around me. When she finished the first dress, she and the matchmaker helped peel it off and replaced it with another.

I was wearing a delicate, off-shoulder gown the color of algae that gathered on still water in summer, of lichen clinging to the bark of trees. It hugged my torso and waist, then fell like water over rock. Sylvie was still pinning when another attendant knocked at the door.

"The Dragon is here, Mistress." She bowed and Estin's tall form appeared behind her in the hall.

The matchmaker thanked the girl, who then scurried away. "I can wait downstairs," Estin offered.

"Nonsense," the matchmaker snipped. "She's clothed."

In the mirror, Estin's reflections moved behind me. His eyes met mine for a moment in the glass, then flicked away to the matchmaker. This morning, he was the Dragon through and through. His lips were set in a firm line as he walked into the room. It suddenly felt like all the air was sucked out of it. Like each mirror seemed to reposition itself just to hold his image.

"I'm surprised you didn't send Asra to fetch her," the woman noted, quirking a brow.

"Asra is busy," the Dragon dryly informed her, straightening his back and folding his hands in front of him.

"We're almost finished." The matchmaker hovered, helping Sylvie finish the hem at the bottom, then tugged the dress tighter across my chest, accentuating it more. "Pin it so that it will lay like this. Cassius won't be able to resist you. His favorite color is green."

I frowned. I needed the Emperor to approve of me, but didn't want to be made irresistible to him.

"Don't you agree, Dragon? Isn't this gown lovely?" the matchmaker asked coyly.

He stood up straighter. "Yes."

The matchmaker stood up straight, craned her head this way and that, and walked around me. "Sylvie?"

"I think it's perfect," the girl quietly observed.

"Go and change, Vayl," the matchmaker told me, pointing to the dressing screen.

She peppered the Dragon with questions about yesterday's training while I stepped behind the screen with Sylvie, who eased the gown slowly up and over my head, careful not to prick me or upset the pins she'd placed. When it was free, I slipped the sky-blue linen dress that Sylvie had brought for me to wear today over my head. She'd taken it in to fit me better, so I no longer felt like I was wearing a shapeless feed sack.

I smoothed a hand down my stomach and sides, marveling at how well it fit. "Thank you," I told her.

She hung the gown she'd just helped me out of and nodded. "Many of the dresses will be ready by tomorrow – in case he comes early."

It was true he'd arrived early to meet me, but he told the matchmaker he would return in a fortnight. "Do you think he'll come *that* early?" I whispered.

She shrugged. "He has before, but he's been a few days late as well. It depends on how long it takes him to accomplish... whatever he's doing."

"How many women has the matchmaker sent to him?"

"I'm not sure how many total, but three in the past few years since I've been here. One each year. There are five matchmakers who procure concubines for our emperor, as well as matching couples within the empire. In fact, a young woman and man are coming in today to meet for the first time." Sylvie gave a small smile. "It's exciting to see the first meeting. The matchmaker is very skilled at pairing, so most seem pleased when they leave this place, but some simply glow. I do hope the couple today is smitten."

"Most?" I asked. "Given her gift, I figured all her matches would be pleased."

She shrugged. "It's difficult to make some people happy."

It would be unnerving being matched to someone you didn't know. What if your mate was awful? Then again, what if they weren't? What happened if you fell so in love with the person you'd entwined your life with, only to have them torn away by fate or misfortune?

Father and Mother respected one another, but I doubted she ever felt dragonflies in her stomach when they touched. I didn't remember her ever mooning over Father, or he over her.

Sylvie took the gown she'd pinned and left the room. Estin glanced in my direction as I stepped out from behind the screen, lifting my heavy hair off my shoulders. I'd need to pull it back before I began my dragon training.

When I looked back at him, he pinned me with a look I couldn't decipher. The muscle in his jaw jumped. Zaire did that when he was mad sometimes... Had the matchmaker upset him? I looked at her, but she snapped at me to get my boots on. As I tied the laces, she shouted for someone to bring the basket.

"Cinnamon rolls, cookies, and scones," she announced as a girl hurried in and placed the handle in my hands as I stood again. She looked to Estin. "I need to be able to reach you if Favian comes for her early."

Aggravation laced his tone. "I'll have what you need this evening. I'll bring it when I see her back."

The matchmaker seemed uneasy, but she nodded. "Very well."

She walked us downstairs, and Estin unbarricaded the door. Even knowing we would be leaving soon, they'd locked it after he arrived. Their precaution made me wonder who we might bump into in the dark and whether the tunnels were truly safe.

Estin offered his hand and watched as I slipped mine into his waiting palm. His fingers tightened with my throat as he led me into the dark and waited until the matchmaker slid the barricade back in place before moving.

He squeezed my hand. "Ready?"

"Yeah."

We walked through the darkened tunnel a little faster than we had yesterday. My feet were learning the path and becoming accustomed to the way he moved, and he let me know if he needed to slow or when to step over a fallen rock by squeezing my hand.

"Why are you upset?" I asked after we'd walked several minutes in silence.

"Why do you assume I am?"

"When I stepped out from behind the screen, you seemed tense and the matchmaker's mood had soured."

He chose his words carefully. "We were just discussing you going to the palace. The very thought..." His steps slowed. In the pitch blackness, he turned to face me. "I have a terrible feeling about this, but I know how to keep you safe, if you'll let me. I could take you to the wall and show you how to climb down the other side."

Gravel crunched under his boots, a gritting sound as he shifted his weight. I wished I could see him, but imagined his gray-green eyes full of earnest concern, the loyalty he felt for my brother extending to me.

"And then what? I fall into the waiting arms of an elvish soldier who deftly slits my throat?"

"If I sent you in elvish armor, they would know you weren't a threat and you wouldn't be harmed."

My lashes fluttered when I realized he was serious. "I appreciate the offer, but I don't want to do that. I don't want to run."

Running meant that someone else would have to do what I had the perfect opportunity to accomplish. Running meant Favian would live to see another day he didn't deserve. It meant their sister would remain imprisoned, even if she had built the formidable cage herself. It meant that war was as close as Estin was now.

His thumb brushed the back of my hand. "I feel like I'm betraying him. Zaire would hate me for helping you with this. He was my very best friend," his voice croaked.

"You're wrong. Zaire never underestimated me. He would have done exactly what you're doing now."

I heard him swallow. Heard each of his breaths in the darkness that entwined us. "He loved you so much, Vayl. He only ever wanted what was best for you. He planned to take you to Thanias, the kingdom of the elves, after your father died. He knew you wouldn't leave him in his condition, and your father couldn't have made the journey, but I know Zaire was grateful for all you did to care for your father while he was away. Despite their difficult past, he loved him."

I knew he did. I'd always known it. For a very long time after he left in anger, I wondered if harboring such a feeling only fed it, or if over time it would burn itself out. I'd hoped for the latter, not knowing what my brother's true motives for enlisting were.

Zaire's desperate apology resurfaced. He'd admitted to everything and didn't even know Father couldn't hear his heartfelt words.

Zaire loved my father enough to put his life at risk to avenge him. Not by a hasty thrust of his blade, but by cutting the Emperor and Favian much, much deeper.

He loved me, even when I was difficult and didn't understand him in return. Even when I wondered if I should risk Rata's wrath and light the taper each night or pray that he would find his way back to us on his own.

I didn't even know he'd given any thought to our futures. He certainly never mentioned taking me to Thanias. Were humans even welcomed in the elvish kingdom? "Why would he think we could go to Thanias?"

"Zaire loved Thanias and visited it often when he carried messages to and from our mother. My sister's magic is debilitating to our kind, and since it resonates from the wall itself, we can't get near enough to send word to her, but there are limitations. Zaire found that it can only deter elves. It doesn't bar humans from crossing in either direction."

I steadied myself with a hand on the rough stone wall of the passage. I had no idea humans could pass through the magic. Did others know? My breathing shallowed as my heart raced. I pictured Zaire running toward the imposing structure, knowing full well that he was welcome on Estin's side.

"If you need to send word to your mother about your sister's location, or what we're going to try, I could carry a message for you," I offered. I'd already carried Zaire's message to him, and if his mother knew where Kirsi was, maybe she would show mercy to the innocent humans who lay in her path.

Estin's hand tightened around mine. "You're doing enough."

"I'm not," I quickly and adamantly argued. "Not yet."

He hesitated for a moment before suggesting we press on. The dragons were waiting.

Estin began walking again, keeping the pace slow as we spoke. "Zaire thought you might find a love match with an elf, though we don't have matchmakers in Thanias. Elves are free to pair themselves, but such a decision is not to be taken lightly. Once bound, they cannot be unbound."

"Even after one of the two perishes?" I asked.

"Love does not perish with death," he said ominously.

After we'd found our new house, I often wondered if Father would request a new match. He never did, but I thought I knew why. He didn't think a woman would agree to the match because of his condition.

"What was Asra busy with this morning?" I asked conversationally.

"What?" he asked as if confused.

"Asra. You told the matchmaker he was busy and couldn't come for me."

He was quiet for a few steps. Every movement and sound echoed through the hollow vein we traversed. "Would you prefer he come instead?"

"No, I... I was just making conversation. I don't like the quiet sometimes, and the sound of our boots on the rock doesn't count as noise."

I could almost hear him smile. "Then let's talk. What would you like to know?"

"What are we doing today?"

"Breakfast to begin with, more work with knives, running for speed and endurance, swimming if you're up for it, and most importantly, thwarting random attacks."

"Random attacks?" I asked.

"Yes. We will each attack you once at some point today, and you'll have to be on guard and defend yourself."

I groaned. "Do you have any idea how long I had to rinse my mouth last night to get all the sand out?"

Estin's laughter echoed through the tunnel. "You have to learn to anticipate the unexpected, fight when you don't see the blow coming – and survive."

WHEN ESTIN PROVIDED the loose itinerary, he didn't mention that he would be absent for most of the morning. When I asked where he was going, he vaguely answered that he was procuring something for the matchmaker. I remembered his promise to bring her something when he returned with me this evening and couldn't stop wondering what the item was and where he had to go to get it.

When I walked into the small encampment, I immediately realized what Asra had been busy doing when he walked out of Indri's tent, shirtless, stretching his back, his hair mussed from... sleep.

Indri followed with one eye still closed, yawning, wearing a short chemise.

Grady clapped his hand on my shoulder. "Let's have something to eat from that basket while those two rabbits wake up and hopefully wash up." He said the last part louder.

Asra answered with a laugh, eliciting a grin from Indri. "Race you to the water!" She was already running before the last word was out of her mouth, but he caught up with her almost instantly.

"Those two are made for one another," Grady told me with a smile, then led me to a broken palm tree that made a perfect bench. I uncovered the basket's goods and held it out for his inspection. The giant of a man rubbed his hands together before gingerly plucking a cinnamon roll from the bunch. I took one too, and we ate while Asra and Indri splashed.

"When you're finished, your clothes are ready," Indri yelled. "I washed them and hung them out for Ventus to dry. But eat as much as you can first. You'll need it today!"

SHE WASN'T LYING. After I'd dressed in the same trousers and vest I borrowed yesterday, Indri waded from the water and changed into trousers and a tight-fitting, sleeveless top. Asra ran to his tent to change as she led me to the dummy, repeating the motions of where to stab to incapacitate my opponent. Yesterday, she showed me how to grip the knife's handle properly and how to jab, stab, plunge, and twist the blade. Today, she focused on where to aim it to kill – slowly, or as quickly as possible. The last, she emphasized, was the most important for me to learn. The rest was just fun.

I smiled and shook my head.

To Indri, death was a game she didn't intend to lose. She practiced every move relentlessly and trained her body to be strong, lithe, and quick like her mind.

She used Grady and Asra to show me where on the body to jab, explaining the dummy wasn't a precise enough example. Since Grady was a much larger man, she showed me how I needed to adjust where I hit him, compared to someone smaller like Asra.

From my periphery, there was a flash of movement an instant before I was knocked sideways onto the sand. The knife I'd been holding landed a few feet away. Indri had warned me a hundred times to grip it tight enough that it couldn't be batted or wrenched away, and the first time something surprised me...

I scrambled to it and reached for the handle when a boot fell on my wrist. A shadow fell over me as the owner of that boot crouched down. "At least you don't have a mouth full of sand," Estin teased, then quirked a brow. "In all fairness, I warned you to expect the unexpected today."

The unexpected, yes, but I thought it would be from Grady or

Asra – someone who was near enough to strike but within my sight. I didn't expect an attack out of the blue. "How did you just... appear out of nowhere?" I grabbed the blade's handle and curled my fingers tightly around it.

"Did I?" he asked, offering me his hand and helping me up.

"You did. I'm certain of it." Estin plucked a stone from his pocket and tossed it in the air. "What is that?" I asked, curious.

A glacieris stone was pure white, like the ice and snow that capped the northern mountains and just as frigid to the touch. This stone was teal, the color of the sea where the sand fell away and all that was left beneath for many fathoms was more ocean.

"*This* is what the matchmaker demanded this morning. I need to take it to her. Be right back," he chirped. Then he disappeared.

My mouth gaped.

Indri laughed at my awestruck expression. "It's a little unsettling to see at first."

"Unnerving," Grady added.

"Human minds don't want to accept that magic exists. They just can't comprehend it at all," Asra chimed in.

None of them were wrong.

I knew what glacieris could do. The crystal was a gift from Zairitus. Frozen water encased in crystal. Not only could it inscribe frosty messages upon flesh, the crystal could freeze a body of water solid – regardless of its size. I glanced at the ocean, imagining it frozen to the very bottom of the deepest trench, every creature immobile in its icy clutches. Every ship, still and stuck upon its slick surface. Would the sea-battered sailors climb down to skate upon it?

Busy daydreaming, my heart leapt when Estin suddenly appeared in front of me. I clutched my chest, my heart pounding. "It's called intervallim. It allows for travel between points. You simply break the crystal and the pieces will forever call to one another, anxious to fuse again. I gave the matchmaker one, kept one for myself, and..." He unfurled his fist to reveal a beautiful necklace. Set into a teardrop pendant, framed with delicate, silver filigree was the other third of the intervallim. "This is for you. I asked the jeweler to remove the original stone and replace it with part of the intervallim instead."

"He cut and polished it rather quickly," I noted dryly.

Estin's stormy eyes met mine. "He did."

The dragonflies flitted in my stomach.

"If Zairitus made glacieris, which god is responsible for the creation of something so powerful and rare?"

"Urit," he answered. "The god of storms and lightning allowed those who knew how to wield it the power to move as fast as one of his bolts."

"How much did that cost you, Estin?" Asra asked sharply.

"That's my concern," the Dragon snapped back at his brother.

Grady excused himself, explaining that he'd spent enough time playing the role of my victim and needed to fish so we would have another mid-day meal as good as yesterday's. I still hadn't seen any hint as to what his gift might be.

Asra nodded toward the sea and wagged his brows at Indri. "Take a break with me?"

She glanced at us once over her shoulder with a sad smile on her face. I wasn't sure what was bothering her.

When they were out of earshot, Estin held the necklace out. "Would you like me to help you put it on?"

I nodded and moved my hair to the side for him. He looped it around my neck and fastened the clasp. The silver setting was cool at first, but my skin warmed it quickly.

"How much *did* it cost you?" I asked warily.

"Only a favor, and not nearly as much as Asra implied." He glanced at his brother, who swam happily with Indri at his side, grinning as the two cut through the water like fins. "That's what Zaire wanted for you: a love that was carefree and as light and easy as breathing."

"Did he ever have that?"

The Dragon took in a heavy breath. "The way he talked, he might have once, but it didn't last. The girl's father did not approve of a soldier for his daughter, and then he was assigned to the dungeons, and slowly, he became our ally."

And now my brother would never have the opportunity to find a love that bridged days, years, and decades. He wouldn't have a thousand simple, happy moments like Indri and Asra shared. His heart would never feel light as air.

If I survived this, I vowed to find that with someone. To appreciate and enjoy every second that Zaire would miss and never take a single one for granted.

Life was too precious to treat indifferently.

Estin's eyes traced the delicate necklace hanging from my neck. "Do you know how Zaire managed to set us free without being caught?"

I shook my head.

"Because he called no attention to himself. He did as he was told. Never did anything exceptional until it counted. He watched and listened and learned the movements of the people who might see him, or us. Only when he knew them by heart did he take a chance."

It was the same thing the matchmaker had said to me. Be quiet and listen. Act when it's right. Be patient. It worked well enough for him when he set the dragons free, but not when he heard that Kirsi was near. Perhaps she was the one who caught him.

"He risked himself when he learned of your sister."

"I worry that it was Kirsi," he said, breathing life into my hidden suspicions.

"It could have been her, but we don't know that."

He scrubbed a hand over his face. "I don't know otherwise, either."

"It could have been one of the favored, or Favian himself. We could speculate all day and never know the answer, and Zaire is no longer here to give it."

He wet his lips and stared at the sea. "What if it *was* her?" he asked. I saw the war raging in his eyes. It was the same battle I fought within my chest. I wanted the person responsible for Zaire's death to share his fate. He said Favian had cut him down – but did someone else focus the Lion of Kaan upon his prey?

Estin wanted to avenge Zaire, too. They were best friends. So close that the Dragon, who seemed so cold sometimes to others, called him a brother. He was warm to me, helping me out of respect for Zaire and his loyalty to him. But he also had a responsibility to his sister. Not only because of the familial bond, but because she was Thanias's future queen.

"Let's hope she had nothing to do with it," I told him, brushing my fingers over the intervallim stone. I wondered how it worked and wished that instead of taking me to its pieces, it might take me straight to the one who caught Zaire snooping around the palace.

Slogging through another run, I was huffing and puffing by the time I made it to the top of the peak. That was when Asra loosed a war cry and tackled me to the ground. My breath escaped in an 'oof'. I slapped at his burgundy curls. "What was *that* for?"

"Estin made me do it," he quickly revealed.

I glared at the Dragon. "Did he, now?" I had no idea how I was going to get him back, but I would. Oh, I would.

Asra jumped up, spry as a jackrabbit and offered his hand. "Swim with us before you go back?" he asked.

I looked at Indri to make sure she wanted me to tag along. "Will it just be the two of you?"

Indri smiled. "Well, Grady is already down there. He might wade in for *you*."

It was obvious Grady hated the water. It would take decades for him to wade in to his waist. "I'm not sure," I hedged.

"Suit yourself," Estin told me with a grin.

My head ticked back in surprise. "*You're* swimming?"

He shrugged. "I'm hot."

"Don't you have mystical errands to run?" I teased.

"None too pressing." With that, he took off running. Asra quickly gave chase. Indri and I jogged down the mountain together.

"Can you swim?" she asked.

"Yes. There was a river near my old house with water deep enough in spots that you couldn't touch the bottom."

"Anyone? Or just you?" she teased, referring to my height.

"Zaire couldn't either," I told her.

She and I ground to a stop at the base of the peak. "You being here is helping him," she said.

"Who?"

"Estin. Learning that Zaire died hurt us all, but not like it hurt him. When Zaire set us free, Estin changed. He felt guilty that we'd all been caught and poured his every breath into finding Kirsi. He allowed himself to become the Dragon everyone knows and fears, a man bent on revenge. But with you, he's different. He's like he was... before."

"It certainly doesn't seem like he's feared among you," I noted, looking at Estin and Asra stripping their shirts off, their tan skin gleaming in Rata's warm light.

"Only because we know the real him."

"He should let others know the real him, too," I told her.

She nodded kindly. "You've only seen him with the matchmaker; he's different with her because she knows his heart. It's the ones who don't that fear him most. Estin can be quite intimidating when he wants to be. He works hard to keep that reputation, among our kind and yours. He wants to drive the Lion mad trying to find him, wasting their resources and precious time."

"Why?"

"Because if the Lion chases him, he's not circling Kirsi." My eyes snapped to hers as realization dawned. She looked at me curiously. "What?"

"That's it!" I took off running toward the water. Sand sprayed in my wake, and then suddenly, I was chilly and wet and submerged beneath the waves that rolled over my head. I planted my feet in the sand and pushed against it hard, surfacing with a gasp. Pushing my hands down to keep afloat, I glanced all around, surprised to find myself in the ocean when I'd been running along the shore only seconds ago.

In a blink, Estin was in front of me with a look of wonder on his face. "You used it."

I meant to tell him something, but all thought escaped me as my mind struggled to process what had happened. "What?"

"The intervallim!" he whooped, splashing the water with his palms.

He was chest deep, but I couldn't touch. I started swimming toward the shore.

"Wait!" he said.

"I can't touch."

He moved toward me. "I thought you could swim."

"I can. I mean – I have – in a river. But not in the ocean, and certainly not in waves taller than I am." My eyes widened as one built just behind him. He easily bobbed over its surface as the crest rolled toward my face. I closed my eyes, ready for it to bowl me over, when two strong hands clamped onto my waist and lifted me above the frothy summit.

My hands found his shoulders. They were solid and my fingers spread, wanting to explore a little further. Estin's lashes were thickly separated by the salt water. I thought of how tumultuous the short amount of time we'd known each other had been, and how our emotions still ebbed and flowed like the tide strokes and strides away.

"This okay?" he asked carefully.

"Yeah," I told him, then remembered why I'd raced toward him in the first place. "Listen, I have an idea. We need to distract Favian and Cassius, right? When I get to the palace, we need them to be looking elsewhere..."

He abruptly let go of me, and I hurriedly hooked an arm around his neck. "Don't!"

His hands returned to my waist. "I won't let you go if you don't want me to. And yes, I agree. Let me think about how we can distract them."

I wiped the water from my eyes, nervous about being so far in the ocean. "The place Zaire and I used to swim was shallow, for the most part. Even when it swelled after heavy rains, the river bed was only a few inches below where I could touch. I could go under and know I could push myself back up." I knew I was babbling, but it was the only thing I could do to distract myself from the leagues of water all around me.

"This is no different."

I shook my head. "This is *very* different. The ocean is fathomless. A wave could tug me out so far, I'd never find the bottom and make it back to the top still breathing."

He smiled. "It's not fathomless where we stand."

"I'll head back to the shallower water," I told him, unhooking my arm from his neck.

But he held firm, his fingers flexing. "Stay."

I swallowed thickly, hoping he couldn't see the effect he had on me, praying his elvish ears didn't hear it over the roar of the wind and waves. I took in the stubble growing on his jaw, lip and chin, giving him a hint of a shadow, mesmerized by the way Rata's light made his dark hair look darker and his skin appear more bronze than flesh. How he made me feel powerful when all other men with the exception of my brother had always sought to trample any ounce of spirit I might have had.

They failed.

My strength was never ruined; I just hid it away until now – when I needed it most.

I'd forgotten Asra and Indri until they waded out of the water. I watched Indri rush into her tent for a moment to grab a blanket. She spread it on the sand and she and Asra lay upon it, holding hands and enjoying Rata's warmth as they dried under her rays. Asra whispered and Indri replied in throaty giggles. They curled toward one another as if each was a fragment from the same piece of intervallim.

As Estin and I bobbed together in the waves, I asked, "How far is the town of Sparrowing from here?"

"What's in Sparrowing, other than the Imperial Army?"

"My mother's grave."

He quietly apologized.

I shook my head, not wishing him to feel guilty. "There's

nothing to apologize for. I just wish the intervallim could take me there in an instant. You already know the boulder that marks the grave of my father and brother, but another stone marks my mother's. One day, I'd like to find it. I left something under it when we left. I wonder if it's still there."

"What did you leave?" he gently asked.

"My favorite, and only, hair ribbon."

"What does her stone look like?"

"It's striped. Black, white, and gray, in that order. I said those words over and over when I was little so I wouldn't forget them," I added with a sad smile. "She's buried near a willow, but far enough from its roots to not be disturbed. She lies close to where we lived when we were small."

"Zaire told me about that night," he admitted.

"He blamed himself for not being able to get us out," I told him. "He told me he was sorry before he died. I told him it wasn't his fault, but I know in my heart he didn't believe me." I looked to the sky where Rata burned, confined in the great fiery orb that was powerful enough to cast light over the earth. To burn us, even as far away as she'd been cast.

Rata was destruction, unfavored even by the other gods. The only one who hadn't abandoned her was Trayton, but even when he pulled her from the inky abyss, he kept her at a distance and set her where she could be captured again.

Without Rata, we would freeze to death or starve, because without her light, our crops wouldn't raise from the rich soil. But if she was ever allowed closer than she crept now, she would ruin us all. Perhaps Trayton protected us from more than just the darkness. Perhaps he guarded us from Rata as well...

I lifted my leg in the water. "That night, the fire burned my thigh. Did Zaire tell you that?"

He nodded again, watching me carefully.

"Did he tell you that Rata claimed me in that moment and healed me the next?"

Estin's brows kissed. "He didn't tell me that."

"I hate her," I breathed. His hands tensed on my sides,

surprised by the vehemence in my tone. "I hate her with every fiber of my being. She healed me, but killed my mother."

"I can't even imagine," he rasped, reeling me in and hooking an arm around my back. If he feared Rata's wrath, he didn't say it. He just held me tight in Zairitus's cool sea and kept me from drifting away.

I wrapped my legs around his waist, hooking my ankles. "I wish Zairitus had seen fit to claim me, too," I revealed, unable to keep the bitterness from my tongue. "Rata could have doused her flames, but she wanted our house and Mother to burn, for me and Zaire to cower, and for Father to forget her. The only reason I can think of for doing that was to punish me."

"You were only a child. What could a child possibly do that would be worthy of such a dire sentence?" he whispered.

"Maybe it wasn't something I did, but something I have yet to do." *Something I'm destined for...*

I probably sounded crazy. Mother used to speak as if she knew the things I would do in the future. Maybe Rata saw them too and disapproved, so she struck Mother down to change the woman I would become.

The gods chose each being – elf or human – while we were still in the womb. We wouldn't learn which one had cast their lot with us until it was revealed at some point in our lives. Some learned in infancy, their parents relaying the great sign to them later when they could understand. Some didn't learn until they lay upon their deathbeds. I didn't understand the gods. Why did we matter to them at all? Why did they bother to meddle in the affairs of mortals? Was this all a game to them, and if so, did they play us against one another, or were they playing us against our neighbors?

"You can probably guess who claimed me," he lightly offered, lifting us both over a bulging wave.

"Trayton," I replied easily.

He nodded.

"How did he reveal it?"

"When I was only a boy, I got lost in the woods. I was shivering and hungry. The stars shimmered in the sky with silver light, but as they grew larger, I realized he was descending."

"He came down to you?" I asked incredulously.

"Not fully. He stayed in the sky where I could see him and led me out of the darkness."

His revelation was beautiful. Instead of instilling fear, Trayton had come to help him, showing he valued Estin and wanted him to survive another day.

"Did you see Rata in the flames?" he breathed, as if the gods couldn't hear our every utterance.

"If she was there, she did not reveal her face. I relive that night often in my dreams and every time, I search for her in desperation. I keep thinking that if I can find her, maybe I can beg her to change what happened and let Mother live. I pray that when I wake, things will be different. I felt the swipe of her hand over my burnt, blistered skin and knew which god had claimed me the instant the pain stopped. Within seconds, the blisters sank back into my flesh and the angry red skin the fire had licked faded away until nothing was left."

His eyes studied mine carefully as we floated over another swell. "We make quite a pair, you and I."

I cocked my head to the side. "What do you mean?"

"Would Trayton have a purpose if Rata had not been cast into the dark night? He was destined to battle for her. Now I know why he does it," he mused, staring at the sky as if he could sense the dragon god flying above us despite Rata's fiery light. He fastened his eyes on mine. "What is a dragon without fire in his lungs?"

His words coupled with the look in his eyes stilled my breath.

Hands cupped, Grady called to us from the shore. "Fish is ready!" The normally jovial Grady wore a scowl and flashed a look of warning at Estin as he carried me to where I could touch. We emerged from the sea together, but Grady had turned his back and was already walking away.

Indri dusted little seams of sand off her clothes, now mostly dry. Asra stretched and followed the behemoth to a large flat rock where he'd laid out a platter of cooked fish, wilted greens, small bread rolls, and the basket the matchmaker had sent with us, half-empty of the sweet rolls.

Indri blessed the food and that strange crackle snapped in the air and settled around the flat rock. We divided the food between us and settled down to eat. Grady offered small bowls for the greens and passed around forks that had seen better days. He was quiet; his lips were thin, his brows drawn.

Asra's eyes flicked from Estin to Grady, a silent question shimmering.

Indri kept quiet, so I did, too.

"Grady, what's the matter?" Estin finally asked after a few minutes of tense silence.

Grady's face mottled a moment before he flung his arm in the air. "What do you think you're *doing*? She's here to train so she can handle the absolute hurricane she's about to walk into. She's not here for you to paw all over!"

Estin went still. Asra and Indri shrank back, the Dragon's brother muttering something under his breath while I held mine.

"We were swimming. Nothing more," Estin replied sharply.

"Swimming?" Grady stood from his seat. "*Swimming* does not require arms around one another, or legs, for that matter."

"We were just talking, Grady. I promise," I hastily added. "I couldn't touch the sand beyond the breakers. If I didn't hold onto him, I would've gotten tossed around and would've had to just wade in the shallow water."

"Better you do that," he yelled, "than the other!" He wagged a finger at us. "The last thing any of us needs is tangled feelings. Not now."

Estin slowly rose and stalked toward Grady. The Dragon matched his height but not his bulk. Despite that fact, Grady shrank from him. The apple in his throat bobbed as he swallowed thickly.

"I was talking to her about Zaire, and about the gods, if you must know. There was no pawing. Nothing untoward. But if there had been, it would be none of your business, Grady. None!" he roared.

Grady pointed at me. "I know you don't want to be, Vayl, but you *are* the Emperor's property. In a handful of days, you'll be delivered into his hands. I wish on all the gods that you succeed in what you plan to attempt, but if circumstance prevents it, if things aren't as easy as we all hope they'll be, you will have to do whatever it takes to survive. That will mean..." His voice broke and he took a moment to compose himself. My throat stung and tears built in my eyes. "It'll mean that you'll..."

"I know what it means, Grady." I stood and walked to the men, facing off and putting myself between them. I hugged Grady and told him I would be okay no matter what happened, asking him not to worry for me.

"I can't help it." His massive body shook as he cried. "And it's not just you I worry for," he croaked, looking at Estin. He straightened and pulled away, wiping his eyes. "I'm a mess."

"It's okay to be a mess sometimes," I chided.

"Took me months to warm to Zaire. I didn't trust him while he wore the Emperor's insignia, even if he was helping us. But you... Two days in, and you've turned me to absolute mush!"

I turned to look at Estin over my shoulder, but he'd fastened his eyes on the sea. He strode away without a word.

My shoulders fell.

"He'll calm down," Grady told me. "Eventually."

Asra blew out a tense breath, then took a bread roll and bit a chunk out of it. "Never a dull moment around dragons," he told me with a wink. He was trying to break the tension. It didn't work.

Indri cleared her throat and looked at me. "Grady's right. You need to be careful about getting too close to him."

"To Estin?"

She nodded once. "If he develops feelings for you... he'll get himself killed trying to free you and lose sight of Kirsi altogether."

"He doesn't strike me as the type to get attached to someone so quickly," I argued.

Indri gave me a sad smile. "You're the last piece of Zaire he has left, and those two were fast friends. Estin trusted Zaire and told him things he'd never even told us, back before we'd been around your brother long enough to be comfortable with him. He wasn't being facetious when he said he considered Zaire a brother. But the way he looks at you sometimes... he certainly doesn't consider you a sister."

"I shouldn't come here anymore," I breathed.

"Yes," Asra said sternly, "you should. You need to learn all you can from us before you go. Whether you can free our sister or not, you need to be able to fight. War will come if Kirsi continues to weaken, and when it does, our mother will assume that all concubines are loyal to Cassius."

"There's no way I can stand against one elvish soldier, let alone many." And they all knew it. The elven army's might was legendary. If not for Kirsi's power alone, they would have laid waste to Kaan long ago. "I could train my whole life and not be prepared well enough for that."

CHAPTER 13

After lunch, Asra worked with me on how to break holds, which I was honestly terrible at. He would grab me from behind, but no matter how I tried to plant my feet and throw him off balance, he was too big and strong for me to move.

No matter if he wrapped an arm around my waist, hooked an elbow around my throat, or just grabbed my arm or wrist, it was the same result with each maneuver. I couldn't make him budge. Before long I was pouring sweat, the only testament to the fact that I was sincerely trying.

"Stop," he finally said when I gritted and tried to bury my shoulder into him. "I'm teaching you wrong. Ignore everything I just said. Don't hold anything back. Pretend I'm Zaire and do to me what you'd do to him if the two of you were play fighting."

I wiped my brow. "Are you sure?"

His eyes lit up. "Positive. It was what worked with Grady yesterday, wasn't it?"

Indeed, it was. "You might get hurt," I warned.

"Duly noted." He chuckled, then grabbed my wrist. Instead of slamming the heel of my hand down on his joint, I jerked his hand to my mouth and bit him. Hard.

Asra swore, his eyes wide when he wrenched his hand away, shaking it for good measure. "That was perfect!"

"I bit you," I deadpanned.

"So?" he whooped. "You broke my hold. You did it!"

When he circled me, I sidestepped and moved to match his pace. In this lesson, there was no fun to be had. I knew that if I ever had to break free of someone who meant me harm, there would be no playful smiles. No dares painted in my opponent's eyes.

The thought terrified me, but I knew I wouldn't be careful then. I'd bite. I'd claw and gouge and kick and stomp to get away, and hope it was enough.

He grabbed the tender flesh of my upper arm, keeping his grip firm but gentle. I brought my hand up as if I was going to pry his fingers away, but when he focused his attention there, I brought my knee up, dangerously close to his groin. He sucked in a sharp breath, then let it out shakily. "Thank you for stopping. I want to have children one day."

I laughed as he released my arm. "It's much easier imagining it's all for fun," I told him. "Zaire and I fought all the time as children."

Asra's easy demeanor shifted in an instant. He tensed and his smile fell away as he glanced over my shoulder. I knew who was standing behind me. "Hey," he said to his brother, his tone curt.

Estin replied in kind, then glanced at me. "The matchmaker is waiting."

I nodded, not ready to leave yet, but knowing that what I wanted didn't matter.

Soon... soon my life will be my own, I vowed.

"Thank you, Asra."

"Welcome," he bit out tensely before turning and walking away – to find Indri, no doubt. Grady warily watched from the water where he waded.

"Did you figure out what his gift is yet?" Estin asked, jutting his chin toward the giant.

"Not yet."

"I'm sorry I left like that," he said. "I'll apologize to them all."

I shrugged. "You were upset." It was better than punching a palm tree, I supposed.

He shook his head, finding each of his dragons along the shore. "That's no excuse. I'm responsible for how I behave and react. I shouldn't have lost my temper in the first place." He pulled the intervallim from his pocket and clasped my hand. "Touch the stone and think of the matchmaker. Take us to her."

I wasn't sure I could. This afternoon, I hadn't meant to be drawn to Estin. I was thinking about him... about telling him something. I didn't actively choose to blink to his side. I touched the stone pendant, closed my eyes, and felt a barely-there brush of delicate, downy feathers. A moment later, the two of us appeared before the matchmaker, who was already seated at her finely set table.

"Vayl!" she said, startled. "You... what are you wearing?"

I cringed when I realized I'd forgotten to change. "I can't train in a dress," I replied sheepishly.

Her brow popped. "You certainly should be! Do you think you'll be allowed to don trousers in the palace of the concubine?"

"I insisted on her apparel change," the Dragon offered. "Trousers allow for more fluid movement. Once Vayl is adept in self-defense, she can practice what we've taught her while wearing one of her dresses."

"Very well, Dragon. You've done enough for the day," she said, primly folding her napkin over her lap and gesturing to the chair. I took it, silently apologizing to Estin for her rude dismissal. The storm in his eyes raged. Green and gray, forest and smoke.

He disappeared a moment later.

I tried to focus on what the matchmaker had taught me last night, only stumbling twice. I could learn this...

She was terse and contrary throughout the entire meal, which made me long for the dragons' easy company. Even when they argued and fought, it was passionate and done out of love. The matchmaker just seemed sour today.

But given that I only confused two of the forks, she was as

pleased as anyone in her mood could be. "You need to bathe and then get as much sleep as you can. Sylvie has finished making your white dresses. You'll need to try them on in the morning."

My brows scrunched in confusion. "White?"

"You'll wear them as an outward sign of your chastity, until..."

I swallowed, toying with my napkin's seam.

"Then you'll be able to wear whatever color you'd like, but never white again. And black is reserved for sacred days."

I nodded, then excused myself from the table. A tub of hot, steaming water waited for me, just as I expected. The matchmaker anticipated everything, it seemed.

Washing quickly, I toweled off my hair and body and slipped into a silken night dress the color of bright yellow daisy petals. I hurried to my room and slipped into bed.

The matchmaker knocked twice at the door just after I closed my eyes.

I sat up.

"Vayl," she began, then stopped herself. She sat on the edge of my bed, the mattress accommodating her weight. "I worry for you with the Dragon."

"He isn't as bad as he seems," I told her, tracing the blanket's stitching.

Her hand pressed against mine. "That's not why I'm concerned. I know he isn't cruel. It's just... I can feel your heart and his."

"I'm not in love with him," I rushed to say. Though I had to admit that something in my belly stirred when he was around. I liked his smile and his strength. I admired his loyalty. But love? I didn't love him.

"You cannot deny you are attracted to him," she volleyed. "That you care about his fate. You wouldn't want to see him dead."

"I don't want to see anyone dead."

"You know what I mean," she pressed. "But you must know that nothing can come of it. If you care for him at all, if you respect him, you cannot allow it. Cassius, while he treats his concubines well, can be unbelievably cruel to those who cross him. He's very particular about what he believes is his, and you already are."

I nodded, unable to speak. I chewed my lips.

It was the same warning Grady, his brother, and his friends had given us this afternoon, but it felt far more dire coming from a Heart Reader. She patted my hand and the motherly gesture hurt to the marrow. Then she left the room and slid my door closed while I sank back into the soft sheets and wiped foolish tears away.

I wouldn't let myself fall for Estin, and I would make sure he didn't fall for me.

If she saw an attraction, that was simple enough to squash now, before the feeling turned into something significant. Even if I wondered what it would be like to love the Dragon.

Flames crawl up the wall like a swarm of millipedes. There is only a faint rapping sound, then a soft whoosh as they climb the thin sheets that act as curtains and stretch up the door frame. I see myself curled up asleep on the cot, Zaire on the other side of the room fast asleep on his, but the other version of me that stands just outside the door chokes as smoke fills my nose.

Dark gray tendrils coil along the ceiling before pluming in undulating waves of impenetrable smoke. Across the room, I watch my child-self blink awake. She screams for Zaire, who startles awake.

He and young Vayl take in the fire that has already eaten its way into their room.

Ignoring the children, I hunt for the one who sent the flame. "Rata!" I yell, cupping my hands to make the sound carry.

She does not answer.

I search for her face along the flame-eaten walls, in the scaling, brittle wood. I call out her name, daring her to face me.

Sanity and self-preservation... I've thrown them away.

The fire intensifies. Across the room, Zaire and a younger Vayl rush to plan their escape, garnering what little courage they can. The ceiling beams groan as fire begins to consume them with angry, grasping fingers of flame.

"Run!" I scream at the children, who crouch together on the floor. Zaire's arm is around young Vayl's back. He uses his small body to shield her, promising it will all be okay, but that they need to run.

They stand and make a break for it, pushing toward me, and then, there she is. Rata emerges from the flame. Not whole, only her arm, but when she clamps her fiery hand onto young Vayl's thigh, both she and I scream out.

Father coughs from the other room. My eyes dart in that direction as the beams overhead creak. The thatched ceiling is lit like the head of a torch that roars above us all. I search for Rata again in the sweltering heat, but she hides her face from me.

"I saw your hand!" I shout, running into the room to save the children. "I saw your hand. I know you're here and you can make it all stop. Put it out! Put the fire out, Rata!"

My words incite her anger and the inferno grows in response. Zaire weakens, his breaths too shallow to feed his lungs. Beside him, my small voice cries and screams for someone to help him.

I rush heedlessly into the flames for them, taking Zaire out first, cradling his head in the crook of my shoulder the way Mother had. Then I return for myself, startled when I don't see a child wreathed in flame, but a woman dressed in a fine yellow nightgown that's torn at the knee. One strap has broken, and the silk fabric lays limply on her chest.

I cannot see her face. Her hair has melted and hangs over it in a thick tuft. She sits on the dirt floor with her hand hovering over the burn on her leg, lacking the strength to move but crying for help. She begs Rata to stop this.

But the god of fire shows no mercy.

Her thigh is red, blistered white, and she hisses as the pain lances through her flesh. I run to her and hoist her up, hauling her arm around my shoulders to carry her away, but Rata appears and blocks the door. Her lithe, fiery form fills our only exit.

"Let us out!" I scream.

The goddess of flame shakes her head, smoke curling from her locks.

The woman I brace goes limp. I lay her on the ground and brush the dark hair out of her face, finding my mother's empty eyes looking back at me, her skin blistered and red, shiny and charred. I scream and scream, unable to stop the pitiful sounds from spewing over my lips. I cover her with my body and then... I burn with her.

STRONG ARMS WRAPPED AROUND ME, but I couldn't raise my lids to see who had come.

"Look at me," a man pleaded.

That scent. Like a thunderstorm had drawn near and the earth was giddy to feel the torrent and wind.

"I'm taking her back with me."

"Are you sure?" the matchmaker asked.

My teeth chattered. "Burning..." I muttered.

"You're not burning," the man assured me. "You aren't in the fire."

I felt softness all around me, but instead of being pleasant, the velvet raked over my charred, blistered, melted skin and I screamed.

Even the sea's voice couldn't drown me out. Waves crashed onto the shore, draining away, then rising again. Ever persistent. Dogged. Determined.

My eyes slowly opened and Estin's form materialized. He was carrying me, and though I could see the gleam of Trayton's scales, I could not count them. The Dragon's steps sloshed into the water and suddenly... blissful cold surged all around me.

"Gods, Vayl. You're shaking so hard.... Indri!" he shouted, carrying me deeper into the sea's cool embrace.

Indri crashed into the waves, but she stopped short when her eyes met mine. "Oh, gods... What happened to her?"

"Rata. She dreamed of Rata." Estin's voice was an anchor. I chained myself to it and hoped it held fast. "In her nightmare, she was on fire."

"Her skin isn't burned," Indri noted. "Are you hurt, Vayl?" She pressed a hand to my head and hummed.

I squirmed to get down. "Let me go!"

Estin carried me into shallower water and gently lowered my feet. I scurried away from them. "Why were you there?" I shouted, raking my hands through my sweat-soaked hair. "Why – How did you know to come?"

He pressed his eyes closed, his lips pressed in a tight line.

Oh my gods. "That's your gift, isn't it?"

His chest rose and fell in time with mine, wild terror still coursing through our veins where blood once had been. "I am a Dream Walker, blessed to roam the imaginations of others, yet cursed to walk their nightmares."

Tendrils of smoke still curled from his shoulders. "Did you come into my dream and pull me out of the fire?"

He nodded once. "Yes, and when I freed and tried to wake you, you began screaming. The matchmaker rushed in, flanked by all her attendants. She knew of your nightmares."

I blew out a shaky breath. Wonderful. I was sure the matchmaker was eager to rid her home of me.

Indri's eyes lit. "I'll warm some water and make some of her tea to soothe you, if you think it'll help." Her eyes trailed to my hands, which trembled like the legs of a newborn doe. Not that my own legs didn't look the same.

When I nodded, she slogged out of the water and met Grady, who was adding wood to the fire he kept stoked along the shore, fanning it to urge the beast to spread. Asra rushed into the woods and returned with fresh water. After pouring it into Indri's kettle, he placed it on Grady's fire to warm.

Stumbling to the edge of the sea where the waves barely kissed, I collapsed with my head in my hands and my elbows on my knees. "I can't do this!" I cried. "My dreams will ruin us all."

Estin slowly sank down beside me. "Your dreams won't bother you there."

"And why wouldn't they? They torment me no matter where I sleep." I turned to him. "Can *you* give me something to help?"

Since he was a Dream Walker, maybe he knew of an herb or stone that would keep them away. We could add another pebble to the necklace fastened around my throat.

"I'll help. I promise I'll find a way. But for now, just focus on calming down."

My trembling troubled the water that lazily swept around us. "What does it feel like – to enter someone else's dream?"

Estin turned his head to look at me. "Depends on the dream," he replied with a wink.

I laughed, my teeth chattering.

His eyes sparked and he angled his body toward me. "Are you familiar with the bug called a water strider?"

I gave a small smile. "Zaire used to chase them when we swam in the river. If he caught one, he'd try to fling it into my hair."

"I'm sure he paid dearly for it later."

I laughed again, my teeth chattering afterward.

"Water striders touch the water but don't submerge. Their legs let them skate over it. In a way, I skim dreams the way they skim a pond, but I can go into the water if I must. I can pull myself back up onto the surface as well."

"Have you ever entered a dream and thought you were drowning?"

He swallowed thickly, his smile falling away. "Once."

"How does it compare to burning?" He'd felt both now, thanks to me.

"I'd rather drown."

I rubbed the gooseflesh of my arms and took in the state of my charred, dirty nightgown, one of the straps torn the same as it was in the dream. "Me too." I plucked at the fabric on my knee, mystified by the reality of the dream. "I've never had this happen. The nightmares have always been so real, but I've never felt pain from being burned by the fire. Is it because you brought me out of it?"

He shook his head. "This time Rata was there, and she was angry with you."

My eyes widened. "Did you see her?" I gasped, angling myself more toward him.

"Only her hand, but I felt her, and... that's when your dream changed. The fire goddess altered it."

My lips peeled apart in surprise. "How do you know this one was different?"

Estin looked out at the sea. "The last time Zaire came to visit you, when he brought the red silk, I came to find him because we needed him to relay a message to our mother. I saw your dream then, but I stayed hidden until the end. I'm not allowed to interfere unless the dreamer's life is in danger."

My heart felt heavy enough to sink to the bottom of the sea.

"I didn't recognize you at the matchmaker's because I only saw your dream that night, and in it, you were a child." He brushed a strand of wet hair out of my face. "You're freezing. Do you feel like you can stand?"

I nodded, but he leapt up before I could get my feet under me and offered his hand. I took it, grumbling, "I'm fine, Estin."

"Let's go sit on the palm trunk."

I nodded and Estin shouted to his brother to bring a blanket. Asra was gone and back in a flash with a doubled quilt, which he draped over my shoulders. I clutched the ends under my chin, thanked him, and blew warmth into my fisted, frigid hands.

The Dragon and I slowly traversed the sand. There was something I felt in my bones but needed to hear.

"So, Zaire carried your message and then... out of the blue was sent to the palace dungeons? Could someone have seen him crossing the wall?" I asked carefully.

He scrubbed his face. "I suspect someone must have, and that they told Favian. It would explain why he sent Zaire to the palace – so he could catch him working on behalf of Thanias."

It made sense. But then, why let Zaire live to carry his message home? Was that part of the Lion's plan, or had Zaire surprised him by stealing the stallion?

We reached the palm trunk. Numbly, I sat down and peered up at Estin, seeking to put coherent words to my tumbled thoughts. "Imagine that you're Kirsi," I began. "That you love Cassius more than anything, that you gave up everything you loved for him – your kingdom, your crown, and the duty that comes with it. You forsook your own people for him, along with your family. And he tells you they value your safety among all others... only to place you among his concubines. The women he keeps for the pleasure you can't seem to provide him. In that single move, he tells you that you aren't enough, and you realize that he's not enough for you, either."

"So, you're saying her heartbreak is what's bleeding her magic away?" he mused, rubbing his jaw.

"And she lets it," I finished for him. "Maybe she's ready for someone to come for her, but she's afraid to take the first step toward reparation." We were both quiet for a moment before I added, "She knows she trapped you in Kaan, or else she would've moved you out with the army and your mother. Is it possible that she found out you were imprisoned? Could she be searching, or having someone she trusts, look for you and Asra?"

He blew out a tense breath, and I was certain he'd asked himself that same question countless times. "I don't know. I would've thought she'd know we were near and could sense our magic from the dungeons, but I'm no longer sure. She's so weak." He shook his head. "I don't know whether she knew that Cassius had imprisoned us, or just didn't care."

"She couldn't have known," I told him confidently. What sister would allow it?

His fingertips found the now-rounded tip of his ear. Kirsi didn't know her lover's brother had mutilated hers. Favian could have killed both brothers as he killed mine, and she would've been none the wiser. Or would he only take them to the brink, fearing she would sense the loss of her kin and risk her dropping her magic and laying waste to them all? Would she have done so for Estin and Asra, or did they not matter to her?

Grady walked toward us. "How are you?" he asked me warily.

"I'm okay."

There was worry in his eyes, coupled with fear.

Indri brought over a steaming cup of tea. The scent of the herbal mix hit my nose when she walked close and handed it to me. My hands still trembled.

"Thank you." Clutching the ends of the blanket with one hand and the cup with another, I wove my fingers through the handle to hold it steady. The ceramic was thick and sturdy in my palm, warm from the liquid inside. Sipping carefully, I hurried to get the concoction into my body. Within seconds, I relaxed. The mixture worked better and faster than it ever had before. I tilted my head, shrewdly looking toward Indri.

"I might have enhanced it a tiny bit," she admitted with a small smile.

"I'm glad you did. Can you enhance the rest?"

She crouched beside us, bracing her forearms on her thighs. "Of course I will."

Even though I could barely hold my eyes open, I was terrified to go back to sleep. Overhead, Trayton's scales glittered.

"You need rest," Asra softly observed.

"I don't want to sleep – ever again," I insisted stubbornly.

He gave a sad smile, then looked to Estin. The Dragon sat taller beside me. "I will stay with you. I can hold your dreams at bay."

"Do you have to be awake to do that?" I asked, finishing off the tea.

He shook his head. "I was asleep before I came to pull you out of the fire. I think the intervallim somehow allowed me to feel your panic."

I sat the cup in the sand and brought my fingers to the teal stone of my necklace, so glad it hung around my neck.

"You can have my tent," the Dragon offered. Grady, Asra, and Indri all went still and turned to him. Exasperated, he said, "Grady, she can't be near you. Your snoring would wake the dead. And I don't think she would want to be near either of *yours*," he said, wagging a finger between Asra and Indri. The two unapologetically smiled at their leader.

I shook my head. "I'm not taking your tent."

"You need to rest," he insisted.

"And you don't? Even dragons sleep, Estin."

"Then we'll make a separate sleeping space for you," he said tightly.

Asra quirked a brow and Grady's ire returned. "Not a good idea," the giant protested.

Estin flung his hands out and then raked his hands through his dark hair. "Vayl is safe with me. We simply need to rest. Besides that, I respect her and would never..." he trailed off uncomfortably. "We all know that her virtue must remain intact. Cassius would cast her out, otherwise."

For the briefest second, I let myself envision Estin hovering above me, pulling one of my knees up to hook around his waist as he dove in for a kiss.

"I trust you," I told him. "I knew I could trust you the moment Zaire told me to find you, and not to share the message with anyone else."

Asra smiled. "Not even me."

"Not even you." I looked up at Grady. "I just need dreamless sleep."

The giant reluctantly nodded, then stuffed his hands in his pockets. "I think we could all use a few more hours of shut-eye."

Grady's tent was nestled in the trees, not too far from Indri's. Asra's was pitched beside hers. Estin's was farther away, down the beach, built on the powdery, thick sand. It was far enough from the water that the tide wouldn't reach it, but close enough that the salt spray dusted us as we walked to the front. Estin held up the flap, pinning it back so cool white light illuminated the small interior.

I ducked inside and found it incredibly tidy. Zaire was never so careful with his things and flung them everywhere. They often migrated to my side of the room beneath our room's dividing curtain.

Like Indri, he'd laid a carpet down. It was soft gray, the color of a dove's wing. He'd made a small bed from blankets and a pillow from another, rolled and folded to fit his head. There were a few leather satchels, two large and one small, situated in the corner. Other than that, the space was uncluttered.

He rushed to pull a blanket from his pile and remove his makeshift pillow. "You don't have to go to any trouble," I insisted. "I have the blanket around my shoulders."

"And you'll need it. The wind is cool tonight." In seconds, he'd made a soft bed for me. He gestured awkwardly to it. "It's not as nice as the matchmaker's rooms, I'm sure."

"It's perfect."

He let the tent flap down and sat on his own blanket. "I'm sorry I have no pillow to offer you."

"I don't need one," I told him.

I spread the blanket Asra had wrapped around me over the bed Estin had prepared. It was still wet in spots, but it was warm enough. Nestling inside was easy. Closing my eyes wasn't. I was uncomfortably aware of Estin in the small confines of the tent. His unique scent; a mixture of lightning and fresh soil. His proximity. Every rustle of his clothing as he moved through the cramped space.

Even Zairitus's roaring sea and sleek, glittering Trayton hovering above couldn't detract from the one they called Dragon. He drew his tunic over his head and every muscle in his back echoed the motion. He settled in his bed, facing me, only a few feet of carpet dividing us, and drew his blanket up to his chest.

For several long moments, we stared – me at him, and him at me.

"Vayl," he finally said.

I blinked at the sound of my name on his lips.

"Hmm?"

"Close your eyes, or I won't be able to sleep."

CHAPTER 14

Trayton freed Rata, though as far as I could tell, she'd done nothing to deserve it. Her light spread solidly over the exceptionally calm sea before she showed her face. I waited and watched, remembering Zaire's claim about watching her last ray dip below the horizon and wondered if the same rules applied to her first. If I might see a brilliant, fiery ray before the others joined it.

Just then, a flash of bright, blinding light.

Worth waiting a lifetime to see, Zaire had described it.

He was right. My heart thundered, grateful, and an unsettling emotion washed over me.

"Why show me this now? Why did you claim me?" I quietly asked the goddess of flame.

She rose quickly, gathering her rays as a woman might an ample skirt to avoid tripping. As if running from the question, and from me.

"Are you sure it was Rata who burned you?" Grady asked.

I hadn't even noticed him standing in the water as I walked along the shore, as if chasing the goddess of fire to demand that she finally answer me. "What do you mean?" The salt breeze toyed with my hair, ruffling it this way and that until it began to tangle.

"Well," he started, "Zairitus brings the rain and controls the waters, but he's here. Ventus pours his breath over the land." He pointed at my flailing tresses to prove his point. "Yenza's flesh is our soil. Urit only comes by briefly to watch over us, hurling his bolts toward the ground to light our way in the harshest storms."

My brows kissed, unsure where he was going.

"Trayton hovers over us. The warrior god in the sky. His purpose is to fight, yes, but mostly to give us hope. We see his back because he faces the dark abyss. And we know that we can conquer hard things if we are brave enough to fight, too. He fights to free Rata, because we need her warmth and light."

"Do you belong to Trayton, too?" I asked.

He shook his head. I wanted so badly to ask to whom he belonged, curious to discover his gift.

His eyes flicked above us. A few of the dragon god's scales remained visible, flickering happily in the pastel sky as if lingering to catch sight of Rata.

"All I wonder is whether Rata is capable of doing the things you accuse her of doing from so far away. She was cast from the earth, and while she's bright enough for us to see, she's distant. Fire remained on the earth because *we* kept it ablaze. She taught us to spark and kindle and coax a flame so we could eat and stay warm when she was too far to do it for us. I just... I wonder if the fire that night could have been a simple accident, but that blaming her is easier than accepting that it was no one's fault."

"You think she's powerless from her perch?"

"Rata is different. She is constantly tugged and dragged under just when she's gotten her breath. I'm not sure she has the energy or strength to intentionally cause harm."

"She had enough energy to claim me that day," I insisted.

"Just because she can reach out through flame, doesn't mean she ignited it with malice in her heart just to hurt you," he said, quietly shrugging. "I think about the gods a lot. Too much, some would say. I'm probably sputtering nonsense."

"No you're not." I just didn't want to hear him make excuses for Rata.

"You and Rata aren't so different, you know," he mused. When I bristled, he hastily added, "I only mean that you were both cast into an impossible situation. Both of you are struggling to free yourself. Neither of you are capable of giving up." He smiled. "Both of you have dragons fighting for and with you."

I swallowed thickly.

Beside his calf in the water, something moved. I waded in, struck by the sight of a small swarm of fish swimming all around him. My mouth gaped. "You belong to Namina..."

He nodded. "I can call creatures to me. I hate to harm them, but Namina is gracious and wishes to nourish us."

He bent down and scooped a fish from the dozens schooled at his feet. It went peacefully still in his hand. I watched as he gently threaded it onto a line tied to a belt on his trousers. He repeated the motion until the line was full.

"I thought you were a fisherman."

He smiled proudly. "Am I not? Does it matter whether I use hand or hook?"

I laughed, my soul at ease for the moment.

"Did you rest easy?" Worry was inlaid beneath his words, like the patterns of gold threaded into the matchmaker's tile floor.

"I slept soundly, for once." I looked out over the water, glancing at Rata, then at Indri and Asra as they raced down the shoreline, laughing as they battled to see who would reach us first. Asra easily won. "Is speed your gift?" I asked him.

"One of many, but not the gift you're itching to know," he tutted, winking arrogantly.

"Is he always like this in the morning?" I asked Indri.

She grinned. "He never runs out of energy."

Grady groaned and turned back to his fish. "We don't need to hear another detail from either of you."

Indri hooked her arm into mine. "I have other clothes you can borrow. You won't need trousers for the lessons you'll learn today."

I slumped. "Please tell me it doesn't include salad forks."

She threw her head back laughing. "I'll leave that to the matchmaker. Actually," she led me from the water, "I thought we might do something fun. I saw the way you looked at my bow."

"Yes, please. I love watching you shoot," Asra added, kissing Indri on the cheek and giving her a lustful look.

"Maybe I'll send you on an errand," she teased, her smile wide and playful.

Mock indignation crossed his handsome features. "You wouldn't do that."

"Why is that?" She tugged me along with her to bump into him.

He grinned. "Because you like it when I watch." He'd clearly won, because Indri raised no further objections. She released my arm to smother him with a kiss that started out fun and tentative, but quickly turned into something more passionate. I left them and walked ahead to Indri's tent. After a few minutes, she joined me.

"Where'd you go?" she asked breathlessly.

I laughed. "Does the whole world disappear when he kisses you?"

She nodded. "It really does. In those moments, we lose ourselves and everything falls away until nothing exists but us. Neither the sky above, nor the earth below." She rummaged through one of the bags in her tent. "I've never felt like this about anyone. He makes every inch of me happy, and I don't just mean when we lay together."

My face heated with her brazen talk.

Her hands found what she was searching for, and she pulled out a rather revealing fuchsia dress.

"Where did you get that?" I asked, fingering the gorgeous material.

"From a merchant in Cerulean. Isn't it brilliant? It's constructed of fabric woven together like reeds in a basket." She tossed the garment at me. "It can be easily adjusted to fit anyone, so I can take it in for you."

"And I thought the vest showed too much of my skin..." I muttered, holding it up this way and that to see how to put it on.

Indri quietly stood. "Vayl, you'll be wearing far less than this in the palace. This dress is modest in comparison to what I've heard about the concubines and their attire."

"Then maybe it's best I get used to it now," I said grimly.

She gave me an encouraging, but fake, smile. "I think you're right." After telling me to strip, she helped me dive into the ensemble. The fabric was thicker around my breasts and hips, but gauze-like and thin around my stomach, and from my upper thighs to the ground. Indri gave me a ridiculous grin. "You look amazing."

I didn't feel it. The filmy fabric was another reminder that I'd soon be forced to wear something I didn't want for someone I didn't want to wear it for.

"Today's true lesson has nothing to do with archery. You have to become a concubine, but that doesn't mean that you allow them to drag you to the palace and shove you into pretty things, waiting meekly and dreading the moment when Cassius announces his plans to get acquainted with you. You have to *want* to be there. Favian must believe you're not afraid. That this is what you chose, not what has been chosen for you."

I raised my chin proudly. "I made him believe it once."

"How long were you in the Lion's presence?" she challenged, crossing her arms.

"Only a few moments," I admitted sheepishly.

"Can you replicate the façade you presented him with indefinitely and without fail? Because your disgust for him is not only visible, it's palpable. If you let that show through even for a second and the Lion, one of his men, or one of the concubines notice, you're dead and so are our plans to remove Kirsi from Cassius's presence."

I swallowed thickly and lowered my eyes. "I've said it a thousand times, but I don't know if I can do this."

"It's too late for that now," she chided gently. "The horse you ride is galloping at breakneck speed. You have no reins. All you can do is hold on and let him carry you or wait for the perfect moment to jump."

I froze for a moment. Had Estin told her he offered to take me to Thanias and hide me safely beyond the wall, and that I'd refused?

Indri took my hands in hers. "Vayl – if you survived anything close to the nightmare you had last night, you can do anything."

She was right. I'd been burned in that fire more times than I could recall, relentlessly reliving my mother's death over and over. The hole in my heart should have healed and calloused over but I refused to let it, mourning her every day since because I loved her and missed her.

Changing the subject, Indri offered, "We don't have cinnamon rolls today, but Grady has bread and fish and fruit. You need to eat."

"Why is everyone always trying to feed me? I went from having nothing to–"

"Because you need it. Your body needs it, Vayl. I can already see the effects of good nutrition on you."

"Because you bolster its nutrition," I replied wryly.

She shrugged. "I can only do so much. You have to remember to take care of yourself while you're in the palace. No one will be there to remind you then."

No one there would care whether I ate or starved, she meant.

Other than Zaire, I'd never really had a friend before. But Indri cared for me beyond what I could do to help her future queen and her homeland of Thanias. Indri accepted me the moment Estin and Asra brought me to this place.

I smiled. "What kind of fruit?"

Indri scrunched up her pert nose. "The kind that keeps through the winter, unfortunately. Dried apples feel a little leathery when you chew them, but they're still sweet." She stepped around me and pushed her palm between my shoulder blades. "Head up. Shoulders back. From this moment on, you must walk like the empire of Kaan and everyone in it owes you a debt you will one day collect. Because they do, and one day you will." She picked at her nails. "I've never been inside the palace, but I know Cassius's character. He would sometimes bring his concubines along when he visited the dungeons where we were imprisoned."

"The twins?"

She nodded once to confirm it. "And others, but most often them."

The fury I felt to my bones settled in my stomach and entwined with disgust, but I managed to maintain my neutral expression.

Indri quirked a brow. "You didn't curl your lip."

"It's difficult to refrain," I told her in an easy tone, "but I'm capable."

"Yes, you are." She smiled. "Later, I'll tell you what I know. I'll ask the others to contribute as well in case there's something I've forgotten – accidentally or on purpose. For now, just practice your posture and on keeping a neutral expression."

"I didn't offer Favian a neutral expression when I met him at the matchmaker's," I told her as we left the tent and stepped onto the sand.

Her brows inched toward one another. "What *did* you offer him?"

Other than myself? Anger. Pride. Confidence.

"Who?" Estin asked from just behind us. My heart clapped against my ribs as his eyes slowly raked down me, taking in the revealing dress that clung to my curves. I pretended Indri's hand lay between my shoulders and raised my head high.

"I met his eye and held it as if he were beneath me."

Indri coughed a laugh. "*That's* what you did? And you lived to tell the tale?"

"The matchmaker said that several of the newest concubines have been found dead. Favian asked her to find one who could hold her own against the other women. I had to show him I wasn't afraid – not even of him."

Indri shook her head, the shells lining her braids chiming. "I wouldn't have been so brave."

"It wasn't bravery; it was desperation," I admitted. "I had the opportunity to get close enough to kill him and seized it. He told the matchmaker that instead of sending for me, he will personally escort me to the palace. I'd planned to strike him along the way, but now I'll wait until after I find Kirsi." *And drag her out of there, whether she wants to or not...*

"If he's traveling with you, it might be your best chance. Maybe your only one," Estin warned, letting me know that if I wanted to kill Favian, I could forget Kirsi and follow my own plan.

"True, but if I don't free her, then Zaire died for nothing," I answered. "He wanted her freed. My wants can wait until I see that through."

The three of us walked toward Grady and Asra, who were gathered around the flat stone.

Grady noticed us out of his periphery; his head swiveled my way and did a double take. He opened his lips to speak but his eyes flicked over my shoulder, releasing only a strangled noise. He covered it with a cough, then a smile. "Don't you look lovely, Vayl."

Indri feigned hurt, clutching herself and scoffing.

"And you as well, Indri," the gentle giant added. He handed me a small plate. In its middle was a cooked fish laying on a bed of wilted greens, little dried apples fanning out from around the catch like the petals of a flower.

"Thank you."

"I'll have something new for dinner," he promised.

"This is delicious," I assured him. "But I'll probably be expected to dine with the matchmaker this evening."

"You have more dresses to try on, but you can eat where you'd like," Estin noted, accepting his plate with a grateful nod. "You can sleep where you'd like, too."

My hand froze between my plate and mouth. Everyone else stilled, too. Until Grady graciously began plating Indri's food, breaking the tension. Asra was served after her and the two settled beside one another. Grady took a portion for himself and lowered onto a nearby trunk without another word.

Quiet lay like a thick blanket between us. Last night was intense. I was grateful Estin had come for me. I wasn't certain Rata wouldn't kill me for the insolent things I'd screamed at her lately, but the last thing I wanted was for their kindness toward me to cause a rift between them.

Estin finally cleared his throat. "I'd like to ask you for a favor, Vayl, but if you don't feel comfortable or safe doing it, please say so."

"What kind of favor?" I asked.

"I need someone to carry a message to my mother. I think *she* can provide the distraction we need for the Emperor and his Lion."

I tilted my head. "Then consider it done."

"It's not without risk," he hastened to add. "If someone saw Zaire, they might also–"

I tipped my chin up regally and kept my voice steady and stern. "I know the risks. I'll carry your message."

I wondered what their mother looked like. Did she give Estin his dark, straight hair or was she the source of Asra's burgundy curls? There was a resemblance in the young men's faces. Did she share their pointed chins? Asra's laughter, or Estin's seriousness?

"What's your message?"

"We need a new way to communicate with her, and we'll need her to launch another attack on the wall when we give the signal." He calmly took a sip from his water skin.

Asra's grin was feral. "With their eyes on the wall, they won't be watching Vayl. Brilliant."

Indri raised an apple as if toasting the plan.

Grady nodded, his eyes glazed over as if picturing it. "It'll make me worry a *little* less for you," he told me, pinching his fingers together, but leaving a sliver of space between the pads.

I offered a wan smile before remembering I was supposed to be solid and stoic and strong. "When do you want me to carry the message to her?"

"Now," Estin answered.

Everyone went still.

"Darkness provides at least some cover," Asra argued.

Estin glared at his brother. "We're out of time. Besides, you and Indri will draw their attention elsewhere."

Asra considered his brother's words. "So, we're going to do to the army what you want Mother to do to the Emperor?"

"Yes," Estin answered simply.

"What's the diversion?" Indri asked with a smile.

"You'll remove their leaders. There are three regiments. Three colonels. Three kills."

Asra groaned. "Such a simple task you give us."

"You can't handle it?" Indri teased. "I can take out all three if you're not up to helping."

Burgundy brows rose to meet her jibe. "Oh, I think I can contribute."

She shrugged a slender shoulder and looked away from him.

"First to kill gets to pick whose tent we use tonight..." he challenged.

"Choose the farthest from mine, for the love of the gods," Grady begged, reaching onto the stone for another filet.

Fighting a smile was sometimes as hard as hiding my disgust or anger. When everyone was finished eating, Grady faced the forest and let out a shrill whistle. Moments later, two enormous mares galloped from the woods and trotted through the sand to him. Indri and Asra hid daggers up their sleeves, in their boots, and in small sheaths inside their trousers. Indri shook out a tailored jacket emblazoned with the crest of Kaan, the same one that every Imperial soldier was given and expected to wear to represent the kingdom. She threw it at Asra, who caught it and pulled it on.

"Do I want to ask where they got those uniforms?" I asked the Dragon, who had sidled up beside me.

Indri dressed to match Asra in an Imperial soldier uniform fitted to her smaller body.

"Your assumption is likely right, but if you'd like details, you'll have to ask Indri. She procured the garments," Estin answered, his back straight and his arms folded in front of him as we waited. "You're doing well," he noted.

"At?"

"Becoming one of *them*..." His sideways glance slid down the fuchsia dress again.

I tipped my chin. "It's only fabric, Estin."

"I wasn't talking about the dress. Your demeanor is different."

"It has to be." It was explanation. It was an apology. It was a promise. I could do this. I had to – for Zaire. For the dragons. Thanias needed her future queen.

"What happens to Thanias if Kirsi refuses to return?"

Estin swallowed, then stretched his neck in a circle as he considered how to answer. "Thanias must have a queen. If Mother dies and Kirsi refuses to take her place on the throne, another will be chosen. Kirsi will be banished, and the gods who blessed her with magic will take it away from her and give it to another they deem worthy."

"She knows this?"

He nodded. "Each day, I wonder why they haven't done it yet."

Perhaps Kirsi didn't realize that she'd lost herself in Cassius and she was somehow innocent in all this. It was bad of me to think, but I hoped her reticence was a result of him drugging her. That she wasn't consciously choosing him over everything she once held dear. Maybe that was why the gods had been patient thus far.

Asra and Indri deftly mounted a dappled mare. Estin climbed atop the second one, then bent far down to lift me up. A smirk played at the corner of his mouth. "Don't," I told him, settling in front of him. "Don't make fun of my size."

He fought a full grin. "Never, my lady."

Estin took hold of the reins and guided the horse toward the wall. Grady gave a shout and both horses took off, sand spraying in their wake.

~

WHEN WE WERE close to the wall, Indri and Asra left us to cut through the woods while Estin kept near the trees. He dismounted and lifted me down, then stroked the brown mare that had carried us with ease at Grady's request. "Would you stay here for us?"

In response, the mare closed her eyes and nuzzled his hand.

We made our way closer to the wall and in minutes, were standing just inside a copse of trees, staring at the imposing, stacked stone. A soldier paced at its top. "We need to go somewhere else," I whispered, watching the man's every movement.

"It'll be fine," Estin assured me. "You can cross over right here. There are soldiers all along the wall, but they're about to desert their posts..."

"How do you know that?"

I'd barely gotten the last word out when an explosion erupted, and not one created from the elves. One on Kaan's side of the wall.

The guard atop the wall screamed an order and all the guards atop the wall ran toward the violent noise and erupting smoke.

Estin grinned. "They'll strike the colonels during the commotion. Let's go." He took my hand and we ran to the wall. "There are divots for hands and feet. Hurry!"

We scaled the wall, every movement fueled by adrenaline. Fear. Excitement. When I finally stood on the top, I let my eyes drift over the length of the structure that separated our people. It curved along the earth like a snake slithering over hill and valley, mountain and moor.

"There are similar divots on the other side. You'll walk a few feet before you cross my sister's magic. Zaire never mentioned feeling the barrier, so you may not either," Estin instructed. "An elvish soldier *will* find you. Make sure to keep your hands in the air and shout that you have a message from Estin."

I nodded as nervous butterflies erupted in my stomach. "Message from Estin. Got it."

"Remember what we need from her?"

"Yes."

"Tell her that both her sons are well and then tell her your plan. She will help you," he promised.

I nodded again, then blew out a breath before throwing my leg over the wall, searching for the divot and hoping Indri's dress didn't trip me up. Bare feet helped with climbing, it turned out. Before I knew it, my soles touched soft grass. It was perfectly green, like it was springtime. The breeze was even warmer on this side of the wall.

I lifted my hands and started forward. "I bring word from Estin!"

Repeating myself several times, I walked further into the Kingdom of Thanias. As I moved, the hair on the back of my neck rose. I wasn't sure if it was because I had walked through Kirsi's barrier, or I was being watched. Just then, there was movement in the trees.

"Estin has a message for the Queen!"

A female elf with golden hair and pointed ears left her position behind a nearby tree and approached, an intricate silver spear clutched in her hands. I felt like a fish swimming too close to a skilled fisherman. "Fetch the Queen!" she shouted.

I relaxed a little, but not too much. She kept her spear trained on me. The sweet smell of wildflowers filled the air just before a middle-aged woman appeared, gathering her heavy skirts and striding confidently toward me. "You bring word from my eldest son?" she asked.

Her hair was dark like Estin's with a burgundy sheen reminiscent of Asra's, sleek and straight as a blade of grass and shinier than the glass windows in Starcrest. She was tall and regal, and her features were sharp but beautiful.

"I do."

"What's become of Zaire?" she asked, then tilted her head. "You favor him."

She saw our shared features, despite our differences. "He is my brother."

"Where is he?"

It was still hard to speak the truth. "Zaire is dead. He sent me to deliver a message to Estin, and now Estin has asked me to come to you for help."

"With what?"

"Zaire found Kirsi." The striking elf drew in a sharp breath and clutched her chest. "We know where she is. I plan to free her so Estin and Asra and the dragons can bring her home. But we need you –"

"Where is my daughter? Where is Thanias's future Queen?" she asked.

"In the palace of the concubines."

The Queen of Thanias nearly choked and fury flooded her eyes. It was then that I noticed a silver sheen to her skin. It intensified the longer she stood silent.

"I am the Emperor's newest concubine," I declared. "I'll be taken to the palace in a matter of days, and I'll do everything in my power to free her."

"She is the one who conjured this wall," the Queen noted, keeping her eyes trained on the sky above us instead of the blocks beyond. "Do you honestly think you can make her drop it and return home to us?"

"Would you rather I not try?" I asked dryly.

Her lips pursed, then her gaze drifted over me. "You are no warrior. You're weak."

"In body, yes, but not in wit," I retorted. "Will you help us, or will you deny your son?" I finally asked. She was wasting precious time.

"What does he need from me?"

"A new way to send messages back and forth so the two of you can communicate without the use of a human messenger. Also, an offensive launched at Kirsi's magic when we need to draw the Emperor's and Lion's attention away from Kirsi and focus it on the wall."

She smiled. "My clever eldest son.... Tell me, what of my reckless, younger boy?"

"Asra?" I guessed. "He's well, and just as clever."

She nodded slowly, warily watching me as if she didn't know

whether to trust me or not. Finally, she clapped her hands together and held them tightly. When she did, silver seemed to shimmer in her palms. When she parted them, a raven walked onto one of her fingers. She held it out to my shoulder and it climbed on.

"He will receive and deliver words from Estin and Asra only. My sons only need to whisper in his ear, and he will fly to me and relay their words. In the meantime, I will prepare to strike the wall again. If Kirsi's magic falls, all the better."

A shiver scuttled up my spine at the implication. She'd been waiting for this battle for years, and it was so close now. She hungered for it. The anticipation shimmered in her eyes.

"What is your name?" she asked.

"Vayl."

"Do what you must to get her out. If you must injure her, so be it. She can be healed. If you must kill her, the gods will resurrect her. Just – don't leave her there with him." She raked the back of her fingers down the raven's back, soothing the beast's ruffled feathers.

"I have a favor to ask in return for my effort, even if I don't succeed."

"Very well," she allowed.

"If I can't manage it, I want you to kill the Lion of Kaan and tell him that you do it in my name, in Zaire's, and for our father."

The elf replied with a bloodthirsty smile. "The one who maimed my sons?"

I nodded. "The same."

"I hope you survive this," she said earnestly, then looked at the stone wall. "You should go now."

I didn't hesitate, knowing she could sense things I couldn't. I dug my toes into the divots and pulled my weight up with my fingers, the bird balancing on my shoulder. Estin was at the top when I arrived.

"We have to run," he announced.

We scurried down the wall like beetles beneath an overturned piece of bark and ran into the woods, panting and smiling at one another as though we shared a secret. He noticed the bird.

"A messenger," I explained. "Only you or Asra can whisper words into his ear and he'll take them to your mother."

"Was she nice?"

"She was terrifying," I admitted, "but fair."

He smiled. "That's good. It means she likes you."

"How does she treat someone she doesn't like?"

Estin held a tree branch back so I didn't walk into it. "You don't want to know. And it doesn't matter now that she approves of you."

"She tolerated me delivering your message. I wouldn't dub that approval, Dragon," I scoffed.

He laughed. The brown mare trotted toward us from out of the woods when we approached. He swept me up onto her back and we rode back to the sea and our encampment, the raven still perched upon my shoulder.

Asra and Indri were in the waves, their mood intense, their passion palpable. I swallowed uneasily as I watched her wrap herself around his body, tugging his hair to ease his head back and kiss him like she'd waited a lifetime and couldn't hold back any longer.

Estin lowered me to the ground, then dismounted. Grady met us. He ticked his head toward the ocean and let his voice roar above the sound of the waves. "They succeeded in the task you gave them, in case you couldn't tell."

Asra chuckled and kissed Indri once more before pulling her from the water.

"I thought they only recently gave in to the attraction between them," I noted softly.

Grady nodded as they walked closer. "They did. Used to be that they'd come back and pick on each other all evening. We could barely stand to be around them. Now, they..." His words trailed away and he stood up straighter. "Well. You know."

Asra's attention slid to my feathered friend as he and Indri approached. "You brought home a new friend, I see," he teased, moving to pet the raven on my shoulder. The fowl nipped at his finger.

"Hey!" he complained, jerking his hand away. "That's not nice, raven."

"Did you leave our dear Favian a note?" Estin asked.

Asra smiled. "Of course."

"What kind of note?" I asked.

Indri laughed. "When we strike Favian's men, we leave a little token so he knows who's responsible."

"As if there'd be any doubt," Asra scoffed, crossing his arms and rolling his eyes. He scuffed his boot in the sand.

"We leave behind a piece of elvish parchment embossed with a silver dragon," Indri divulged. "He gets raving mad every time he finds one."

"Got a stack of them in his tent," Grady added with a chuckle.

Asra patted his pocket. "I never leave home without a few. Just in case."

"Hey, guys?" Indri said nonchalantly. "We need firewood."

Grady's head swiveled to his supply, neatly stacked – and plenty of it, from what I could tell.

"When she says that, it means she wants us to leave," Asra informed the group.

"Well, just say so, Indri," Grady grumped. "We'll give ya space if you need it."

"Actually," she sang, "Vayl and I need it."

"More girl time?" Asra whined.

"Just a little," she chirped. "But I'll make it up to you later."

His smile flared as she dragged me away from the men. Estin rubbed the back of his neck, watching our retreat with an unfathomable look on his face.

She led me to her tent and pulled me inside, then sat down on the rug and patted the space across from her. I sat and waited.

"Do you have any questions about how it all works?" She picked at her cuticles. "I know your mother died when you were too young to speak of the marriage bed, and... well, I know you aren't being matched, but thought you might want to talk about what to expect. I'd rather you be fully prepared. Just in case."

My lips parted. "I know how it works," I told her stiffly.

"The concubines drink a tonic each day to prevent pregnancy," she said.

My cheeks burned and I looked down at the rug. "You said you saw Cassius with them..." I led.

Indri nodded. "More often than not, he travels with Satira and Gaila, the twins. They are dark and beautiful, with glossy hair that flows to their calves, silky skin, full lips and hips, and large breasts. Their looks are what drew Cassius in, but what keeps him close is their unwavering loyalty. They've killed for him – and not just other concubines."

I gasped. "Do you think he had them kill the other women?"

"I think they killed them. I'm just not sure whether he gave the order or they took it upon themselves. The matchmaker knows that some of the girls she's sent recently have died, but I'm not sure she knows how many of the others have."

"How many concubines are dead, Indri?"

The girl had the good grace to look sheepish. "Close to one hundred, the last we'd learned. But our source within the palace hasn't been heard from in days."

My back went rigid. "A hundred?"

"Give or take."

"Over the course of how many years?" Indri didn't answer at first, and the more seconds that passed, the more nervous I became. "Indri?"

"Weeks. Maybe a couple of months," she admitted. My mouth gaped. "I'm not sure what's sparked it, but there seems to be a war raging among the concubines."

My mind struggled to process the reasons why such bloodshed would occur. "Why would they battle each other?"

She shrugged. "Why does any battle begin? Envy. Pride. Anger. Who knows? I wanted you to know these things because the moment you enter the palace doors, you'll be on your own against them all."

I told her what the matchmaker told me about the last girl she'd sent. How she'd been poisoned so thoroughly that even the flies that tried to feast on her corpse shared her grisly fate.

Indri nodded grimly. "The dungeon cells where we were imprisoned lined three of four walls. Against the empty fourth wall was an ornate chair reserved for Cassius. What kind of man insists on having a throne located in the dungeon's torture room?" She shook her head. "He would come to visit us occasionally. And by *visit*, I mean he'd have us dragged out one by one and flogged or beaten, or worse if he was in a bad mood. Through it all, Satira and Gaila would perch on his lap to watch. They either loved it or were the best liars I've ever seen. They cheered when the tips from our ears were sliced off. They drank champagne and laughed and made a party of it."

She ran her tongue over her teeth. "He ordered a servant to nail the tips into the mortar of the wall behind Cassius's throne so that every time we looked out of the cell, we'd see them."

I pressed my eyes closed, trying to control the bile that inched up my throat.

"I just wanted you to know who you're about to encounter and why it's so important for you to not only be aware of your expression at all times..." she looked at me meaningfully and I schooled my expression with great effort, "you'll have to act like them, too. You may not be invited to the dungeons, but you'll have to cheer as the ears of other elves are figuratively or literally sliced."

She rolled her shoulders. "If you don't become one of them, you'll become an even greater target than you will be by stepping foot into the viper den the first time. But... act as they do, pretend that Cassius is a god – the most funny, clever, strong, brave, perfect man to ever grace the surface of the earth – and you just might be taken into the fold. It won't be easy for you or us to stomach, but we know your heart, Vayl, and your reasons for behaving however you must. Estin does the same when he becomes the cruel Dragon."

"I'm glad you won't have to witness it," I rasped shakily.

"Just don't forget to get out of there as quickly as possible." She squeezed my hands tightly. Worry painted her smooth brow and then her lips parted. She glanced toward the woods.

"What is it?" I asked.

Indri gave a wan smile and shook her head. "I thought I heard something outside." She blew out a long breath. "Look, I'll just say this, and if you don't want to speak further, so be it. Some men are gentle. Some are anything but. I don't know how Cassius is or if he will come to you before you find Kirsi. But if he does... take your mind somewhere else if you can."

Easier said than done, I was sure. Being intimate with Cassius would be akin to being burned in the fire once more, a fresh torture I prayed I wouldn't have to bear.

"You're braver than I would be," Indri added. "To be in his presence again, every ounce of the fight in me would have to be beaten away. They'd have to drag me before him."

I knew Favian's reputation, but this was the first time I'd ever heard anything about the Emperor. Perhaps that should have served as a warning that Cassius was more depraved than his Lion brother.

CHAPTER 15

Indri and I had just left her tent to rejoin the men when Sylvie appeared on the beach. "Vayl!" she cried, searching all around until her eyes snagged on me. "Vayl," she panted, "the Lion... he's early."

"What?"

"He's waiting for you with the matchmaker. We have to go *now*."

I'm not ready! my mind screamed. No one was. My eyes met Estin's over Sylvie's shoulder. The young attendant waved for me to come with her and I turned my attention to the elves who had quickly become my friends.

"Thank you, Indri, Asra, and Grady," I told them. "I'll never forget what you've done for me in these last few days. It's more than a lifetime of what I deserved."

Grady pinched his lips together and inclined his head. He rocked on the balls of his massive feet.

Asra wiped his palms on the legs of his trousers, chewing his cheek, then walked to me and gave a brotherly hug. "*Valor* is your name now and what you have to become. You must battle in spite of the fear in your heart," he murmured.

I nodded, unable to speak. My throat clogged with emotion.

Indri took my hands and whispered a blessing. "There will be no more trembling," she promised. "Remember what I said about your strength. Draw on the fire. The flames will put things in perspective for you. Nothing can burn you again. Rata took your burns away. She saw you through.... Rata chose you for a reason, Vayl."

I nodded again.

Estin was suddenly in front of me, his every muscle taut. His face twisted between anguish and fear, his eyes haunted and frantic at the same time. "Do what you must to survive," he said into my ear as he gathered me in his arms and hugged tightly. "Don't give us away."

I pulled back, my brows kissing.

"Asra has a very special gift," he answered cryptically. "Just know you're a dragon now, and dragons don't fight alone."

Sylvie worried her hands. "We must hurry. The matchmaker is stalling him, but you must dress and be ready to leave soon. His patience is thin as frost."

Estin waved for Sylvie, who scurried over the sand and took my hand. "Can you take us back?" she asked, eyeballing my necklace.

"I can."

"We need to appear in your bedroom."

Estin's stormy eyes were the last thing I saw before I grasped the intervallim and it whisked us both back to the matchmaker's home. As the feather-soft feeling came, I wondered what his last whisper meant. I consoled myself with the fact that Estin had the final third of the intervallim and could find me at any time. Then again, that could prove deadly for him...

This was terrible. We weren't prepared.

Sylvie hurried with me behind the dressing screen and helped strip off Indri's fine gown. "See that she gets this back," I told her. As she hung it over the back of a small chair, she promised she'd care for it until she could return it on my behalf.

The ivory riding gown was made of thick, woolen fabric that would be too hot for the first part of the journey to the palace, but wouldn't be thick enough for the harsh, frigid mountain passes that led to it.

A thick cloak trailed behind me. Sylvie explained that I could wrap it around my body when it got too cold, like a blanket. It felt like a heavy yoke tying me to a future I didn't want.

She quickly raked my hair back with a comb and twisted the tresses, coiling them into a bun at the back of my head and pinning the thick mass there. "He didn't bring a horse for you," she whispered in warning. "I think he means for you to ride with him."

The thought of being so close to the Lion repulsed me. Sylvie carefully studied me for a reaction and in the mirror, found none. She nodded her approval, powdered my face, and swept rouge onto the apples of my cheeks. With a final spritz of perfume to camouflage the sea salt on my skin, she placed her hands on my shoulders.

"A carriage will arrive in a few hours to carry your trunk, but that means you will reach the palace before it does. They'll have things for you to wear, but you'll be without what you need, and I'm not sure for how long."

That meant I wouldn't have the false bottom that stored the armor or Zaire's blade.

"Is it packed well?" I asked, hoping she knew what I meant.

She nodded.

I reached up and placed my hand on hers. "Thank you, Sylvie."

Footsteps trailed down the hall toward my room and the door opened. The matchmaker walked in, her eyes flooded with fear. "Good. You're ready, then?"

"Yes, Madame."

She smiled and walked forward. A small folded cloth lay in her hand. "Good. I have a gift for you to wear to the palace – a little token to remember me by." She unfolded the cloth to reveal four delicate, silver hairpins, each capped with a small dragonfly. "Allow me?"

I inclined my head and turned so she could tuck them into my hair. Instead of her prized peacocks, she'd chosen dragonflies to remind me of her – yes – but also of the days spent with the dragons, letting me know I was one, too. I thanked her, my voice as strong as my resolve and fear.

"Bravery does not require fearlessness. It simply means that you forge ahead with the fear trailing behind you," the Heart Reader intoned solemnly, brushing my cape back.

I nodded, unable to speak.

Her gaze flicked to the door. "Lord Favian is waiting."

It felt like the boulder that lay over our home and my family had tumbled again, this time settling in the pit of my stomach as I left the room. I left Sylvie, and Zaire's blade behind to come face-to-face with the Lion.

He stood in the front parlor, glancing out the window at the lush gardens with his arms crossed, his leather armor encasing his muscular form. I wondered if he slept in it, fearing someone might attack him as he slumbered. Irritation flashed over his features until he saw me walking behind the matchmaker. His arms fell to reveal the lion etched over his chest and he stood straighter. "Valor," he greeted.

I inclined my head and dipped into a curtsy. "Lord Favian."

He glanced at the matchmaker. "I'll see that another portion of gold is brought to you when her trunk is collected."

"You are far too generous," she fawned, bowing to him.

"Come, Valor," he said. His fair hair was half-damp, half-dry, as if he'd bathed before coming here. The scent of his minty soap struck my nose as he stepped close and proffered his elbow.

We walked down the hall together. This time I noticed each and every attendant who had blended into the walls and curtains. Favian found them, too, his eyes catching on every girl who stood with her eyes averted, waiting for instruction. Did he suspect that his missive was stolen from someone in this house?

I didn't say goodbye to the matchmaker and didn't look back as we left her home and crossed the walkway, her golden fence closing behind us. Three men waited atop their own horses. One held the reins to a fourth horse Favian would command. My heart sank when I saw the stark white stallion. It seemed the Emperor's horse had been found and captured once more.

A sudden wave of fury tumbled through my flesh, heralded by the sight of the horse and furthered by the sight of Favian among his men. This was the man who maimed my father and was responsible for filling his every movement and step in his remaining years with pain and anguish. This was the man who mortally wounded my brother.

I had no idea how Zaire managed to get away and make it as far as our home. Surely the gods must have cleared his path. Favian had taken everything from me. His every breath and heartbeat was an insult.

The Lion of Kaan mounted, then held his arm out for me to take. I clasped his forearm and he pulled me up, positioning me in front of him and waiting as I smoothed the riding skirt's flaps over my legs. His hand found my side, then slithered toward my navel.

Taking the reins in his other hand, he gave the command to ride. The busy men of Starcrest parted like the sea to allow us through, respectfully placing a fist over their chest and bowing their head to the Lion.

If loyalty required that they honor him, fear held their heads and eyes down a few beats longer.

As we rode away, Favian's men silently flanked us, one at each side and one behind. Wagons hastily swerved out of the way, those driving urging the horses to an abrupt stop. In front of the market, the blind beggar still sat. His head rose as we approached, and his clouded eyes inexplicably found mine and tracked me as we rode past. I could feel his stare even after he was long behind us.

Why had the Lion come for me so many days earlier than he'd told the matchmaker? Did the disturbance at the wall rush his plans? Why leave in the afternoon? Night would soon fall, and we wouldn't be able to see the paths that led north.

We left Starcrest for the foothills that were arranged like rows of sentinels guarding the entrance of the Angris Mountains. The palace was situated somewhere among its tallest peaks. Rumors swirled through the countryside that it was made of pure gold, that its pinnacles could pierce the very clouds, and that the snow was so thick it would be taller than our horses in places. But the Emperor's soldiers maintained a path worn between frozen walls just wide enough for a wagon to pass through.

The Imperial city was supposed to be a glittering jewel itself, with bridges made of ice and walls formed from blocks of packed snow. It was rumored that during the wars, Cassius stole elvish light stones and hoisted them in lanterns that hung on posts throughout his city as a reward to those allowed to live so close to him, but that also served as a nightly reminder of his power.

If he could steal the magic of the elves, what else was he capable of?

Favian did not speak. Nor did the three men riding with us. But they were aware of every sound, alert to every movement.

I kept still and quiet, listening.

~

DARKNESS SOON WRAPPED its arms around Rata and pulled her away. I hated her, but she was mine. She chose me before any other god deemed I was worthy. So, despite our tumultuous past, the fact that the goddess who wanted me was absent and had no idea what was happening to me for hours each night made me uneasy.

Warmth poured from the Lion's body behind mine, but I didn't relax into it. I sat up straight and when I caught myself dozing off, pinched my arm to stay awake. I couldn't let my guard down around him, even for a second.

"You should rest," he finally said after I startled again, having closed my eyes a moment too long. I didn't reply. "You may speak," he allowed.

But I didn't have anything to say to the Lion. The conversation I yearned to have with Favian would be spoken with swords and memorialized in blood.

Irritation hardened his tone. "We'll ride through the night."

When I remained silent, he gritted his teeth, snapped the reins, and drove us faster. For hours, he sipped from a small flask, the astringent smell of alcohol wafting from his breath behind me.

It wasn't until he was taking another sip in the heart of the forest and his swallow was so loud that I realized there was no other sound. Not from Ventus's wind rattling the curled, dry leaves that still clung to the branches that bore them, though they quivered. Not even from our horse's hooves.

Leaning over to get a better look, I nearly fell off. Favian caught me easily. With a shock, I realized the horse's hooves weren't touching the ground. They were enchanted.

"Elven magic," Favian noted arrogantly.

And because he'd given me that small, but rather obvious piece of information, he expected me to converse. "You recently lost your father, is that right, Valor? Or was it your mother?"

I wondered if answering him would make him tell me something he shouldn't. I wasn't sure he should've told me about the horses' enchantment, but the alcohol had loosened his tongue.

I swallowed thickly. "My mother died when I was ten. I recently lost my father."

"No siblings?"

The matchmaker had told him all of this. He was testing me to see if our tales matched. Perhaps he saw it for what it was – a lie.

"I have no living siblings, my lord." That was the truth.

"Ah. Many a woman buries a child soon after they bear them," he quietly observed, waiting to see if I would confirm his suspicion.

I wanted to claw the skin off his arms and tell him my brother was no infant when he died, only days ago; that it was *he* who'd killed him and taken him from me. I wished for Zaire's dragon blade so I could sink it into his thigh, then plunge it into his heart.

The soldier to our left suddenly slowed.

Favian, following suit, pulled on the reins.

The man, barely a few years older than me, used his hands to speak, forming signs and gestures Favian interpreted. Favian looked at me, the moon catching on the craggy planes of his face. "We can make a very brief stop, I suppose."

Favian's men were already gulping hands full of cupped water from the stream along with their horses before Favian dismounted, lifting me down from the saddle as if I weighed nothing. I turned to walk into the woods for privacy and so that for a moment, I could feel like I could breathe freely when something tugged at my hair. I felt the careful bun Sylvie had wrapped, but it was still firmly in place. I turned to find Favian holding one of the dragonfly pins the matchmaker had given me.

"What an unusual choice for adornment." He twisted the delicate silver back and forth, watching me instead of the trinket. "The *dragon*fly."

I gave him a small smile, surprised by the lie that flew smoothly from my lips. "Many flew over the matchmaker's lawn. I think they liked her fountains, but regardless of what drew them there, one got caught up in my hair one evening and I screamed until she plucked it out. It was a surprisingly thoughtful gift from her," I told him easily.

He held the bauble out for me to take, pinched between his finger and thumb. I took hold of it, but he held it tight when I tried to pull it away. I looked toward him only to find him carefully watching my face.

"Allow me to tuck it back into place," he offered.

"Thank you," I said, then turned around.

He tucked the pin into my bun in the spot from which he'd taken it. When his hand fell on my shoulder, I barely suppressed a shudder. He stepped close, pressing his front against my back as if we hadn't ridden for many miles the same way. The difference now was that such contact wasn't necessary. We weren't sharing a horse. And, I realized, his men weren't watching us.

"Valor... I am my brother's closest friend and advisor. He

invites me to the palace often. I think I should like to visit you there, once *he's* become acquainted with you, of course."

His repulsive implication coiled heavily in the air. In my mind, I formed it into a sword and cleaved him the way he'd cut my brother down. Watched him crawl to get away from me, that same sword raised to strike again.

He let his fingers trail over the back of my neck. My hair rose in reply.

Without another word, the Lion peeled away and ventured into the woods. I collected my thoughts and walked proudly in the opposite direction, pretending he hadn't rattled me. And I lifted my head and thanked Indri, wherever she was, thankful the trembling in my hands, in my very soul, had not returned at his touch.

THE NEXT MORNING, Trayton freed Rata once more. For the first time in years, I was relieved to see her rays and watch her climb into the sky little by little. With her growing light, I didn't feel completely alone. The trees had thinned, only pines remaining now. A crusting of old snow littered the ground, but the horses left no prints in it as they galloped over the air.

We mounted our horses and prepared to ride. "We will arrive at the palace in a few hours," Favian said, drawing my cloak over my shoulders. "The wind will howl from now until then."

The wind tore at his pale yellow hair. In my periphery, one of his men rode alongside us, but when I glanced that way, I stiffened.

Asra rode alongside us, his burgundy curls twisting and flailing in the bitter wind. He stared straight ahead as if he didn't notice me at all. That was when I saw the image laid over him like a shroud. With a start, I realized his gift was camouflage.

The Lion only saw his trusted soldier flanking us, but I saw a warrior loyal to me and to the Kingdom of the Elves riding at our side.

I smiled and pulled the cloak tighter under my chin.

Glancing to the right, I found Indri hidden beneath the skin of the man who'd ridden in his position yesterday. A glance behind revealed that the Dragon lay beneath the flesh of the hind rider. I wasn't sure where Grady was...

A raven soared overhead, then tilted and disappeared from sight.

I pressed my eyes closed as my heart swelled. They were close.

They were here and I wasn't alone.

Estin had said not to give them away, and now I knew what he meant. I wracked my brain for when they could have taken the place of Favian's men, realizing it must have been when we stopped last night. While Favian was toying with me, the dragons were devouring his men and using magic to don their skin.

It must be as hard for them to be in Favian's presence as it was for me. Especially after what Indri said about Cassius and their ears...

Relief and excitement pumped through my veins, but something else was there... dread and fear. What if I could never get close enough to achieve either of my goals – killing Favian and rescuing Kirsi? What if Cassius had already moved Kirsi out of the palace? What if someone caught me searching for her, or one of the concubines decided they didn't want a new girl in their number? So much could go wrong, and only a few things right.

Still, the dragons were here, and if I failed, they could take up the torch and continue on without me. If I failed, their mother would uphold the bargain we had negotiated as soon as Kirsi was weakened enough that she could tear down the magic of her wall like a curtain torn from its hangers.

A sliver of fear cut through me like a winding vein of gold through rock. Estin said that their magic weakened the closer they were to Kirsi. It was how they were imprisoned and kept there so long until Zaire released them and helped them escape. Would Asra's glamour magic hold the closer we drew to the palace?

Asra wound a scarf around his mouth and head, leaving only

his eyes uncovered as Ventus's breath tore over the mountains. Indri tugged her hood up so I could only see her mouth. Were they already worried Asra's gift wouldn't hold? I wanted to turn and see Estin riding behind us, but I kept still and quiet as the roaring wind rattled the evergreens and lifted snow into the air, scattering it before us.

CHAPTER 16

The palace, even from the base of the mountains, was striking. Spectacularly massive, it was nestled in a craggy nook that once likely held part of the range itself. It glittered golden in the snow, thanks to Rata. Diverging from a shallow river with water so perfect and blue it looked like something that could only exist in a dream was a quaint town filled with tiny stone houses and a path that wended up the mountainside to the palace of gold.

Was Trayton with us?

Was Zairitus present in every flake of snow, every slick piece of ice, every drop of the vivid blue mountain stream? Did the god of great waters recognize the blood I shared with Zaire?

The horses carried us easily up the mountain, where we passed in and out of clouds, our vision obscured for moments only to emerge from the mist to see scenery so beautiful I couldn't find words adequate to describe it.

Majestic.

Resplendent.

Heartbreaking.

"The other concubines I've brought here focused only on the

golden palace," Favian laughed. "But you can't peel your eyes from the mountains."

The palace could not outshine them, no matter how brightly it gleamed in Rata's light.

I'd never seen anything like this. Zaire and I climbed hills when we were children and to my small, weak legs, they felt as large as these mountains, but in reality, they were nothing like this. These ice-covered peaks were even infinitely taller than the ones Grady made me climb.

The Lion gave a shrill whistle and the horses slowed to a stop. "The three of you ride on without us," he instructed his men. "I need to speak privately with Valor."

Favian noticed nothing amiss with his men's appearances as Asra, Indri, and the Dragon rode past us so that Favian could speak to me in confidence.

While I was glad that Asra's magic allowed me to see past their visages, I was afraid it might cause problems. What if I accidentally called them by their names? Favian and Cassius would know the names of the dragons they so fervently hunted. They were on the list the little thief had stolen and I'd given Asra.

I watched as my friends left us and rode on ahead, the hooves of their horses never touching the loose pebbles that peppered the pathway. When they were far out of earshot, Favian spoke. The horse stood perfectly still for him, breathing easily under our weight.

"You'll be guarded until Cassius arrives. The three men traveling with us are among my most trusted."

That meant Cassius wasn't currently at the palace, and it sounded like the Lion would be leaving soon. Maybe the gods *were* smiling on us. Or maybe it was a well-laid trap.

"You might have noticed that they don't speak. It is because they cut out their own tongues to prove their loyalty to me so they could never speak of anything I told them in confidence," he boasted. The very thought turned my stomach. "That sort of dedication is difficult to find, but I found it in them."

After a moment, he dismounted and stood on a snow bank

beside me, watching every blink of my eyes. "The Heart Reader said that I can trust you. My gut says I cannot."

Would he cut out my tongue to keep me quiet? Would Cassius encourage it?

Irritation mottled his face. "Speak, woman!"

I cleared my throat. "Trust me with what, my lord?"

Tension bled from his shoulders; aggravation leached from his facial features. "I need your help. I rarely depend on anyone else, but now I have no choice, as circumstance prevents my presence within the palace for longer than brief visits with my brother."

He glanced up at the golden, gleaming palace now looming before us, even larger than I realized when I stood beside the river that carved a blue vein in the snowy valley far below us. "Many concubines have been found dead of late."

My lips parted. The matchmaker already told me of the deaths plaguing the Emperor's polished palace, but it was shocking to hear him talk about the deaths of these women as if their dying was an annoyance. I schooled my features, internally reprimanding myself for allowing the slip of disgust to show through – even though Favian hadn't noticed. At some point, he would.

"Do you know that the concubines guard the Emperor at all times?" he continued. "He takes at least two with him everywhere he goes, even when he travels throughout Kaan. He's particularly fond of a set of twins who were trained in the art of warfare from a young age." His deep blue eyes watched and waited, searching my face.

"I had no idea," I lied smoothly. "The matchmaker said that once the concubines arrived at the palace, they never left."

"Most don't," he advised, "whether by their choice or not." He shifted on his feet. "I want to know who among them killed the others. Whomever is doing so is a threat to my brother."

Something dark swam in his eyes. Not concern, but suspicion. But who would the Lion suspect, and why would it matter if a few concubines died at the hands of one of the others? That person wouldn't be a threat to anyone but other concubines...unless the murderer was one of the two who traveled with the Emperor.

"You suspect the twins?"

A slow, pleased smile spread over his lips and his cold eyes glittered with approval. "Why do you assume that?"

I tilted my head. "Why would they hurt the Emperor when he shows them favor?"

"Perhaps they wouldn't, but the twins especially are very jealous of any other woman who takes Cassius away from them. I fear their envy and obsession will ultimately turn them against my brother."

He was using me as bait.

My life meant nothing to him at all.

Neither did Father's.

Or Zaire's.

Or the countless others he'd killed or had killed to further his schemes and purposes.

I opened my mouth and thought better, but not before Favian noticed. "What were you about to say?"

"Only that the Emperor does not belong to the twins," I said quietly, keeping my tone light and subservient.

He smiled. "Indeed. So, will you keep watch for anything that seems amiss?"

I nodded.

"And if the twins try to lure you to a place where you'll be alone with them..."

"I won't allow it."

He pursed his lips and gave a satisfied nod.

"How can I send word to you?" I asked.

"I'll find you, Valor." The same lust-filled promise curled between us like dark smoke, his stare echoing his intention. "Be on constant guard within these walls," he said, his voice surprisingly soft as he reached up to toy with my frozen fingers.

They stung at his touch.

If I died at the hands of these ruthless women, he wouldn't lose a moment of sleep. But if I managed to avoid them and learned their secrets, he wanted them in his hands so the necks of those I tossed to him would be at his mercy.

Perhaps it was Favian who wanted his emperor brother dead. Did he plan to use the cunning women against Cassius?

Weak men exploited others to keep their own hands clean.

Just then, a cry came from a raven circling above us. Goosebumps rose on my arms as Favian took note of the creature. "They don't usually fly so far north."

THE ROAD to the palace widened as we dipped into its shadow. Favian rode to the small number of men he'd ordered ahead, my dragons hiding within them, and doled out their orders.

Suppressed rage poured off them so violently, I imagined it unsettling the snow, separating the powder from the rock it clung to and sending the Lion roaring down the mountain. He would crash into the valley or be buried alive. Either way, no lion could survive an avalanche.

The palace doors looked like they'd been poured from pure gold and stood as tall as two houses, thick and impenetrable. Guarded well, I noted. I was under no illusion that I'd be able to leave this place by waltzing through the front doors, but hoped all entrances weren't made or watched so well.

The outer walls were built of precisely cut rock that glittered under Rata's light. It was the same rock used in the matchmaker's walkway. The people of Starcrest would see the stone leading to her door and think of how lucky she was to receive such a gift from the Emperor. They wouldn't know that the flecks of glassy crystal were reminders of the man to whom she belonged. She may not live in the palace, but her fate belonged to Cassius all the same.

From the valley, the palace had seemed like a small diamond sparkling in a grand, intricate setting, its glimmer barely noticeable next to the dazzling mountaintops beside it. Standing at its steps, the perspective changed entirely. The palace was the crowning jewel here.

I glanced up at the windows and saw several curtains flutter.

A few of the women didn't bother hiding themselves, but openly glared. Perhaps they were sizing me up. Perhaps they would take bets to see how long I survived among them.

Searching for Kirsi would be nearly impossible with so many curious eyes watching me. Maybe instead, I could become a diversion; something to keep the concubines and guards busy so the dragons could find her on their own...

Two bundled soldiers tugged on the door handles and they parted without the slightest creak. Favian strode toward me with wide steps. "The men need rest. I have some matters to attend, but first... let's warm ourselves by the fire."

He rubbed his hands together and blew his hot breath into their middles. It escaped in fine plumes. As he led me to the doors, I fought the urge to look at the dragons I knew would not be sleeping as they were told.

The palace was remarkably warm. I expected it to be as drafty and frigid as the mountains surrounding it, but my skin prickled as the heat from many fires warmed it. Favian allowed two servants to swoop in and remove his cape.

The doors loudly slammed closed and the two guards keeping watch inside slid a broad bar into place, locking them.

A slight, elderly woman appeared and silently waved me into a private parlor before motioning for me to move close to the fire. Within seconds, the clumps of ice that were stuck to my skirts and cape began to melt. The water dripped onto the stone floor all around me as I stood in front of Rata's flames, far enough back to avoid her grasp, but close enough for her warmth to soothe the frost from my skin and chase the chill from my bones. My cheeks and nose burned as she thawed me.

Favian came to stand at my side, too close for me to be comfortable. He held his hands out to catch the heat rising from the hearth.

Why doesn't Rata burn people like him? It crossed my mind that the Lion might also belong to the goddess of fire and light.

When he brought his frost-bitten fingers to my cheek, I suppressed the urge to smack them away.

"Color is returning to your cheeks. You looked very pale when we arrived. I apologize for not warning you of the manner of travel sooner, so you could better prepare."

Liar. If he wanted that, he wouldn't have come to retrieve me earlier than anyone could possibly prepare for such a journey, even if riding on enchanted horses.

"Do not fear me," he whispered. Lust sparked in his eyes. The fingers that traced my skin drifted into my hair, down the side of my neck...

"I don't," I told him honestly.

"Everyone does," he said hoarsely. His eyes met mine. "Everyone."

Wasn't that what he wanted? To be feared. For everyone to cower when they heard him called the Lion?

"Why do they?" I quietly asked.

"Because I am the Lion of Kaan. Because they know only of the beast, not the man."

I considered my next words carefully. "How do they differ?"

He looked to the fire. "The Lion does what he must. The man does what he will."

"And which would you rather be if you could only choose one?" I asked brazenly.

"Valor –" He stepped closer, twisting his body toward me. His hand tugged firmly on my arm until I faced him. "I prefer to be both." He lowered his head. "But I wonder, if allowed the choice, would you still choose Cassius over me?"

Scruff had grown over his jaw and lip. His cheeks weren't hollow. Nor were his deep blue eyes. They held depths of emotion, fathoms of questions.

I looked down at his breastplate and traced the careful, etched lines with my eyes. They caught on every nick. Every scrape. He knew his brother had claimed me, so I wasn't sure why he kept touching me and looking at me like that. Not with hunger exactly, but almost with determination.

Was he testing my loyalty, or his restraint?

The servant woman returned with her head down, and with

her hands, spoke to Favian. Had she given her tongue as well, or had the Emperor demanded it in exchange for her place here in the palace? She was withered, the arduous years bowing her back and making her thin skin wrinkle over delicate bones.

After demanding that she see I was cleaned and made presentable for dinner, Favian strode out of the room, saving me from giving him the answer he sought. His loud footsteps softened with the blissful distance put between us.

The woman waved for me to follow her once more and led me down a hallway where alabaster busts of the Emperor lined the walls. In varying poses, he watched us. The details of his face were captured perfectly in the rock, identical from sculpture to sculpture.

The woman's thin, gray hair spilled delicately down her back, the ends fluttering as we walked. What color had it been in her youth? Was she brought here to serve at a young age, or was she among the concubines in her prime and found a new purpose and position as she aged? If either were true, my hopes of escaping this place dwindled with each step.

The woman took the steps one at a time, propping a hand on one knee and using the wall to steady herself. "Would you like my arm?" I asked carefully.

She went rigid, then turned to look over her shoulder at me with wary eyes. She shook her head and brought a single finger to her lips. *Quiet... Be quiet,* she said with her eyes.

I swallowed thickly and fell into step behind her.

The dragons are here somewhere. They won't leave me behind. I won't be here long, I told myself. But every click of my boots upon the glassy floor mocked my thoughts. This place was built to carry noise.

The woman came to a set of intricately carved doors. A scene had been captured in the wood, exquisitely and painstakingly detailed. In a field of wildflowers that bent in the wind and craned toward high-flying Rata, stood a doe. Her head was up, ears perked, as if she'd heard something and was waiting to see if danger lurked too near.

On the far left of the double doors, something dark lurked behind a tree, watching the doe. Looking closer, I saw that it was a man. He wore a crown.

The woman pushed until the doors parted, then stood to the side and ushered me into a chamber of rooms. The echoing snap of the doors as they closed made me flinch. The woman noticed. Instead of looking at me with contempt, pity swam in her warm brown eyes. Understanding. Compassion.

Someone had built fires in each room. There was a fireplace in the bedroom and another larger one fitted between the bathing room and parlor. The suite was lushly furnished with plush couches and chaises, a bed so large it could comfortably sleep six, desks with matching chairs, and tables that held golden vases filled with fresh-smelling, long-stemmed white roses.

The matchmaker said it would be the only color I was permitted to wear until the Emperor came to me... Several dresses in shades from the purest white to creamy ivory hung on a gilded rack in the corner of the room. The woman walked into the bathing room and waved for me to come with her. I trailed behind.

Everything in the suite was white. The walls, bedding, and the fabric stretched over the chairs and couches gleamed. Even the floor boards had been washed to look pale. The rugs, towels, tub, and counters in the bathing room were blindingly white, along with the stools perched in front of two large, white-framed mirrors. Every tile. Every detail.

Molten rage slithered through me with an intensity that Rata must always feel.

I wasn't the first girl to sleep in this bed, but I vowed to be the last. I imagined lighting the doors on fire and asking Rata to coax the flame as well as she was able. This high, we were closer to her. Maybe her power over flame was stronger on the mountain.

The tub was full, but the water was as cold as the rest of the room felt. Like the matchmaker's tub, there was a place beneath it to build a fire. The woman stacked the wood into a small tower, then struck a piece of flint with a blade she'd kept tucked in her apron's pocket. She held her hands around the small flame as it spread over some of the shaved kindling and thin pieces that splintered off the nearest piece of wood.

The budding ember and trickling flame winked out, and thin trails of smoke slithered from where they'd just burned. She struck the flint again, casting more sparks into the tinder. One caught, but it burned out, too. She became nervous, casting worried glances at the door.

Did she think someone would come in to inspect her progress? Were we pressed for time?

She struck the flint harder each time, but nothing caught.

With great difficulty, the woman rose and took one of the small slices of wood to the hearth in the bedroom, holding it into the fire.

I sank to my knees and held my breath. *Rata, this woman needs your help. If you will not help me, please help her. She's frightened. I can imagine many things that might be the cause, but there are likely many more I can't yet fathom.*

Just then, the small bundle of tinder beneath the tub caught, a flame growing from its middle like a heart on fire, hungrily spreading to the other tiny pieces until nothing but a bright ball of flame remained. A gasp escaped my chest as it spread slowly to the lowest pieces and climbed, feasting on the snack as if it was a delicacy to be savored.

Rata heard me. She helped, though I hadn't expected her to.

Thank you, Rata.

The woman returned from the bedroom's hearth with one hand cupped around the flame atop the piece of wood she gingerly held. When she saw the fire roaring beneath the tub, her mouth gaped. She tossed the small stick into the blaze and waved for me to stand.

She glanced from me to the fire and back, a question in her eyes. "I was chosen by Rata," I admitted.

She nodded, trailed her hand through the water, then placed a hand on her chest.

"Zairitus claimed you?"

Another cautious nod.

Keeping her hand in the tub, I could see the water calmed her. Tension bled from her back. She dried her hand on her apron and walked to the corner where a dressing screen sat folded against the wall. She stretched its joints and waved for me to step behind it. I left the tub and untrustworthy fire and joined her there. She helped me unfasten my cloak and neatly folded it, placing it on the floor, then motioned, indicating that she would scrub it.

"Thank you."

She inclined her head and moved behind me where she tried to unzip my dress. "I can bathe and ready myself," I told her.

She shook her head. Pointed at her chest.

I didn't understand. "I can care for myself. I promise to scrub well."

She shook her head, pointed at the door, and pressed her hands together as if begging. Worry lines deepened the creases in her face. Like everyone else, she feared Favian. He'd told her to see that I was cleaned and made presentable for dinner, and she was afraid not to do exactly as he'd instructed. I presented my back to her. "I understand," I whispered.

When she went to unfasten the necklace Estin had given me that held the intervallim stone, I placed my hand over hers. "I'd like to keep it on, please."

She let loose of the clasp and instead dragged my zipper down.

After my skin was red and raw from being harshly scrubbed, the woman helped me into a thick, white robe and led me over to the rack of pale dresses, gesturing to them. It was my choice which one to wear.

All the dresses hanging on the rack looked alike, for the most part. They were soft and made of warmer, thicker fabric than we could buy out of Starcrest. Not that we were able to afford it more than a handful of times, and only when I grew so tall the hem would strike my knees and the sleeves crawled up to my elbows.

Before Zaire left, Father used to send him around to ask the neighbors with daughters if any would want to buy my old dresses. There was always someone who needed them. They tried bartering with food, knowing we were hungry, but when I needed material, Father wouldn't accept anything but coin. Ears of corn couldn't buy even the cheapest bolts of fabric.

I pointed to the dress nearest me and the woman reached up and brought it down. She helped me don it, styled my damp hair into a twist at the nape of my neck, and painted shimmer onto my cheeks and red onto my lips.

Watching the mirror, I reminded myself that the Emperor wasn't here and I didn't have to worry and panic about him yet. But that didn't mean I didn't have other things to be concerned about.

"Do all the concubines dine together?" I asked.

Her eyes snapped to mine. She shook her head and held up two fingers.

"Only two of them?"

More head shaking. She pointed to my chest, then lifted one finger.

"Me?"

She nodded, then pointed at the door. Did she mean the other person who would dine with me was Favian? She raised her hands and snapped her teeth. The Lion.

"Lord Favian and I will be dining alone?"

She nodded and took hold of my hand as I stood, patting it and giving a small, wary smile. I didn't want to be alone with the Emperor's brother again. Each time we spent more than a moment together, he became bolder with his words and actions.

With dinner would come wine. The matchmaker said it poured from fountains here, but I hadn't seen them yet. Outside, the liquid would freeze. Perhaps the wine fountains were in the dining room.

Either way, I wasn't safe in the presence of the Lion whether he was sober or not.

CHAPTER 17

I wished I knew the name of the woman who had been helping me. Knowing that Zairitus looked over her was a small comfort. I decided that if she remained my handmaid, I would try my best to convince her to teach me to read the hand signs she gave.

The fear in her eyes when she thought I wouldn't comply and allow her to fulfill Favian's order made me wonder if she would risk teaching me, for fear of being caught.

I came here wondering where Kirsi might be hidden, but a thought struck me as the small woman slowly led me to dinner. Kirsi might not be hidden at all. If Emperor Cassius wasn't here, who was to say she wasn't with him or wouldn't join him the moment he stepped back inside the golden doors? Who was to say I wouldn't see her this very night? She could pass us in the hall or be lounging on one of the many chaises scattered about and I would be none the wiser.

Estin said I would know her by her smile, but I wondered if concubines ever had a reason to smile.

It hurt to think that Father would have marveled at this and believed this was better for me than a life I could carve out in the countryside. Rural life was hard, yes, but there, even a single woman had moments of freedom. I could wrap myself in thoughts and enjoy the simple things: Rata's warmth on my skin, the feel of moist soil crumbling between my fingers, the muddy bottom of the cool creek bed between my toes, the scent of flowers and vibrant colors of plants, the licks and antics of playful pups who escaped their own farms for a time to visit mine.

Even the soft clucking of chickens as they slowly pecked their way over the ground and the bleating of the hateful goat. Father's rhythmic snoring. The way I would wonder where in the empire Zaire might be and what things he might get to see and tell me about – if I woke to see him when he came.

I missed home. I hadn't tasted freedom since I left it.

The old woman took the steps back to the bottom floor one at a time, again bracing herself against the wall. I wanted to offer my arm, but wisely held my tongue. My words might get her in trouble in this quiet place.

I raked my teeth over my tongue, wondering again if the concubines had been silenced the way the guards had been.

The old woman was winded and stopped on a step to gather her breath. Glancing over her shoulder, I looked at her and waited, lifting my hand just a little so she knew my offer stood. She nodded and reached her frail hand out, placing it on my waiting forearm.

Her skin was cool and her grip weak, but it did help having something to hold onto with each hand. She quickly took her hand away when we reached the last step and straightened a little as two soldiers drew near.

She saw Favian's men, but I saw Indri and Asra hidden in their skin. Asra's magic still held.

There were eyes on all of us. I could feel them even now. Just walking down the hall, someone, or several someones, watched.

I stumbled, unused to the combination of slippers with pristine soles and polished slick floors, but caught myself. A shadow on the wall moved a moment before a throaty, feminine chuckle floated down from the balcony just overhead as we entered an intimate dining room.

Tall, white candles lined the dinner table between Favian's place setting and mine. I never expected to be grateful for flames, but they provided a glowing barrier between me and the Lion. Favian wore a smug smile. He rose when I approached and dismissed the woman who'd helped me bathe, dress, and led me there with a flick of his wrist, then held out my chair, pushing it in as I lowered myself.

He had bathed. His mint soap wafted through the small space as he reclaimed his seat. He'd combed his still-damp hair back and shaved the scruff from his jaw and lip. I couldn't help but wonder why the throne had not passed to him, or why he hadn't fought his brother to claim it. Maybe I was wrong, but I didn't think more than a year separated him from Cassius.

Perhaps he'd fought for it at one time and lost.

Servants moved around us, but I feared losing sight of the Lion crouched in front of me, every candle a concealing blade of grass.

Water was poured. Then wine. Plates of steaming, salted meat and vegetables were uncovered, their savory spices making my mouth water.

Suddenly, I was grateful for the matchmaker and for the dragons. They'd taken in a starving girl and fed her so the pangs and desperation were gone. I could think clearly again, my mind free of the fog that settled when all you could think about was where your next meal might come from and when, or what it might be. When even blades of grass looked appetizing.

Favian called a servant over and ordered him to try a sip from our glasses and take a bite of the tender meat, along with a sliver of carrot and potato. The man took tiny portions from both our plates and small sips from our cups. Nothing happened.

"It's safe," Favian declared.

The matchmaker's warning of the girl flashed through my mind. I imagined her in the white room, surrounded by a hoard of lifeless flies, their tiny, bent legs pricking the air. When Favian cut into his meat and chewed ravenously, it struck me... he was hungry. Not starved, but he needed to eat. He was a man like any other.

And no man could escape death.

"Do you question my judgment, Valor?" he asked, swilling his wine.

"No, my lord." I picked up the only fork and knife at my place setting and began to eat.

"What's the matter, then?" he prodded, irritated.

Thinking quickly, I explained, "It's just that the matchmaker showed me many forks and spoons and… the table is different from what she taught."

He smiled then, as if thinking I was a simple girl overwhelmed by her surroundings.

Good.

I smiled back.

"When my brother returns, all her tutelage will have been worth it. He prefers to complicate even the most basic things to preserve decorum."

I took a sip of water. "And you don't?"

"I prefer simplicity."

The way he looked at me made me draw my feet in from where I'd outstretched them, every inch of me desperate to stay out of his reach.

"May I ask a question?" I blurted.

He inclined his head. "You may."

"What is expected of me here?"

His sharp brow rose.

My face heated and I rushed to explain, "I know what is expected of a concubine, but what about when the Emperor is gone? What am I to do? How should I busy myself? Am I to inquire after him, or is that not my place?"

Favian took up the wine bottle and filled his glass again, then began to chew more of the food that lay on his plate. "There is a library if you enjoy reading, and a courtyard if you enjoy spending time outdoors. Some of the women like to embroider things. Some have small window gardens. Others paint. There is a room with game boards set up at small tables. You only need a partner to enjoy them." He cleared his throat. "All find hobbies to occupy their days. Just know that there are many concubines, so you will find that the days drag on between my brother's visits. And you may inquire after him if you'd like, but no one is required to answer."

"Where is he now?" I asked.

Favian narrowed his eyes. "How do you know he's not here?"

"I assumed that if he was, he would be dining with us." I returned my attention to my food, half gone.

"Cassius had to travel to Sparrowing for a few days. It seems a change in leadership was needed among a few regiments."

Needed? I wanted to laugh. Asra and Indri had slaughtered three colonels. Cassius must have had to leave to choose their replacements. Still, I wondered why Favian hadn't been assigned to choose, since the Lion commanded the army.

"Some things, Cassius insists on doing alone," he added as if intuiting the direction of my thoughts.

"Do you choose each concubine for him?" I asked. That seemed to be one thing for which the Emperor didn't make time.

Favian's eyes drilled into mine. "You know that I do."

"Why did you choose me?"

He chewed on his cheek. "I could simply answer that I chose you because of your beauty."

"That's a lie, though." I was tip-toeing closer to the tall grass the Lion crouched behind.

He finished the last of his wine. "You share something with a few of the others that I think might serve you well here."

"What's that?"

"A hunger... to survive, of course," he recovered.

"So you brought me here because I was starved?" I bristled, unable to stop the words.

"Valor." His tone demanded that my eyes return to his. "I chose you because you're keen, intelligent, and like your namesake, brave. No other woman – including those cloistered within these walls – has ever looked me in the eye as you have dared."

"And does Cassius share your admiration for daring women?"

He leaned forward, braced his forearms on the table, and opened his mouth to answer. Then his eyes fell on my necklace, on full display now where the riding dress had kept it hidden. "What sort of jewel is that?" he asked.

"Oh, I'm not sure," I replied airily.

"It was a gift, then?"

I smiled. "Yes."

"From the matchmaker?"

"Yes. To match the hair pins."

A sudden draft tore through the room, blowing the candles' flames sideways. A few winked out, leaking smoke into the air.

I thanked Ventus for the interruption. Did Favian only suspect or did he know the crystal in the setting was intervallim?

Favian leapt to his feet, reaching for the handle of the sword he always wore on his hip. He wore no armor. His pale shirt flapped in the frigid breeze sailing through the palace. Abruptly, doors slammed down the hall, severing Ventus's wind.

There was a sudden commotion. Favian waved for me to join him just outside the dining room. A flurry of color erupted along the balcony as more women than I could count rushed toward the staircase and lined up along its ornate balustrades as if their positions were predetermined, arranging themselves like flowers. Different feminine fragrances hit my nose, each heady and strong. Each unique despite them mingling together.

Every part of the empire was represented. Cerulean women with glistening, dark skin and hair adorned with shells like Indri wore. Palts from the western coast with hair as fiery as Rata's light in the evenings and skin like goat's milk. Women from the countryside like me, with thin frames and hair like night. The girls from Sparrowing nearly all had freckles and hair the color of a fresh puddle of mud, while the girls from the Imperial City – which I still hadn't glimpsed, though it was tucked into the mountains someplace nearby – had golden hair and sun-kissed complexions like Favian... and Cassius.

The Emperor and the Lion shared many similar features, which I now bore witness to as Cassius strode into the foyer.

Servants quickly removed his fur-lined cloak, matted with snow and ice and grit from the journey he'd taken. His eyes weren't as dark as Favian's. They were a shade of vivid blue like deep water trapped in a pond frozen over in winter, while his hair was a shade warmer than Favian's.

From behind him slithered two beautiful women with identical, heart-shaped faces, pouty lips, and harsh, dark eyes. Their long, wavy hair was silver, but not because of their age. They were a few years older than I, but not old enough for their hair to turn. The servants rushed to rid them of their fine, snow-coated cloaks as well.

Their eyes fastened on me, noting my white dress. Even their sneers matched. Satira and Gaila, otherwise known as the Twins.

Cassius's favored.

Where were they from? I'd never seen silver hair before. *They almost look...* I quietly gasped when I saw the pointed tips of their ears. The twins were elves.

I searched the entryway to see if Kirsi had traveled with them but only saw the three of them, along with two soldiers who had entered the palace. As the soldiers peeled fur-lined gloves from their hands, Indri's warnings flashed through my mind.

Keeping my expression neutral and my head slightly bowed, I waited patiently at Favian's side as Cassius made his way to us. If it wasn't for Indri's magic, I would have trembled uncontrollably. I'd stomached riding on the same horse with the man who slayed my brother and disabled my father years ago, who put such fear in him that he never admitted to it even when he was sure he was dying.

He touched my hair, my skin.

I'd dined with him, spoken to him while sipping wine from a bottle he'd uncorked.

But as intimidating as the Lion could be, Cassius was a force all his own and in his presence, I felt unsure and diminished. My senses dulled when I needed them sharp.

The Lion addressed his emperor. "I'm glad to see you've returned safely, brother."

Cassius clasped Favian's hand and clapped his shoulder, a curious smile tugging at his lips and making his eyes gleam as he watched me instead. "Who is this?"

Hadn't Cassius asked the Lion for a new concubine? Had Favian at least written to tell him he'd found one?

The room had been made ready, the dresses were prepared... Or were they always there for when the Lion took someone new away from their lives at a whim?

Favian stood proudly next to me, his hands folded behind his back. "This, brother, is Valor."

"Valor..." the Emperor repeated, moving to stand in front of me. "Raise your head."

I followed his order and watched him take note of me. "What a pleasant surprise. Allow me to welcome you to the palace."

"We only arrived a couple of hours ago. We are weary and in need of rest, brother. The road was long," Favian told him, going on to describe a harrowing, days-long journey we never took. He was lying to his brother, his emperor. But why?

"Any trouble along the way?" Cassius asked, his eyes flicking back to the Lion.

"None, sire," Favian answered.

"We have much to discuss," Cassius told his brother in a grave voice. "I'm afraid that, despite your exhaustion, there are matters that cannot wait."

Favian bowed at his waist. "As always, I am at your service."

Cassius seemed satisfied. "I will introduce myself more thoroughly soon, Valor," he promised. He strode away, the women deflating as he failed to look over them despite how much effort they'd put into their appearances and how they'd all come to welcome him home.

Favian motioned for his guardsmen, beneath whose visages lurked Indri and Asra, to see me to my room and position themselves outside it. As the women retreated into the palace, they slowed their steps to get a better glimpse of me. I walked like

Indri showed me with my shoulders back, like the world owed me a debt I would soon collect. I met their narrowed eyes and did not cower. I would bow my head to the Emperor if I must to save my neck, but never to my equals.

Indri and Asra waited until the staircase cleared, then escorted me back to my suite. Indri hissed at the engraving on the door and Asra gave her a grave shake of the head. We weren't safe to speak even here. But I had to know where Estin was. Had they seen any signs of Kirsi's presence here at all?

I looked at the Dragon's brother, beseeching him silently. Asra closed his eyes and tilted his head as if he were laying down to sleep.

Estin would come to me tonight – in my dreams.

The older woman waited inside as the guards closed the doors and shut us inside. I didn't fuss this time, and instead let her help me get ready for bed. I wanted to see Estin, but I wasn't sure I could bring myself to shut my eyes.

My friends were here but in grave danger. As if that wasn't enough, I was in the palace with at least one who wanted me dead and was shackled to the Emperor who owned me.

He was busy at present, but I dreaded the moment he found his hands idle and his curiosity piqued.

CHAPTER 18

Estin looks concerned when he turns and finds me standing in front of him. We are surrounded by fire, the flames hungrily eating Mother's curtains. They devour the furniture Father made when he and my mother were matched. They take and take and in their midst, we are smothered.

"I can't wake you. We need to talk."

Wringing my hands, I panic, the dreaded feelings from that night clawing to the surface once again. The fire destroyed everything around me, but didn't burn away the memory of that night. "Can we at least leave this house?" I pleaded.

"The dreamer controls the dream, Vayl." His eyes lock with mine and I realize how much I've missed their hue. He shakes his head. "I think the reason you repeat it is that there's something Rata wants or needs you to see."

My eyes widened in surprise. "She's sending them to me?"

He nods. "Other than you, she's the only thing I can feel when I enter your dreams. Your attention is always on your brother, your mom, and what you feel, but you need to look beyond them. Look with your heart, not your mind. Your mind can only bring up the fear you felt that day, and seeing through your fear is nearly impossible."

My family isn't here now. Only Estin, me, and Rata dwell in this fiery terror. I try to search for her with my eyes and my heart, but find only the oppressive heat. It presses water from my skin and beads upon my brow and lip, sliding down my back and between my breasts. We can't linger here forever. The beams will soon break.

"Where are you?" I ask, worried.

"Hidden in a servant's skin at the moment. Asra has moved us around many times to avoid suspicion. We're fine. Don't worry."

"And Grady?" I shout.

"He rode to gather all the other dragons."

I shook my head, fighting the panic that threatened to consume me. "You, Asra, and Indri are taking too great a risk. You need to leave. Meet Grady and return with the other dragons."

He leans in and raises his voice over the rapping flames. "You'd be alone, then. I would never leave you behind, and even if I gave such an order, they wouldn't listen."

I shook my head. "You're the Dragon. They respect you. They love you, Estin."

He gave a wistful smile. "It doesn't matter how much they care for me because they also care for you. You're one of us, now. I told you that dragons don't fight alone. I meant it."

My eyes dry and turn gritty as the moisture is wicked away. Every blink rakes uncomfortably. "I haven't seen Kirsi as far as I know," I admit. I haven't been here long, but I don't have the freedom to move about as I please, either.

"Neither have we. Indri and Asra are searching for her now."

My stomach drops. "They left the door?" If the Lion sees...

"Favian's men are there," Estin added. "They won't remember anything about being overtaken. Asra's magic is powerful. He and Indri have taken on different skins so they can move more freely. But we must leave this place as quickly as possible. I have a terrible feeling."

So do I.

"Favian is being overly kind and attentive to me," I reveal. "It seems out of character. He asked me to figure out who is killing the concubines and report back to him. He thinks Cassius is in danger."

"He wants you to report to him, but puts you in danger to gain the knowledge?" Anger flares in his eyes.

I flinch when a wooden table crashes to the floor, its legs eaten away until they couldn't bear weight anymore. Estin glances at the door. We have little time left. A dragon's scales might protect him from flame, but not from a house collapsing on top of him.

I search for Zaire, but he isn't here. His cot burns wildly behind Estin's back, but he doesn't seem bothered in the least.

"What else?" he asks quickly.

"Favian lied to Cassius about how long it took us to travel here. Favian used elvish magic to enchant the horses, but how did he get it?"

He shook his head and rubbed the back of his neck, but had no answers to give.

"I think he recognized the intervallim."

Estin went still. "I'm not sure you should wear it again, but I'm terrified for you to remove it."

I felt the same, unsure what to do or what trouble wearing it might bring for me or the matchmaker.

Suddenly, over his shoulder, I can see through the wall behind him and into the room where Father sleeps on his broken chair. I walk around him to get a closer look. Estin turns and walks with me. He sees it, too. He watches...

Father's arm jerks violently in his sleep. The motion upsets and knocks over his small table, sending the contents careening to the floor. A cup of water glugs onto the dirt floor, leaving a small pond that quickly soaks in. Beside the dark mud spot is an overturned candle holder and the candle it once held rolls slowly across the floor, still lit. The flame catches on Mother's curtains...

My hand presses against my mouth.

Father started the fire. He never admitted it, but he knew what he'd done. He... he wouldn't look at her when she died because he felt guilty. Ashamed.

He tries to stand quickly, but winces and clutches his back, falling into his chair again. He tries again, but his cane was propped up against that table and now lays on the floor, out of reach.

He has nothing to help him up.

A tear falls from my eye. I always wondered why he wouldn't speak of it – of her, but now I know it was an accident. A terrible, tragic accident of which he was the cause.

The wall solidifies again as flames spread over the spot we were just looking through. One of the beams overhead creaks. It burns and chars the wood, turning brittle and dry like the bark of a tree after lightning strikes and ignites it.

Suddenly, child-me stands in the middle of the room with her brother, who stands a head taller. They are small and afraid, but bravely plan to run out the door. The frame is on fire, but worse than the flames, the smoke chokes them. The girl makes a break for it, but when she gets near, Rata's hand emerges from the flames and catches hold of her thigh. When she screams, her shriek of pain drowns out the noise of a beam that crashes down just outside the door they were about to run through.

I gasp. Time slows.

Zaire pulls his sister back into the room, then huddles in the corner. Crying and in pain, the little girl runs and tucks herself beneath her cot. When her mother calls for her children, Zaire screams for her. She finds him first. She carries him away, leaping over the beam that would have crushed and killed both her children. Smoke blurs their forms.

Their mother returns and calls out for Vayl, who timidly reaches her tiny arm out from beneath the cot. Her mother spots her there and jumps that fallen beam, racing toward her through the flames.

Mother tucks her daughter's head into her neck and runs out of the room, leaping over that same beam again. The flames from it melt her silken dress against her legs.

"She saved me," I breathe. "Rata saved me that day."

Estin nodded. "The beam would've killed you if she hadn't stopped you right then."

I press a hand to my chest. "It would've killed Zaire, too."

It is a lot to take in all at once.

"Vayl –" Estin begins, "with Cassius being in the palace..." His brows draw in and he stumbles over his words.

I lift my hand and put a finger to his lips. The fire around us suddenly winks out. Gone is the whittled, charred memory of my childhood home. Instead, we stand in the soft sand among swaying palms, with Zairitus's endless sea before us and Trayton's glinting armor above.

Estin looks all around us, awestruck, then returns his gaze to mine. "You changed the dream!"

"Estin... I know Cassius is in the palace. I knew and weighed all the risks before agreeing to come here. But..."

"But what?" he quietly asks.

My heart pounds toward him. "Will you do one thing for me?"

His voice turns gravelly as his eyes search mine. "Of course."

The salty wind slides over us, cooling our skin. My hands find his. I hold them for a moment, memorizing the feel of them. My thumb brushes over the calloused and soft parts. The same light that dances upon the water shimmers in his eyes.

I step closer to him. Closer, until my dress meets his tunic. The cool sand slides between my toes. The breeze toys with my pale dress, tousling his hair and mine. I let go of his hands and let mine curve over his shoulders. One threads into the back of his hair while the other blazes a trail downward, settling between his shoulders.

His arm tightens around the small of my back. The other braces my spine and presses me completely against him. I hold him tight, then tilt my head so my lips hover over his.

It's selfish, but I want his lips to be the first ones to touch mine.

We're in an impossible situation, but in my dreams...

Maybe there, at least, we can be free.

I'm pulled toward him and him to me. And then...

I wake.

My heart startled and it took me a moment to remember where I was and recall the dream I'd just left behind. The flames in the hearth roared, casting warm light over the room and projecting a tall, elegant, human-shaped shadow on the wall though no one stood before me.

My heart pounded.

I wanted to whisper her name and see if it was Kirsi, but what if it wasn't? What if one of the favored twins had the ability to make themselves invisible?

Favian used magic to enchant the horses, which meant he knew how to harness it. Could the Lion be prowling at night?

The shadow slid slowly over the wall, soaked into the stone, and disappeared.

I threw the blankets off and rushed to the door, scaring the guards. They herded me back inside with their arms outstretched and their eyes wide at the sudden noise. I craned to look over their shoulders, but no one was in the hall.

I stepped back into my room and rested my back against the closed doors, my pulse thundering, and heard soft rustles on the other side. The guards were likely gesturing about how crazy I was. I closed my eyes for a moment, and when I opened them, something glinted on the floor in front of the hearth.

I padded across the room, quickly tugging on and tying a robe to better cover myself. My heart leapt into my throat when I saw the silver dragonfly hairpins scattered over the floor. The old woman who took them out of my hair had laid them neatly on the table next to my bedside before she left last night. She made sure I saw where she put them.

I picked them up one by one and clutched them in my hand, a delicate silver bouquet, and brought them back to the bedside table.

A few moments later, Favian burst through the door. I clutched the robe over my chest, over the necklace so he wouldn't see it again and question me further. His hair was wild, his eyes bleary. His pale shirt was untucked and his trousers unbuttoned. "What happened?" he demanded.

I tried to calm my breathing. "I don't know. I-I must have been dreaming. I thought I saw a shadow."

He took a step toward me. "A shadow?"

"I'm sure it was nothing," I tried to reassure him.

"What *exactly* is going on in here?" Cassius's deeper voice inquired from the doorway. Two soldiers flanked him with their swords drawn. He took note of the Lion and me, of our proximity, our mussed hair and clothes, of me clutching the robe tightly over my chest, and his features turned molten.

"I had a nightmare and screamed. Lord Favian must have heard and came to see what the commotion was about," I quickly explained.

Cassius looked at the guards who had been posted outside my doors. One began to make words with his hands and pointed to the hall, then back into the room. He gestured to Favian and silently but quickly relayed what happened from his point of view.

"Thank you for checking on Valor, brother," Cassius said, his voice calmer but still sharp.

The old woman servant wobbled back and forth as she entered with her head down, escorted by yet another soldier. She waited for her orders. "You will sleep in here with her until I command otherwise," the Emperor told her. He looked at the guards. "Bring a cot in for her – *now*."

Cassius was dressed in the same clothes he'd worn when he stepped into the palace. His wheat blonde hair wasn't snarled in the least. His eyes were still sharp shards of ice. He had not yet slept.

Cassius held my eyes for a beat before turning and leaving my suite. The guards waited for Favian to exit as well. He rubbed a hand over his jaw, then quickly left the room.

Servants moved a cot with neatly folded blankets piled at one end into the suite for the older woman, but I couldn't stomach her sleeping on the hard slab of wood. There was a thin mattress on top of the cot, but there might as well have been nothing for all the good it would do her. If I slept on it, I would ache in the morning. If she did, she would hardly be able to move.

The soldiers took up their positions outside the door again.

The woman shuffled over and removed the folded blankets from the end of the cot, preparing to spread them. I walked to her and placed a hand on the soft pile, then whispered, “What is your name?”

She motioned with one hand as if she was writing with a quill. I shook my head, embarrassed. “I can’t read.”

She pointed at her mouth. “I know what they did to you,” I told her.

Her eyes lit up. She laid the pile of blankets down and walked across the room to one of the vases that held the silky, white roses. She took one from the vase and held it up.

“Rose?”

She shook her head but pointed at the flower.

“Another flower, then.”

She nodded.

“Daisy?”

She shook her head again.

What flower could she have been named for? “Lily?”

Her eyes lit as she smiled. She pressed a hand to her chest. *Lily.*

“Thank you for trusting me with it,” I told her. “Lily, I don’t want you to sleep on that hard cot. The bed I have is larger than my house in the countryside was. I think we could each take an end and sleep comfortably.”

She swallowed and pointed to the door, then shook her head.

“They won’t come in without knocking, will they?” I asked.

She shrugged warily.

“I’ll ask them not to.” I started toward the door, but her hand touched my arm.

She shook her head, her eyes wide and frightened.

“If anyone comes in unannounced, I’ll tell them I had another nightmare and asked you to sleep nearer to me. Is that okay?”

Her eyes flicked to the door, then at the cot. She quickly made the bed and mussed the covers to make it look like she’d slept in it. I gave her my arm and led her to the plush bed I’d been given.

I threw a few more logs into both the hearths as Lily made herself a comfortable spot in the bed. As I did, I silently offered

Rata an apology. She hadn't caused the fire after all. It was all an accident.

I didn't remember the beam falling outside our door, but I was screaming so loudly, we must not have heard it.

In my heart, I was honest with the goddess of fire and light. I was still hurt that Mother had to die. I still ached for her, though I knew that if Rata had stopped Mother to keep *her* safe, the rest of us would have died in the blaze. Perhaps the goddess had a difficult choice to make and in the end felt that one of us dying was a better choice than three.

What Grady claimed was fair. All the other gods but Trayton were nearer than her. The mighty moon was no god, but a remnant of Rata's great body, cleaved off in the early days of the perpetual battle against the lurking, clever darkness. It gave light even as its fire slowly died. Rata was wounded, but still she fought. Her light was damaged, still it shone.

I hated her after Mother died. I'd feared her, thinking she sent the fire to our home that night and might one day send another. Despite it all, she kept me safe that night and every night since. In this place, I wasn't sure she'd be able to manage it. We were high on the mountain, closer to her than any human could get, yet her fiery rays couldn't melt the layers of ice upon the rock in this cold, desolate place.

I turned to face Lily.

She was so small, she nearly disappeared into the mattress, but her presence made me feel less alone. There was a kindness in her eyes. She was afraid to let that beacon shine too brightly in this darkened place, but I could see its spark and wanted nothing more than to free her, too. I didn't know her past, but her present wasn't what she deserved.

I wished Zaire's blade was tucked beneath my pillow. I wished I could free Lily even if I couldn't free Kirsi or myself.

Eventually, I fell asleep. Rata kept the fires burning throughout the night, slowly consuming the added split wood. And as far as I was aware, no more shadows entered my rooms that didn't belong.

The Dragon quietly watched the water flow in the murky stream near our home because my mind had conjured it. I wondered if he was truly in my dream or I'd conjured him, too.

I stepped toward him and my foot rustled some of the dried tufts of grass. He turned. I was about to tell him about the shadow, but he rushed to me, clutched my face in his hands, and crushed his lips to mine as if he couldn't wait another moment. And like Indri had described, time drifted away.

When we finally parted, he held me close to his chest. "I was so afraid something had happened to you."

"I'm worried for you, too. All of you," I told him, running my fingers over the scales in his armor.

He was frantic. "He's here. I thought we might have some time before..."

When we arrived at the palace and learned that Cassius was away, I thought the same thing. But Estin was right, Cassius was here. And things were infinitely more complicated now.

I insisted he take the intervallim necklace. The Lion suspected, if he didn't *know* what it was, and I needed to calm his suspicions. He pushed the stone out of the setting and placed it in my hand, telling me to keep it hidden but on me at all times, just in case I needed to urgently find him. In case there was no other path, this one would remain open.

He kissed me again and again, and I tucked the feeling he stirred in my heart and memorized the taste of him on my lips so that when Cassius came to me... I could go back to Estin in my mind.

Lily helped me don another white dress, this one with panels of fabric that crisscrossed my torso. In the front, the skirt fell just below the knee, but in the back, it grazed the ground at my heel.

She arranged my hair in delicate braids, then coiled them into a mass at the right side of my neck and pinned them into place. She even used the dragonflies that had littered the white tile floor last night.

When I slid on my slippers, she made the motion of eating and pointed to the door. "Can you come, too?"

She shook her head and pointed to the floor, telling me she would stay here. I wasn't sure when she'd be allowed to eat if not with me. I knocked upon the thick doors and the soldiers perked up on the opposite side, pushing them open.

"Good morning," I greeted. "I'm ready to break my fast."

They waved for me to follow them, and I soon learned that the concubines gathered in one large room to eat, choosing from a variety of foods sent in from the kitchens. The elegant hall, supported by impossibly tall columns and lined from ceiling to floor with gray-veined pale marble was abuzz with movement, laughter, and whispers.

Like the marks of a lion's claws, four long tables slashed the center of the room. Flanking them were smaller round ones that each seated at least ten. Though the room was busy and full, there were plenty of empty seats.

I imagined how the room would have looked before the first concubine was slain.

The women chattered amongst themselves until I wandered further in and they noticed me and the soldiers who flanked me. Favian had ordered them to stay with me and they would not disobey.

The room went quiet, leaving only the scrapes of utensils on plates and bowls. The women had doused themselves in their perfumes again, each wearing a scent distinctive from the rest.

I wondered how many women Cassius kept here, but didn't dare stop to further study them. Even so, I couldn't help noticing many pairs of pointed ears in my periphery as I walked to the front of the room where the various foods had been arranged. How were so many elvish women here? Had Kirsi trapped them all – for Cassius?

The women tracked my every movement as I glided down the line of tables to see what was offered. "Am I allowed to eat in my suite?" I whispered to the closest soldier, who woodenly nodded to affirm that it was okay.

I took one of everything so the others wouldn't know what my favorite foods were. The soldiers reluctantly helped me carry plates back to my room. I offered them something from what we'd collected, but they declined.

In my suite, Lily and I spread the bounty on a small table and ate together beside the warm fire.

I leaned in to whisper to her. "Lily, how are there so many elvish women here?"

She pursed her lips and shrugged, but I wasn't convinced she didn't know. Her eyes were haunted by a fearful gleam. Perhaps there was no way to communicate what knowledge she had.

"Are *all* of them elves?" I hadn't seen each one up close, but the women I'd been nearest to were certainly elvish.

Lily pointed at her ears, then at the door. *The soldiers are listening.* They might hear our conversation. I hadn't spoken loudly, but perhaps she was right. Or maybe it wasn't Favian's men she worried about, but the owner of the shadow that crept in last night. Either way, I didn't press her further.

It wasn't a simple thing to communicate, given the barrier between us. For a moment, my thoughts slid to the second of last night's dreams. I could still remember the feel of Estin's lips on mine, the way his fingers flexed and tightened on my waist, his earthy scent.

When Cassius came to me, if we didn't find Kirsi and manage to escape in time, I would remember Estin and carry my mind back to the creek's edge like Indri advised.

Why had my mind taken us there and not the beach?

It was as if I was tip-toeing closer and closer to home, the place I longed to be even though I was afraid to see it again. Things there had changed since I saw it last.

Zaire would be buried beneath the rock, beside our father.

There would be a mound not heaped by my own hands and sweat. The last person to see the inside of our house would have been the physician. It was hard to tell what shape it was in. Had he even bothered to rake away the blood or burn the mattress?

A servant entered the room and came to take away the plates. Favian arrived just as she scurried out. Lily stood behind me and bowed deeply as he approached, keeping her eyes fastidiously locked on the floor.

"Good morning, Valor," he greeted.

"Good morning, Lord Favian."

His eyes flicked to my empty neck, a pleased tilt curving his lips when he noticed the intervallim necklace was missing. He folded his hands behind his back. "I wondered if you'd like to take a walk around the palace? I can show you the library we spoke of last night."

I smiled graciously, though scorn unfurled in my belly. "That would be wonderful."

Lily remained frozen in the deep, uncomfortable bow until I strode across the room and joined the Lion, taking the arm of the man who murdered my brother and grievously wounded my father. For some reason, the very sight – even the smell of his mint soap – enraged me.

It was entirely possible to hate everything about someone. Favian was living proof.

Outside the room, Favian told his men to get some rest, informing them he would see to my safety for the time being. They left their positions the moment he gave the order. We followed them down the hall, but Favian slowed his steps so they were soon out of sight and earshot. We paused at the landing. I imagined him shoving me down them, tumbling head over foot and bashing every part of my body on the hard stair edges.

"Downstairs are the dining rooms, as well as a few parlors where you can relax." He waved toward the staircase. "The third through eighth floor are suites."

"Is mine the only suite on the second floor?" I asked, realizing I hadn't seen any activity on my floor since I'd arrived.

He started up the steps. “No, there are others. Yours is the only one occupied, though.”

“Did the other women move to higher floors?”

“The other women are dead,” he stated matter-of-factly. “The uppermost floors are occupied by those who’ve been here for quite some time. There is a hierarchy within the concubines, you see. The Emperor’s suite is on the eighth floor. He takes up the entire space.” When he saw I was following along, he continued, “The seventh is for those women who’ve been here the longest and have proven their loyalty. The hierarchy trickles down from there and ends with you, though you’ll be moving up soon enough. There are many rooms empty between yours and the women just above you in status.”

When we reached the third-floor landing, Favian steered us to the right and we walked down the hall. Two women passed us, one wearing a dress a deep shade of yellow, the color of cracked corn in autumn, the other wearing a shade reminiscent of the soft orange inside a cantaloupe. Both greeted Favian with a bow and as they held the position, I noticed their pointed ears.

My lips parted.

Favian gave a sideways glance and offered a smile, though he said nothing of their Thanian heritage.

Moments later we passed a trio of women. Each looked like they were born in Kaan’s varying regions, but all had pointed ears. I didn’t understand. The elves I’d seen from Thanias looked nothing like us. They were luminous and beautiful with sharp, distinctive features. There were no soft jawlines or freckles. They were tall and lithe and strong. There was nothing average or human about them. Could they all be gifted, having both human and elvish blood, but allowed to maintain their pointed lobes?

We approached two open double doors and entered a room lined floor-to-ceiling with varying bound books. Every spine was vibrant red or blue, green or gold. Plush couches were arranged throughout the space, centered around a large hearth where one could curl up and read the afternoon away.

I felt Rata in the fire. Now that I knew what her presence felt like from my dream last night, I could distinguish when she was part of the flame and when a fire was just that: *from* her but not *of* her. She wasn't there when Father upturned the table. She wasn't there as the flames spread throughout the house and into the room, but she came for me at the first sign that our home would buckle. She'd known Mother wasn't there yet and we were vulnerable...

Favian and I took a turn about the room. He pointed out the various subjects about which I could read, what books were his favorites – mostly books about strategy and warfare – and which ones Cassius preferred. His brother's tastes centered around history and fantasy, but included classical stories, folktales, and poetry. "My brother is a romantic, I'm afraid," he said with disdain.

He didn't assume I was illiterate, and I didn't offer that information for him to use against me later.

"You don't respect that about him?"

"I respect everything about my emperor," he quickly corrected.

I looked at him from my periphery. Was the Lion afraid of Cassius? "My mother loved to tell me stories when I was a girl, though my father would scold her and say they were a waste of time; that they set expectations people would never live up to."

"Let me guess – princes and princesses and happily ever afters?" he teased.

I smiled. "Of course."

"And did they do as your father claimed? Did they set expectations you'll never see met?"

"I'm no princess, my lord."

"Yet, you're possessed by an emperor. There is something romantic in that."

There was nothing romantic or beautiful about being a concubine and considered property, and knowing he thought that just punctuated how out of touch he was. Did he think this was an honor? A privilege?

He stopped at a window that stretched between bookcases

and overlooked a courtyard. Despite the cool morning, a few women were walking the stone paths between snowy garden plots. Unless magic allowed it, I wasn't sure how anything grew here at all.

"You can walk the courtyard at any time. It's guarded at all hours."

"Were any of the women from the second floor killed in the gardens?"

He straightened his back. "One."

"Then I'll remember not to entrust my safety to those guarding it."

The Lion didn't comment.

Pressing a finger to the glass, I leaned in to look closer at the ladies walking below us, noting the matching pointed tips of their ears with increasing bewilderment.

He led me around the rest of the vast library and then further down the hall where a smaller art room had been set up with canvases and paints in every color, along with palettes and smocks and brushes with fanned bristles and some with barely any.

Beyond it was a room with reams of fine fabric, threads, and needles. "If you're skilled with a needle, you can make your own clothes. Some prefer that to using the seamstresses we have."

I shook my head. "I can barely sew a button on."

He shrugged a shoulder. "You may have plenty of time to learn and perfect a craft."

Or you might have little, he implied but didn't say.

"Would you like to see the courtyard? If so, we could return to your suite to collect your cloak."

"I won't need one if we won't be out long," I told him. "I'd love to get some fresh air."

A staircase at the end of the hall took us back to the first floor and to one of three entrances that led to the courtyard, which was encased by a tall wall. The only things that could come in and out were the birds.

The raven circled overhead, then gave a loud caw and flew

away. Favian studied it as it flapped its wings, suspicion flaring in his eyes.

"It's far colder than I realized," I said to draw his attention from the raven. I rubbed my arms, aware of the stares of the women who walked the grounds.

"Of course. Let's go back inside where it's warm," Favian suggested, tearing his gaze from the sky.

Many of the doors that had been open this morning were now closed. There was no sound other than the occasional clang from the kitchens or the swish of soft fabric as one of the concubines moved from this place to that. "I assumed there would be children," I told the Lion, waiting to see what he might say.

"The apothecary will mix a tonic to prevent pregnancy. You'll have your first brought to you later today, actually." Favian stopped suddenly, a smile tugging at the corner of his lips. "There's one room I forgot to show you. You wouldn't want to be caught alone in it just yet, though."

My ribs tightened. "What sort of room?"

"Come along," he ordered, striding away and deftly ignoring my question.

Near the kitchens, a small stairwell wound into the earth with torches that lit the dim hallway at the bottom. The hallway ended at a set of double doors engraved with two crossed swords. He pushed them open. The room was lit as well as one without natural light could be. The torches were positioned closely together. The firelight gleamed on every piece of metal on the walls.

"This is the weapons room," he presented with relish, waving me inside. His gaze caught on the bows and quivers, the swords, the spindly daggers, the axes and maces... even slings hung from nails on the wall. "What are you most proficient with?"

"I'm not proficient with any, I'm afraid," I lied easily. "My father had one dagger and he sold it when the metal turned green. He couldn't afford more, and even if he could have, he wouldn't have taught me to wield them."

"He was a man of traditional values, then. One who believes women are weak and better suited to work about the house?"

I nodded. Father was traditional in many ways, but he couldn't have believed I was weak when I did everything he was no longer strong enough to do. I did Mother's work until Zaire left, and then I took on his, too.

Deep down, I think Father was afraid of my strength, and Mother's. That it might not only equal his, but surpass it.

The Lion walked to the wall and plucked a small bow similar in size to Indri's, then chose a quiver filled with a dozen pale-wood arrows. "Try to shoot the target," he dared, pointing at the far end of the room where a bale of hay had been painted with a red circle in its middle.

I shrank away. "I don't think I'd even get close."

"Then move closer," he challenged, holding the bow and one arrow out for me. When he waited for me to take it, I knew he wouldn't take no for an answer.

I took the bow and pretended to be awkward, fumbling with finding where to position my hands. Acting like I didn't know how to nock the arrow, I pretended to struggle pulling the heavy string back. Favian helped me, of course. He told me where to position the string near my mouth when I finally managed to wrench it back, and how to hold my breath so that the movement of my chest and arms didn't send the arrow flying off course.

"When you're ready and you think you've honed in on the circle, let it soar," he breathed into my ear, far too close for comfort. His hand pressed on my lower back. Instead of the warmth Estin's hand left, his chilled me to the bone.

I released the taut string and watched the arrow wobble, striking the stone wall far above the target and clattering to the floor.

"Perhaps the bow is not for you," he noted, amused. "What about a sword?"

Favian walked to the wall and tested the weight of two, deciding on one for me to hold. It was lightweight to him, but felt cumbersome and heavy to me. Metal raked metal as he slid his sword from the scabbard, firmly striking my blade.

I tightened my grip on the handle and prepared for the next time he struck. There was a strange glint in his eye when he did, almost like he was daring me to make a true move. To lash out. A feeling of dread washed over me.

He couldn't know who I was. Could he?

His offensive became bolder, his strikes heavier. I laughed. "I don't think I'm very good with a sword, either."

"The concubines are expected to protect the Emperor, which means you'll have to learn them all. I'll help teach you, if you'd like, when I visit."

I gave a false smile I hoped he thought was real. "That's very gracious, though I'm sure you're very busy."

"Oh, I am, but I'll make time for *you*, Valor."

I swallowed thickly as he took the sword from my hand and wildly threw it into the middle of the room.

"Let's try something else..." He looked at the wall of daggers and walked over to it, then plucked three blades and brought them to me, holding them by their sharp tips in one thumb and striking his palm with the handles. "Have you ever thrown a knife?"

I shook my head.

"No?"

"No," I told him, trying to keep my breath calm though my heart felt like it was beating out of my chest. He watched carefully. "Here. These blades are perfectly balanced. They're forged from elvish metal."

Elvish metal? My heart crashed against my chest.

Palm up, I waited to receive them, terrified he'd plunge one – or all of them – through my waiting hand. He slapped their handles into it instead. "Look at the craftsmanship. Was your father's blade as fine as these?"

My fingers tightened around them so they didn't fall. I looked at the blades casually, though every muscle in my body screamed to run.

In my hands were three daggers with intricately carved dragons on the blade...elvish blades belonging to Estin's assassins. "Father's blade was nothing like this," I told the Lion. "You have elvish blades and use their magic to bolster your horses. How did you procure such things?"

"Procure?" His brows lifted. "Oh, I suppose you could call it that. I *procured* these blades from three different elves. They were members of an assassin group who are intent on killing my brother."

"How would elves get through the wall's defenses?" I asked in mock horror.

"They didn't. They were here when it was built and the magic that sealed Thanias and its greedy queen out, hemmed them into Kaan. We quickly apprehended and imprisoned them after the war's end, but it seems they found the right person to use to further their cause..."

Ignoring his leading remark, I declared, "Well, they must have failed, if you have their knives."

His eyes searched mine. "They call themselves the dragons. And I don't have *all* their knives – yet."

"I'm sure they won't evade you – the Lion – for long."

"Indeed," he agreed, licking his bottom lip. "I thought it would be a shame to let such fine knives go to waste by leaving them to be scattered by whatever animals tore the elvish rubbish to pieces. Don't you think?"

"Did you steal their horses as well?" I asked innocently. "Is that how we could move like Ventus's breath?"

"You don't recognize these blades?" he pressed.

I pinched my brows. "Why would I recognize them? I'm neither elf nor assassin. Obviously," I laughed, gesturing to the fallen arrow and discarded sword.

"Throw one." It wasn't a suggestion, but a command. He pointed at the target across the room.

Instead of hurling it tip-first, I held two in my left hand and took the third by the handle, getting ready to heave the knife like a spear.

Favian finally laughed, his posture relaxing. "You can't throw it like that."

"What do you mean?"

He pinched the pointed tip between his thumb and forefinger, then launched it across the room. The blade flipped end over end until it lodged in the center of the red circle. If the bale could've bled, it would've soaked the floor all the way to our shoes.

I shook my head, my eyes wide and impressed. "I can't do *that.*"

He smiled, took the other two blades from me, and replaced them on the wall. He retrieved and replaced the sword and bow, tucked the arrow back into the quiver he'd pulled it from, and hung it back on the wall spike.

"You will want to avoid this room," he said conversationally as he walked back to me. "The other women are skilled with each of these weapons."

My eyes widened. "All of them?"

"Some embroider, some paint, and some read, but all fight, and all are proficient with every kind of weapon – just in case."

"Is our emperor in danger?"

He gave a sharp smile. "Of course he is. He holds the most power, and power is coveted above all else."

Rata's fires along the wall flared. The Lion noticed and his gaze flicked from the flames to me once more. "Does Rata favor you?" he asked.

"She does," I confirmed. We stopped outside the armory doors and he closed them behind us, the engraved blades meeting up once more. "Which of the gods has chosen the Lion of Kaan?" I offered a curious smile.

"Urit," he was quick to answer, tipping his chin up proudly. The god who struck the earth with his bolts and lit our paths in times of storm.

We approached the steps and he gestured for me to go first. "Do you wish another had claimed you?" he asked. Something dragged along the fabric of my skirt and I turned around in the tight stairwell, looking down and seeing that he held it between his fingers.

"I don't suppose I do. It wouldn't do any good to wish such a thing. Once a god claims you, another cannot. Besides, I appreciate the beauty of Trayton and Rata's story."

He let go of my skirt and his hand fell to his side once more. "Be careful of what stories you romanticize. Rata was cast away because she was a traitor to the other gods. Let's hope you don't share her treasonous heart."

CHAPTER 19

From a far corner in the dining hall, the Dragon's gaze tracked me and Favian as we walked past.

The first kiss Estin and I shared changed everything. Indri's warning took shape in the form of Estin, hiding within the skin of other men, watching me instead of searching for Kirsi among the faces of the other women he should have been sorting through.

He drew nearer and nearer, a moth to Rata's torch fire. I vowed to tell Asra to preoccupy him so he didn't get burned, and I chastised myself to avoid his lips and flee his touch. I wanted to protect him just as fervently, and if he came too close to me, someone would take note.

Favian and I walked in a part of the palace I had not yet seen as he escorted me to a room that held a long table with sturdy chairs placed all around it. Cassius sat beside a window, pinching his bottom lip between his thumb and forefinger. I lowered my head like the matchmaker had instructed.

The Emperor sat up and straightened his tunic when we approached. "Brother." Favian inclined his head respectfully. Cassius turned his attention to me. "Now that you've seen most of the palace, Vayl, I'm curious to learn what you think of it."

I raised my eyes and when he nodded, my head and voice followed. "It's exquisite. I grew up in a modest country home, so the matchmaker's certainly impressed me, but there is no comparison between the palace and anything else I've seen or heard of," I admitted.

"Not even in the tales you were told as a child?" Favian teased, earning a speculative look from his brother.

"No, my lord. Nothing comes remotely close to the grandeur of the golden palace."

"I hope you will appreciate it as much, years from now," Cassius said.

I wasn't sure whether he meant if I survived that long, or if he hoped I would still love my cage after such a long time being cloistered within it.

"I'm sure my feelings won't change," I responded graciously.

He nodded slowly. "We'll see." "I have to attend to a matter in the Imperial City," Cassius began, "but there is a separate matter to attend to here first. A servant was caught stealing extra portions of food."

It was a blow to the stomach. If someone was stealing food, it was because they or their family was hungry.

"I provide them what they need," he explained. "And they know better than to take from my tables. Unfortunately, when this happens, an example must be made. Do you understand?"

Fear and anger ripped through my veins, but I carefully schooled my features and unclenched my muscles as I replied, "Of course, Emperor."

"Good," he said, striding forward and taking hold of the hand still perched on his brother's forearm.

"Bring each of us a cloak," he barked.

Two servants appeared moments later, fastening one around the Emperor's neck and one around mine. He led me to the courtyard where a man stood shivering and naked in the snow. He'd been beaten.

Through swollen lids, he peered at us before falling to his knees and beginning to cry. "My Emperor, please have mercy!"

"Why did you steal from me?" Cassius asked, waiting patiently as the man quaked, whether from cold or fear I wasn't sure.

"Today is my daughter's birthday, and honey cakes are her favorite. I only wished to see her smile, my Emperor, and there were so many left uneaten after the ladies took their first meal."

Cassius pulled away from me and approached the man. "Do you feel ashamed?"

He cowered further. "Oh, yes, my Emperor. Terribly so."

"Will you ever steal again?"

"Never. I give you my word."

"What good is that?" Cassius asked cruelly. "When I brought you here, I told you what was expected, what was forbidden. You gave your word then, yet you broke it today. Why should I trust it again?"

"Sire, I promise, I'll –"

"Have you been properly punished?" Cassius interrupted, crouching before him.

The man reached out to touch him, to beg, when quick as a viper, Cassius pinned him to the ground by his neck. His face was buried in the thick, powdery snow. He held him there as the man thrashed, desperate to breathe. Muscles rippled beneath his pale, bruised skin.

Fixing a neutral mask across my face, I watched in revulsion as the man died before my eyes and asked the gods why... Why would they afford someone like Cassius so much power?

Lord Favian watched me carefully, searching for a chink in my armor, but my features remained impartial despite the horror I witnessed. Even so, I couldn't bring myself to titter and laugh or celebrate as the man's soul left him.

When the man finally stopped moving, Cassius released the man's neck and stood. I took the arm he proffered and walked inside with him.

"Weakness is not something an emperor can afford," he simply stated, as if such a statement justified murder.

~

I SPENT the afternoon in my room because the trembling in my hands had returned after witnessing Cassius callously kill the servant in the snow, and I didn't wish to roam the palace alone right now. Somehow, the whole event felt like a staged warning.

At some point, I drifted off to sleep. I dreamed of Estin, but when I woke, knew he hadn't used his magic to enter my subconscious. It was just my mind creating a world of escape.

In my dream, he spoke of the future and in doing so, freed me from the dread of the present and the sorrows of the past. He lay next to me atop the boulders in the crevice between the hills behind our home – the same ones Zaire told me to hide among if strangers came near.

There, in my dream, it was a sunny, warm spring day. Pink petals rained down upon us in a gentle, swirling curtain. They landed and built up around our forms, caught in the strands of our hair, and softened the mud-colored landscape.

"What do you dream of when you imagine a life you choose?" he asked, brushing petals from my lashes.

"Women have no choices."

"But if you did..." he pressed. "Do you see yourself standing beside the one you love, watching your children chase one another in the yard, sitting with them to read a story before bedtime and kissing your beloved when the little ones have fallen asleep?"

I smiled. "Is that your dream?"

"It is now," he earnestly replied.

"How did you imagine your future before?"

He thought for a moment. "Seeing my sister home. Taking charge of the Thanian armies. Ensuring that Cassius and Favian never harm another living soul."

"Those are all admirable dreams. Why the drastic change? The lives you describe couldn't be more different."

He gave a hopeful smile. "I want something greater. And what is greater than a simple, joyful, peaceful life with the ones I love?"

~

A SOLDIER SLIPPED into my room, startling me awake.

Asra!

He detached himself from the man, whispering magic that made the man's eyes dilate, then stare blankly into the room.

"What are you doing? Are you insane?" I hissed.

"I had to warn you," he explained. "I can't speak through him, so this was the only way. My magic will hold his mind for a moment while we speak," he said, raking a harried hand through his burgundy curls.

Dread coiled in the pit of my stomach. "What is it?"

"I can't find Indri."

"What?" I breathed.

"She's missing. Estin can't find her, either. We don't even sense her. I felt the moment my magic was removed from her, but there was nothing I could do." His chest rose and fell as he paced a tight line.

I looked down at my trembling hands. Asra's eyes followed. He clasped them and pressed his eyes closed. "Her magic isn't helping you anymore."

"Did you check the dungeons?" I asked, hating to even suggest he go back down there.

"Estin has. She's not there."

My stomach fluttered. "Where is he?"

"Hidden," he promised. *But then, Indri had been, too.*

I shook my head. "He's been getting too close to me. He has to fall back and remember why we're here."

"I'll do my best, but my brother is... attached to you, Vayl."

"Then I'll try to distance myself from him." I cursed. "I should have listened to Grady and the matchmaker."

"She warned you, too?" he asked, his head tilted.

I nodded and pressed my eyes closed. "It's Kirsi who has Indri, isn't it? Who else is powerful enough to sever her magic?"

"It must be." He scrubbed his hands down his face. "We

haven't been able to find her, which I don't understand. I sense Kirsi everywhere I turn, but I have yet to see her face."

"What is her gift, Asra?" I asked warily.

"She's our future queen," he answered. "No one knows for certain, but I *do* know that she's not limited to one gift like the rest of us are. Mother has them all. Kirsi might as well."

I gasped. "*All* the gifts?"

My gods. If Kirsi held power over the mind like Asra did and could blend herself in with anyone, she could be any one of the concubines. She could even be the Lion. It could've been her in the weapons room with me earlier today.

No, that was definitely him. He was hunting. Circling me, his prey. Waiting for me to slip up.

The possibilities were endless. If she could sift through dreams, had she been lurking in mine when I spoke to Estin? Is that why her shadow slid over my walls? Why she scattered my hair pins?

She knew they were here, which meant Cassius and Favian knew, just like I feared.

"This was a trap," I breathed, clutching my stomach. "She knew the moment we stepped foot inside these walls."

"But if that's true, then where is she?" he argued. "And why didn't she simply use her power to reveal us and tear us apart, if that's what she wished?" He threw his hands up and I felt his frustration to my marrow.

I told him of the shadow in my room, then of the dragonfly pins scattered on the floor. "Was that her?"

He cursed. "I don't know, but we need to leave."

"We can't just walk out of here, Asra, and we're not leaving without Indri or Lily," I insisted stubbornly.

His head cocked back. "Who's Lily?"

I pointed to a chair where Lily was sitting, completely asleep, snoring softly every so often. "I can't leave her here."

He released a long sigh. "I know your heart doesn't want to hear this, but she'd never survive the journey down the mountain."

I shook my head. "I could keep her warm. Rata will help me," I told him, hoping I didn't speak a lie. "Besides, how do you know we even have a chance to escape?" Not only was the palace guarded by soldiers hand-picked and trained by the Lion himself, but every concubine was a skilled fighter. How did we ever think we could waltz in here, free Kirsi, and stroll back out alive?

He swallowed thickly.

"You and Estin keep searching for Indri during dinner," I told him. "I'll provide a distraction."

"How?"

I picked at my gown and ignored his question.

"Asra, if you find Indri and you need to leave me here, Lily knows some secret passages we can take. There are stairs between the walls, halls that only servants pass through. We'll disguise ourselves and hide in a wagon, then meet you at the bottom of the mountain when we can. There's a little village by the river. Do you know it?"

When he didn't agree to my plan, Estin's words thundered in my mind. *Dragons never fight alone.*

"Be careful, Vayl."

"Don't worry about me. Go." I motioned to the soldier and he slid back into his body, using it to walk out the door undetected.

Lily finally stirred. She'd been sleeping since I returned from the execution. Her eyes lit when she saw me standing there. She slowly stood and walked across the room to where a cedar chest sat.

In my harried state, I hadn't noticed it had arrived, but now a sense of relief washed through me. "My things are here!"

She nodded encouragingly.

I lifted the latch and eased back the lid. On the left, white dresses were folded neatly, stacked on top of one another. On the right were the colorful pieces for *after*. Lily walked to the hanging rack and retrieved some extra hangers. She hung up the white gowns first, smoothing the wrinkles with her hand.

At the bottom of the box were lotions and salves. Perfumes.

Peacock feathers the girls had collected in the yard. I picked them up and ran my fingers over their soft plumes.

Just then, something thumped against the window. I looked up to find Estin's raven. It cawed loudly before flying away, soaring southward.

Estin was sending a message to his mother.

It was time to distract the Lion, the Emperor, and the shadow so we could locate Indri and escape this forsaken place.

I smelled each of the lotions and salves and soaps before lining them up beside the chest, then pushed on one side of the bottom, causing the opposite end to pop up. In the narrow compartment was a folded suit of elvish armor, its dragon scales shining. Beside it was a slender bundle of fabric, tightly wound.

Unraveling it took a moment, but soon, Zaire's blade lay in my palm.

Lily gasped behind me.

I looked over my shoulder and saw her covering her mouth with both hands. She shook her head, tears welling. Would she run and tell the Lion what I had? How did she know about the significance of the knife? Did she know about the dragons?

"It's okay," I soothed. "I won't hurt you." She pointed from me to the dragon on the blade. "My brother's," I told her. She studied my face and I saw the moment when recognition dawned on her features. "You knew him," I whispered. "You knew Zaire?"

Lily slowly inclined her head.

"Lord Favian wounded him, but he made it home to me before he died," I told her. She looked at the door, wary. "A friend of mine is here, but she's gone missing. She's not in the dungeon. Do you know where else she might be?"

Lily shook her head, but I could tell she thought it was too late for my friend.

Suddenly, a knock came at the door. I threw the dagger into the false bottom, gathered the fabric that had concealed it, and mussed the colorful dresses so they covered it all.

"Come in!" I yelled. Lily held a hanger in her hand, hovering nearby as if she was coming to collect another garment when the

Lion of Kaan stepped inside. I stood and gave a slight bow. “Lord Favian.”

His chin jutted toward the cedar chest. “I see you’re settling in.”

I smiled sweetly. “Yes. My handmaid is hanging the dresses the matchmaker sent for me now.”

Lily kept her head down, ever the dutiful servant.

“Cassius asked me to invite you to dine with him tonight.”

“How kind of him,” I replied. “Will all the concubines attend?”

“No, only the two of you, I believe.” He shifted his weight. “I should warn you not to get too attached to my charming brother, but I have a feeling you’ll soon be like all the others.”

“How is that?”

His cold blue eyes were always searching. “Completely enamored.”

“I’m afraid I don’t form attachments quickly.”

“No?” he asked playfully, but there was a sharp glint in the blue depths of his eyes and an icy warning in his tone.

I shook my head.

“I’ll be leaving at daybreak,” he said, crossing his arms.

“Oh?” I let the question linger. Why was he leaving and where would he go?

“It seems my brother wishes for me to remain near our army, which happens to be positioned in the south.”

“The entire army is there?”

He brushed a thumb over his bottom lip. “That’s right.” His head tilted to the side, his curiosity piqued by my line of questioning.

Without thinking, I challenged, “I felt what the elven army is capable of while staying with the matchmaker. Will they breach the wall?”

“I trust the magic will hold, and if for whatever reason it fails, the army will form lines along the wall.”

“If the elven army is as powerful as Cassius fears, could they not decimate the army as well?”

He smiled arrogantly. “We have an advantage.”

This game he was playing, dangling information like a ball of yarn in front of a curious kitten, was becoming tedious. Probably because I was the kitten.

"Dinner will be served when Rata is taken," he advised, then walked to the door. He glanced over his shoulder once more before closing it behind him. Outside, he instructed the soldiers to escort me to the small dining room where he and I shared a meal last night.

Lily wrung the green dress in her hands. She did not lift her head, but I noticed that her hands were shaking. I was well acquainted with the feeling of terror that influenced their quaking. I turned and hugged her tightly. She let the green gown fall to the floor and clung to me.

"Did *he* do this to you? Did he take your tongue?"

Her hands tightened on my back. She didn't have to nod. The way she held me was enough to confirm it. Her frail shoulders shook as she cried.

The only thing I could do was hold her and whisper a promise in her ear. "He will pay for what he's done. I swear it."

I LEFT my suite with Asra by my side, hiding within the soldier's silent form. He'd come back to guard me – a direct order from Estin.

Shadows slithered along the walls, though nothing was there to cast them. Rata had been pulled into the darkness once again and Trayton couldn't be seen. Urit's storm shrouded us. In the countryside, such full clouds would have dumped torrents of rain over the land. On the mountain, they drenched the land in fresh, powdery snow.

Lightning flashed outside the windows as we walked down the first-floor hallway, raising the hair on the back of my neck and arms. Urit was here, god of the Lion.

Rata was not. Flames flickered atop torches lining the stone walls, but I couldn't feel her in them and was terrified.

My dress was cut to draw the eye toward my chest. Cinched at the back, my waist felt impossibly tiny, and the skirt was slit so my thigh was exposed with each step. I needed to keep Cassius busy this evening to allow Estin and Asra time to find our friend, regardless of what *busy* might mean.

Lily had left my hair down and brushed it while it dried in front of the fire. She'd put some of the matchmaker's cherry-scented lotions on the ends to keep it sleek and dusted shimmering powder onto the apples of my cheeks before painting my lips a deep fuchsia.

Favian pushed off the wall across from the dining room when he heard us approaching. He'd bathed. The minty scent wafting from his skin almost made me sick. But it wasn't his wet hair or easy demeanor that gave me pause, it was that he wore his armor.

There was only one reason for him to don it – the Lion expected a fight.

"My brother will be here in a few moments," he told me.

His eyes raked down my dress and I yearned to take the orbs as payment for Lily's tongue. She would no longer speak or taste, so why should the Lion be allowed to see?

Zaire's blade was hidden in a sewn-in panel within my layers of skirts – the work of unimaginably sly, ingenious Sylvie. Lily had found the thick fabric sheath while tugging it down over my hips. When she inspected the other dresses, she noted that each had that convenient feature.

The Lion waved me inside the room, and I saw the table was arranged as it had been the night before. Tall candleholders branched from thick stems, their tapers sprouting and reaching to the sky. Beneath the candles were clear glass vases stuffed with pale roses like those wilting in my rooms, already brown at the petals' edges. Their scent mingled with Favian's mint in a sickening miasma.

Asra lingered outside the door, but listened for the slightest movement. The Lion pulled my chair out and gallantly scooted it in as I sat at the table. He did not sit, but stood behind my seat as a stark sentinel.

There were three settings instead of the two Favian promised earlier. My eyes slid from the third setting and I turned my head to see him, still standing behind me. My gaze caught on Favian's armor again.

"I am leaving tonight," he quietly advised. That explained why he'd donned his armor and set me slightly at ease.

I twisted to see him better. "Why before dawn?"

"There has been another attack on the wall."

I clutched my chest and he watched the motion.

"This was far more ferocious than the one you experienced in the matchmaker's care."

"How so?"

He licked his lips. "I won't trouble you with such ugly details. I will, however, be dining with you this evening before I leave. I hope my presence isn't a disappointment."

"Not at all," I told him quickly, pushing through my revulsion.

"Don't pretend that you feel comfortable with me, Valor. You carry constant tension in your shoulders in my presence." He slid around the side of my chair and let his hand settle between my shoulder blades. "Here."

"How do you know I don't always carry it?" I asked.

He made a non-committal hum, but didn't remove his hand from my skin.

His touch made me want to shudder. It made me want to curl my lip, reach into my skirts for Zaire's dragon dagger, and plunge the blade into his heart. Were its edges sharp enough to pierce the heart of the leather lion on his breast?

He left me to stand behind his own chair as footsteps pounded down the hall. Cassius entered the room and I stood and bowed my head to him, keeping my eyes on the floor as the matchmaker had instructed. Before I did, I noted that his hair was combed back and when it was wet, it was the exact color of wet sand. He didn't smell like mint, but like patchouli and something more familiar ... like the earth in the middle of a lightning storm.

I knew who I would see beneath the Emperor's skin when I

looked up, so I refused to. Fear pressed my head down further. *What is he thinking? Has he lost his mind?*

"Look at me, Valor," Cassius's voice demanded as he seated himself at the head of the table, to my left. I peered up into the face of the only elf I knew who smelled like petrichor, the earthy smell left when rain falls on dry soil. Asra had allowed him to usurp the Emperor's skin so perfectly and thoroughly that even the Lion couldn't see the Dragon lurking beneath his brother's surface.

Estin sat proudly the way Cassius did in the few moments I'd been in his presence. A simple snap of his finger sent a wave of movement rippling throughout the room. Servants poured water, uncorked and poured wine, brought out steaming loaves of bread, and a crisp dish of fresh butter. Golden plates of food appeared in front of us, their lids removed with a flourish as the servants bowed and quickly darted away.

The only way Estin would know Cassius well enough to imitate him in front of his own brother was because he'd spent plenty of time studying him. I hated even imagining the things he'd experienced at the hands of these two men.

I expected tension at the table the moment I realized Estin was there, but not derision. No, that was an arrow nocked by the Lion and aimed at his brother alone.

"Emperor," Favian began. "Brother. A terrible storm has settled over the mountaintop. Perhaps it is best that my men and I leave in the morning."

"The dauntless Lion fears a skiff of snow?" he taunted cruelly.

Favian's eyes flicked to mine for a moment. "Not at all. It would simply make travel easier."

"If you haven't the fortitude, Favian, I can appoint another to lead my army."

The Lion calmly sipped his water. "I do not fear the storm, or the difficulty it will place upon us."

"What *do* you fear?" Cassius asked, his voice as icy as the wind gusting against the windows and walls.

"Nothing, my emperor," Favian was quick to answer.

"Good." Estin pretended to be the Emperor, but the man in power was not so different from the mask he wore as the Dragon – fierce assassin and warrior fighting for the people of Thanias, searching for their imprisoned queen.

I didn't believe Kirsi would stay here of her own volition now that I'd seen the barest hints of what actually took place here. Could a woman born of the same mother as Estin and Asra truly love, or possess, a heart that admired what beat in the chests of these men?

"You've paid my newest concubine quite a lot of attention of late," Cassius casually noted, studying Favian as he sawed a bite of the fowl being served. My fork paused just shy of my lips.

Favian's face turned beet red and his nostrils flared. "Do you question my loyalty?"

"Only that you might wish to have her, instead of me adding her to the number here."

"Not at all," Favian said as if the matter bored him. "Though I'm curious to know how Satira and Gaila have reacted to her presence."

"They're not pleased, as you can imagine," Cassius admitted dryly.

Favian offered his brother a smile and his head swiveled toward me. "You saw them the night he arrived – the twins."

"Warriors, if I recall correctly."

"All the women here have earned that title, but the twins were born with spears in their hands and knives on their belts. They're an absolutely ferocious duo," Favian confirmed. "You'll meet them soon, I'm sure."

"You seem pleased at the very thought of strife between the women," I remarked, unable to bridle my tongue.

Favian's lips thinned. "The turmoil exists whether it pleases me or not."

"You must admit that you thrive upon discord, brother," Cassius noted, raising his wine glass to his lips. "He believes a series of unfortunate occurrences weren't accidents at all. His slanderous theories have upset many of my concubines."

"You and I both know I'm right," Favian said, quirking a brow at his emperor brother.

"Do I?" the Emperor challenged. Estin, through his skin, stared at me for a long moment. "Come here, Valor."

My brows kissed.

"Come here," he repeated more sternly.

I stood, my chair legs raking the floor, and took the few steps to stand at his side. He pushed his seat back and spread his powerful legs a little wider. "Sit," he ordered.

I stepped between them and let him tug me down onto his lap, aware of the warmth pouring off his skin, seeping into mine. Of how intimate the position was. Of Zaire's blade in my skirts. *This is Estin*, I reminded myself. He wouldn't hurt me. He would be proud that I'd armed myself.

"My brother has a new, troublesome theory," he said, brushing my hair over my shoulder. He held my eyes, the green and gray troubled behind the flesh that enshrouded him. He grinned at Favian. "You see, he's uncovered quite a treacherous scheme. He thinks you may play a role in it, but he has no evidence to prove or disprove your involvement."

He commanded the soldier, Asra. "Bring them in."

Asra motioned to someone outside and several sets of feet began to shuffle in the hall. Chains clinked together as prisoners were brought into the room. I sharply inhaled when I saw who walked into the room. The matchmaker's hair was disheveled. Her skin was grimy. Filthy. Her attendants, Sylvie included, were chained to her, and to one another. The only one absent from her entourage was the little thief...

She must have escaped or managed to evade them. Or perhaps she'd been sent out on an errand when the soldiers came for them. I didn't want to think of worse possibilities.

Estin's hand tightened on my side, keeping me tethered. My eyes flicked from his steady, regretful ones, to hers. "Matchmaker?" My voice shook.

The woman did not bow her head in shame, or in respect to

our emperor. She stood with her head high and her shoulders back. She stood the way Indri taught me to stand.

Favian stood slowly, menacingly. “Will you not greet the girl you so carefully procured for our emperor?”

The matchmaker peeled her lips open and a guttural noise emerged. Favian smiled triumphantly. “What’s the matter? Cat got your tongue?”

The matchmaker lunged toward him, the chains straining, but she couldn’t reach the Lion. The attendants began to cry, crystalline tears painting their cheeks, similar deep noises rising from their throats.

My gods. He’d taken all their tongues.

“See them to their new accommodations,” Favian ordered. Asra and the other soldier led them from the room. Each of their steps, every rattle of their chains fell in time with my pounding heart. Each cried out that I was a liar. A traitor. A snake.

“What did they do to warrant such a punishment?” I demanded.

Estin’s hand patted my side, then held it tightly once more. He was trying to steady me. Calm me. But how could I stay calm, given what I just witnessed?

Cassius spoke. “These women have conspired with a group that calls themselves dragons. Favian believes you know of them.”

“Dragons?” I said disgustedly, my eyes flicking to the Lion. “I only know what you told me about the knives in the weapons room.”

“And nothing more?” Cassius quietly asked.

“Absolutely nothing. What can I do to convince you of my innocence?”

“I desperately want to believe you,” Estin told me. His hand slid around my back and pulled me close so that my chest pressed against his. The other pushed hair out of my face, off my shoulders, then slid down my arm and back up. He took hold of my chin. “Prove you are mine and not theirs. That you value me more than their tongues, their lives.”

It was exactly what I imagined someone as arrogant and depraved as Cassius would say.

Frightfully so.

My heart thundered.

Indri warned me about this moment. That I would have to cheer as the tips of other elves' ears were cleaved. That I would have to become one of them in order to best them. I hadn't expected Estin to be here, beneath the Emperor's skin, making it fractionally easier for me despite how hard it must be to not be looking for his missing sister and friend.

I pressed my lips to his. Not tentatively. Not desperately. Confidently. As though he was what I wanted and all I wished for, that he was my choice and the kiss was, too. Cassius pulled away, his eyes searching mine. It was as if Estin was trapped in ice beneath the Emperor's surface and I was the only one who could melt it to reach him there.

I belonged to the goddess of fire and light. Of heat and flame.

My hands slid over his shoulders as he claimed my lips, softly this time, with a vulnerable tenderness I knew was Estin and not Cassius at all. And I melted the ice separating us and lost myself in the cool waters of his touch. His kiss. His heart.

In the hall, the matchmaker and her girls fought the soldiers. Chains rattled, grunts and cries erupted, there was scuffling and terror. They didn't want to go back into the dark bowels of this place, and who could blame them?

I wanted to run to them, to free my blade and defend them – even to the death.

But the noises of resistance faded as they descended into the dungeons.

"Can we please finish the meal before you feast upon her, brother?" Favian grumped. I peeled away from Estin – Cassius – and found that the Lion had taken his seat again, his chest heaving.

I turned my attention to him. "I went to the matchmaker because I had nothing and no one to care for me. It was my father's dying wish. He worried I would be all alone after he was gone. She and those girls helped me learn etiquette to please the Emperor and fitted me for gowns that might catch and hold his attention." A tear fell from my eye. "They taught me how to scrub myself clean because I was too dirty and ignorant to do it myself."

My voice cracked. Favian listened intently.

"They fed me and gave me a soft bed upon which to sleep," I told the men. "I saw no nefarious activity, and no men with blades like you showed me, Lord Favian. I just... grieved and ate and slept and learned."

"You say you saw no *men* with blades?" Estin asked with Cassius's voice.

"No, Emperor," I confirmed.

"What about *women*?" The Emperor cast a knowing glance at his Lion brother, who smirked.

I raised my chin. "Let me be clearer. I have seen no person with such a weapon. The matchmaker and her attendants were the only women I saw at her house. The only men were you, Lion, and the men on horseback waiting outside her gate for you."

Estin was insane, but brilliant. This... this was how he planned to find Indri. By taking over the most powerful man in Kaan and tricking the second most powerful into telling him everything.

CHAPTER 20

The windows rattled and Estin's hand tightened on my hip. "The storm is strengthening."

But his glance at Favian contradicted his words. Favian, who'd just taken his seat to finish his meal, took a large swallow of wine before standing once more.

Was it truly the storm pounding the palace walls, or was Kirsi weaker than she had been only days ago? The lightning bolts had ceased during dinner, and I didn't think this was thunder. I sensed this was Estin's mother and her army, sending a strong message to the Emperor and his men.

"I need to speak with you privately," Favian told his brother. "Now."

Cassius released me and called for a soldier. Estin's eyes promised he'd come to me soon. The Emperor walked me to the soldier and gave strict orders for him to see me safely back to my rooms and ensure I didn't leave them. Favian seemed satisfied.

The man Asra had overtaken earlier was in the hall, but Asra was not hiding within him now. What had happened to make him leave us? Did he see Indri? Kirsi? Or had he found a better opportunity in the flesh of another?

"Favian, meet me in my study." Cassius's cold voice slid over the walls.

A shadow moved across the stone wall in front of us, but no one was there.

The Lion strode from the room as the guard ushered me down the hall. Favian's heavy footsteps trailed away in the opposite direction.

Perhaps I was wrong about the elven assault. Lightning torched the sky beyond the window panes, occasionally flashing white light upon the walls and drenching us in viscous darkness between bolts.

Rata was still not in the flames that clung to the wall torches.

A second shadow crept along the wall ahead of us, slithering through the warm firelight. The soldier walked behind me up the staircase to the second floor. He startled, then flicked at his ear and brushed his forearm as if knocking something off it. Then he whimpered at something on the floor, jumping sideways and rushing down the hall, taking my arm and dragging me along with him.

As we approached the ornately carved door, the soldier abruptly stopped. A blank expression slid over his features and he turned and walked away.

A shiver spread up my spine.

Torchlight flickered over the engraving on the double doors of my suite. I sucked in an unsettled breath.

The carving had changed. The guarded doe still stood alert in the meadow. The beast still stood watching. Waiting. But hanging from the lowest branches of the tree he clung to were two serpents. With their forked tongues, they tasted the air.

The engraving came alive. The serpents bared their fangs at the gentle, cautious doe, protecting the beast.

More snakes appeared in the branches.

All twisted and writhed toward the innocent doe.

Something unseen brushed my ankle, dragging my skirt toward the door as if the delicate fabric was caught upon its scales. But whomever was doing this did not know the nature of dragons. At her home – in her cage – the matchmaker looked me in the eye and told me that dragons did not cower before lions. The same was true of serpents.

"If you have something to say to me, be brave enough to speak it instead of pathetically slithering about with vague, meaningless threats," I said boldly.

One of the silver-haired twins materialized in front of me, her smile wicked and feral.

A tug on my hair.

The second twin stood behind me. She released the strands she held. "And she thinks *we* are pathetic," the twin behind me purred. "Look at *her*."

"How could he possibly want *her*?" the woman in front of me agreed smugly.

"Yet he's responsible for smearing my lip paint," I taunted. I didn't care anything for Cassius, but couldn't reveal that to them any more than I wanted them to sense the fear pulsing through my heart.

"Satira!" the Emperor's voice boomed.

The twin in front of me turned to face the man we'd been speaking of. The Emperor had approached and none of us had heard him.

"Gaila," he greeted.

The twin behind me moved to stand with her sister, but a gleam in Gaila's deep brown eyes promised our conversation was far from over. Or perhaps that the first battle of the war between us had begun.

Both women wore red dresses that crossed from their waists to cover their breasts, tying behind their necks. I'd known one set of twin boys when Zaire and I were little. It was difficult to tell them apart, but one day I realized one was a smidge taller than the other and the taller brother was the thinner of the two. Studying these women, I could see no physical difference in them at all. Not a single beauty mark. There was no difference in their postures. Their heads even swiveled the same way, at the same pace, almost as if they shared a mind.

Perhaps they shared the same envious heart as well.

The Lion suspected them of killing the most recent concubines, but he didn't mention when the killings began or speak of their frequency. Did they all die at once, or did the women fall like dominoes? Why only the new ones? Why hadn't any of the women who'd been with Cassius longest been slain?

The Emperor stopped at my side. I glanced at him in my periphery, expecting Estin to still be wearing his skin, but the Dragon was not within Cassius now.

He bid the twins goodnight, kissed each on their crimson lips, and dismissed them. Both women glared in my direction before obeying and taking their leave. My heart drummed with each click of their retreating heels.

Where had Estin gone? Where were Asra and Indri? Had they found a way out?

The Emperor was quiet for a long moment. He watched the dark walls. No shadows slid along the warm glow between the torches.

His arm brushed mine when he walked past me to part the doors of my suite. Lily stood from where she'd been sitting on the end of her cot. She kept her head averted, wringing her hands nervously as she held them in front of her small frame.

"Leave us," Cassius ordered coldly.

Lily shuffled across the floor, her wispy gray hair lifting and falling with each step. When she went to close the door, her fearful eyes met mine. There was nothing she could do to help me now.

Zaire's blade felt heavier in my skirts.

I moved to stand near the hearth, as close to Rata as my past would permit.

Cassius moved with me, stopping when the toes of his boots were only inches from the toes of my slippers. I watched them, knowing he would soon order me to raise my head.

And then, he did exactly that.

I brought my chin up and craned my neck to meet his crystal blue stare. He began walking, circling me as a vulture might carrion. "My brother tells me we just had dinner. My stomach is full. The taste of wine lingers on my tongue. My left thigh is warmer than the other because he swears you sat upon it during our meal, yet... I don't recall a single moment of the evening or of the kiss my brother insists we shared."

The circle he walked tightened.

"Are you loyal to me, Valor?" he asked, stopping before me.

"*I* am, my emperor." It might get me killed, but the only way for me to keep the dragons safe was to cast doubt upon another, and there was only one other in the room with us tonight: the Lion himself.

His eyes narrowed. "Are you implying that someone is disloyal?"

I kept my back straight, my features neutral. "I have no tangible proof."

He crossed his arms over his broad chest. "Then provide the *in*tangible."

I hesitated, feigning fear.

"Valor – if it is my brother you suspect, know that he has left the palace."

"We both know that he has eyes all over Kaan."

Cassius nodded at that. "I admit you're right, and I know that you fear him." He reached up to brush his knuckles over my cheek. "But, little doc, what you need to consider in this moment is whether to fear the lion who prowls far away, in the middle of the plain, or the beast standing before you."

"If I am the doe, Favian the lion, and you the beast... who are the serpents?"

He smiled seductively. "They are as protective as they are fierce," he said proudly. "The concubines point their venom at any threat to me. If you prove your loyalty, I'll see you transformed from the fearful doe to a venomous snake. Even the mighty Lion wouldn't dare stand against you then. One is a formidable opponent for him, but together, these women could defeat great armies of men."

Had he offered the other new concubines the same? To be

transformed somehow? I recalled their pointed ears. Did Cassius have a way of transforming human women into elves?

"If they are such a force to be reckoned with, why not send them to the wall?" I breathed.

"Because there is no need. The elves will never break through the barrier that severs Kaan from Thanias. I only feign concern to get Favian out of my palace. He likes to stick his... *nose* where it doesn't belong."

"How are you so sure the wall will hold? I felt the power of the elves in Starcrest. They almost brought down the matchmaker's house. Their powerful blasts leveled entire buildings!" I gasped.

"Only the weak fall, little doe." The circling began again. "And I am confident in the magic that separates our kingdom from Thanias, because it is made by the serpents who protect me."

He was lying. The concubines didn't build the wall. Kirsi did. This was a test to see what I knew and would admit.

"Tell me of my brother's treachery and I will reward you unimaginably," he tempted, pausing once more to look me in the face.

"I only know that he lied to you about something simple. When you arrived at the palace and he told you of our journey, what he said was false. He used an enchantment on the horses. We left Starcrest one afternoon and reached the palace the next day at the same time."

He ticked his head back, then pinched his lip. "Why would he lie about something so mundane?" His eyes flicked to mine. "Why would he do that, Valor?"

"To hide a larger lie, perhaps."

"Ah, but which one?" he mused.

His eyes settled upon the bed and lingered there. "I have a few pesky issues to tend to, but I'll return as soon as I can."

I steeled my spine, fusing each vertebra together and forging them into the blade of a sharp, deadly sword. The Emperor turned and strode across the room. When he pushed through the double doors, I imagined shoving that blade through his back in exactly the same spot where my father had been pierced.

Lily was shaking when she reentered the suite. She pointed to the doors, then back at me. *He left, but he will come back*, she tried to say.

"I know."

She stopped in front of me and took my hands in hers as tears fell from her eyes.

"Don't cry for me, Lily." She clutched my hands tighter as a loud crash came from the sky. "That wasn't thunder," I breathed.

Cassius's deep voice boomed from someplace downstairs, quickly followed by more magic snapping in the air. It sizzled, stinging my nose and ringing in my ears.

"I need help," I told Lily. "Do I have a black gown? Something dark?" She nodded and moved quickly to pluck it from the back of the rack as I stripped off the white dress, transferring Zaire's knife over. "I need to find someone while the others are distracted. I don't want you to stay here, though. Is there somewhere you can go and hide?"

She nodded once and took my hand, squeezing it once for luck.

"I'll be careful. I promise."

She shooed me out the door Cassius had left unguarded. The unwatched door seemed too convenient, but I didn't have time to ponder Cassius's motives.

I begged Rata to douse her flames. Though she didn't put the torches out entirely, her flames did weaken. As the light they cast faded, the shadows lengthened. I tried to become one of them, using a staircase I'd seen but hadn't yet taken at the end of the hall farthest from my room. It twisted down to the first floor, into the earth where the weapons room was, then further down...

The dungeon announced itself with the unmistakable stench of blood and urine. The door to this floor wasn't guarded either; I had no idea why Cassius would neglect to post a watch down here, of all places. He couldn't have forgotten his prisoners so easily – unless the attack from Thanias was far more threatening than he let on.

I hurried past the door and peeked into each cell. They were nothing more than cages; iron bars joined to form walls, ceiling, and doors. The floors were dirt, and the stench worsened as I hurried down the row.

Then... something familiar. A flash of teal against a row of bars. She sat with her gaze fixed on the ground.

"Matchmaker!" I cried, dropping to my knees and clutching the bars. Her attendants perked up and moved to the doors of their own cages.

The matchmaker turned to me. Her knees tore the fine silk she wore as she pushed herself onto them. She caught hold of the bars and pulled herself upright with great effort. She struggled, guttural noises pouring from her throat and lips, trying to tell me something.

I shook my head. "I don't understand. I'm so sorry."

"Vayl," someone said from behind me. I turned to see the little thief crouched beside me. Her strawberry blonde hair was matted and filthy like the clothes she wore. "I managed to slip away when they first brought us here and have been watching. They know who you are and why you're here," she said. "They're using you as bait to find the Dragon."

She exchanged wary glances with the matchmaker, who pointed to the ceiling and the floors overhead. Was someone coming?

"She wants you to know it's not Cassius and Favian hunting him, using you as their lure."

The truth struck me like a fist to the stomach. "The concubines," I breathed.

The little thief nodded. "They move the pieces on this game board, despite what our foolish emperor and his cruel brother think," she confirmed.

"Where is Kirsi?" I asked her.

The little thief's brows met, confused. "None of them are called Kirsi."

That wasn't possible. Estin knew his sister. So did Asra and their mother. They knew her magic and felt it strengthening the Emperor and his walls. Such a feat as this had to come from her.

"Have you seen my friend Indri?"

The thief shook her head. "No, but there are levels lower than this one," she explained. "Sometimes we hear screaming from those unfortunate souls."

"What about Asra and Estin? Have they been here?"

She shook her head. "You should go before they come looking for you. They'll find you here."

Just then, calloused, meaty hands grabbed the back of my hair and jerked me to my feet. I hissed at the pain, shoving the little thief back into the shadows behind me. My eyes trained on the Lion of Kaan as he brought my face to his, taking care not to stray toward the girl I prayed would stay hidden.

"Does my brother have any idea where you are?"

"No," I answered, wincing as he tugged my hair harder, exposing my neck.

Favian hadn't left the palace, so either he deceived Cassius, or the Emperor had deceived me.

"Do you often seek out the treasonous, Valor?" he growled.

"I told you. These women helped me when no one else would," I gritted as he pulled my hair. I stood on the tips of my toes to keep him from tearing it out, but I felt strands being plucked from my scalp one by one.

"These women are *filth*. They work with greedy elven rubbish to try to overthrow Cassius and take Kaan for themselves. They helped you only because it furthered their cause, not because they cared."

My eyes met the matchmaker's. When she stood, her girls flanked her.

I sensed movement behind me. *The little thief...* She would be caught if she wasn't quiet.

I used to believe that because I was smaller, I had a disadvantage against someone larger, but the dragons taught me that the playing field could be evened if I fought unfairly. Dirty. Like I would if I was trying to best my brother and everything depended on it. And since everything *did* depend on it, I smashed my forehead into the Lion's nose and shoved him toward the cell of women. He cursed, clutched at his face, and blinked his eyes rapidly to clear away the tears, and maybe his vision.

Seizing upon his moment of weakness, the thief threw a handful of dirt into his eyes. He roared, throwing wild punches in every direction. I narrowly avoided them, but managed to put my shoulder into his belly and ram him against the cage, where the matchmaker curled her forearm around his throat and the girls restrained his arms and legs, all making horrible, grunting noises filled with rage and revenge.

I pulled Zaire's blade from its hidden sheath. The Lion's eyes were irritated and red, but they narrowed when he saw what I held. "Traitor *and* thief, I see."

"I'm neither. I'm not a traitor, because I owe no loyalty to a disgusting pig of an oppressor, and I didn't steal this blade. I inherited it from someone I deeply loved. Someone *you* took from me." I blinked away the tears that gathered. "My name is not Valor," I spat, approaching him carefully. "It is Vayl Halifex."

His eyes flared in recognition.

"My brother was Zaire Halifex. He was stronger than you ever gave him credit for, *Lion*. He made it all the way home to me after you wounded him, where he told me what you did to him and what you did to our father, Strieg Halifex. It was *your* blade that cut into my father's back so thoroughly you crippled him, and with that stroke, our family. I've lived long enough beneath your cruel hand, *and* your brother's."

His eyes flicked between the glinting knife blade and the rage that painted my face.

"I refuse to cower to you anymore. Do you know which god claimed my father, Lion? I hope *he* comes to personally collect your spirit for Oro, and that Urit allows it to wither in the god of the cursed dead's shadow fields."

Lightning fast, I stabbed him where Indri taught me would

kill fastest. He didn't deserve a swift death, but I wouldn't waste any more time on him.

He gasped. His eyes flared wide and his mouth gaped like a fish left out of water too long.

He was trying to say no. Silently begging me to recant the name of the god I'd just invoked.

He looked down at the spot where Zaire's blade was lodged in his chest. Luckily, the edges *were* sharp enough to pierce the thick leather the Lion wore.

If Urit agreed to send Favian's soul to Oro, he would forever be barred from the Solace. He would desiccate and fade into nothingness, as he deserved. The shadowed fields of Oro were reserved for the depraved. For men like the Lion. Like the Emperor.

Blood bubbled from Favian's throat and trickled from the corner of his mouth. When his knees weakened, the women released him and he slumped to the ground. I jerked Zaire's blade from his chest with a sickening squelch.

The air suddenly turned icy; colder than the snow and frigid winds that tore over this cursed mountain range. This was primeval, a chill so cold it felt hot against my skin. The blood on my blade froze.

I didn't see Oro, but I felt something familiar. Something comforting. And I knew that my father was there. He had heard me and went to his god with my plea before coming to personally collect the Lion's spirit.

Favian struggled for his final breaths. I crouched and whispered, "Perhaps the Lion should have been wise enough to know not to start a battle with a dragon."

He choked once more, then went still. His eyes fixed on something far beyond me. I hoped he saw my father's smiling face.

A moment later, Oro's frost and my father's presence receded. Though it wasn't hot in the dungeons before he came, their absence made it feel like a warm tide washed over us.

Rata's flames roared to life on their torches. I wished Trayton would hurry and free her. I could feel her reaching out for me now, yet too weak to catch hold.

The matchmaker pointed from Favian to the open cells down the corridor. If I left him where he lay, he would easily be discovered. A guard would come by at some point and they'd find their precious Lion dead.

"The cell doors at the end of the row are empty and unlocked," the little thief advised, coming to stand beside me.

The matchmaker nodded, panting rapidly and pressing a hand to her dirt-smeared brow.

I wiped my blade on Favian's trousers and secured it within my dress once more, then took him by the wrists and dragged him down the hall to one of the empty cells. The little thief helped as she could. He was heavy and moving him was slow, but we managed to maneuver him into the farthest cell and positioned him against the wall as if he was napping there. The hinges of the cell door squealed as I eased it shut.

I closed my eyes, wincing at the shrill sound, though it couldn't have been louder than our voices were only moments ago, mine sharply parrying the Lion's until, with Zaire's blade, I silenced his tongue for good.

I should have felt elated that he was dead, but right then I couldn't feel anything but fear. Even though we were finally free of Favian, there were many more obstacles to overcome before we tasted freedom.

The attendants reached through the bars to the dirt floor and disturbed it so dust settled over the bloody spot, concealing it from anyone who might walk in.

"They'll kill us all," I breathed, holding a shaking hand on my ribs. The shock of what I'd done was beginning to settle in. I didn't regret killing Favian. If anything, he deserved to die much sooner than he had. But I didn't want these women to pay the price for my actions.

"We helped you," the little thief asserted, translating for the matchmaker. "We helped you because we wanted to, and we will share the blame if it falls upon us. We are with you, dragon."

I shook my head, knowing I hadn't earned the title yet.

I took one of the torches down from the wall and brought it to the cell door, whispering to Rata. "I need your heat to free them."

Fire could melt and weaken. It consumed and made strong things brittle. It reduced many to ash. I held the torch near the door's hinges and Rata came to us. I felt her in the warmth that flooded the room. The burst of molten air was intense, and though she couldn't hold it for more than a few seconds, it was enough. The hinges were old and rusted and broke easily under the ardent heat of her flame.

The matchmaker and her attendants were set free from their cage.

The thief looked to their leader. "She says that we will do whatever you order. We want to be of further help."

I nodded, thinking quickly. "I need to find the other dragons – Indri, Asra, and Estin."

The matchmaker tried to speak.

The little thief smiled. "We will spread out and help you find them. There are many of us."

"Do you read minds?" I guessed of the small girl.

She smiled in response. "It is my gift. Theft is my talent."

"Good. Steal some clothes if you can. Blend yourselves in with the concubines. And if you see any chance to escape, take it."

CHAPTER 21

Two of the attendants dared to search the lower levels for the missing dragons.

The rest, including me and the matchmaker, climbed the stairs to the second floor, followed by the third, fourth, fifth, and sixth. At each level, one or two from our small party peeled slowly away to cloak themselves as best they could and aid in the search...until I was left alone with the matchmaker. I promised her I would be careful and asked her to promise the same. She gave a wary nod and walked down the seventh-floor hall.

The intervallim lay at the bottom of the sheath Zaire's blade occupied. I was contemplating whether to take both out and demand that it take me to Estin when I reached the Emperor's rooms.

Cassius's suite took up the entire eighth floor. Favian hadn't lied about that, at least. At the landing was a single set of double carved doors. There was no hallway, and only one torch burned dimly at either side.

Engraved in the wooden door, another scene emerged from the wood. A beast, split down the middle by the space between the doors. He stood with his arms crossed and his sharp teeth bared, flanked by the twins, Satira and Gaila.

Spread out in a deep V behind the trio was a likeness of every concubine, each peeking out from behind the one in front of her. I wondered if those who'd been killed were still in formation, or if the twins had used their magic to alter the image the way they had the doors to my room.

Hurried footsteps echoed behind me and Cassius's voice rose from one of the floors below. "I want her found. *Now*."

My stomach sank, knowing my absence had been noted.

I pushed the doors open and quietly slipped inside. Cassius, for all his darkness, appreciated light. Inside his rooms, the torches on the wall were positioned closely together. Candles flickered from his desk, the table at the entry, and a small dining table in the far corner. Faint, warm glowing light came from rooms I couldn't completely see into.

Slipping into the next room, I found that it was a study lined with books. Just then, someone clapped a hand over my mouth, stifling my scream.

"Shhh."

"Estin?" I spoke around his fingers. I hadn't needed the elvish intervallim after all.

"What are you *thinking* coming in here?" he rushed, hugging me to his chest.

"I'm looking for you and Asra and Indri. Cassius is ordering his men to search the halls as we speak. He's a couple floors below us, but I don't know how fast he'll move."

His hands drifted to rest on my arms. "Asra has gone missing, too. I can't find either of them anywhere. I don't know if they've been caught, or if Kirsi has used her power to push them back into Thanias...or worse. That's why I had to run. I was flung from Cassius and only had moments to escape."

"Kirsi wouldn't hurt Asra, would she?"

He blew out a tense breath, his eyes raking over the tomes lining the walls. "I honestly don't know. I never dreamed her capable of any of this."

"I killed Favian," I admitted quietly.

The Dragon went completely still. His lips parted as he searched my face. “Does Cassius know?”

“Not yet. I had the opportunity and I took it. I don’t regret it,” I insisted stubbornly.

He pressed his lips to mine. “Woman. Warrior... Dragon.”

After regaining my senses, I admitted, “The matchmaker and her attendants helped. They’re searching the palace now for the three of you.”

“We know. We found your little rats,” two throaty voices chimed in harmony. Satira and Gaila stepped into the room. “Cassius!” they shouted.

I drew Zaire’s knife at the same time Estin drew his sword. His grip suddenly failed him, as did his knees. His blade clattered to the floor a moment before he fell. I tried to catch him, but could do little more than cradle his head and keep it from banging on the floor.

Something silver gleamed at Satira’s foot.

My heart sank.

In trying to help Estin, I’d dropped Zaire’s dagger.

“We’ve been searching everywhere for you, Dragon,” the girls purred in unison. “If we had known a simple country girl could lure you here, we would have done so years ago.”

A thunderous noise crashed outside. The girls’ focus temporarily snapped to the window.

Footsteps pounded up the steps, through the sitting room, and into the study. Cassius appeared, flanked by concubines dressed in every color of the rainbow.

“The Dragon, Cassius,” Gaila presented grandly, stepping toward him with a proud, radiant smile painted on her crimson lips.

Cassius’s pale blue eyes sparkled, catching Rata’s firelight, along with Estin’s sword behind him. Satira moved Zaire’s dagger away, and two of the concubines collected our blades for him. The Emperor crouched in front of Estin, placing his elbows on his thighs. “*You* are the great Dragon who has evaded the Lion of

Kaan for so long? I remember you well. You are Kirsi's eldest brother."

"Yes, and I've come for my sister," he gritted. Some unseen force held him, crushing him.

"I believe she's made it quite clear that she does not wish to return to Thanias. Duty or none," Cassius smirked.

"Please," Estin spat, grunting beneath the pressure, "I only wish to speak to her."

"That is a lie, *Dragon*," the Emperor enunciated mockingly.

"It's not," Estin insisted. "Just let me see her and speak to her, then return my brother and friend, and I'll leave. I'll let Kirsi send me back across the wall and vow to never again look back to Kaan."

His eyes flicked to mine, reminding me I knew the way. He wanted me to leave Kaan for Thanias. I would have a home amongst the dragons.

The Emperor smiled. "You actually believe that after all the time, resources, and lives you've wasted, I would just let Kirsi send you home? That you'd suffer no consequences?"

More footsteps thundered down the hall, followed by two panting soldiers pushing into the room. "Sire... it's Favian."

The Emperor went still, his posture rigid. His icy stare sliced them so that the truth poured from their mouths. "We found his body in the dungeon. We were looking for some of the prisoners that escaped and discovered him in a cell."

The Emperor turned slowly to the Dragon.

Estin confessed at the same time I shouted, "I did it!"

Cassius's head swiveled to me and he gave a mirthless laugh. "*You*?"

I held my head high. "*I* killed him," I insisted.

The Emperor shook his head. "You must love this scoundrel very much to be willing to die for him," he said of Estin.

"I'm not saying it to protect him; I'm telling you that *I* was the one who killed him. I plunged my brother's blade into his heart as deeply as his leather armor would allow. Then, I beckoned Oro to come and drag him away."

The Emperor froze. “What did you say?”

“It was fitting, killing him with my brother’s knife. After all, it was the mighty Lion who cut him down. But it was even more fitting that my father come to reap him for Oro. His cruelty slowly killed my father, too. His name was Strieg Halifex. My brother was Zaire Halifex. Perhaps you remember them.”

The Emperor most certainly remembered them. He seethed at the mention of their names.

The look he gave me was one of pure hatred. “Bring them both to the throne room,” he commanded his soldiers.

Estin’s eyes met mine the instant before the soldiers hauled us from the room. Whatever magic held the Dragon seemed to suppress his movement. *He* couldn’t fight, but I wasn’t so restrained. I thrashed and bit and kicked until the guard balled up his fist and slammed it into my nose with a sickening crack. A blinding, overwhelming pain left me unable to do anything but focus on its pounding rhythm. My head swam and I saw stars as they dragged me down the steps. Blood dribbled from my chin, leaving crimson spots on the gleaming white tile.

I wished I could see the sky through the windows so I could watch as Trayton freed Rata. I wished she would burn this palace to the ground. It wouldn’t even matter if I was inside this time. I had a feeling neither of us would leave this mountain alive.

“Vayl!” Estin gritted. “Vayl. Don’t go to sleep.”

What was he talking about? I couldn’t sleep. There was too much pain. With each step, my knees and shins banged against the sharp floor. The guards were doing their best to wrench my arms out of their sockets. But my head... I couldn’t hold it up anymore.

CHAPTER 22

The first thing I noticed when I came to in the throne room was the shrill ringing in my ears. Maybe I should have fixated on the golden columns or the realistic painting of the afternoon sky on the ceiling, complete with birds soaring across the expanse in a great wave. Or the throne itself. It was solid, as if gold had been poured into a mold and left to cool.

With the first blink, that grand chair sat empty. When I blinked again, Cassius occupied it.

Countless concubines lined the dais behind him.

My ears still rang. My nose stung; part of the bridge had already swollen, going blissfully numb. It was definitely broken. The water that had been leaking from my eyes finally stopped and I could see clearly, despite the pain and the incessant ringing.

Cassius said something, but I couldn't hear him. His words were muffled. Muted.

I scanned the faces of each concubine and blinked. Despite their different hair, the varying tones of skin, the builds of their bodies... the eyes of each woman were the same stormy gray. The shape of their ears was similar, too. Broader than Indri's and a little more petite than Estin's and Asra's, but the same basic form.

My lips parted. He said I would know her by her smile...

Every woman in the room shared the smile of the Dragon and his brother. Every concubine, the twins included, was not only elvish... they were *her*.

Laughter bubbled out of my chest and I swayed on my knees. Blood coated my teeth and left sticky trails across my lips, chin, neck, and chest, staining my dress over my thighs and marring the pristine floor. When the guard who broke my nose curled his fingers as if he might do it again, my laughter evaporated.

"What's so funny?" Cassius demanded. I kept still. "Answer me."

My voice was scratchy. "It's just that we came here to find Kirsi, and she's been right here the whole time. All around us. Haven't you?" I asked the women.

Estin's brows pinched in confusion, thinking my head had been knocked harder than he realized.

I glanced at him. "They're all her. Look closely at their smiles and you'll see your own, Asra's, and your mother's."

How had I not seen it before? I knew the twins appeared identical, but realized all the concubines looked so alike now that I saw them gathered together, up close.

Estin's mouth gaped in surprise. "Kirsi? What have you done?"

"Nothing she didn't *offer* to do. Nothing she didn't *want* to do," Cassius interjected.

"I'm talking to my *sister*!" Estin shouted.

A soldier kicked him in the small of his back and he buckled forward, catching himself with his powerful arms.

The twins slithered forward. They started toward him and he gritted his teeth, panting as they pinned his chest to the floor. He was a bug beneath their fine slippers. Kirsi was far more powerful than I thought, yet as a person, she was weaker than anyone in the room.

"You don't deserve to touch him," I growled.

Their heads and attention swiveled to me. The tall windows behind the women revealed the impending dawn. Rata was so close. But was she more powerful than Kirsi? Could she protect us from the damned elvish queen? Rata had strengthened the torches to help the matchmaker and her girls escape the dungeons, but Kirsi was no rusted hinge.

"You don't deserve to be Queen of Thanias," I spat, "or to wield the power the gods bestowed upon you. Each one gave you a little, didn't they?" I ticked my head toward Cassius. "Does he know that if you continue to forsake your birthright, they'll strip it all away? Will he still want you if you are powerless?"

Suddenly interested, he straightened on the throne. "What is she talking about?"

The twins flanked me. Satira grabbed the back of my hair and pulled me up roughly.

"He doesn't love you. He doesn't want you," I seethed. "He only wants what you can offer him."

Rage contorted her lovely features. Satira curled her lip and gritted her teeth so hard, her jaw shook.

The truth came to me in a flash. "He wanted the girls he brought here, but you didn't like that so you became them for him, didn't you?"

She took my head between her delicate, deceptively strong hands. I fought her, but she was like iron, stronger than Grady.

"*That's* what weakened your magic," I continued. "You spread yourself too thin to become what he wanted. But don't you see? You were enough, Kirsi. It's *he* who's not worthy. Not you."

She squeezed my head and black spots danced in my vision. One jerk, and I would lay in a dead heap on the floor.

"Kirsi, no, please," Estin begged. "Don't hurt her. Please. I'll do anything." Gaila watched him carefully from where she pushed him down on the floor. He raised his hand, still trying to reach me. "Please."

"Did you watch when they sliced off the tips of his ears? Did you watch when they did the same to Asra?" I spat. "How could you allow it? For *him*?" I asked derisively. "He's *never* been worth it. But even though they were maimed as you watched and laughed, they never stopped looking for a way to save you."

A crystalline tear formed in Satira's eye. It spilled down her cheek at the same time a matching one slid down Gaila's.

"Your brothers love you, Kirsi. Cassius will only ever love himself."

The twins sniffled.

Slowly, Satira relaxed her grip on my head and stepped away.

With Kirsi's deep, agonizing cry, the windows that stretched from floor to ceiling exploded and Ventus's frigid wind gusted into the room, dragging in Zairitus's snow from every direction. The fire in the hearths roared, and in them, I felt Rata's strength. The mountain upon which the palace was situated shook with Yenza's displeasure. Clouds formed outside, spreading in dark plumes. Bolts of Urit's lightning flashed all around us, and from the city that was closer than I realized, Namina's animals of every kind brayed, bellowed, and bleated.

There was a great flash of light, followed by a thunderous noise. I covered my ears and huddled into a ball on the ground. Estin crawled to me and covered my body with his. He was free from the invisible bonds that had held him, but if Kirsi's rage wasn't contained, we would all perish on this mountaintop.

The noise suddenly stopped, but my ears still rang. The staggering power of the gods faded away, and when we raised our heads, there was only one woman standing between Cassius and us.

"Kirsi," Estin breathed.

Cassius stood and wormed his way toward us from behind his golden throne where he'd sought refuge during the tumult.

"Where is my youngest brother?" she asked in a voice that could freeze bone. "Where are his friends?"

"He's safe," Cassius, his palms up in supplication, quickly offered.

"Where?" Her icy voice carried through the hall, over the peak.

He dropped his hands to his sides. "Now, Kirsi. *You* were the one who taught me never to reveal all my secrets while some could still be valuable."

His soldiers who'd been standing in a cluster just inside the doors, rushed into the room to stand before their emperor. With one flick of her wrist, they fell like pieces swept across a game board. She would not move one stone at a time, but demolish them all.

Cassius snapped at her. "Have I not made you happy?"

"No!" she shrieked. "You gutted me over and over and over. You certainly have *not* made me happy!" She clutched her stomach, moving toward him. "I molded and shaped myself into what you wanted, every woman you craved, to please you. I shielded your empire, your armies, your golden palace. And what did you *ever* do for me?" She tilted her head, walking faster toward him.

He kept his eyes trained on her, matching her pace as he fled. But she suddenly moved like lightning, stopping before him. Her teeth lengthened into viper-like fangs and her eyes narrowed into slits. She lunged for his neck. He screamed and fought, writhing as her venom entered his flesh and poisoned his blood.

Kirsi dropped him on the ground and called for Oro, demanding that the god of the cursed dead come to collect Cassius himself.

Fractals of his frost, like footprints, spread over the tile from the open window pane to the Emperor's body when he came to collect Cassius's spirit. His feet crunched the shattered glass that littered the floor like diamonds. It was all I could do not to scream from the frigid air Oro brought. It was a thousand times colder than the air that howled in from the mountaintop.

This time, I couldn't feel Father at all. The god of the cursed dead himself had come to collect what Urit had given him.

Kirsi fell to her knees, placed her head on the ground, and wept. She begged for Oro not to take her spirit in penance for what she'd done.

Inwardly, I raged. Did she think she deserved her slate to be wiped clean after all she'd done?

Oro paused near Cassius's body, breathing in the cold that emanated from the Emperor's discarded corpse, and then retraced his steps. Frost covered my skin, lashes, and hair when the god of the cursed dead passed me the second time.

Rata soon melted them away, but the cold feeling didn't evaporate like the frost. It made me shiver to the bone.

Estin stood and carefully made his way to Kirsi, placing a hand on her shaking shoulder as he crouched beside his sister.

"How can you stand to even look at me after what I've done?" she asked him mournfully.

"Because I love you," he answered. "You're my sister, even if you lost your way."

She let him pull her into a hug. "You should have given up on me." Her eyes fell upon the harshly sawed curves of his ears and she covered her mouth in fresh horror. "It was like a dream. Like I was there, but it wasn't real." Her tear-filled eyes grew wide. "I killed them. I killed many, many women, Estin. I couldn't maintain the wall and split myself any further, so I..." Her anguished cry echoed over the room.

His hand on her back stilled. "I know. I know what you did."

"And still you came."

"Family is loyal."

Kirsi clutched her chest. "As are dragons," she sobbed. "We used to pretend to be them as children. Is that why you chose the emblem?"

With a nod, he offered a small smile and sat back on his haunches. "I won't promise there won't be repercussions for what you've done. I don't know what Mother will recommend you do to atone, but you should, Kirsi. You can't possibly make up for all you've done, but you should try."

She nodded, then wiped her cheeks dry. "I will."

Perhaps my anger clouded my opinion, but her apology felt insincere. I was convinced she was lying. That she remembered every moment of torture her brothers and their friends had endured. That she recalled laughing and drinking wine as she watched their ears being nailed to the mortar. Kirsi was willing to forsake everything – even herself – for Cassius. Why her brother actually believed she wasn't fully conscious of what happened, even while split into more women, was more than I could stomach.

I stood close to the hearth, close to Rata, and wrapped my arms around my middle to stave off the cold.

Kirsi's gray stare finally met mine. I wondered if she could see the flames writhing within me. Rata was in the hearth, but she was also in my heart.

"You didn't come here to give yourself to Cassius," Kirsi aimed at me, letting Estin help her up.

"No. I came here for me. For him," I told her, jutting my chin at Estin. "And for Asra, Indri, and Grady, and for countless dragons I haven't even met yet, but whose names I saw on the Lion's paper. He was hunting them to keep you under his thumb, and you let him." I couldn't keep the derision from my tone or maintain the neutral expression Indri had worked so hard to teach me while white-hot anger coursed through my veins.

"You came for me, too," she noted, a hint of hope still evident in her tone.

"No." I shook my head and glanced at Estin. "I didn't come for you. At one point, I thought I was, but I was wrong."

"What do you mean?" she asked.

"I came here thinking you might be innocent in all this, but you're not. And I don't believe you when you tell your brother it was all a dream for you, that it felt surreal." I swallowed thickly. "I think you were aware of every second, Kirsi."

I hated her.

"Estin's friends, his dragons, for years have fought all over Kaan to free you. Our friend Grady went to round them up. They're likely on the way up this dreadful slope to fight in your honor."

My hands began to shake, but this time, they didn't tremble like a frightened hare. They quaked, like the earth god moving mountains and casting them into Zairitus's turbulent sea. I moved toward her slowly.

"My brother died for you. Did you know that?" I kept my eyes locked on hers without blinking. "He befriended the dragons, helped them escape the dungeons where you and Cassius had penned them, then later overheard them talking about you. Favian caught him looking for you, fully intending to set you free, because he believed that the sister of such good men as Estin and Asra couldn't possibly be evil like the Emperor and his Lion brother. Zaire is dead because of you. He may not have died by your hand, but he died trying to save you when the last thing you wanted was to be saved."

Kirsi slowly stood, anger glinting in her eyes. Estin, in a low tone, spoke a warning to his sister. "She's a dragon, with every right to tell you what she's gone through, sister."

A small, rhythmic scuffing noise came from down the hall, slowly growing closer until at the doorway, a tiny woman with long, wispy gray hair peeked into the room.

"Lily?" I rushed to the old woman, then hugged her to me and cried. I wasn't sure where she'd hidden or if they'd found her and hurt her, but I was glad to see her.

I speared Kirsi with one more terrible glare before walking away. If I didn't leave the room, I would likely die at her hand when I attacked.

Estin jogged after us. "Where are you going?"

Instead of answering his question, I replied, "Go with Kirsi to find Indri and Asra."

"Where will you be?"

"I don't know yet," I lied. "I hope they're okay, Estin. My hands are shaking again, despite Indri's blessing." Tears filled my eyes. I had a horrid, ominous feeling in the pit of my stomach when I walked away from him.

GRADY FOUND me in the suite I'd been given. As I'd vowed earlier, I took a torch to the disgusting doors. They burnt from floor to ceiling, but the stone around them unfortunately put the fire out. He inspected the damage before striding further into the room.

He was a welcome sight for sore eyes.

"Sorry I wasn't here sooner. The dragons are all here, just in case..." he added sheepishly. "Estin filled me in on what happened. He also mentioned that you wanted to leave."

"*We* do," I told him, gesturing to Lily, who was asleep by the hearth. "I need help ensuring that she survives the journey."

"I can see to that," he promised quietly. "Can I ask why the sense of urgency?"

I could have told him I wanted to see where Zaire was buried, or that I wanted to travel to Sparrowing to find Mother's grave stone and see if the red hair ribbon I'd placed beneath it all those years ago might still be there. I could've claimed I needed to start healing and I couldn't do that in Kirsi's presence. All of that was true, but it wasn't the whole truth. The whole truth was...

"I can't stomach her, Grady. I know she's important to you all, but when I look at her, all I see is Zaire's face before he died. I know he gave his life for the dragons, but he gave it for her too, and she wasn't worth it."

He swallowed thickly, then pursed his lips and nodded rapidly. "Of course. I understand, Vayl."

"I'll wake her and we'll finish packing."

"Estin wanted me to ask you what you thought we should do now that Cassius is dead. No one knows yet. We can repair the palace and appoint someone new. You could choose them."

"And perpetuate another lineage of men who inherit the empire because of who their fathers are and not because they deserve to lead it?" I scoffed.

"He thought you might have ideas for a new way, a better way."

The blind beggar's words resurfaced. He'd told me this world was built to silence me and that I shouldn't let it. I retorted that perhaps it was time for a new world.

"I don't, but I know someone who might," I replied honestly, then told him where to find the blind beggar. "He has hope for a future I can't even envision. And if Kaan needs anything, it's that. It's him."

Grady inclined his head respectfully. "The matchmaker and

her attendants are ready to leave, but she'd like to see you before they do."

Lily stirred awake and her eyes widened when she saw Grady. "He's a friend," I told her. "He's safe. This is Grady, and he's going to take us home."

Lily patted her chest above her heart, letting me know she'd been afraid but was okay now.

I told her I needed to go see the matchmaker and her girls before they started home, and she pointed from the dresses to the trunk. I nodded. We were taking everything we could to sell in the towns so we could fix up my house and wouldn't starve this winter. It wasn't a glacieris stone, but what we could gather would have to sustain us for a very long time.

I followed Grady through the burnt-away doors of my suite to the first floor where men and women in elvish armor lined the walls. Near the golden entrance, the matchmaker waited in a fine, thick dress. Her attendants wore similar gowns, along with furs wrapped around their thinner frames.

During their short time here, they'd gained an understanding of what starving meant, but unless I cut my own tongue out, I'd never know how they felt now. How it would feel to be silenced the rest of their lives. Guilt washed over me in waves and settled heavily in my chest.

I should have seen the Lion's trap and told them to run the second he took me from her fine lawn. They could've taken the tunnels to the beach and hid on the shore. If they had, they would still have their tongues, their words, and their voices.

I approached the Heart Reader tentatively. "I'm sorry."

She held her back straight and regal. Her hair was perfectly combed back and arranged in a tight bun. In her hair, tiny silver dragonflies perched. Tears pricked at my eyes and throat when I saw them. She was still with me. Even though I had failed her.

"I'm so sorry!" my voice cracked. The next thing I knew, I was running to her and throwing my arms around her gaunt frame.

She patted my head and back, holding me tight as I cried. When she pulled away, she tipped my chin up to remind me of what she taught me, who I was, and who my mother imagined I might one day be. She clasped my hands and squeezed them before pointing to the doors. She was leaving.

I didn't blame her. I wanted out of this palace, too.

Away from Kirsi. I didn't trust her words, claiming that she'd suddenly come to her senses. That she wasn't evil like Cassius and Favian. Or that she still might not claim the empire as her own and slaughter us all.

The matchmaker stepped between her girls and led them past the gilded, solid doors, out into Rata's light.

"Keep them safe," I begged the goddess who'd claimed me.

Just then, there was movement on a small, winding staircase situated in the shadows behind the great doors. Asra's burgundy mop of hair emerged from the lowest levels of the dungeons, from rooms even Estin's horrid sister claimed she knew nothing about. Kirsi and Estin climbed the steps behind him.

Asra blinked when Rata's light hit his face. Eyes watering, he held up his arm to shield his eyes. His expression held hints of what haunted him and the merciful relief that it was all over.

Indri followed him. Alive, but only barely. She was listless, hollow.

Kirsi healed her body, but there was a blankness to her eyes, an unnerving quietness when she stepped from darkness into Rata's light behind her dragon and in front of his awful sister. I wondered if Kirsi's magic could heal her mind and spirit as well, because my beautiful, once vibrant friend seemed broken in ways I couldn't fully comprehend. Asra moved to stand beside her and held her hand, smoothing her hair back and assuring her again and again that she was safe and the ordeal was over.

Kirsi pushed the golden doors open with her magic and called upon a red-tailed hawk that came wheeling inside to perch on her arm. "I am safe. I am coming home," she told the fowl. "I am dropping the wall. Do not hurt the people of Kaan for what I have done." The hawk flew southward at her command, far faster than any bird should be able.

She watched me as she uttered those words, as if a single

sentence could forgive a lifetime of wrongdoing. As if her apology could bring Zaire back.

Estin once had asked me – what if Kirsi *was* responsible for orchestrating the entire affair and was responsible for all of it – even Zaire's death. What then?

Now we knew.

He had already forgiven her, but I wasn't capable of it. I may never be. Where that left us, I wasn't sure. All I knew was that he needed to see his sister home and mend their broken family. Everything else had to wait.

While he longed for closeness, I wanted to be as far away from Kirsi as possible. Everything I'd suppressed during my journey for vengeance came roaring back. It weighed heavily on my shoulders, pressing me hard to the earth. I was tired to my soul and wanted to go home.

I was taking Lily with me, and Indri, too, if she wanted to go.

I held a fur up to my elvish friend. She looked from the soft pelt to my face and back again. "Do you want to come home with me for a while? My house isn't nice. The floor is dirt, not tile. The roof leaks. The furniture isn't comfortable, and... well, I set fire to part of it before I left home. But we can get more. There's a stream nearby and a small garden, and with a quick stop along the way, we'll have a goat and our chickens back. It's not much, but you're welcome to share it with me for however long you want."

It *wasn't* much, but it was mine. It felt safe there, even if that sense of security was false.

My arm grew tired of holding the fur up. I was about to draw it back to my chest when Indri reached out and took it from me, wrapping it around her shoulders.

Asra's mouth fell open in shock. "You're going with them?"

Wordlessly, she moved to stand with us.

Asra was torn. He would go with her to the ends of the earth, I knew it. But he also had a duty to Thanias.

I gave him a wan smile. "You can come when you want, Asra. You're always welcome."

ASRA ESCORTED INDRI to the carriage and helped support Lily as she climbed the steps. "I'll come as soon as I check in with my mother," he vowed. "Only to spare you from her coming to find me."

Grady stood with the horses, ready to use his magic to take us safely home. The wheels of the carriage were spiked with iron to punch through the ice, though I wondered if they would even touch the ground once we were off.

Estin lingered nearby, the hardened mask of the Dragon settled onto his face. "So, you're just going to leave?" he asked.

"You need to see her home." I nodded toward Kirsi. She'd barely let Estin out of her sight and watched us even now. I recognized the feel of her stare. Whether she was one or many, it felt the same.

Not only did he need to see her home, he needed to make sure she stayed in Thanias.

"I don't know what to do. It feels like my heart is being torn in two," he whispered.

"Don't let it. I'm just... tired and I want to go home," I admitted. "I don't know what else to say. I need some time to work in my garden and sit by my family's graves and mourn them."

"You're still a dragon," he rasped, opening his arms to hold me.

I walked into them gratefully, then wrapped mine around his strong back and squeezed. "Thank you."

"I'll come to you when I can," he promised, kissing the side of my head. "But if you want to come to me..." He held out the intervallim necklace, the stone reset and ready if I chose to use it. I wouldn't. He knew it. I could see it in his eyes.

Zaire always said something similar when he left in the quiet of night – until the day he warned it might be a long time before he saw me again. Somehow, I think he knew that whatever he was being sent to the palace for would be the beginning of the end for him. As much as Favian suspected Zaire, Zaire was suspicious of the Lion, as well.

Did he sense that he'd been seen climbing back over the wall?

Did Favian escort him quickly to the palace in a failed attempt to lure the Dragon to the mountaintop to save his friend? Did the Lion even know the Dragon was Kirsi's brother all along?

No one would ever learn the full story behind how each of the game's players strategized their victories, though I couldn't discern that anyone had won. All lost in one way or another. All but Kirsi, who perhaps above all deserved to lose the most.

I climbed into the back of the carriage where Lily and Indri sat, still as statues, and watched as Estin fastened the door. His eyes met mine before he nodded to Grady. The gentle giant climbed onto the driver's seat of the carriage and whispered to the horses before we smoothly glided forward.

Grady's magic, granted by Namina herself, was stronger than whatever enchantment Favian had placed upon the horses that carried me up the mountain the first time, because we reached the base, which was bracketed around a vibrant blue river and nestled beside that quaint stony village, faster than I ever imagined. The horses might as well have sprouted wings and flown us down into the valley.

"Won't be long now!" Grady shouted. He was covered head to toe in fur that was matted in snow and ice, but he seemed jubilant.

Lily nodded off on the bench across from me and Indri, seemingly content with the next chapter of her life, while my friend stared blankly out the window for a long time, speechless. Eventually, she slumped to the side and fell asleep, too.

It was a small victory to feel comfortable enough to shut your mind off for a time. I held no such victory. I sat up and held vigil with Grady, watching and listening.

We made it to Starcrest in record time, then veered right down the muddy road that led into the countryside where farm after farm dotted the land. Winter still hadn't gripped the land here yet. Autumn held it at bay, chilly but not frozen like we soon would be.

When the farms became sparser, he stopped the carriage and

asked me to join him on the bench up front. "Where'd you say your livestock is?"

"At the physician's house. I can show you. It's not far from here."

THE PHYSICIAN OPENED his door on the warm, sunny afternoon I returned and glanced from me to the Imperial carriage and the behemoth Grady guiding the elvish horses that pulled it. "Vayl! What a surprise. You look well."

He lied well.

"I need my livestock back."

"O-of course," he stuttered, obviously flummoxed at the sudden reappearance of someone he thought he'd never see again. "They're in pens in the back yard."

I nodded. "Set them free and guide them to the road. They'll follow us home."

The physician's brows pinched. "Vayl, I'm not sure they'll just..."

But I'd already turned around, leaving him with his argument and assumptions, and climbed back up to sit beside Grady. We waited until he freed the chickens and dragged the stubborn goat by his horns into the muddy road. Once Grady whispered to them, they all clucked and plodded along behind the carriage, following us home without complaint.

Ventus's wind toyed with the physician's gray, wiry hair as he stood at the end of his lawn, scratching his head as we ambled away. His wife spied from the window.

CHAPTER 23

Grady helped us get settled. First, he located the half-rotted ladder Zaire had propped behind our house and fixed the rungs that wouldn't bear his weight before climbing up to look at the roof. He couldn't find a hole, per se, but a part of the thatching could use sprucing up. So... he spruced.

Fortunately for us, Lily had friends in the palace. Friends who loaded our chests full of finery we wouldn't need but could sell, as well as adding a chest full of salt-cured ham, wheels of aged cheese, and more smoked, leathery venison than we could eat in a year into the carriage. Rolling around the bottom of another chest were potatoes and carrots. They'd hurriedly gathered what they could into aprons and sent anything that would keep.

The physician had done an admirable job straightening the house after my hasty departure. After wiping dust from the flat surfaces, I stocked the larder and tried to make the house feel like a home for my friends. Once everything was unloaded from the carriage, I brought buckets of water from the stream and set about making a fire to prepare dinner.

Indri lay in my cot, curled up and facing the wall. Tonight, Lily would take Zaire's.

Grady worked quietly and watched me closely, likely the

Dragon's unnecessary orders. He cared for us and worried for Indri.

Eventually, when the shock of the ordeal wore off, I hoped she would speak. But until then, I would feed her as best I could, offer her my bed, and let her soul take the rest it so desperately needed.

~

Lily quietly raised her spoon and sipped the last of her broth from the rich stew I'd made. She lifted her bowl and smiled at me from across the fire.

She fussed when I told her where she'd be sleeping, insisting she'd take the floor, but I wouldn't have it and my stubbornness won out over hers. After eating, she made her way inside and laid down on Zaire's cot.

Grady studied the boulder as he ate a second bowl. His gaze briefly roamed both graves, the heaped, freshly dug earth richer than the packed soil around it.

"Father is on the left," I told him, remembering exactly where I'd dug and placed him. "Zaire lays on the right."

"I'm sorry, Vayl," he told me sincerely.

"You lost him, too."

He shook his head. "That's not what I meant. I meant that I'm sorry you went through all that because of Kirsi. Estin told me what you said to her. You had every right to."

My eyes welled. I knew I did, but hearing it from Grady brought the emotion surging to the surface. "What hurts most is that the gods still favor her."

He cleared his throat, spooning more stew into his bowl. "I'm sorry for that, too. They shouldn't." Grady's eyes settled on Rata's flames as the fire I'd built flickered between us. "I'll leave at first light to find the man you told me about. The blind man."

I nodded. "Good. Would you check on the matchmaker and her girls, too?"

"Of course."

"I'm not sure if she'd be willing to step foot anywhere near the palace again, but if she went with the blind man, I wager the two could create a world I might one day be happy to live in."

He inclined his head. "I'll ask, and I'll send them your love. I'll come back as soon as I see it through, Vayl."

"I know you need to check on them," I told him.

He shook his head. "Estin and Asra can handle themselves. I want to see what's going on for my peace of mind."

I couldn't help but think that finding Kirsi – the thing that once united the dragons – at last was what broke the warriors apart. What purpose did they have now that she was found, made whole, and returned to her people?

"Did he order you to stay with us?"

"I told him where I was going," Grady admitted. "He didn't try to dissuade me, but he didn't order me to come with you." He stirred the stew with his spoon. "I am your friend, Vayl. And Indri's. And now Lily's. Friends, like dragons, stick together. Friends look out for one another in good times and in bad." He was quiet for a moment before adding, "He cares for you, you know."

Through the pain in my heart, I tried to smile. Estin did, on some level, care for me. I cared for him, too. But his familial duty and our circumstances had diverted our paths.

I missed his steady presence. Even though my friends were here, the world was a little lonelier with Estin gone.

I slept outside beneath Trayton's scales and beside Rata's flames, across the fire from Grady, who snored loud enough to keep any predators at bay if the fire wasn't a great enough deterrent.

I did not allow myself to dream.

GRADY LEFT the following morning to collect the blind beggar and ask if he would, for a time at least, help figure out a better path for our empire. Our friend told us he would return as soon as he was able, once things were settled. I wondered if he knew that might take a lifetime.

Indri stepped outside after he was gone. She sat by the fire we used to stave off the bite of late autumn, but she did not speak.

When Lily woke and joined us, I rambled for hours... about the boulder and how it fell, explaining the graves. I pointed to where the stream was and described the swimming hole and how deep it seemed when Zaire and I were kids. I told them how I remembered our mother and our home in Sparrowing, and how I missed the smell of it. It always smelled sweet. The house here didn't smell sweet at all, but with the honey and sugar we would now be able to buy, maybe it would.

I reminisced about coming here and admitted how scared I was and how for weeks, I worried that we might catch the plague from the dead man whose house we stole and whose body we burned. How I cried every night because we'd left Mother and her stone behind. I told them about the red ribbon I left behind to mark her grave and asked if they thought it would have rotted by now.

I brought out the ream of red silk Zaire brought for me and told her about the dress I wanted to make with it. The cool softness calmed me and somehow made me feel close to my brother despite the insurmountable distance between us now.

Describing the game of Scales was complicated, but Lily seemed to understand. I even brought the dusty game board out from beneath Zaire's cot and she and I tried to play a game; her armies were represented with pale stones, mine with dark.

I wondered if Indri listened as I chattered, but Lily did. She listened until my droning made her lids droop and her chin fall.

In the afternoon, with Rata watching from above, the three of us napped.

After being tense with fear for so long, it felt strange to relax.

That evening, I prepared a small dinner for us and described how Mother would sing when she worked in her garden, and how when she wasn't singing, she hummed. How butterflies loved to perch on her arms or clothes. How I'd only seen a dragonfly a few times before arriving at the matchmaker's home. I told them of the lie I had to quickly spin for Favian when he took the pin from my hair and questioned me about it.

Until that moment, he never indicated that he suspected me, or her, of treason, but in hindsight, I wondered if in that moment, with that tiny silver hair trinket, I ignited his suspicion.

Before I went to feed him and the chickens, I told the women how the goat loved, and never rammed, my mother. I didn't remember him bothering me at all until one day, Mother set me on his back. I clung to his neck, but I didn't ride long before sliding off and hitting the ground. That was the moment the old goat turned on me. He'd hated me since I tried riding him like a pony, and he would hate me until he or I died. Maybe even longer than that.

Sitting beside Indri, Lily watched to see if the goat would chase me. He did not disappoint. His disdain for me seemed to have grown since leaving him with the physician. Perhaps he'd finally been happy with him, although the doctor would've slaughtered him to fill his table.

My friend and former handmaid smiled when I returned, winded and with my heart quickened from running away from his horns, climbing the fence just in time to avoid his thick skull ramming into the rung my foot had just pushed off. The old woman raised her brows and pointed at the goat as if to say he almost got me, and he might get me yet.

I laughed and thanked the goddess Namina for holding him back so I could escape.

In late autumn, darkness came sooner and snatched Rata away before we were ready to retire, but I still felt her in the flames by which we warmed ourselves. Lily yawned and stretched her back, her worried stare cutting to Indri, then pointed toward the house. She was going to sleep.

The sounds of shuffling feet over the floor led into the bedroom I once shared with Zaire. Then, they went quiet as Lily settled into his bed.

Indri stared blankly at the flames. I wasn't sure if she saw them at all, or was visualizing far worse things tucked into the dark corners of her mind.

"My father, now a servant of Oro, took Favian's spirit to the shadow fields. He'll wither and fade among his kind there," I told her.

Her eyes finally moved to mine and held.

"I did what you showed me. I plunged the knife through the lion's head on his armor, right through its mouth, and pierced his heart," I admitted. "Before I left, I didn't know I would be strong enough to do it, but you taught me well."

She watched me, something dark glittering within her gaze.

"What did he do to you?" I whispered. "I would kill him again if I could."

Her lips peeled apart. "He didn't touch me. None of them did. Kirsi was the one who tortured us." Her voice was scratchy from disuse. "Our cells were pitch black. We couldn't see her, but we sensed her. You know the feeling you get when you're alone and something evil creeps too close?"

My mouth twisted in a grimace. "I know the feel of Kirsi's attention."

Indri's lower lip quivered. Tears finally fell. "She used her magic to delve into my mind so all I could see was Asra being flayed, then dismembered piece by piece. All I could hear was his screaming. I think he saw the same thing of me, but felt his sister's magic and realized it was all an illusion. That it was all her doing and I was fine. But it didn't feel like that to me."

"You love him."

She nodded once. When she did, the iridescent shells lining her braids clinked together. Then she looked back to the fire and was quiet again.

She sat with me as I made another dinner of stew, then slowly sipped her portion, though with more energy than I'd seen her display since she'd stepped into the carriage with me. I promised her I would figure out something else to cook before tomorrow. Then she went inside and laid down in my cot again, facing the wall.

Alone for the first time, I sat with Rata. I was grateful Indri had spoken, that she'd listened all day even when she likely wanted to tell me to stop my incessant prattling.

The only way to move forward was one day, one step at a time.

~

WHEN I HEARD footsteps approach in the darkness, I slid Zaire's blade from the makeshift sheath on my hip. These footsteps sounded like his had when he came home, so much so that a knot the size of my fist formed in my throat. *But Zaire is dead*, I reminded myself, glancing at his grave.

It wasn't my brother who emerged from the darkness. It was Asra.

"Where is she? How is she?" he asked, crushing me to his chest when I stood to tuck my blade away.

"She'll be better now that you're here." I told him as he pulled away, then pointed to the door. "Her room is through the door and to the right. She's sleeping."

"Should I wake her?" he asked, worried.

"You should absolutely wake her, Asra. I think you're the only one who truly can."

He blinked rapidly, nodded, and walked to the door.

I overheard his soft, reassuring words when he told her he loved her for the first time and vowed to never again leave her. He had already told his mother and Estin as much.

I tugged my makeshift blanket – which I'd torn from the windows behind where Father's chair used to sit – tighter around my shoulders and took solace in Rata's flame.

~

WEEKS PASSED and the bitter chill of winter settled over the farmlands, chasing us inside but for the vital tasks that drove us outside: drawing water to drink and wash with, or bringing in firewood from the stack I'd made earlier in the year.

Long ago, Zaire had taught me how to fell trees. How to divide them and cut the divided parts into smaller and easier-handled pieces of wood. How to stack them so they dried out for winter. He told me never to let the stack dwindle too far, though I hadn't exactly mastered that part yet.

Asra helped, felling and cutting and replenishing as we emptied our stacks. Daily, Asra reassured Indri that he, and she, were fine and that all would be okay from now on.

The morning after he returned, Asra told me Estin was helping in Thanias and he would come when he could.

For days, I looked for him. In the fields that lay across the stream from our home, at the spot where the muddy, rutted road bent toward Starcrest, in the now-bare trees on the hills behind the house.

Days turned into weeks.

Every time I walked past his grave, I remembered the words Father had shared with me more times than I could count. *Only the weak and ignorant dared hope. Hoping for something you don't have is a fruitless waste of time.*

When I was younger, Zaire told me not to listen to him, that he only told us those things in an effort to instill an appreciation for what we had, a sense of gratefulness instead of covetousness. But maybe his insight was broader than that. Maybe it *was* silly to put your hope in others.

CHAPTER 24

More weeks passed, and finally Grady returned with news that while the blind beggar had been shocked to receive such a nomination, he humbly accepted it and promptly ordered the demolition of the golden palace on the peak.

He and the matchmaker planned to establish a council where an odd number of people, nominated by the citizens of Kaan, might govern her fairly. He had renamed the Imperial City to Mountain's Bluff and planned to invite this new council to send a single representative to meet with him in Starcrest, which was where the council would convene. It was a city central to all the provinces and close enough to Thanias that if contact with the elvish kingdom was necessary, it would be easy enough to initiate.

Grady's roof repairs held. When it snowed, the cold didn't seep in from the rotten corner of the roof. When it melted, the water didn't race across the ceiling beams or trickle down the walls.

Grady brought provisions in his wagon, pulled by two head of cattle. Father couldn't afford to keep such large beasts, but Grady promised we would have plenty for them and promised he could always get more – animals, feed, whatever we needed. He brought bales of hay for them and the goats. Bags of cracked corn for the chickens. Barrels of wheat and oats for us to make bread. Bags of finely ground flour. Jars of jellies and jams and honey to coat the bread. Corked containers of cinnamon, sugar, dried rosemary, and vanilla bean pods.

He brought an arsenal as well. Spears, bows taller than I was, arrows with ends threaded with fine feathers, swords, knives, axes, and a mace, then hung it all on the walls. The fact that they weren't bare anymore made my heart fill up a little. Crammed in our tiny home, there was a lot of love.

We had become a small family.

Lily doted on each of us, offering mother-like smiles and encouraging pats on the back. Indri had slowly come back, too. She laughed, talked, and mostly loved. Asra only left her side when necessary, and that was a rare occasion.

Winter's chill fled into the mountains, giving way to more of Rata's warmth and light. The buds on the flowering trees that dotted the countryside began to bud. Soon, the pink blossoms erupted and rained over the land in scented waves.

I DIPPED my bucket into the stream and watched as the gurgling water filled it, hauling it out when it was full. Then I filled the second, losing track of the chore to watch pink petals gather on the water's surface and ride down the currents, clumping together only to separate or sink.

Walking back up the path that led to home, pink blossoms outlined everything. Pathways, homes, fences, rocks. It coated the roof, gathered around the boulder's base, and painted Father and Zaire's graves.

The petals stuck in the sills of windows. They built into tufts inside the chicken's coop and goat's pen. The hills beyond the house blushed.

I was about to set the buckets down to admire it all when

someone rushed toward me, taking the weight and bucket handles from my hands. “Thank y—” I started to say, but my words caught in my throat. I thought it was Asra who’d come to help me, but it was Estin. My heart crashed against my chest.

He sat the buckets down.

So many thoughts rushed through me until I couldn’t discern where one stopped and the other began. Questions. Like where had he been and what happened? Why he was here? Why now?

Observations. Like how handsome he looked. How looking upon his face was better than all the pink petals in the world.

Then there were the things I longed to say but never would. Like *please don’t leave again. Please stay.*

I wondered if he could feel them raging inside me. “Are you really here?” was all I managed, blinking away tears that built and flooded over.

He didn’t answer with words.

Instead, he wrapped his strong arms around my back, lifted my feet from the ground, and kissed me like it was all he’d thought about for a season.

His kiss was everything.

His lips were soft, but pressed hard against mine. His strong hands braced my back, crushing me to him in the gentlest way. The way he sighed and kept kissing me, even as he slowly let my feet touch the ground again, melted my damaged heart.

“I missed you,” he told me. “I missed you every moment of every day.”

“Where have you been?” I asked.

His green-gray eyes met mine. “I went to the temple and begged the gods to strip my sister of her power and title, and then asked them to give both to someone more deserving.”

My lips parted in surprise, though I didn’t dare to hope. “And?”

“They did,” he said breathlessly.

“Who did they choose?”

“A new queen. She’s kind and fair. My mother has been

working with her, teaching her to use the powers she's been entrusted with."

Ventus's wind picked up dozens of blushing petals and spun them around us in a gentle cyclone. Estin watched, transfixed, with a smile on his lips. That smile fell away as the wind died.

"Mother kept me close, hoping that the new queen and I would form a bond." He smiled. "But I told her my heart belonged to another...though I didn't know how entirely it was yours until we were apart." I swallowed thickly as he brushed my tangled hair from where it caught on my eyelashes. "What is a dragon without fire in his lungs?"

I smiled and kissed him until our friends emerged, playfully groaning.

Indri snuggled into Asra's embrace and Lily smiled from the doorway.

Grady grinned as he slapped a meaty palm over his eyes. "Are we going to have to build separate houses now?"

CHAPTER 25

Pink petals caught on Estin's eyelids. They built around him, outlining his form as he lay next to me atop the boulders perched in the crevice between the hills that undulated behind our home – the same ones Zaire once told me to hide among if strangers came near.

It was sunny and warm and perfect... except that he hadn't said a word since leading me here.

I was growing worried.

Sometimes, when what you needed to say might hurt someone, you put it off to give yourself time to build the strength and courage to inflict the wound.

He propped his head up with his hand and watched me. "What do you dream of when you imagine a life you choose?" he asked, gently brushing petals from my lashes.

My breath caught. "What?"

"When you imagine a future, a life of your choosing, what do you envision?" he rephrased.

This was exactly how it unfolded in my dream, but I was sure he hadn't been there with me. Even so...

"Women have no choices," I rasped.

"But if you did..." he pressed. "Do you see yourself standing beside the one you love, watching your children chase one another in the yard, sitting with them to read a story before bedtime and kissing your beloved when the little ones have fallen asleep?"

I smiled, wondering if somehow Rata had sent me a small glimpse of my future when I dreamed of this moment in the heart of the palace. Was it she who reminded me that this life he spoke of was worth fighting for? "Why, is that *your* dream?"

"It is now," he earnestly replied.

"What did you used to imagine for your future?"

He thought for a moment. "Seeing my sister home. Taking charge of the Thanian armies. Seeing that Cassius and Favian never harm another living soul."

"Those are all admirable dreams. Why the drastic change? The lives you describe couldn't be more different."

He gave a hopeful smile. "I want something greater. And what is greater than a simple, joyful, peaceful life with the ones I love?"

I leaned forward and kissed him. His hand found the curve of my waist, then settled on my hip. "Elves are free to pair themselves, but such a decision is not to be taken lightly. Once bound, they cannot be unbound."

"You told me that once, reminding me that love does not perish with death..."

His lashes fluttered. "I... I wonder, if given the choice, you might choose me, Vayl."

"I already have," I admitted.

We came together beneath Rata's brilliant warm light in a storm of pink petals, in a place only marginally safer than Estin's arms. We chose each other, and a simple, joyful existence I prayed would be peaceful.

"What happened with Kirsi when her powers were stripped away?"

Estin scrubbed a hand down his face as we sat near the fire.

Asra, Indri, Grady, and Lily waited to hear as well. "She flew into a rage," he answered.

Unease slithered through my friends almost as a tangible force. "Where is she now? How can you trust her not to harm the new queen?"

"She wouldn't have the power to," Estin said confidently. "She has been imprisoned for her crimes against your people and mine... in a cell next to our father's."

I gasped. "Your *father*?"

He nodded. "It wasn't until after Asra was born that Mother caught him searching for a way to siphon her power away so he could rule the kingdom." He looked at me with a curious expression. "Did you assume he was dead?"

"You never spoke of him, so yes."

He grinned. "One day, you will hear so much of my stories you will have grown tired of me repeating them. Until then, enjoy them afresh."

"When that happens, we'll just have to make new ones. I hate being bored."

Estin kissed me and because we were mates, even Grady did not groan.

I'd been practicing my stitches on a sturdy piece of fabric and was mentally preparing myself to sew a dress from the red bolt of fabric my brother had given me. Until now, I'd been too afraid to ruin it. But if I left it on the ream, the red would rot away, and I couldn't let that happen either. I searched everywhere I could think of for it one drizzly morning, but couldn't find it anywhere.

Neither Asra nor Indri knew where it was. Grady had no idea what I was talking about, and Lily just shrugged when I asked her.

"Estin needs you to go to him," Asra said breezily from just outside.

"Where is he?" I called.

"He said you'll need to use your intervallim."

My hands stilled, ceasing their search within one of the many crates lining the walls. I touched a hand to my necklace and thought of him.

The elvish stone took me to him in an instant, though it took me a moment to realize where we stood. I appeared in the middle of a field of fragrant wildflowers that Yenza saw fit to grow and whose blossoms Ventus's breath swayed. We stood beside a giant willow, its weeping branches bending sideways in the gentle wind. A large striped rock stood between me and Estin.

Black, white, and gray, in that order.

I covered my mouth as tears filled my eyes. He'd found Mother's grave. My knees gave out and Estin fell with me, holding me steady as grief and relief battled for dominion. It had been so long since I'd seen this place. This rock.

When I finally calmed, he wordlessly lifted one side of the marker. Crushed into the soil so hard that an impression had been made in the earth, brittle with age, was my favorite red hair ribbon.

I let my fingers glide over it one time before asking that he cover it again. There could have been other black, white, and gray striped rocks. Other willows. But there was no other ribbon. This was my mother's resting place.

ESTIN SAT with me beside her grave for as long as I needed, then helped me clear debris from Mother's final resting place. He stood with me as I placed the wildflower bouquet I'd collected atop the soil for her and Yenza to enjoy. And when I told him I was ready to leave, he reminded me that I could come back any time, and he would be honored to return with me.

When he brought out his intervallim crystal and reached for my hand, we were swept to a familiar garden where peacocks strolled and dragonflies buzzed. The matchmaker was already waiting with a pleased smile on her face. Estin thanked her for all she'd done to establish the council and for working with Edmund, the man I knew only as the blind beggar, to make a better way of life for the citizens of the new Republic of Kaan.

I barely let him finish before running to her and throwing my arms around her neck once more. She hugged and rocked me, smoothing a hand down the back of my hair. And when we released one another, she placed a hand over her heart. I mimicked the motion to tell her I loved her, too.

Sylvie stepped out of the house, holding a folded piece of … red fabric.

Estin smiled. "When I told the matchmaker and her attendants about your brother's final gift, Sylvie wanted to help make it special for you."

A knot formed in my throat. I placed my hand back on my heart for the tiny seamstress. After what happened to them because of me, I was surprised any of them would ever want to see me again, let alone do something as extraordinary as this.

Sylvie slowly unfolded the dress so I could take in her delicate hand-stitching. She'd embroidered dragons, cherry blossom trees, peacocks, and even dragonflies over the red silk.

"There aren't enough words to thank you properly, Sylvie."

She simply smiled and extended her handiwork to my grateful hands.

The intervallim took us home. And as I lay next to Estin beside the hearth that night, listening to Rata's flames snap and dance in the darkness to remind us she was still fighting, helping Trayton in his endeavor, my heart was finally full. Through the heartache and strife, the tender joy of finding and being separated from love, and all the terrible things from my past, I realized all my steps led me to this beautiful future I never would've imagined, much less have the courage to create.

I couldn't help but wonder if this... this was what my mother envisioned for me.

ACKNOWLEDGMENTS

I'm ever thankful to God for his mercy and blessings in my life. I thank my family for their constant encouragement, my friends for their support, and fans for loving my characters and stories as much as I do.

Thanks to Alessia of AC Graphics for designing this beautiful custom cover that captures the heart of this twisted retelling of Mulan, a woman with a fierce spirit despite her circumstances.

Thanks to Stacy Sanford for waving her magic red pen over my manuscript and polishing it until it is as sharp as Vayl's dagger.

Thanks to Steffani Christensen for illustrating Estin and Vayl in all their beautiful ferocity. I love your creativity and working with you is effortless.

Thanks to Cristie Alleman and Amber Garcia for reading this book before anyone else and helping me make the story better. I appreciate your time and keen eyes.

Thanks to A. Lonergan and Elle Madison for reading this while it was still being polished and offering endorsements to make her soar.

Lastly, thanks to you, the reader. Whether you're a member of the Bondtourage Reader Group, social media follower, or this is your first Bond book, I appreciate you reading the story that bled from my soul.

ABOUT THE AUTHOR

Casey L. Bond lives on a rural farm in West Virginia with her husband and their two beautiful daughters.

She writes phoenixes – gloriously flawed and morally gray characters that fiercely rise from the ashes of their circumstances.

She thinks thunderstorms are better than coffee and that watching a meteor shower is the closest thing to magic you might ever see.

She's a firm believer that every amazing book needs a world you want to wrap yourself in, a character you want to win, and a love you would fight for.

ALSO BY CASEY L. BOND

HOUSE OF ECLIPSES & HOUSE OF WOLVES

The Shadows of Neverland Duet: The Last Lost Girl & The First Lost Boy

When Wishes Bleed & The Omen of Stones

Gravebriar

With Shield and Ink and Bone

Things That Should Stay Buried

The Fairy Tales: Riches to Rags, Savage Beauty, Unlocked, & Brutal Curse

Glamour of Midnight

The High Stakes Saga: High Stakes, High Seas, High Society, High Noon, & High Treason

The Harvest Saga: Reap, Resist, & Reclaim

The Keeper of Crows Duology: Keeper of Crows & Keeper of Souls

The Frenzy Series: Frenzy, Frantic, Frequency, Friction, Fraud, & Forever Frenzy

www.ingramcontent.com/pod-product-compliance
Lightning Source LLC
Chambersburg PA
CBHW020339310726
48979CB00015B/2432/J

* 9 7 8 1 0 8 8 0 1 4 5 1 6 *